To my wife Patricia (my Caroline), with all my love

CHAPTER 1

Danny Carroll was sick of the cold, despite it being June. It seemed every day was getting harder, especially since Pete died a week ago. Now he had no one left to share a bit of body warmth. The two of them had hung out together for years, but now, without Pete, he felt lost. Preferring the outdoors to the shelters, their favourite hideout had been a culvert by the abandoned railway line. He smiled to himself when he thought of the first time Pete had stuck his head into it and let out a curse, staggering back as a skunk appeared at the mouth and trotted away. When they'd cautiously poked their heads into the culvert they couldn't smell any trace of the skunk.

"Stuck up little critter," Pete had said. "Probably couldn't abide the smell of us. Maybe we should have a shower at The Shelter tomorrow."

Danny was 64 years old, quite a few years older than Pete. Older than nearly all the other guys he saw at The Shelter. When the doctor had examined him there not long ago, he had shaken his head in amazement.

"I don't know what it is that's keeping you alive, considering all the drinking you've done. If you can stay off the drink you could last several more years."

In fact, a year previously, Danny had very nearly died. It was summer and he'd been drinking with Pete on the banks of the Elbow River, not far from downtown Calgary. Their litre of cheap wine had run out and Danny had fallen asleep, but a short time later Pete shook him awake.

"Danny, I've got some really good stuff here. Home-made hooch, the real McCoy. Got a great kick, too."

"How'd ya get that?" Danny asked.

"Never mind. Here, have some." Pete had passed him a plastic two-litre container.

Danny tasted it and Pete was right, it had a great kick. Between them they finished it.

Sometime later Danny found himself throwing up on the grass. There was nothing new about that. But this time something was really wrong. Somewhere in his fogged brain an alarm bell was going off and Danny knew he needed help. He shook Pete awake. It wasn't easy, but somehow he got Pete on his feet and they stumbled away from the riverbank towards the street.

He passed out and came to, briefly, as a crowd of white-masked faces hovered over him. He felt himself quickly hoisted and then dumped onto another surface. He lost consciousness again.

He learned later how lucky he and Pete had been. A patrol car had found them, out cold, in a back alley a block from the river. The doctor told him that the home-made booze he and Pete drank contained methanol. The container had been used to store windshield washer fluid and hadn't been rinsed out properly.

"The police found two more victims on the riverbank. Same kind of containers nearby. They didn't find them in time," the doctor told him.

As Danny lay for five days in the hospital bed, feeling rotten, he didn't say anything about the strange occurrence that had shaken him while he was having his stomach pumped and they were feeding him oxygen. He waited a few weeks before he went to the library to look for books on what he had heard were called near-death experiences. He was amazed to find how many people had reported similar stories.

Nobody knew for certain what had happened to them, but many believed that they had died and had somehow come back. Several had become convinced there was an after-life. Although near-death experiences varied, most had common elements, and Danny's matched many of those reported in the books. He recalled passing through a tunnel, a warm, brilliant light, a voice saying, "He's gone." Most remarkably, he found himself floating freely, looking down on himself on the bed. He was sure it hadn't been just a dream. It was far too vivid.

Danny was still very skeptical about any after-life, but one thing he was certain of: he no longer feared death and, even more surprisingly, he found he no longer feared living. In one book he read that a lot of people who experienced a near-death experience were so affected by it that their lives were changed completely.

He didn't tell anyone about what had happened to him, not even Pete. Pete wouldn't have understood. He'd have laughed. Danny didn't understand it himself but, like the books said, he felt changed. He'd quit drinking and had even taken a few day-jobs that had come up at The Shelter employment office.

A week ago, on the day Pete died, Danny had taken a job with a landscaping company for the day. When he got back to The Shelter where they'd agreed to meet and have supper, Pete wasn't there. Danny wasn't too worried. Pete had probably gone off drinking somewhere, but two hours later when he still hadn't shown up, Danny had gone looking for him. It took him until nearly midnight, but he was too late. Pete was dead.

Pete had liked to drink cheap port and although Danny had found it awfully hard to be around him when he was drinking, he'd stuck by him. It had been a mighty struggle but Danny had managed to stay off the booze. He thought he might be able to save up a little money, now that he wasn't drinking. Soon he'd also be eligible for his Canada pension money although he'd heard some talk that the buggers in government were thinking of moving up the age for collecting it.

Collecting bottles and pop cans paid for most of the food he bought and when the recycling programme had been introduced by the city, he and Pete had done well. They had a regular route through a number of back alleys, hitting the recycle bins before the truck arrived, liberating the bottles and cans from bins whose owners were too lazy to take them back to the bottle depot. On a nice day, they'd often buy a sandwich with their bottle money at the Subway and take it to the woods by the river to eat.

He had breakfast at the Christian Mission this morning after lining up for an hour to be let in. Today, Wednesday, was recycling day and Danny found the back alley trek long and lonely without Pete. It took him much longer and the recycling truck had arrived before he'd completed the route. Danny was still mourning Pete, and not having the heart to stick with it, he wandered away from their usual route.

Today there was a cold wind from the mountains. Tomorrow he might head to the library. It was warm there, and Danny loved to read. He kept a list of the books he'd read and often scanned the book reviews in the newspapers in the library and added them to his list. He was currently reading *The Road* by Cormac McCarthy. When Pete was sober, Danny sometimes read aloud to him. Pete's favourite book had been the kid's book, *Charlie and the Chocolate Factory*, by Roald Dahl. Pete had liked it so much, Danny knew passages off by heart. Danny had laughed out loud too, when he read it.

He found himself outside a long, low building, on a street he wasn't familiar with. The sign outside said *Cavandish Long Term Care Home*. He pushed his shopping cart in amongst some thick bushes and walked across the lawn to look in the large windows of the entrance. Beyond the double doors, the entrance opened into a lounge area where a number of people were sitting on couches and comfortable chairs. Some were dozing, others were watching a large flat screen TV, set in a corner of the lounge. Over half of them were in wheelchairs. A sign on one of the glass doors read, *Visitors: Please do not assist anyone to leave by holding the door open for them unless you are accompanying them.*

As he stood there, someone walked up the path behind him and said, "Excuse me." It was a middle-aged woman and she glanced back at Danny and smiled, holding the door open. "Coming in?" The sign on the front door had said not to help anyone leave, but said nothing about letting people in.

"Uh, thanks," Danny said and stepped in behind her. It felt warm inside. The woman walked on, leaving Danny, who glanced about at the TV watchers. Only one or two registered his presence before turning back to the TV. The TV was tuned to some religious programme, which was calling for donations. He was glad he'd taken the time to shave and put on a clean shirt after breakfast at the mission. He slipped off his knapsack where he kept his belongings. On a small couch dozed a skinny, grey-haired man wearing thick glasses. Nobody looked at Danny as he settled himself at the other end of the couch. He'd just stay a while, warm up and move on.

He glanced down the hallway, which ended at a long desk with a high counter. He could just catch a glimpse of the top of the heads of two women, whom he guessed might be nurses. One of them was on the phone. He turned back to the TV, but before long he too fell into a doze.

Danny woke with a start.

A woman, wearing a pale pink uniform, was clapping her hands and calling, "Snack time." Her name was Nina, according to the badge pinned to her lapel. She paused to shake the shoulder of his sleeping companion, asking loudly, "Do you want to come for your snack, Charlie?" Charlie opened his eyes, yawned, looked at Danny and nodded, as Nina moved on.

"Coming for a coffee and a cookie?" Charlie asked as he eased slowly to his feet.

"Sure," Danny said. A coffee would be great right now, he thought.

He picked up his knapsack and walked slowly beside Charlie as they moved down the hall towards the desk, along with about half a dozen other seniors. A couple of them were using walkers, and Nina and another woman pushed residents in wheelchairs.

Beyond the desk were entrances to the dining room, according to the sign above each doorway. Danny expected he'd be challenged at any minute, but no one said anything as he followed Charlie into the dining room. Corridors branched off from each end of the desk, two at each end, and Danny assumed that's where the residents slept. The dining room was about half full. A woman was playing a tune on an old piano in one corner – Danny thought he recognized *When Irish Eyes Are Smiling*. About half of those sitting at the tables were in wheelchairs. Charlie stopped at an empty table, pulled out a chair and nodded at Danny to do the same. Danny sat, placing his knapsack beside him on the floor. An attendant was serving coffee and juice, while another followed with a trolley serving a large cookie on a napkin to everyone.

"Coffee?"

"Yes, thanks kindly," Danny said to the attendant.

"Cream and sugar?"

"Just cream, thanks."

She poured coffee for him and Charlie and tossed a couple of packets of sugar and cream containers onto the centre of the table.

Danny helped himself to a container of cream and poured it into his coffee, stirring it with a plastic stir stick as he pushed the other cream and sugars to Charlie.

"Charlie Bannister," Charlie said, extending his hand to Danny, "and you?"

"Danny Carroll. You been here long, Charlie?" Danny asked as they shook hands.

"Too damn long. Coming up to five years. You?"

"Just got here," he answered.

The cookies arrived and when Danny smiled and said, "Thanks kindly," again, the attendant smiled back. He noticed when she'd gone that he'd been given two cookies, but Charlie had only been given one.

Danny sipped his coffee. Not very strong, he thought, likely decaffeinated. Probably don't want the residents staying awake at night. Still, it was warm and the cookies were sweet. He'd slip out as soon as he finished and maybe head downtown for supper at The Shelter.

THE GRAND GETAWAY   5

"Are you going to watch the game?" Charlie asked. "You have a TV in your room?"

"Um, no." Danny wasn't sure what game Charlie was talking about. He wasn't much into sports. Was hockey season still on? Mid-June – must be football.

"I've got a TV," Charlie said. "You can come back to my room when we finish here if you want. Not a lot on, probably some soap, but it kills time before supper. Sometimes that nature channel has some interesting stuff. Saw a good show on monkeys in India. Monkeys running wild all over a city – Delhi, I think it was. Robbing food, stealing all sorts of stuff. Cheeky little bastards." Charlie laughed.

They finished their coffee and cookies and Danny followed Charlie down to the last room on the left near the end of one of the corridors. As they walked down the hall they passed several people, mostly women, sitting in wheelchairs, dozing or staring at the wall opposite. Danny noticed that most rooms had two names outside the door but when they reached Charlie's, there was only one – Charles Bannister.

The room had two single beds, and a TV resting on a small chest of drawers between them.

"Grab one of those chairs from out in the hall and bring it in," Charlie said. "I'll see if there's anything worth watching." He sat down in the only other chair in the room and turned on a nature show about elephants.

"This doesn't look too bad. I like elephants," Charlie said, as Danny sat down beside him. "So what wing are you in? You said you just got here."

"I did. I'm just passing through, so to speak," Danny replied.

"Oh. Just for a few days? Where are you going then? Hope it's somewhere better." Charlie shifted in his chair. "Look at that elephant, it's huge. They had to dart him to get him loaded into the truck. Moving him to another sanctuary. Poachers killing them off like flies, even inside the wildlife sanctuaries, hacking off their tusks and making a fortune selling the ivory to the Chinese, the buggers. Rhinos getting killed off too. They think the rhino horn will give them a hard-on. Stupid bastards. So, what sanctuary are *you* moving to?"

"Charlie, I won't tell ya a lie. I just walked in off the street to get warm. I'm homeless, so I usually sleep wherever I can. I'll be on my way. If I leave now I'll make it to The Shelter for supper."

"So you sometimes sleep outside?"

Danny nodded.

"Well that sounds a bit more exciting than being cooped up here all the time. We hardly ever get out into the garden even on a warm day. Too much trouble wheeling all those wheelchairs out and back in again."

"I should go," Danny said. "It was nice talking to ya."

"Wait! Don't go. I haven't had anyone to talk to in a long time! Stay a while. I can maybe get you in with me for supper."

Danny sat back down his chair. It was cozy here, and supper sounded good.

"Just stick with me. The staff changes almost every day. New girls appear all the time. The new ones don't know us from the visitors. One of the new ones asked a visitor if he'd had a bowel movement. Bowel movements are a big thing here – they're fixated on them! If you don't go two days in a row, they shove a suppository up your ass.

"I make sure I lie if I haven't gone. I kid the cute ones, tell them I haven't gone for a couple of days, then say, 'I'm kidding, I know you just want to fondle my cute ass.' I would have liked that at one time, but now? Haven't any interest. But the young women here don't know that. Think I'm a horny old bastard. It's good for the ego. So if you stick around, make sure you tell them you've had a crap if they ask. Those suppositories make you stick close to the toilet unless you can move fast."

"Thanks for the tip," Danny said. "Where's your room-mate?" He pointed to the other bed.

"Don't have one. Jimmy died about a month ago. Diabetes and heart problems. Snored like a bugger. They haven't found anyone to share with me yet. I'm probably too ornery."

They watched the nature programme on elephants for another half hour. A programme on oceans came on, but Charlie had dozed off by then.

Danny looked around the room. Beside the window at the head of Charlie's bed was a black and white wedding picture of a much younger Charlie and a dark-haired buxom girl with a wide smile. A 2001 calendar from an auto parts dealer featuring big cars and big busty girls hung on the other side of the window beside a hand-made card with a stick figure, a cake with candles and the words *Happy Birthday Grand-dad* printed in large letters with coloured crayons.

Someone poked their head in the door, called "Supper time," and left.

Charlie stirred, stretched and yawned.

"They just called supper time," Danny said. "Look, I don't want to cause you any trouble."

"Hang on. Just wait a few minutes. They always call meal times far too early. If you go right away, we'll be sitting there for 20 minutes or more before they put anything in front of us. They take the wheelchairs down first. Best to go when it's getting crowded. There's an empty chair at our table. I share a table with a couple of good old gals. Betty and Caroline. Betty has some heart problem and Caroline has dementia. Betty's sharp as a tack, but Caroline, God love her, does a lot of rambling. Still real pretty. Fit as all get-out but doesn't remember much. Just sit with us and they'll drop a plate of food in front of you. They like us to eat fairly fast 'cause this is the first sitting and they have to do it all over again for the second crowd. Caroline's a slow eater. Sometimes I think they rush her too much. Me and Betty look out for her."

"That's Betty and Caroline's room," Charlie said, pointing to the names Betty Danglemeyer and Caroline Gilchrist posted outside the room next to his.

THE GRAND GETAWAY   7

They strolled slowly down the hall, avoiding wheelchairs that were being pushed towards the dining room.

"Table 13, our lucky number, Charlie said as they entered. "We always sit in the same place." He nodded towards a table near a wall with a blurred representation of a stream and woods that looked to Danny like it was somewhere in Italy. He was sure he'd be asked who he was, but everyone seemed to be bustling around. Two nurses hurried around, dropping off pills in front of some of the people already seated. Other attendants pushed the last of the wheelchaired residents to their respective tables. As Charlie and Danny sat down, one of the nurses dropped a tiny paper cup with three or four coloured pills in front of the woman he guessed was Betty.

She was a fairly heavy-set dyed blonde, who took a sip from one of the glasses of tomato juice that had been placed on the table and swallowed some of the pills. Beside her chair was a walker. A slim woman with short, grey hair, clear complexion and brown eyes, was rearranging the knife, fork and spoon. She looked much younger than Betty. She paused in her cutlery rearranging, smiled at Danny, and then went back to her task.

The room was quiet except for the chatter of the attendants settling the last residents in place and a low whine that Danny thought sounded like a jet, far away but warming up.

"Betty, Caroline, this is Danny," Charlie said.

Betty finished swallowing her pills and took another sip of tomato juice. "Hello Danny."

Caroline was still rearranging the cutlery but smiled, and said, "Oh you. There you are."

An attendant approached, handing out large bibs.

"Take a bib, Danny," Charlie said.

The attendant placed bibs in front of Charlie, Betty and Caroline, hesitated at Danny, but gave him one when he held out his hand. Danny put on his bib, then helped Caroline and Betty with theirs.

"We finally have a gentleman at our table," Betty said, looking pointedly at Charlie. He grunted in response.

The whining noise started up again from a nearby table.

"What's that racket, Charlie?" Danny asked.

"Oxygen line unhooked, or a tank getting low. Happens all the time."

The whine went on for a few more minutes until an attendant came over and adjusted a plastic tube at the back of one of the wheelchairs at the next table. Plates of food were placed in front of them. There was mashed potato, carrots and some kind of meat covered in gravy. Danny picked up his knife and fork and sampled it. It tasted fine, but more importantly, it was hot. The attendant came back with a glass of tomato juice for Danny.

"They call it Veal Panceretti," Charlie said. "That's what it says on the menu posted outside the door, but I'm not sure what it really is. We have our main meal at noon. Today we had Cape Capensis. Know what that is?"

"Never heard of it," Danny replied.

"Neither has anyone else, but the cook told me it was cod. I think it's fish, but it tastes like all the fish we get. Could be anything from snapper to sardine for all I know."

Caroline was rearranging her carrots on the plate and seemed to be talking to them. Then she speared a piece with her fork and put it in her mouth, chewing slowly.

Betty looked at Danny and nodded, "You finally get a new room-mate, Charlie?"

Charlie, his mouth full, hesitated then nodded.

"Don't take any crap from him, Danny, and don't snore whatever you do. Rumour is Charlie smothered poor Jimmy. Complained so much about Jimmy's snoring, we're all sure that's how Jimmy died."

Charlie snickered. Caroline looked up from her plate with sad eyes. "Oh no. Did he die?"

Betty patted her hand and said, "Just joking, Caroline," and laughed. "Eat some meat."

"Oh yes," Caroline said. "I know you," and smiled as she speared another carrot piece.

Danny looked at her and smiled. Charlie was right. She was really pretty. He tried to guess her age. Maybe 62, he thought.

"So Danny," Betty asked, "where were you before this?"

Before Danny could reply, some kind of chocolate pudding in small dishes was placed on the table. An older guy wearing a hair net over his mostly bald head poured coffee into the plastic mugs on the table in front of them.

"Thanks, Mario," Charlie said. "This is Danny."

Danny, his mouth full of mashed potato, mumbled his thanks to Mario as his coffee was poured.

As Mario moved off, Charlie added, "Mario's a good guy. Sometimes he slips us a bit of extra stuff we like."

Somewhere further away the whining noise went off again as someone's oxygen line detached. Betty was helping Caroline get started on her meat and potatoes, as the arrival of the pudding and coffee had distracted her. She seemed confused over what to eat next.

"So Danny, I was asking where you were before," Betty persisted. Danny could only mumble, but Charlie came to his rescue.

"Danny came in today from Purple Springs Hospital," he said. "Had a problem with his ticker for a while." He lowered his voice and whispered hoarsely, "Doesn't like to talk about it. I'll fill you in later. Give him a chance to get the lay of the land."

"Okay," Betty said. "Did you warn him about suppositories?"

"I did."

"Well that's something you did right."

"What's that supposed to mean?"

"Hmmf," was all Betty said and went back to helping Caroline.

As residents finished their supper, those that could walk ambled off. Charlie and Danny finished eating about the same time. Betty was almost finished and was encouraging Caroline to finish her pudding.

Charlie nodded to Danny. "Ready to go?"

They walked slowly back to Charlie's room, weaving in and out of wheelchaired residents who had been pushed back into the hallway or were maneuvering themselves.

"Game will be starting in about five minutes," Charlie said as he switched on the TV, keeping the sound low.

"Thanks for getting me the grub, Charlie, but I think I'd better be going now."

"What's your hurry? Watch the game, Montreal and Edmonton, pre-season action. Where do you have to be anyway?"

"Well, The Shelter closes about 9:30, and if you're not there by then they lock the door. I'd have to sleep rough. That's no big deal. I'm used to that. I actually prefer it, but it's best to settle in before dark. I was thinking of staying at The Shelter tonight. I like a shower."

"There's an extra bed here. Stay overnight."

"And what's gonna happen when they come to tuck you in and find me still here?"

"I usually get myself into bed. Somebody just sticks their head in about nine. If you get into the other bed they probably won't even notice."

The game came on and Charlie turned up the sound. They watched, mostly in silence with the occasional comment from Charlie, but with Montreal up 24-3 over Edmonton at the end of the half, they lost interest in the game, and Charlie began telling Danny a bit about himself.

"Born in New Brunswick. Worked on the railway all my life, CP. Freight conductor. Back when they still had cabooses. Been all over the country, northern Ontario, Quebec, an' all across. Vancouver, nice city, but it rains too much. Knew every bump and shimmy in the tracks like the back of my hand."

"And what about Betty and Caroline?" Danny asked.

"Betty is a tough old nut. Been here at least five years. A widow or divorced, I've never been sure. Doesn't have much good to say about her ex, dead or alive. Hates this place. Always talking about getting out and doing something exciting."

"With a walker?"

"Betty can get to her feet when the mood takes her. Usually just uses the walker as a prop. She really doesn't need it. She had a slight stroke some years ago. When she's tired she sometimes drags her left foot a bit."

"And Caroline?"

"Ah, Caroline. Dementia got her. Usually smiling, but I've seen her cry too when she can't figure out something or she's looking at an old photo. She's fit. Used to ski a couple of years back, cross country, but doesn't remember much now. Had a husband who took her out four or five days a week, but he got killed in a car accident driving here to pick her up one day in a snow storm. She hasn't been out since. I think she still misses him. See tears in her eyes when she rummages through an old pile of photos she has, but it's hard to say."

"How old is she?"

"Had her birthday last month. She's 74. The staff keep track. Gave her a big birthday card and sang *Happy Birthday* at breakfast."

"I thought she was maybe early sixties." Danny said.

"Yeah, she kept her looks. Only her brain let her down."

"What about yourself? That your wife in the photo?"

"Yeah. Margie. Gone nine years now. My daughter and her husband were scared shitless they'd have to look after me after I had my minor heart attack. Couldn't wait to get me into a home. Her husband got transferred to Newfoundland. Works on an offshore rig. So they moved there with my 6-year-old grand-daughter. She's 11 now. Haven't seen them since they moved." He broke off, then turned off the TV. "Near enough to bedtime. I'll get my pajamas on and slip into bed. You need some pajamas? I've an extra pair in the closet."

"Thanks," Danny said. "You sure this is gonna be okay?"

"If you're still nervous, get these pajamas on and slip under the bed." He tossed Danny a pair of blue striped pajamas. "One of the women will stick her head in in about five minutes. I'll have the light off and once she sees me in bed, she'll leave us alone. I'll give you the all clear and you can get into bed and have a good sleep. I don't snore like Jimmy. You might hear the odd holler from someone down the hall during the night, but I'll bet it's quieter than that Shelter place."

"What about the morning?"

"We'll let that take care of itself. You should be used to that."

Danny put on the pajamas, shoved his clothes into his knapsack and scrambled under the bed with it as Charlie switched off the light. It was only a minute before the door was pushed open and Danny caught the silhouette of a woman by the light in the hall. Charlie feigned sleep and the door was closed.

"All clear," Charlie whispered, and Danny came from under the bed and climbed in.

CHAPTER 2

He awoke to Charlie shaking him. "It's ten to seven. If you need a quick pee now's yer chance, then duck under the bed again. Someone will look in to see if I'm still alive, but I'll be up and dressed."

Danny quickly used the bathroom and ducked under the bed again. Charlie finished dressing and switched on the TV and sat in front of it. Someone poked their head in the door.

"Ah you're up, Charles," a female voice said. "You feeling good?"

"Fine, fine."

"Did you have a bowel movement?"

"Sure thing. Regular as clockwork."

"Good."

Danny heard her walk away.

"You can come out now and get dressed and shave if you want. You got a razor?"

"Yeah." Danny rummaged in his knapsack, retrieved his razor, and carried his clothes into the bathroom. When he came out Charlie was watching the news.

"Another earthquake in Japan. No one killed. Sit down and we'll wait for breakfast. No one will bother you. I'm lucky to have an end room. If you're not in an end room, you have to share the bathroom with your next-door neighbours. There's a door on both sides of those bathrooms."

They repeated the same procedure they used at suppertime the day before, arriving for breakfast just before the last residents. Caroline and Betty were already seated.

"You two look like you've been up to something," Betty greeted them.

Caroline had opened one of the miniature plastic cream containers and looked like she might pour it onto the table. Betty noticed and took it from her to pour it into her own empty coffee cup.

"Like what?" Charlie asked as they sat down, and he and Danny put on the bibs they found on the chairs.

"I dunno. I watched an old movie on TV last night. Black and white. Only caught the second half but it was about prisoners breaking out of a prisoner of war camp in WWII. Somewhere in Germany or Poland, I forget. By the guilty look on Danny's face I'd say you two have hatched a plot to break out of here."

"What's for breakfast?" Charlie asked. "No, don't tell me. Let me guess. The usual porridge, small bowl of scrambled egg and... toast."

"Boy you're good," Betty said, "considerin' we've had the same damn breakfast for the last six months. Yeah, the usual prison food. What I'd give for a good cup of coffee."

"I was just about to say that," Caroline said, smiling.

"Don't they take you places?" Danny asked.

The porridge, scrambled egg and toast were placed in front of them by one of the attendants.

"Oh sure," Betty said. "Mostly to fast food restaurants, Burger King, Dairy Queen. We pay from our so called 'Comfort Fund' if there's any money in your account. Haven't had any in mine for months. One trip to the park down the street for a picnic. One trip to the zoo. I missed out on that, the only trip I really wanted to go on. They said they could only take seven in their bus. Said I signed up too late, but I know I was third on the list when I did. Probably thought I'd be too much trouble. Anyway, I'd sure like to go to the zoo, but not on their damn bus. I don't want to stare at the camels and the elephants. I'd like to just sit in that plant place, what do they call it, observatory or somethin'?"

"I think it's called a conservatory," Charlie said.

"Yeah. Be nice to sit and smell some real plants for a change. Eat your porridge, Caroline. That's enough stirring."

"Oh yes," Caroline said, but went on stirring her porridge until Betty gave her the first spoonful. She put the spoon back in Caroline's hand and Caroline began feeding herself.

"I haven't been to the zoo in years, myself," Danny said. "I hear it's expensive."

"Well it would be nice for a change before winter sets in," Betty said. "But I'd still like to know what you two are up to."

It was four days later and Charlie and Danny were sitting in Charlie's room when Betty came in pushing her walker. "Okay let me have the whole story. I snooped and there's no file on Danny. You must be desperate if you checked yourself in here. You're free to leave anytime. Charlie put you up to it didn't he? He's been real lonely since Jim died even if he did complain about him all the time. You're just passin' through, aren't ya Danny?"

"Yeah. You got me. I've been telling Charlie I should move on, but he keeps saying, wait until after breakfast, after supper, stay one more night. It has been nice to have three meals a day and a warm bed. I can get that at The Shelter, but sometimes I don't get much sleep. Real noisy. I often sleep out."

Charlie laughed. "I was having a little fun. Adding some excitement to my life. Seeing how long we could get away with it. It's been four days now and no one's said anything. They're even doing his laundry along with mine."

"Jeez, Charlie. That's a gas." Betty chuckled. "But if you're going keep it up much longer, you'll have to do a few more things. Let me help."

"How?"

"Well for one thing, put his name up outside the door beside yours. I'll make one up tonight. He needs a file in case someone checks."

"How you gonna make up a file?" Charlie asked.

THE GRAND GETAWAY   13

"Now hang on," Danny said. "I don't want to cause any trouble. I wandered in from the cold a few days ago and it got outta hand. In a few days I gotta do my bottle run or someone else will steal my territory if I'm not there to cover it."

"But you can come and go," Betty said. "Sign yourself out. There's a book on the front desk. Just write in the time you think you'll be back. Let's see how long we can carry this off. Come on. Let me in on this. It sure beats sitting in the hall on Friday afternoons, singing, *Home On The Range* or, even worse, *Show Me The Way To Go Home*. Sure, we'd all go home if we could. I'll make up the sign for outside the door and make up a file for Danny. I need a few details. Oh, and if you're gonna get your own clothes back from the laundry you'll need your name on them. I'll grab a few labels today and you can stick them on your shirts and stuff."

Betty was as good as her word. That night a genuine looking sign that read "Daniel Carroll" was taped up beside Charlie's, and at breakfast the next morning Betty gave them a thumb's up. "I sneaked into the office last night and filled in your admittance form. Had to do it at 4:00 a.m. when Loreen was the only nurse on duty and Luis and Wanda were making out in the laundry room."

"You're kidding," Charlie laughed.

"No, I got it done, but I'm a slow typer and I had to duck down when someone down the hall pressed their call button and Loreen walked past."

"No, I mean about Luis and Wanda." Charlie started laughing again.

"Well it's true. I've known about them for weeks. When they're on shift together, they usually grab a quickie around 3:30 to 4:00. I was awake one night and heard this moanin'. I thought it was Caroline at first and when the moanin' went on, I got up to go check on her, but she was fast asleep. I was standing beside her bed when I realized the moanin' was comin' from the laundry room across the hall. A minute later it stopped, and Wanda came out adjustin' her panty-hose and a minute after that, out comes Luis."

"Oh yes." Caroline said, "It was over there. Right there." She pointed across the table.

"Here Caroline, here's your juice. Drink this first." Betty put the glass into Caroline's hand.

"Oh, by the way, Danny, they might give you some low dose aspirin every day. I forgot to ask what your medical problem was, and I had to put something on your form, so I said you had a slightly weak ticker."

"Thanks, but I'm not sure I should stick around much longer. They're sure to call the cops when they find out I'm a phony."

"I doubt it," Betty said. "They wouldn't want any publicity. They hate publicity."

"Yeah," Charlie said. "They don't like anything in the papers. They'd most likely just throw you out."

"Did you label your clothes with the labels I gave you?" Betty asked.

"I did and I've got lots left over. I don't have a lot of clothes. Well, tomorrow I'm going out to do my bottle run. I hope my shopping cart is still outside in the bushes where I stashed it."

"Why don't you check on the zoo when you're out? The weather forecast for the next week is good and I'd sure like to try for the zoo," Betty said.

"But how would you get there, if there's no actual bus going from the home?" Danny asked. "And then there's the cost of getting into the zoo."

"It's only two blocks to the CTrain that takes you right to the zoo. I could make it that far with my walker. Let's make a plan. Give me somethin' to dream about."

"You mean you want me to find a way to get you out of here? Get you to the zoo and then get you back?"

"I'll work on getting us out of here. But, yeah. That's exactly what I want. But not just for me. We'd take Caroline and Charlie too. All four of us."

"What! You're crazy. How far do you think we'd get before they caught us? Then I really would be in trouble with the cops."

"Jeez, Danny! Relax!" Betty laughed. "We're just four old people going on an outing. By ourselves with no minders."

"God, but wouldn't it be great?" Charlie hit the table with his fist. "Let's make a plan, Betty. I'm excited even thinking about it."

"Oh yes," Caroline said. "A plan is good. And Smucker's. Smucker's strawberry jam. Jam. Straw... Strawberry." Her eyes had fallen on the plastic jam packet beside her toast and she picked it up and read the label slowly out loud again, her fingers tracing the lettering. "Smucker's – Straw – Berry – Jam."

CHAPTER 3

Danny found his cart in the bushes where he'd left it. He'd signed himself out in the notebook he found on the desk when no one was behind it. He only had to print his name, the time he left, and the time he expected to return. No other details were asked for. He went back to his bottle collecting route but kept mulling over how he could help the others leave the home, get them to the zoo and back again without causing some uproar. Betty and Charlie were supposed to be working on a plan but the biggest factor, even if they all left unnoticed, would be money. Taking a cab would be the easiest, but at that moment, all he had was ten bucks.

He stopped by the United Church office, hoping he might pick up a couple of transit tickets. He hadn't been there for quite a while and a notice on the door said, 'The Church no longer gives out transit tickets. Please contact Social Welfare.' There was a phone number. Danny knew that was a lost cause. There would be questions, form filling, proof of a doctor's appointment or some other real need. The Social Welfare office was downtown, and that would require transit tickets to get there and back – or spending his ten bucks. Better to hang onto that for now. Maybe Betty and Charlie could come up with some cash.

Danny got to the service station where he usually used the bathroom. Haifa was behind the counter and he had to wait until she finished with a customer. Haifa was Hamid's wife, and he didn't know her nearly as well. They were Iraqis who had seen hardship in their former country. Hamid had always been gracious with him and Pete, while Haifa was more cautious. Danny wasn't sure she'd approved of Hamid giving them the key to the washroom.

"You want washroom key?" Haifa asked.

"Er. No. Yes. But could I use the phone, please, first?"

"Phone?" Haifa hesitated. "Local number? You know number?"

"Yes, I have the number. It's the zoo. I need to borrow your phone, please."

Another customer came in. She picked up a couple of packets of chips from a shelf and went to the counter as Danny waited patiently until she left.

"It's the zoo," Danny said to Haifa.

"Zoo? What is zoo? I don't know this number." Haifa was looking at him suspiciously.

"Er, sorry. It's..." Danny looked at the slip of paper in his hand again. With Haifa's eyes on him he had trouble reading the number quickly. "It's 613-555-0100."

"Call, local?"

"Yes. Local. Area code 613."

"I dial number, 613." She looked at Danny as she started to dial the number and paused for him to repeat the rest.

"Er... 555-0100."

Haifa dialed each number very slowly as she kept glancing back at Danny. Only when she heard the beginning of the recorded message from the zoo did she hand the phone to Danny.

He heard, '... *open seven days a week with admission gates open from 9:00 a.m. to 5:00 p.m. and the zoo closing at 6:00 p.m. If you would like to purchase your admission in advance please visit our website at www...*' "Holy shit," Danny muttered, glancing at Haifa who was frowning at him, her hand poised to take back her phone. Danny pressed the phone to his ear. '... *or stay on the line for one of our service representatives. For admission prices please press 1. For —*' Danny pressed 1. '*Our admission prices are as follows and do not include sales tax. Adult admission $22.50. Adults 60 and over $20.50. Children ages 3 -15, $14.50. Children under 3 are admitted free.*' Danny pressed end. "My God! It's $20.50 plus tax. Each!"

Haifa almost snatched the phone from his hand as he handed it back and another customer came to the counter.

"Thanks," Danny said as he walked out, shocked by the cost of the zoo admission. He was still muttering to himself and a long way from the service station when he realized he'd forgotten to use the washroom. He relieved himself behind some bushes in a park.

Danny finished most of his bottle run and turned in the cans, bottles and juice containers at his usual bottle depot. He looked at the bills and coins in his hand. Twenty-eight dollars and fifty-five cents. Below average. With Pete he'd done better. Pete never missed any recycling containers.

He bought himself a sandwich at a nearby Subway. As he ate, he mulled over the idea of getting all four of them into the zoo. They'd need at least $100 for this trip. He'd see if Betty and Charlie had any ideas or could come up with some money. He made it back to the home just in time for snack time, a half hour earlier than he'd written in the check-out notebook. No one took any notice of him when he put a check mark beside his name.

He found Charlie heading for the dining room. "Where's Betty?" he asked.

"Sleeping," Charlie said. "She usually has an afternoon nap."

Caroline was sitting alone at a table, folding a paper napkin and then unfolding it and spreading it flat on the table again, smoothing it with the back of her hand. Charlie and Danny sat down beside her.

"So, what did you find out?" Charlie asked.

"It costs a hell of a lot of money to get into the zoo."

"How much?"

"More than $20."

"Sounds a bit high. But I guess prices have gone up. I haven't been to the zoo in years. The price of nuts for the monkeys must have gone up, or maybe they feed them bananas. Still, I suppose it's not bad for the four of us."

THE GRAND GETAWAY   17

"The four of us! Hell! That's the admission price for only one of us and that's the senior's rate."

"Holy! We only want to look at the monkeys, not adopt one and take it home. Let's see what Betty has to say at supper time."

Betty had a lot to say, but it was not what Danny had thought she'd say. He expected her to throw in the towel and forget about it, but she seemed even more eager to go. "It's a challenge," she said. "We'll just have to find a way to get in. It'll be all the more excitin'."

"But how do you think we're going to get in without enough money?" Charlie asked.

"Bluff!" Betty laughed.

"Bluff?" Danny asked. "You mean just B.S. our way in? What would you tell the guy who asks for our ticket? That we are all new zoo employees? Or maybe veterinarians come to check out the elephants? Apart from not looking anything like employees or vets, we'd need some kind of I.D. and Caroline here can't even say her own name."

"Yeah," Charlie laughed. "Betty, maybe you could tell him you're a lion tamer from the circus. You know how the lion tamer in the circus fends off the lion with a chair? You could tell them you just brought your walker along instead of a chair and were hoping to get in a little practice."

"Oh shut up, Charlie. Look. I've been reading this old book I found in the library. After watching that old WWII movie, I thought I'd look for some books on the topic, and I found a book in the library about these two English pilots who escaped from a prison in Germany. They walked through Germany into France and managed to find the French Resistance who helped get them back to England. They walked for weeks and were able to bluff their way through whenever they were stopped."

"But that was over 60 years ago, and I bet they spoke some German and French," Danny said.

"Yes, one spoke a little German and the other a little French."

Charlie laughed. "The problem's solved. We won't need either language to get into the zoo, and we can probably bluff our way in with our broken English!"

"Will you be serious, Charlie. Here Caroline. Let me help you cut your meat."

"Oh, yes," Caroline said.

"I don't suppose we could get hold of a real zoo pass and forge four copies? The two escapees had some forged documents," Betty said.

"I think that was before they had scanners. Everything has a bar code now and everything gets scanned," Danny said.

"Well we'll just have to bluff our way in. Come up with some story."

"Like what?" Charlie asked.

"I don't know yet. Maybe we gave our passes or tickets to Caroline and she lost them. Maybe they'd take pity on us and let us in. What's letting four old people into the zoo goin' to cost them?"

"Eighty-two bucks," Danny said.

Nobody said anything except Caroline, who said, "82, 82, 82."

"If we couldn't bluff our way in, we'd need some kind of distraction. Maybe use poor Caroline in some way. No..." Betty said.

"What?" Charlie asked.

"Well, after you get off the train, there's that long tunnel you have to go through to buy your zoo tickets at the ticket booth. There's someone probably scannin' your tickets, like Danny says, and you'd have to get past that person. I was just thinking if Caroline would run past, we could all rush after her, claiming she'd get lost if we didn't catch up with her. But it wouldn't work... Caroline wouldn't take off without us, she'd stand there waitin'. Why don't we just go and maybe we'll get a brilliant idea once we get there? Come on. Let's have some fun. Let's pick a day."

CHAPTER 4

They decided to try for the zoo on the following Monday. The long-range forecast was good with above average temperatures, but nobody had come up with any plan to get in. Betty was adamant that they weren't going to pay.

"It's one for all and all for one," she declared. "We all make it or nobody does. It's a day out, well, maybe not for you Danny, but for the three of us, it'll be an adventure! A bit of excitement. Let's see what the four of us can get away with. If we get caught, I'm sure we'll only get a good talkin' to. And if we do become celebrities and get our pictures plastered over the front page of *The Sun*, it'll give the rest of them in here something to think about. We may even get ourselves on TV and if that happens, I'll bet we'd get an all-expense paid trip to the zoo, anyway."

They planned to leave right after breakfast.

The first part of the plan was to leave without being noticed if at all possible. At breakfast, Betty quietly snipped off Caroline's plastic security bracelet with a pair of manicure scissors so she could slip it into her dresser drawer before they left. There was no way they wanted the alarm on the door to go off when they left or returned. Betty was hoping to get herself and her walker, along with Caroline, out the front door without arousing suspicion. Danny and Charlie would leave separately after she and Caroline had left.

After they finished breakfast, Betty took Caroline's hand and pushed her walker towards the front desk as a number of wheelchair residents were being brought back to their rooms. They passed the desk and, before ducking into the small library off the main hall, Betty passed Danny her handbag. Charlie and Danny were standing by the notice board pretending to read the notices and Danny set Betty's handbag on the floor in front of his feet. Betty stood with Caroline just inside the library door, out of sight of the front desk, waiting for Danny's signal that the coast was clear. Danny nodded and Betty urged Caroline out of the library towards the front door.

To Danny, their pace was agonizingly slow, and they were only half way to the door when he heard Charlie begin speaking to someone. He knew one of the nurses had put in an appearance behind the desk. "There was no toilet paper in my bathroom just now and I had to go looking for some yesterday too," he heard Charlie say. "I was getting desperate."

"If you have to go now, just get a roll from another bathroom, Charles," the nurse said. "I'll ask housekeeping to get some for your bathroom."

Danny could see that Betty and Caroline had reached the front door. Betty was struggling to hold the first door open while trying to get both her walker and Caroline into the area between the two sets of doors. She had to push Caroline out and then block her from coming back in with her walker. Luckily someone opened the outer door to come in just then and Caroline stepped forward, allowing Betty to catch up with her and hustle her outside. Charlie was still mumbling about the lack of toilet rolls and the nurse was losing patience. Betty and Caroline still had to walk a few metres down the front pathway before they could turn and get out of sight of the front desk. Danny heard the nurse say, "Okay, Charles, okay, I hear you." To his relief, he heard the phone ring and the nurse picked it up. Betty and Caroline had disappeared.

Charlie sauntered into the front lounge and sat on a couch near the door. Danny walked down the hall and dropped Betty's handbag beside Charlie. Danny stood in the centre of the hallway, pretending he was interested in what was on TV, but keeping one eye on the nurse at the desk. When she hung up the phone and stepped into the office behind the desk he said, "Go!" to Charlie, who picked up Betty's handbag and was outside and hurrying down the path in seconds.

Danny had stashed his knapsack behind a planter near the front door, but now he walked back towards the front desk. There was still no one behind it as he scribbled all four of their names in the notebook, with slightly different times of departure and return after each. He skipped a couple of spaces between their names. It was Betty's idea that anyone else going out might fill in the spaces and then it wouldn't look as if all four of them had left together. He walked to the front door, nonchalantly picked up his knapsack and went out. The residents watching TV paid him no attention.

Charlie had caught up to Betty and Caroline who were about half a block down the street. Charlie took Caroline's arm as Betty led the way pushing her walker. Danny caught up to them as they reached the end of the block and he helped Betty maneuver her walker off the sidewalk, cross the intersection and get back on the opposite sidewalk. He was surprised she was able to move so fast considering she spent a lot of her time with her walker. They were still a long block and a half from the train station. It was a bright sunny day, but quite cool this early in the morning.

"I've got enough cash to buy us transit tickets, but we'll only have enough left to get one of us into the zoo."

"Keep your money, Danny," Betty panted. "We'll wing it. Forget buyin' transit tickets, we'll just get on the train. I'd rather have an ice cream at the zoo. No one's goin' to hassle four oldies at rush hour."

"I hope you're right," Danny said. He remembered when he and Pete were short of cash and had been unceremoniously thrown off the train half way into the city centre when they couldn't produce tickets. The two transit cops hadn't cared how old he and Pete were. In fact, they were about to start writing out tickets for fines which would have used up days worth of their bottle collecting money, when the cops got a call about some disturbance on a train just coming into the station. But before the two cops jumped onto that train, one of them said, "Don't let us catch you on the train again without paying. We've got a good memory for faces."

THE GRAND GETAWAY   21

They had been as good as their word and had checked him and Pete twice in the last year when they found them on the train, but, luckily, Danny had been able to scrounge some tickets from the United Church. He only hoped the transit cops wouldn't be on their route this morning.

They reached the station and Betty maneuvered herself onto the escalator while Charlie and Danny helped Caroline. The escalator took them up above the tracks, and then they had to take another down to the platform. Charlie was having trouble getting Caroline to step onto the steps moving downwards, until Danny took Caroline's hand and stepped on ahead of her. When they reached the platform, a train was just coming in.

"Let's get on the front coach," Danny said. "We have to change trains downtown and if we get on the front coach there too, we won't have far to walk to the zoo entrance." Danny was also hoping that his hunch was right that transit cops were likely to jump on somewhere in the middle of the train.

The coach was packed but a couple of people got up and gave up their seats under the sign that said 'Reserved for Disabled' to Betty and Caroline. Danny and Charlie hung onto the overhead straps as the train moved off. About three more stations along, some passengers got off. Danny got a seat beside Betty, and Charlie found a seat opposite.

"So, what's the plan, Betty?" Danny asked.

"I'll figure it out when we get there."

Danny shook his head.

Betty laughed. "Haven't you heard, **gettin' there is half the fun!** I haven't felt this free in ages! But then, I guess you're free all the time, Danny."

Danny laughed. "We may not be if we break into the zoo."

Caroline sitting on the other side of Betty, laughed too. "Oh yes, the zoo, the zoo."

"That's where we're going, love," Betty said.

"Oh, don't talk to her," Caroline said. "She doesn't know who she is."

Betty smiled. She turned to Danny as Caroline went on talking to herself. "What's that song? You know. Janis Joplin sings it. The *Me and Bobby McGee* song." She sang the line about freedom, then laughed. "Even if we don't make it, I'm lookin' at this as an adventure. The day is full of possibilities."

The train pulled into City Hall station. "Here's where we change," Danny said, as he helped Betty to her feet and the train stopped. He took Caroline's hand and they waited until most of the passengers had left before he helped her out the door while Charlie guided Betty with her walker.

The train taking them to the zoo arrived almost immediately and once again they got into the front coach which was half empty. As the train pulled away, Caroline waved at the people standing on the platform.

"So, Betty," Charlie asked. "Have ya come up with a plan yet?"

"I'm still thinkin'."

At the zoo station they climbed off the train and a few others, including a couple of young women with kids in strollers, got off too. Caroline started talking to one of the babies as the mother smiled at her and then pushed her stroller after the other woman who had started down the tunnel.

"Okay," Betty said. "Stand over here for a minute out of sight. Here's all I can think of. You two go into the mens. Don't show yourselves until you're sure we are past the ticket checker and almost at the end of the tunnel."

"But how are you and Caroline gonna get past?" Danny asked.

"Here's our story. I'll be struggling with Caroline and my walker and I'm goin' to tell the guy that you two, our husbands, have the zoo passes, you're just in the washroom. Don't start down the tunnel if we're not past him because if he holds us at the gate and makes us wait for you two, we're screwed."

"So what happens when we get there?" Charlie asked. "If he lets you and Caroline through and we can't come up with any passes, we're buggered. There's no way he'll believe us and let us in too."

"You've got to be able to bluff your way through. Stall until we're out of sight. That way he won't call me and Caroline back. You'll have to tell him that I have the passes and I must have forgotten."

"God, Betty, that's a lousy plan. If you and Caroline get in and we can't, you two will be in there on your own," Charlie said.

"Look," Danny said. "You'd better take a little of my cash, just in case. That way if you're lucky, and we're not, then maybe you an' Caroline can get a bite to eat or at least that ice cream you wanted. If we don't get in, Charlie and I will have to wait out here until you two show up again. Any idea how long you'll be inside if you make it?"

"Mmn. I think we should start back to the home about 3:00. You have your watch, Charlie?"

Charlie nodded.

"Count to about a hundred then go into the tunnel. Make sure you can be seen before you go into the washroom. Then Danny, you keep an eye out, peek out the door, to see how we make out. If Caroline and I are turned back, we'll meet out here again. Wish us luck. Come on, Caroline."

"Oh, yes," Caroline said.

"Start countin', Danny." Betty took Caroline's hand, pushed her walker ahead of her and the two disappeared into the tunnel.

"One, two, three, four, five, six, seven..."

Charlie snorted. "Some plan this is. Damn that Betty. There isn't a hope in hell this is gonna work."

"Ten, eleven, twelve, thirteen, fourteen..."

"We shoulda had a plan made up before we left the home."

THE GRAND GETAWAY   23

"Twenty-two — shut up, Charlie, you're making me lose count— twenty-three, twenty-four..."

"What are you and I gonna do if we don't get in? You're not suggesting that we just lay out here on the grass for the next five hours? We've gotta do something ourselves, go someplace."

"Thirty-six, thirty-seven... We'll have to wait until we see how Betty and Caroline make out. If it doesn't work, we'll regroup here and make some other plan. Maybe go somewhere else. I've lost count. Stop yapping. I must be at about fifty. Fifty-one, fifty-two, fifty-three."

"Go? Where? Betty had her heart set on the zoo."

"Jeez, Charlie. Would ya shut up? Just shut up. I think I'm at sixty-nine, maybe higher. I've lost count completely. I think we'd better go now. Come on."

They rounded the corner and entered the tunnel, walking slowly. A few more visitors entered behind them and Danny motioned Charlie back to let them pass. He made sure he and Charlie walked down the centre of the tunnel in full view where the ticket checker was sure to see them. When they were opposite the washrooms, he stopped Charlie and pointed to the men's room. Charlie nodded and followed Danny. There was no one else in the washroom. Charlie went immediately to a urinal and had a pee while Danny stood at the door holding it slightly ajar, looking down the tunnel.

A train had just arrived and about 15 people were walking down the tunnel in scattered groups. A few stopped at the ticket office to buy tickets but most of them moved on down the tunnel and Danny figured they must have annual passes.

"What's happening?" Charlie whispered behind him.

"I don't know, I can't... Ah there they are. They're second in line. Now they're talking to the guy. Looks like Betty's pointing back this way. The guy is looking this way, keep back. Betty is arguing with him and the line behind them is getting longer. Now I can't see them, there's too many people in the way."

"So now what?" Charlie asked.

"Someone's coming. Go back to the sink," Danny hissed, letting the door close as he went to the paper towel dispenser. Charlie was washing his hands again. A man entered and immediately went into one of the stalls. Danny grabbed for the door again and took a peek.

"Come on, Charlie. Betty and Caroline are nearly at the far end of the tunnel. They made it. Let's go."

They left the washroom and started down the tunnel. "Walk slower," Danny said. "We don't want to get to the ticket checker guy until Betty and Caroline are outta sight."

"What are ya gonna say? We need to have the same story," Charlie said.

"Yeah. I know," Danny replied. "Be on the same page, as they say nowadays."

"Jeez I hate those stupid sayings," Charlie said. "Like, *From the get-go*. What the hell was wrong with *From the start*?"

"Well," Danny said, "we don't have time to argue the finer points of the English language right now."

Betty and Caroline had just turned the corner at the end of the tunnel and disappeared when Danny and Charlie reached the barrier. There was a young mother with a little kid in a stroller, and an elderly couple just ahead of them.

"So, what are ya gonna say?" Charlie hissed.

"That Betty has our passes."

"Holy shit!" Charlie said, causing the elderly woman to turn and glare at him.

The young woman with the kid in the stroller had gone and now the woman in front of them was complaining that she and her husband would have to pay for parking. "When we bought our season's passes, I thought parking was included. It's outrageous."

"Sorry Ma'am," the ticker checker, whose name tag showed his name was Brad, replied. "I just work here. But there's a pamphlet that explains that."

"It's ridiculous," the woman snapped. "Come on, Hector, we have to hurry if we're going to see the penguins on their walk."

"Your tickets, sirs?" Brad asked.

"Oh yeah," Danny said. He patted his pockets then turned to Charlie. "Did Betty give them to you just before we went into the washroom?"

"No... um." Charlie looked a bit nervous.

"Daaad," a little girl behind them whined, "are we gonna see the *elphi-nuts* soon? Why can't we go? You promised we'd see the *elphi-nuts*."

"We will, honey, in just a few minutes. You'll get to see the *elphi-nuts*, um elephants." He grinned sheepishly at the people waiting just behind them. "She's always called them *elphi-nuts*."

"I'm sorry sirs," Brad said, "but I can't let you in without tickets."

"But we have season's passes," Danny argued. "Look, our wives just went on ahead of us with our passes. They just forgot to give them to us."

"I'm sorry sir, but as a matter of fact they said that you had the passes and I let them through."

"I want to see the *elphi-nuts* now, Daddy! You promised." The little girl stamped her feet and started howling. Danny could feel the crowd behind him and Charlie growing restless.

"Sirs, if you would just step aside, I'll let some of these people through," Brad said.

It took about another five minutes before the line-up had passed and Danny was ready to give it one more try.

"Look, Brad. My wife is getting a bit absent minded and she thought we had the passes. She just forgot to give them to us."

"Sorry sirs. But I can't let you in without tickets. I've already let your wives in and if I let you in too, I could lose my job."

"But we didn't have tickets," Danny said. "These were season's passes. We're just four old folks out for a day. Have a heart, Brad, we can hardly get by on our pensions. We can't afford to buy more tickets."

"Yeah, that's right," Charlie chimed in, finding his voice. "We bought our passes on voice-mail."

"Voice-mail?" Brad asked. "Do you mean on the internet?"

"Yeah, that's it. I have trouble getting my head around all this new-fangled stuff," Charlie mumbled.

Danny glared at Charlie.

Some more people arrived, and Brad scanned their tickets or passes while he went on talking to Danny and Charlie. "I can't do any more. You could try making your case at the ticket office. If you get the girl there to call security to find your wives and they have your passes, then we could let you in, but otherwise... I'm sorry."

CHAPTER 5

Danny and Charlie walked back down the tunnel. When they reached the ticket office, Danny glanced over his shoulder. Brad was busy checking tickets. Danny and Charlie walked on out of the tunnel.

"So, what now?" Charlie asked. "You think that kid was on to us?"

"I guess so," Danny said. "Especially when you said we booked our zoo passes on voice-mail," Danny laughed, "and what was that about not being able to get your head around those new-fangled devices? I thought you said you hated those stupid sayings."

"I was just trying to speak the kid's lingo. Be hip, as they say."

"I think they say cool, nowadays." Danny chuckled.

"Whatever," Charlie said. "What happened to Betty's *one for all and all for one* – we all make it or nobody does? But jeez, I sure hope they don't call security to look for Betty and Caroline. It would be really crappy if they got thrown out. It'd be nice if they got a chance to look around for a while. So what do we do now? I guess there's no way we can get in."

"There might be," Danny said. "Just give me a minute." He looked at Charlie. "You're pretty skinny, like me. There's just a chance I might be able to find it."

"What? A hole in the fence?"

"Not exactly. We have to walk around to the other side of the zoo."

"I don't mind walking." Charlie said. "Let's go. Betty will be getting anxious. You're not going to try the same story at the other entrance gate, are you?"

"No. How are your knees?"

"My knees? Why? I could probably crawl through a hole in the fence, okay."

They walked to the other side of the zoo, past the entrance gate and Danny began to scan the brush on the far side of a wide ditch. "I may not be able to find it. The brush has grown up quite a bit."

"But if you're looking for a hole, shouldn't we cross the ditch and walk along the fence?"

"It's not a hole I'm looking for. There used to be an old culvert near here. Pete and I used it to sleep in a few times but not for a few years. They expanded the zoo and they may have taken it out. Pete and I quit coming here when they started construction. Too much activity. There was an old lilac bush not far from the culvert, a seedling from somebody's garden. Wait! That could be it. It's still got a few dead blooms, but it's grown a lot since I was last here." Danny scrambled into the dry ditch then disappeared behind a bush growing on the far side.

He reappeared a moment later. "Come here, Charlie. Quick. We don't want to be seen."

THE GRAND GETAWAY   27

Charlie staggered into the ditch and Danny pulled him in behind the bush. "Here it is."

"Holy smack! How are we going to get in there? It's awful skinny."

"It is. But so are we. Pete and I were able to squeeze into it and we'd bed down end to end on dry grass. It used to be outside the zoo but now it goes under the fence since they made the zoo bigger. I'll take a look and you follow me if I keep going, okay?"

"Crawl on our hands and knees into a god-damn culvert barely as wide as my ass, in the dark. What if we get stuck? I think this is a piss poor idea, Danny."

"Okay. What's yours?"

"Hell, I don't know."

"Well, I know there's no way we can climb over the fence. It's real high and the top has three strands of barbed wire. And I guess you don't happen to carry wire cutters. So this is all I've got. The culvert. And... unless you can come up with something better, Betty and Caroline are waiting inside wondering what we're doing. Betty has her heart set on this. You want to give it a try or not?"

"I guess. I'd never hear the end of it if Betty knew I chickened out."

"Okay then." Danny got on his hands and knees, which was a little difficult because the lilac bush had grown so much. "It's real dark. I can't see much. After I go in, stick your head in and I'll give you the okay if I think we can make it." Danny took off his knapsack and shoved it into the culvert before scrambling in after it.

Charlie knelt down and took a look inside as Danny's feet disappeared.

"Hey! Danny, can you see the other end?"

Danny's muffled voice came back. "I can see a little light, but I think there's just grass growing over the other end. You follow. I think it's okay."

Charlie nervously poked his head inside the culvert, then using his feet, he pushed himself inside. It was pitch black but he could hear Danny scrambling ahead of him. He tried to follow, wriggling himself along. "Jeez, it's hard on the elbows and the knees. Damn!"

"What?" Danny's voice came back to him.

"I just bashed my head," Charlie grumbled. "Are you sure there's enough air in here? It's kinda hard to breathe and awful dusty."

"God! Don't go having a heart attack. Rest for a minute," Danny called back.

"How long is this culvert anyway, Danny?"

"I can't remember. Maybe six, seven metres. What's that? Twenty feet? Pete and I never crawled all the way to the other end. We usually backed up to get out again."

"Jeez! I don't think I could back up," Charlie said. "God! It's hot in here."

"It's not hot. You're just warm from crawling. I can see the end now. Oh."

"Oh what?" Charlie called.

"There's some kind of a grill over the end."

"Jeez. I feel like a sardine in here and there's not enough air."

"Don't tell me you suffer from claustrophobia now, Charlie. It's a hell of a time to go telling me that. We'll have to back up."

"I don't think I can do that, Danny."

Danny could hear the panic in Charlie's voice.

"Just lie still. It'll be okay. I'll take a look at this grill. It's only a couple of feet away. There's lots of air coming in. You won't suffocate."

Charlie heard Danny move ahead again as he lay still, taking slow breaths. He sure hoped Betty would appreciate the efforts he and Danny were making. How long, he wondered, would Betty and Caroline wait for him and Danny to show up? Betty said they would head back to Cavandish about 3:00. God! That was about four and a half hours from now. What if he couldn't back up? He'd never last four and a half hours in here. He tried wriggling backwards but was sure he hadn't moved a bit, maybe had even gone forward. He was now convinced the culvert sloped downhill towards Danny and backing up would be impossible. If he couldn't back up, then Danny would be trapped too. They'd both die inside the damn culvert and never be found.

"What are you doing, Danny?" he called.

"Trying to get this grill off the end of the culvert. I'm not having a lot of success. It's a bitch. If I can't get it off, we'll have to back out again."

Danny heard Charlie groan.

"Stop moaning for a minute. There's a couple of rusty screws coming through a plate holding it on."

"So how'll you get the screws off with your bare hands? Aren't the heads of the screws on the outside?"

"Yeah they are. But I had a pair of pliers in my knapsack along with a couple of other things. I always carry a few tools. If I can snap off the ends of the screws, I might be able to force the grill off."

"If you have a pair of pliers, why in hell didn't you just cut a hole in the fence with them?"

"We'd be standing outside the fence for a week trying to cut a hole with these pliers – they aren't exactly heavy-duty. Now shut up and let me try to get this bugger off."

Charlie heard Danny grunting as he strained with the screws. "Come on. Come on," he heard him mutter. "There you bastard! That's one." Danny grunted again.

Charlie heard more panting and grunting and some cursing and when he heard a clanging sound, he called, "What's happening, Danny?"

"I'm bashing on the grill with my shoe. I got the screws broken off but I had a hell of a time reaching my shoe. The grill is kinda rusted on but I'm getting it loose. There!" He heard the satisfaction in Danny's voice. "Got the bugger off. Now crawl after me."

THE GRAND GETAWAY   29

Charlie heard Danny move ahead and he got back on his elbows and started pushing himself forward. Suddenly the culvert seemed flooded with light as Danny scrambled out the far end. Then he could just make out Danny's face peering in at him.

"Come on. You're nearly there. Keep moving. You'll make it."

Danny's face seemed a hell of a long way off, but gradually it got closer and then Danny's arm shot in and caught the back of his jacket and pulled. Charlie's head popped out into the air. Danny pulled some more and he was free. He scrambled to his feet, gasping for air.

"We made it. I thought I was gonna die in there. God. We're pretty dusty looking. What the...?"

"What?" Danny asked.

"That black thing," Charlie whispered hoarsely. "Holy! We've come up inside the panther cage. And it's moving this way. A black panther." Charlie was pointing and his face had gone white.

Danny saw a bush moving slightly and caught a glimpse of a black-haired creature, and an eye peering at them through the bush. Danny looked at the culvert, hoping they could make their escape out the way they had come, but Charlie was already running for a nearby fence.

"Shit!" Danny gasped, then quickly ran after Charlie, knowing he'd have to help him over the fence. There was no other choice now. They would be sitting ducks if he tried to stuff Charlie back into the culvert.

Charlie had reached the fence but was making little progress in climbing it when Danny got to him. Charlie wasn't able to get a foothold on the vertical bars.

"Here!" Danny gasped. "Put your foot on my hands and I'll bunt you up. But hurry for God's sake, hurry!"

Danny cupped his hands together and Charlie quickly placed his foot on top of them. "Grab for the top of the fence when I heave you up. Go!"

Danny heaved upward on Charlie's foot. He surprised himself with his own strength and Charlie shot upwards. He staggered a bit, but Charlie must have got a hold as the weight left Danny's hands and Charlie was floundering over the top. Danny lunged for the top of the fence himself and was surprised when he made it. The thought of having those razor-sharp teeth sinking into his rear gave him the strength. The damn panther can probably jump half way up this fence too, he thought. He saw Charlie tumble to the ground then pick himself up as he reached the top himself. He got one leg snagged on a top bar for a second as he realized that the fence wasn't particularly high. Strange, he thought, as he struggled to free his leg. Then Charlie was laughing.

"It's okay. It's okay. I got it wrong. The sign says..." Charlie started laughing again as Danny managed to swing his leg over the top of the fence. "It's a beaver." Charlie was pointing to the sign on the outside of the fence and still laughing. "It's not a black panther."

Danny hit the ground and swatted at Charlie. "You stupid bugger. I almost shit myself!"

"Thank God for small mercies then." Charlie chuckled.

"What!" Danny snapped.

"That we didn't get any suppositories at Cavandish, this morning. Now that would have been disastrous."

"You bugger. Let's get out of here and go find Betty and Caroline."

CHAPTER 6

"God! What happened to you two? It looks like you've been dragged through a sewer pipe." Betty gasped. She and Caroline were sitting on a bench near the elephant enclosure.

"You're not far off the mark there," Charlie said, slapping at his pants and jacket, causing a cloud of dust to drift away in the breeze.

"It's just a little dust." Danny laughed. "Your plan, *who has the zoo passes*, didn't work. I think that kid knew he'd been conned by you already and wouldn't let us in, so we had to find another way."

"Caroline and I had almost given up on you. We got tired of hangin' around the penguins. When they took a few on the penguin walk across the bridge, Caroline wanted to pick one up. I'm sure the keeper thought we were tryin' to steal one. We've also looked at the elephants. We've been sittin' here a while, so I think we could manage a walk through the African jungle. Maybe we can get a bite to eat. Then I think I'll just take Caroline into the tropical plant greenhouse, sit on a bench and relax until we head back to Cavandish."

"Okay," Danny said, "give us a sec to clean up in the washroom over there and we'll go."

When Danny and Charlie came out of the washroom, they all walked the short distance to the African savanna building and went inside. "God, this is as hot as the dinin' room at Cavandish," Betty said. "I wonder if the maintenance man who runs the boiler moonlights here on the weekends?"

They watched a large family of red river hogs scamper about. Caroline laughed at the baby hogs running back and forth. Then they moved on to look at a couple of hippos.

"Oh, little boy," Caroline said, and bent over to talk to a small boy walking with his mother. What she said next didn't make a lot of sense, but Betty smiled at the mother who listened to Caroline for a moment, then smiled and moved on.

"Caroline likes watchin' little kids more than the animals," Betty said. "I guess it comes from her years as a grade one teacher. I must say the kids are more interestin' than these hippos. Look at them, just lyin' there."

They moved on to look briefly at the giraffes and finally the gorillas who were a little more active, but the steamy heat of the building drove them out into the fresh air. The smell of chicken and hamburgers attracted their attention.

"Do we have enough to buy somethin' to eat?" Betty asked. "That food smells good. I haven't had a burger in ages."

"Probably not the best thing to eat in our condition," Charlie said.

"Hell, Charlie. You only live once. That food smells too good, and when we get back you can eat all the pureed carrots and crap you want. Come on. If you think a burger is goin' to kill you, at least you'll die happy."

Betty ordered a burger for herself and a chicken burger for Caroline. "Caroline really likes chicken," she said. "And I'm having a real coffee to go with my burger. I'm tired of that brown, hot, decaffeinated water they call coffee at Cavandish."

"What the hell! I'll have a burger too, with all the trimmings," Charlie said. "As long as I don't have to crawl out through that god-damn culvert to get out of here again. And a real coffee too."

Danny had a chicken burger and added a couple of orders of fries to share between everyone. The sun was warm, and they found a picnic table close by. While they ate, Charlie related the episode in the culvert.

"I'm eating this burger to celebrate my close call with death by near suffocation – not to mention my last-second leap over the fence from the jaws of that panther."

"You mean the beaver!" Danny said. "He said there was a panther chasing us. I nearly killed myself scrambling over the fence, and I had to get this bugger over first. You'd think with all the nature programmes he watches he'd know the difference between a beaver and a panther."

"It looked black, and my eyes hadn't adjusted to the light after crawling in the dark in that culvert. And, by the way, just last week, on the news, I heard a guy in some former Russian republic, one of the *istans*, was killed by a beaver when he tried to photograph it."

"What, the beaver mistook him for a tree?" Danny asked.

"I don't know. I only know he bled to death when the beaver bit him."

"Balls!" Danny said.

"Is that where the beaver bit him?" Betty laughed. "But I think Charlie is right. Some guy did get killed by a beaver somewhere. I heard it on the news. Caroline and I will stay away from the beavers. Now, would you two help me and Caroline get to the, what is it called? Oh yeah. The conservatory. I think we'll just relax and smell the flowers and plants."

Danny and Charlie escorted Betty and Caroline into the conservatory. The smell of vegetation and the sound of running water greeted them as soon as they entered.

"Now this is more like it," Betty said. "Not hot and sticky like that African animal house. Just warm enough to be comfortable. That bench by that banana tree and those lovely red flowers will suit me and Caroline nicely. If you two boys want to scout out the zoo for a while, me and Caroline will be happy here for an hour, anyway. And look, isn't that lovely? There's a blue butterfly."

Danny and Charlie left Betty and Caroline on the bench, Betty finishing her second coffee and Caroline greeting little kids who happened to come by with their mothers.

THE GRAND GETAWAY   33

"Let's go see the lions," Charlie said. "It feels good to be out in the fresh air instead of breathing that stale air at Cavandish, like being cooped up in an airplane forever."

They followed the direction the sign pointed for the lions, and found a lion and two lionesses lying on some large flat rocks taking in the warmth from the sun.

"Not much happening here," Danny said. "I think maybe they've just been fed."

"Yeah," Charlie said. "Let's sit and watch them for a little while. I like lions. Do you know that in the wild, lions feed only once or twice a week?"

"I didn't know that. And what do they do the rest of the time?"

"Not much," Charlie replied. "Mostly sleep. They sleep up to 20 hours a day."

"Well then, if they've just been fed and they've just fallen asleep, I'd say we're in for a hell of a long wait before they move. Not much different than sitting and watching some of the residents at Cavandish."

"It's nice here anyway. Let's just sit awhile. You could kill a little time telling me a bit more about yourself. I've known you for nearly two weeks now and you haven't said much."

"Not much to tell." Danny sighed.

"You surely haven't been living on the streets all your life?"

"Just about, when I think about it. The years fly by. Yep, the years fly by."

"But what about when you left school? Did you get a job?"

"Before I finished school, my old man had left. He had a drinking problem. I think my mother probably threw him out. I never saw him again. I was about ten at the time."

"Brothers or sisters?"

"No. Just me. My mother did her best. Didn't have a lot of education. She worked as a cleaner in schools. Saw to it that I finished. Not the highest marks or anything but I finished. The trouble was, I fell in with some kids who were into joy riding. They'd steal a car, ride around for about an hour, then abandon it. Never did any damage. No vandalism. Just borrowed the car. I liked cars. Got a charge out of grabbing a car and soon I was an expert at getting into cars. We got caught three times by the cops. We were still juveniles and mostly got our wrists slapped. My mom was real mad and tried to ground me for a while. One night I snuck out. Met Mick and Kenny, my two buddies. They'd found a real hot sports car, a hard top, but couldn't get into it. I figured it out. It was a two-seater and Mick and Kenny wanted a ride in it first. They were supposed to meet me after about twenty minutes. They didn't. They hit a gravel truck just a block away from where we were going to meet. I heard the crash, saw the sports car under the body of the truck, the top sheared off, the truck driver screaming. Truck driver musta called an ambulance, cops. Then the sirens. I knew Mick and Kenny were dead. I ran home and never stole a car again. Blamed myself because Mick and Kenny wouldn't have had the car without me."

"Jeez that's tough," Charlie interjected. "But they could've died anytime. So could you."

"Well I didn't. It was Mick and Kenny."

Danny fell silent. He didn't tell Charlie that before he'd run, he rushed to the car. He recalled again the horror of finding Mick's headless body and Kenny with his neck twisted grotesquely, his mouth open. Blood spurting from a torn artery had splashed onto the front of Danny's jacket. That's when he'd screamed and ran.

Danny paused, not saying anything to Charlie about how Kenny's blood spurting onto his jacket had left him with a fear of getting anything spilled on his clothes. Every spill or stain brought back that terrible moment, including the time he'd spilled a cup of coffee onto the front of his shirt in a McDonald's. Funny, he thought, I haven't had a panic attack in a long time now.

Danny continued, "I had finished school, but I had a juvie record. Went to tech school and really ate up mechanics. Loved it. Wasn't sure I could get a job without a clean sheet. But I did. Apprentice mechanic at a local repair shop. The owner knew about my past but gave me a break. My mom was pleased. I was doing well."

"But then I started drinking," Danny went on. "On Fridays some of us went for a beer after work. I guess I liked it too much. Started drinking other nights. Showed up hung-over a couple of times for work. My mother didn't find out about it. She was in hospital. Cancer. My boss was decent. Gave me a number of chances after my mother died, but then my work got too sloppy and I didn't always show up. He had to let me go. I got one or two other jobs. Held them for a while, but not for long. Tried AA, but always fell off the wagon. I had no staying power. Followed the NASCAR circuit for a while. I even got taken on as a mechanic with Ford team, but I got busted and that career was over. Can't be drinking on a race car team. That's about it. Never did settle down. Only recently got off the booze and that just about sums things up."

"Holy jeez," Charlie said. "What about women? You hook up with any?"

"Not really. The women I kept running into had the same problem as me." Danny lapsed into silence.

A loud roar snapped Danny out of a nap. He leapt to his feet, convinced he was about to be pounced on by a lion until he saw all of them still inside the fence. Charlie was standing just outside the low barrier, leaning forward, his face as close to the inside fence as he could get. The lion roared again but remained lying on the rock with his head raised and turned towards Charlie. The two lionesses had raised their heads too and were looking in Charlie's direction.

"What the hell did you do to rile up that lion?" Danny grabbed Charlie's arm.

"Nothing! I just stared at him a while. Maybe he doesn't like me."

"Good grief! How long have you been staring at him?"

"You've been asleep for about half an hour. 'Bout that long, I guess."

"He gives me the creeps. But you musta given him the creeps first. Let's go find Caroline and Betty."

The lion gave one more roar, then seemed to lose interest, rolling on his side to go back to sleep. About a dozen school kids, attracted by the noise, ran up with a breathless teacher in tow.

"Come on. Let's go." Danny pulled Charlie's arm. I don't know what you did to that lion, but I don't think we want to be accused of irritating the animals."

They found Betty and Caroline still sitting on the same bench in the conservatory. Caroline was asleep on Betty's shoulder.

"Ah, there you are. We both dozed off and I just woke up. What have you two been up to?"

"Charlie was annoying the lions," Danny said.

Caroline stirred, opened her eyes and lifted her head from Betty's shoulder. She smiled at Danny and Charlie. "How did you get here?" Then she watched as a fairly large red and black butterfly settled on her hand. "Tickles," she said. The butterfly flexed its wings then flew off. "Gone," Caroline said.

"Well maybe we should be gone soon, too," Betty said. "It won't be much fun on the train if we get caught in rush hour. We've had a nice day, but I think we should start makin' tracks."

"Do you think we should go by way of the tunnel?" Danny asked.

"Well I'm sure as hell not crawling through that culvert again," Charlie said.

They made their way slowly back towards the exit tunnel, stopping briefly when Caroline looked at some monkeys and then the penguins. When they got to the tunnel there was no sign of Brad, the ticket checker. There was a girl standing in his place and she showed no interest in those that were leaving.

The two blocks from the station to Cavandish seemed a long way. Betty was dragging her left foot a bit and having a tough time walking without stopping for short rests.

When they made it to the front doors, Danny and Charlie decided they would go in first and create a distraction in case any questions were asked about why Betty was escorting Caroline back in.

They had timed things well. The afternoon snack and coffee were being served in the dining room and only one nurse was behind the front desk. Charlie checked off all four names without the nurse even casting him a glance and Danny strolled back towards the front doors as Betty coaxed Caroline into the lobby.

At supper that evening they toasted their successful day out with a glass of cranberry juice.

CHAPTER 7

About three weeks later, Danny had just returned from his recycling route and started towards Charlie's room, when the nurse at the desk behind him called out, "Oh, Mr. Carroll, Brenda has been looking for you."

Danny turned and said, "Okay, I'm just off to the washroom."

"I'll tell her you're here," the nurse called.

Well that's that. I'm busted.

Charlie was just coming out of the bathroom when Danny got to their room. "Guess I'd better get my belongings and get out of here," Danny said.

"Why? What's up?"

"Brenda, the accountant, wants to see me. It's pretty obvious it's about money. No doubt she's discovered I've been living at Cavandish for about five weeks without paying a cent."

"Darn. Could be. But see what she says first. Jeez we're gonna miss you if you get booted out. Maybe you could tell her the cheque's in the mail or something."

"Mr. Carroll." It was Brenda. She was standing in the open door of the room. "Could I see you in my office for a few minutes?"

"Sure," Danny replied.

Brenda waited, so there was no hope of stalling or hatching any brilliant plan with Charlie. 'The cheque's in the mail,' was a no hoper, and it was too late to gather his stuff and just walk out. Brenda was waiting to walk him down the hall. When they reached her small office she closed the door behind them.

"Have a seat, Mr. Carroll."

Danny picked up on the 'Mr. Carroll'. Usually, Brenda had called him Danny whenever she'd seen him in the hallways. She had his file on her desk and she opened it. As she looked at it, Danny studied her, waiting for the questioning to start. She was a slim, dark haired, attractive woman in her mid to late thirties, who usually wore a business suit with tight fitting pants. Charlie often commented on her cute ass. As Danny waited, she brushed her dark bangs from her eyes and studied his file. He knew there couldn't be a lot in it. Betty hadn't asked him many questions and Danny suspected Brenda was no dummy. As she scanned his file, he noticed a smile flick across her face. She giggled, put her hand over her mouth, became serious and looked up at him.

"Mr. Carroll, Danny. That is your real name?"

Danny nodded.

"You know Danny, I've been checking up on you and I can't find much about you. Much, that is, that seems to be true. For example, it says here your doctor is Mark Hop..." She scanned his file again, "Hopwood. Is he, Danny?"

"Er, I'm not sure." Danny scanned his own memory. Was Hopwood the name Betty had said she had used?

"Well, Danny. I checked with Dr. Hopwood's receptionist and she says they have no record of anyone named Danny Carroll, never have, and she's been with Dr. Hopwood for over 10 years. So, either you've been surprisingly healthy for the past 10 years, or you just picked some doctor's name out of the phone book."

Danny guessed now that that's what Betty must have done.

"It also says here that you transferred in from Purple Springs Hospital. They've never heard of you. You've been here now for about five weeks. I don't know how you did it, and the owner, Mr. Darlington, would give me hell if he knew you've been free-loading. Mr. Darlington hates to lose money. In fact," Brenda let out a hoot of laughter, then got it controlled down to a snicker, "he'd be really pissed off, excuse my language. Sorry. I've been having a little celebration with some friends at lunch time. So how did you do it? Okay, I can guess. We have a huge turn-over of staff, so it was easy to fool new staff members and I was away for two weeks holiday and I didn't catch on. But heavens! Five weeks! I suspect you had a bit of help. Charlie Bannister and, perhaps, Betty Danglemeyer?" Brenda paused and smiled.

"I admire your guts, Danny, and I bet Charlie and Betty had a good laugh at my expense. Well, not really mine, more like Mr. Darlington's. I've been onto you for about a week, but I wanted to be sure. I saw the book at the front desk and saw you were out today. I looked back a few weeks and I see you usually go out on Wednesdays. I noticed a few weeks ago you, Charlie, Betty and even Caroline were all out at the same time. You all went out together, didn't you?"

Danny nodded.

"I hope you all had a good time. Where did you go?"

"The zoo," Danny said.

"The zoo! God, I haven't been there for years. Well Danny. I must tell you. This is my last day here. And I think it better be yours. I'm taking up a new job at another care home and I'm looking forward to it, but I couldn't leave here knowing you were scamming Cavandish. It wouldn't look good on my record. It would be *a cop on my blotty book!*" Brenda snickered. "Oh darn, what is it? A blot on my copybook. What the hell did I say? Never mind. Anyway, I couldn't have it come out that you were living here free of charge on my watch. You understand, Danny? It wouldn't look good."

"Yeah," Danny said. "I'm sorry if I caused you any problems."

"You didn't really. But you would be a problem if you stayed. I must say your arrival gave Charlie a new lease on life. He hadn't been the same since his roommate Jim died, and when you came along, he perked up. Betty too. The staff really noticed it. But it's over. You have to go. Sorry. You understand?"

"Yeah. Sure."

"So tell me, how did you do it?"

"I just walked in. Had a coffee and stayed."

Brenda laughed again. "God, Danny, you've a nerve. But thank God I found out about you before I left. Now, I'm not going to blow the whistle on you. If you promise to go quietly, I'll say nothing. But you must be gone before supper time. Here's what I'm going to do. I'm going to shred your file. Pretend you haven't existed, or at least haven't been here. You can get your things, say goodbye to your friends. Do you have a place to stay?"

"I can find a place. I'll be okay."

"You sure?"

Danny nodded.

"Okay, Danny. At snack time, tell Charlie and Betty you're leaving. Then gather your things and just go quietly. I'm going to tell my friend, Carmen, who works here, what happened, and she'll know if you try to sneak back in. So, are we agreed?"

"Yeah, thanks. Could I still visit?"

"Yes. But I suggest you don't come every day. Maybe stay away a while. We have some new staff coming in next week and it might be good to stay away so not so many of the staff ask questions about you."

"I'll leave as soon as I get my things and tell Charlie and Betty. And thanks."

"Just slip out after coffee break time." Brenda stood up and extended her hand. "Good bye, Danny." She hiccupped again. "And good luck."

The piano lady was banging out some tunes and trying to get the residents to sing along.

"I'm gonna miss you, pal," Charlie said. "We all are. Betty will be mad we didn't wake her up to tell you were leaving, but she'd be mad if we did wake her up. It was fun while it lasted." Charlie chuckled.

"Fun, fun," Caroline repeated. Then she studied the cookie on her napkin and began counting out loud the number of chocolate chips. When she got to five, she repeated it, broke the cookie, and put a piece in her mouth.

Danny sipped his coffee and patted Caroline's hand. She smiled back at him.

"Brenda suggested I stay away for a while, sort of lie low. There's a bunch of new staff coming in who won't know me and ask too many questions. Well, I'd better get going. Better not overstay my welcome. Coffee break's just about over."

"Yeah," Charlie said sadly. "Keep us informed of what's happening in the real world out there."

The piano lady was playing and singing, *We'll Meet Again*.

"See you Charlie, Caroline." Danny stood, picked up his knapsack and left.

Caroline smiled and waved.

Charlie called after him. "See you soon, Danny."

CHAPTER 8

Danny stayed at The Shelter for the first couple of nights, but found getting a good night's sleep difficult. He was woken the first night when there was a scuffle over the ownership of a pair of shoes. The second night he was startled out of his sleep by the guy occupying the mattress next to him, who sat bolt upright and began rocking and droning some kind of prayer mantra that lasted for half an hour, waking up half the residents who yelled at him to 'Shut the fuck up!' Unfortunately, he woke up twice more during the night and repeated the whole performance. The next day Danny sought out the culvert under the railway bridge.

Since leaving Cavandish there had been two recycling days and Danny had retrieved his shopping cart and done the rounds. He missed the companionship with Charlie, Betty and Caroline. The days seemed to drag, but he heeded Brenda's advice not to visit too soon.

When he did return, a couple of the staff recognized him and greeted him by name, but no one asked where he'd been, and it was obvious there were several new staff members who didn't know him. There were also a few new faces among the residents in the dining room.

He found his three friends seated together and Betty greeted him with, "God we've missed you. I'm sure Charlie has been telling me the same joke for a month. It's time to plan another breakout."

"Hi, Caroline," Danny patted her hand and she smiled at him.

He was given a coffee and cookie.

"So, what's new?" Charlie asked.

"Not a darn thing. I've missed you guys too. Slept rough most of the time. Too noisy at The Shelter."

"People are dyin' like flies around here," Betty said. "Another outbreak of pneumonia but mostly bored to death. I don't want to die in this place, Danny."

"Yeah," Charlie said. "Betty was really ticked off when I told her you got the boot. Her hatred of this place hit a new high. But she's cooled off a little, although she's still grouchy as hell."

"Oh shut up, Charlie. Since our outing to the zoo, I've been thinkin'. I don't want to die in here. There's more to life than this, and if I can find a way to make it happen, I will."

"Make what happen?" Danny asked.

"I'm workin' on it. It'll take more plannin' than the zoo trip. It's just a dream at the moment."

"Anything I can think of costs money," Danny said. "Funland, Heritage Park, fancy restaurants."

"I've got bigger dreams than Funland or Heritage Park. This would be a long outing. Right now it's just a dream that needs a lot of plannin'."

"A longer outing!" Charlie scoffed. "You were beat after the trip to the zoo. If it had been any longer, we'd have had to carry you back. I've seen you reading those old *National Geographics* from our so-called library. You're not thinking we could make it to the mountains and back, for God's sake!"

"No. I'll tell you when I think about it a bit more. Just leave me be for now. I don't want you telling me it's impossible."

"So you think it's possible?" Danny asked.

"It's possible. I keep hearin' this song in my head *The Impossible Dream*." She sang the first line. "I don't remember anymore, I just know that line. I've no idea when or how it got stuck in my head."

"Yeah. Well we all have dreams. Most of them impossible," Charlie said, "like me winning millions in the Lotto."

"Of course it's impossible, you dummy. You never buy a ticket." Betty snapped.

"*Man From La Mancha*" Danny said.

"Did he win the Lotto?" Charlie asked.

"It's from the musical based on the book by a guy called Cervantes."

"What are we talking about here?" Charlie asked. "I'm lost."

"The song stuck in Betty's head," Danny replied. "It's from a musical based on a book. The book is called *Don Quixote*. He's the hero. It's a famous book. A classic."

"How come you know so much?" Charlie asked. "Did you read it?"

"Half of it. It took me a while, but the public library is a good place to stay warm, and reading books passes the time. So is it an impossible dream, Betty?"

"If I tell Charlie, here, it will be. I admit there are a lot of things to figure out for it to ever happen."

"Well, sometimes sharing the problem can help," Danny said.

"You'll laugh if I tell you. Right now I guess it really is an impossible dream. Still, it helps me forget I'm stuck in this place. Makes me feel happy thinkin' about it. You have any real happy memories, Danny? Like, what was the happiest time of your life?"

"I suppose the time I was at tech school training to be a mechanic and then the first time I got the job working in the garage. I was pretty happy for a while. Made my mom real happy too. But I let her down when I got into drinking and lost the job. Let myself down too. Thought I could shake off the booze habit when I got the break with the NASCAR Ford team."

"How did you get that job anyway, Danny?" Charlie asked. "You couldn't have had great references."

"Nah. Not a one, but I ended up in Chicagoland Speedway in Illinois where there was a NASCAR race and I made it to the track one day when they were training Security wasn't like it is nowadays and I hung around the pits. A bunch of mechanics were going over the engine of a Ford Mustang, wondering how to solve a problem with the carb, and I said you should try a little different mix of air and gas. I can't remember what it was I said but it was something simple. The head mechanic said, 'Okay let's give it a try.' They did, drove it a few laps and it worked. They got an extra five miles an hour. I was watching from the background when the head mechanic came looking for me. He'd thought the suggestion had come from one of the team, but someone pointed me out to him. He asked me what I knew about cars and said he'd try me out on the team. That was a really happy time. I'd been given a big break but I screwed that up with the booze again and that was that. But I was real happy while it lasted. What's your happiest memory, Charlie?"

"Oh I dunno. I guess I really liked travelling 'cross the country on the trains. Loved going through the mountains. That was probably the happiest time ever. No wait – it was when I was a kid and I went fishing with my dad on the Miramichi one day, salmon fishing it was. I'd only been once before and I never caught anything. I was just 13 or 14, and my dad said he would show me how it was done. Trouble was, he never let me try anything on my own. He was an expert at everything. But I'll never forget the look on his face when I landed a 15-pound salmon.

"I was fishing downstream from him, behind some bushes and he couldn't see me. We'd both got mad at each other. He'd shown me how to cast a few times and I wasn't doing it exactly the way he said. He kept telling me I'd never catch anything. I swore at him when I couldn't stand his bellyaching anymore and I wandered further down the river. When I hooked the fish, I couldn't believe the pull on the line, but I didn't yell out to Dad. I knew he'd just start telling me I was doing it all wrong, taking over my rod and landing the fish himself. I thought I'd never land it. It took me nearly half an hour, and it felt like my arms would be pulled out of their sockets. It wasn't until I got the salmon into the shallows and I knew I had him beat that I yelled out to Dad to bring the net. You shoulda seen the look on his face. Yeah, that was a great day. Makin' my dad smile. He was a miserable bugger, with never a kind word, but that day I think he kinda liked me." Charlie grinned.

"And you, Betty?" Danny asked. "Your happiest time?"

Betty looked away like she was studying the blurred picture of the woods and stream on the wall by the table. Danny heard her sigh. Then she sat back in her chair and closed her eyes.

"It was the day Arnie Thorkleson showed up on his motorcycle. An Indian. The bike, not Arnie. He was a blue-eyed blonde just a couple of years older than me. I was just turnin' 17. I heard the rumble of his bike long before I saw him. I was sittin' in the long grass in the ditch beside our hayfield." She opened her eyes, smiled at Danny and continued. "I don't know how many bales of hay I'd slung onto the trailer that day with my older brother, but I was hot and tired. There was hay down the front and back of my shirt and I was sick of haulin' bales. So when my dad turned the tractor and trailer and headed for the farm yard, I slipped off the back of the trailer into the long cool grass by the ditch.

"I hadn't any plans. I just wanted to cool off. Get some of the itchy hay off my skin. I knew if I walked back to the farm yard, probably more than half the bales would already be unloaded. They'd curse me for not being there but there'd be a lot less for me to haul off the trailer.

"Then I heard the bike again. I guess I stood up, listenin'. The rumble became a roar when he got to the top of the hill. He wasn't wearin' a helmet but had some kind of red bandana wrapped round his head and was wearin' dark sunglasses. He must've seen me, but he didn't slow down. I gave him a wave when he got to me and all I saw was a white flash of teeth as he gave me a nod. Then he was roarin' down the hill at the end of the straightaway. I stood there listening to the roar fadin' as he moved further away from me.

"*Freedom! Escape!* That's what I was thinkin' as I stood there listenin' to the sound of his bike getting fainter. What I would have given at that moment to have some way to just up and go, get away from the drudgery of life on our two–bit farm, and Dad's constant bitchin' that I wasn't pullin' my weight around there, despite the fact that I did most of the cookin' and cleanin' since Mom had died a year before. Dad had pulled me out of school before I graduated. Said I was needed at home with Mom gone. I was feelin' real sad as the sound of the bike got fainter and fainter. I sat back down in the cool grass and began to pick bits of hay out of my shirt. I wondered where he was headed. Anywhere would be better than here, I was thinkin'. I could still hear the bike. Maybe he'd stopped. I stood up again to listen. The sound was definitely gettin' louder. He was comin' back."

Betty fell silent and nobody spoke except Caroline who was having a quiet conversation with herself.

"Go on, Betty, don't keep us in suspense. Tell us the rest," Danny urged.

Betty looked at Danny. "Ah... It was a long time ago."

"So. Tell us," Charlie said. "It sounds a hell of a lot more interesting than me catching a fish."

"Well, okay. I can still see him crestin' that hill and pullin' up beside me. He switched off the motor and for a minute I thought he was just gonna ask for directions. But he didn't. He grinned at me and asked, 'Wanna ride?' Then he took off his sunglasses and I saw those beautiful blue eyes. I think I just stood there open mouthed, sayin' nothin', and he picked a piece of hay outta my hair. I felt like a real hick.

"I was only thinkin' about gettin' him to take me as far as Bentley. Rimbey was the next town, just down the road where I'd gone to school. We roared through Rimbey, and when we got to Bentley he bought me a milkshake. I'd no idea how I would get back, but when he said he was headin' south, far south, I wanted him to take me along. And he did."

"Bloody hell!" Charlie gasped. "You had a lotta guts, just takin' off like that. How far south did ya go?"

"The Grand Canyon." Betty smiled wistfully then started studying the picture on the wall again.

Danny and Charlie looked at each other but said nothing for a minute until Danny broke the silence by asking quietly, "Is the Grand Canyon the dream you have now?"

Betty nodded. Then she turned away as she wiped away a tear.

"Jeez," Charlie muttered but Danny shushed him.

Most of the residents had left the dining room and the last of them were being ushered out as the tables were being cleared off.

Betty turned to Caroline and got her to finish her cookie.

Danny looked around. "I'd love to stick around to hear more of your story, Betty, but Brenda said if I hung around too long, I'd be over-staying my welcome, so I'd better get going now that this place is clearing out. I'll get back here again as soon as I can."

CHAPTER 9

It was several days before Danny made it back to Cavandish. He'd woken up at The Shelter and was cleaning up, preparing to go when he realized that it was recycling day. He'd been thinking about Betty's story so much, it had completely slipped his mind. He'd spent a couple of hours at the library studying an atlas and locating the Grand Canyon. It was a good 2000 kilometres south.

Was it really Betty's dream to go and see the Grand Canyon again, or just to find this Arnie Thorkleson? Was Arnie Thorkleson even alive? Betty said he was a couple of years older than she was, and Betty was well into her seventies.

He'd got a couple of photocopies of the map pages from the atlas in the library and taped them together to follow the route she and Arnie might have taken. It would have been quite a ride on a motorcycle. He was looking forward to hearing the rest of the story.

When he got to Cavandish just before snack time, he found Charlie sitting in the front lounge, looking anxious.

"Good to see ya, Danny. Betty took an early nap. She wouldn't tell me another word about her motorcycle trip until you showed up. Said she didn't want to tell the story over and over."

"Do you think that's really her dream?" Danny asked. "To see the Grand Canyon again?"

"I dunno. I think she nodded when you asked her. But if it is, then between you and me, I think she is crazy."

"Well don't go telling her that and making her mad. I want to hear the rest of her story. Letting her tell it her way is good for her, even if she can only relive it in her mind. Here she comes now with Caroline."

"Glad you're here Danny." Betty smiled. She had Caroline's arm and was leading her towards the dining room.

"Oh, there you are." Caroline smiled at Danny and said, "That's what she said."

They sat at the same table as before. Betty helped Caroline get seated. She took a glass of juice for herself and Caroline, while Danny and Charlie asked for coffee. Danny added a container of cream to his coffee and stirred it as the cookies arrived. "I'm hoping you'll continue your story of the motorcycle trip, Betty. You said you made it to the Grand Canyon."

"We did. I have no idea how many days it took us to get there — I was just enjoyin' myself. Funny thing is, I didn't even worry about goin' off with a stranger like that. Arnie was so sweet, lookin' after me, like when he bought me a few things — some sun tan lotion and a head scarf to keep me from getting burned by the wind and the sun. I was already a bit burned from workin' on the hay, but a wind burn on

THE GRAND GETAWAY   45

a bike can be pretty bad. He had some campin' gear, a small pup tent. I think we made it to Montana the second day."

"Did you have any trouble crossing the border?" Charlie asked.

"I don't think so. I can't remember any problem. It's a long time ago. I think they just waved us through when we said we were Canadians."

"Much different nowadays," Charlie muttered.

"I remember some of the places we camped," Betty continued. "Somewhere near Great Falls in Montana. I remember bits of Yellowstone Park. We saw Old Faithful, that famous geyser, and there were hot springs. It was all magic to me. Arnie paid for everything, the food and so on. I didn't have a cent. I remember his tent was sure small, really only big enough for one, but we squeezed in. He cooked breakfast every mornin'. Sometimes we'd stop at a drive-in for lunch, and he'd cook supper over a campfire at night.

"We had some trouble findin' a campsite when we got to Salt Lake City, but we just scooted through and found a spot somewhere by a little creek. I remember it was getting pretty hot, it was July. Arnie had bought me a couple of blouses and a pair of shorts at some gift shop on the road. Some place called Jackson Hole."

Danny pulled the photo-copied map from his pack and spread it on the table and studied it. "Here's a place called Jackson. It's just after Yellowstone."

Betty peered at the map. "I can't see that too good. I'd have to use my magnifyin' glass in my room. Can I borrow that map?"

"Sure," Danny said. "You can keep it."

"Well after that I think we went to some national park with really red rocks, a canyon. But it wasn't the Grand Canyon. It had some other name. I don't think I've ever seen anythin' so red."

As Danny peered at the map, Charlie, said, "I think it was probably Bryce Canyon. I saw a *National Geographic* programme on TV a few months ago. It's in Utah."

"Yeah, you're right. I found it, here it is," Danny said. He pushed the map over to Charlie.

"I remember we camped right at the edge of the Grand Canyon when we got there. The colours, especially in the early evenin', were so beautiful," Betty said, "the blues, purples, reds."

"Blues, purples, reds, oh yes. That's what she said," Caroline repeated.

Betty patted her hand and continued. "And the canyon was so deep and wide. Arnie and I lay down at the edge and looked down at the river so far below. It was beautiful, but I was kinda scared. We stayed there three whole days. By then I think I was in love with Arnie Thorkleson." Betty broke off and stared at the wall.

Everyone was silent, including Caroline who was nibbling on her cookie.

Betty said softly, "Arnie never took advantage of me. I was an innocent girl, but I gave myself to him that first night at the Grand Canyon in our little tent. He was very gentle. He must have known it was my first time. It was probably his first time too. Things were different then." Betty stopped talking again and they waited.

"Anyway, that was that. We had made it to the Grand Canyon. I was feelin' a bit guilty 'bout leaving my dad and my brother, without tellin' them I was goin'. I was sure they'd be worried. I'd sent a postcard from that place Jackson, sayin' I was okay. Arnie had got where he wanted to go and only had a little money left for gas. So he decided we should head back. He was going back to the oilfields up north again. A week later he dropped me off at the very spot where he'd picked me up. That was the last I saw of him. He promised to write, but he never did. For months I checked the mail lookin' for a letter."

"What did your dad say when you showed up?" Charlie asked

"Not much. I think he said, 'Thought you'd be back. Got all the hay done, no thanks to you.' My brother was glad to see me because he'd had to do the cookin'. They'd lived on canned beans and potatoes when I was away."

"So you've never been back? To the Grand Canyon, I mean," Danny asked.

"No, never have. Dad died in an accident with the old tractor and I looked after my brother while he looked after the farm. I got a job at a fast food place in Rimbey, then I took the notion to go up north and cook in one of those oil camps."

"Were you looking for Arnie?" Charlie asked.

"I guess. In a way. Never ran across him though. Worked in the camps for nine years 'til I met Roy."

"That's a great story, Betty. Here, keep the map. See you all in a few days."

"Thanks for listenin', Danny. You too Charlie. You didn't laugh at this old gal's memory, anyway."

Charlie cleared his throat. "That's okay Betty. Like Danny said, it's a great story."

Danny kept mulling over Betty's tale in his mind for the next few days. He got a map from the library and studied it some more. He suspected a lot would have changed since Betty first made the trip and wondered how she thought she could ever get to the Grand Canyon again. He wouldn't mind seeing it himself. Betty's age, lack of money and difficulty travelling would be three huge strikes against her. Going by Greyhound, even if it was possible, would cost one hell of a lot of money. It might be possible to fly if she had the money. Hell, Betty hadn't even had enough to pay the entrance to the zoo. Hitch-hiking would definitely be out, he mused. He chuckled to himself imagining Betty standing beside the highway with her walker and her thumb out. Then again, maybe someone might feel sympathy seeing an old lady hitch-hiking with a walker. And she was feisty enough to push her walker out in front of a car if she got fed up waiting for one to stop.

Danny spent a couple of nights at The Shelter, but again retreated to the culvert. He made a list in his head of what would be needed to make Betty's dream come true, and money topped it. His list, besides money, consisted of transportation, accommodation and food – and those all required money. Winning the lotto seemed like their only hope.

He returned to Cavandish a few days later. He was a little late getting there and found the trio already in the dining room drinking coffee.

"Charlie and I made up a list." Betty smiled and waved an envelope.

Charlie looked up at the ceiling and started humming what Danny thought sounded a bit like the *Impossible Dream* song.

"I should never have taught you that tune, you bugger. I thought you were goin' to humour me," Betty snapped.

"Bugger, bugger, sugar, sugar, sugar," Caroline chimed in.

"Sorry Betty," Charlie said. "I'll try not to rain on your parade. Betty's been making me go over her list…"

"Our list," Betty interjected.

"Okay, our list. For the past three days," Charlie continued. "She calls it, The Problem Solving List."

"And you haven't contributed anythin' towards solving the problems. You only make them worse," Betty said.

"Can I see the list?" Danny asked

"Okay, so it's still just a fantasy," Betty backed off. "But it's fun to think about it." She passed the envelope to Danny.

The list read, Money to buy:

> Vehicle.
> Registration.
> Gas.
> Food.

Danny said nothing for a moment. "Assuming you somehow bought a vehicle, do you have a driving license?"

"Caroline has," Betty answered.

"Caroline!" Danny gasped.

"But we were hopin' you might have a license or could pass a test and get one."

"Okaaay." Danny paused. "This is just a fantasy, Betty, isn't it?"

"At the moment, yes. But so was the zoo trip."

"But the zoo trip is a hell of a lot different from a trip to the Grand Canyon," Danny said. "I mean I thought it was just you who wanted to go there. Now it sounds like you want to take Caroline along."

"Yes, and you and Charlie, if you're game."

"All four of us!"

Charlie was rolling his eyes and looking up at the ceiling again.

"You wouldn't happen to have a license, would you?" Betty asked. "Come on, Danny, at least play along for now. What are you gonna do all winter? Wouldn't you like to go somewhere warmer? If the three of us stay here, we may all be dead by spring, from boredom or pneumonia. Caroline got pneumonia twice. Once one or two get it we're all in danger. It spreads like wildfire. Every illness does. Come on, help us think through some of the problems."

Danny took a breath. "Okay, Betty, I'll play along, but I wouldn't want you getting your hopes up too high. Let's consider one thing at a time. First, where would you get enough money to buy a vehicle? Do you have any?"

"A little. We wouldn't need a whole lot. We could maybe raise it somehow. Take a look at this." Betty produced an ad torn from a newspaper.

Danny took it and read – *Malone's Vehicle Auctions. Sales every Saturday from 9:00 a.m.* There was an address and telephone number and at the bottom of the ad he read, *Come and check out our vehicles during the week. We are open for viewing from 9:00 a.m. to 5:00 p.m. Monday to Friday.*

"I assume you've considered other ways of getting there, Betty, besides driving. Like Greyhound bus or flying."

"We have."

Charlie snorted.

"I have," Betty corrected. "The Greyhound just wouldn't be the same and would probably cost as much as an old vehicle, and flyin' would be out of the question."

"Getting there is half the fun," Charlie interjected.

"Well, I don't know that you'd get much of a car for the price of a bus ticket," Danny said. "It wouldn't be in great shape."

"We thought with your experience as a mechanic, maybe you could fix it up," Betty said.

"I haven't worked on any kind of a vehicle for years. They've changed a lot, and even if I knew how to fix an old one, it would need parts. I've no idea what it would cost, and where would you get the money?"

"We're not sure... I'm not sure, yet," Betty said. "We thought you might be able to go to the auction place and see what's available. I looked up their web site on the computer. They have some cars as low as five hundred bucks. Could you just scout out what's there and then we could maybe see if we could raise some cash?" Betty asked. "I know this all sounds crazy."

"You can say that again," Charlie said. "But it beats watching soaps on TV."

"It's about time for me to go," Danny said. 'I'll take this with me and think about how I could make it out there to have a look. I might be able to get a bus. It's right at the edge of the city. I can't promise anything. One step at a time. I'm sorry Betty. I agree with Charlie – this sounds completely nuts. But I'm willing to go look and report back."

"Thanks, Danny. I knew I could count on you."

"Well, Betty, as long as you realize it's the impossible dream at the moment. I don't want you to be disappointed. Let's treat it as a challenge for now. Will you be happy with that?"

"I will, Danny, I will." Betty patted his arm.

"She will, she will, she will," Caroline repeated.

Danny patted her hand. "See you soon, Caroline."

Caroline smiled. "Soon, soon, soon."

CHAPTER 10

Danny spent the next couple of days checking out the bus route to the auction place, which was some distance from downtown. He also extended his usual collection route, adding several more alleys. Keeping just ahead of the recycling truck, he hit the jackpot at the back of one house and found several boxes of empty beer bottles. He then added a few more plastic bags to his cart, tying them to the handles and along the sides. It was a hard haul back to the recycling depot, but he got over $50 for the returns, one of his biggest hauls ever. He slept well that night in his culvert.

Next morning, he bought himself a Subway sandwich for lunch, then caught a bus that dropped him off at the closest stop to Malone's Auctions. All around were open fields, but the driver pointed to a gravel road a little further ahead. "Malone's is about half a mile down that road, you can't miss it. You'll see all the cars and a big metal building. Their sales are on Saturdays, but you can look around today."

"Thanks," Danny said. "I'll take a look."

It was a decent summer day. He hadn't gone far down the road when he caught a glimpse of a metal roof reflecting the sunshine. A little further on he could see rows of vehicles surrounding the building. There was a trailer on one side of the huge yard with a sign over the door that read, 'Office and Payments'. As he walked into the office a young woman was sitting behind a counter talking on the phone. A pile of booklets listing the vehicles for the upcoming Saturday auction lay on the counter and Danny picked one up and scanned it. The first thing he noticed on the front page was the statement — '$500 Deposit Required On All Vehicle Purchases'. There was also a list of buyer's fees according to the vehicle's selling price, the lowest being $60 for vehicles up to $975.

The woman put down the phone and smiled. "Can I help you?" she asked.

"Eh. It says here to check with the office staff if you need to know a vehicle's reserve," Danny said.

"Actually, most of the vehicles have their reserves written on the windshield. A few have no reserve and it says that too. Have a look around. The keys are in the ignitions if you want to start one up, but you can't drive it around if you start it, okay?"

"Okay, thanks," Danny said. "I'll take a look. I can have one of these lists?"

"You sure can. That's the auction list for Saturday, but we sometimes get a few late additions. Good luck."

"Thanks."

Danny went outside and began walking down the first row of vehicles. He quickly saw it was pointless even looking at the vehicles, as the reserves ranged from $2500- $4000. Most were passenger cars, with a few vans and a sprinkling of half-ton and one-ton trucks. The next row was much the same. The cheapest reserve he

THE GRAND GETAWAY   51

could see was $1500 for a 2003 Ford Taurus – probably not a bad price, although he wasn't really up on the price of autos and that was just the reserve. It might well sell higher. He opened the driver's door, climbed in and turned the key; the engine fired right away. It sounded fine to him, but he knew he was just killing time. He turned off the engine and climbed out. Perhaps he could get one of those *Auto Trader* booklets to get a better idea of vehicle costs?

Sauntering down the next row of vehicles he found a few with no reserve, but even the worst of them looked like they'd bring more than $500, just for parts. Plus, there would be the buyer's fee of at least $60. And there was also the issue of a license and registration. *This is a real wild goose chase, he thought. What am I doing here?* He climbed into a ratty looking SUV and took out his Subway sandwich. Even if they had a vehicle, they sure as hell wouldn't be able to come up with money for gas, never mind cash for food and accommodation. As he ate his sandwich, he chuckled to himself. What a hare-brained scheme this was. Betty could fantasize all she liked, but there was no hope of it ever coming true. He wondered if her dreams were the only thing that kept her going.

He'd given up on dreams himself. He had no ambitions, and just took each day as it came. For a long time that had been enough, but now he found himself mixed up with Betty, Charlie and Caroline, life was getting more complicated. Still, he thought, it is more interesting. Having finished his sandwich, he rested his head on the back of the seat and felt the warmth of the sun through the side window. He dozed.

Danny awoke with a start. Someone was tapping on the window beside his head. It was the young woman from the office. She gave him a relieved smile when she saw he was awake, as if she might have thought he was dead.

He stepped out of the vehicle. "Sorry," he said. "I guess I fell asleep."

"That's okay, just wanted to make sure you were okay. I'm just out marking on a few reserves." She paused to look at a sheet and then scrawled $1200 with a white marker on the windshield of the vehicle he'd just been sitting in.

"Do all the vehicles that sell meet the reserve, or do they ever sell for less?" Danny asked.

"Not usually. A lot of these vehicles are on consignment, so there is usually a minimum reserve price agreed on by the owner. I think the prices are pretty realistic. But sometimes, like if it's a repossession, a bank may just want to get rid of it and not care much about a reserve. Anyway, I've got to get back to the office."

Tomorrow he'd go to the library and see if he could find an *Auto Trader* magazine. At least he'd have something to show Betty. Maybe convince her that it was going to take a lot more money than she expected.

Apparently *Auto Trader* was only published online now, so the librarian showed him how to find it on a computer. He was slow and lost his way a few times, but he managed to make a short list to show Betty. Nothing on it even came close to meeting the low price she was hoping for.

"We've come up with $580." Betty announced triumphantly.

"What!" Danny was startled. "How did you come up with that?"

"Sold a few things," Betty replied. "Things we don't need anymore."

"Like what?"

"A little bit of jewellery," Betty said. "Just some useless stuff."

"I don't know about that. My watch wasn't useless," Charlie said.

"No, it wasn't entirely useless," Betty retorted. "We got 50 bucks for it."

"And the rest?" Danny asked.

"My old weddin' and engagement rings. Like Charlie's watch, they were just sittin' in a drawer and there sure was no sentimental value in them."

"Who did you sell the stuff to?" Danny asked.

"Betty convinced me to go downtown with her to see this jeweller friend she knew," Charlie answered. "But we found out he'd died five years ago and the store was a thrift shop now. We ended up at a pawn shop."

Danny sighed. "Well, I'm sorry to give you bad news, but that's not nearly enough to get you anything that you'd consider decent transportation. I went out to Malone's and spent a couple hours there. I couldn't see anything that you could possibly afford. I doubt you'd find anything that would take you as far as the zoo, never mind the Grand Canyon."

"Oh Danny, I hope you're not gettin' like Charlie here, the born pessimist. Maybe you missed somethin'?"

Danny could see Betty was thinking, and then she suddenly blurted out, "We should take another look."

"What? Who?" Charlie asked.

"All four of us. Maybe you missed somethin'. Look, it'll be another outin'. We could all go on Saturday."

Charlie snorted.

"It's a hell of a long way," Danny said. "We need the bus, and we can't skip paying like we did with the train."

"We'll come up with the bus fares," Betty said firmly.

Danny groaned inwardly. He knew she was adamant about all four of them going. He didn't want to think about the journey there, but on the bright side, maybe going to the auction would finally convince Betty it was a hopeless fantasy. He'd show up Saturday and get it over with.

When Danny was about half a block from Cavandish he caught sight of the three of them crossing the street towards the bus stop. Charlie waved. Betty didn't have her walker.

THE GRAND GETAWAY   53

When the bus arrived it was half empty, and all four of them found seats just behind the driver as soon as Betty paid the fares.

"What did you do with your walker, Betty?" Danny asked.

"I'm feelin' pretty good today and I thought it would just be a nuisance."

Danny wondered if the walk down the road to Malone's would be a bit of a problem for her, but then again, they didn't have to arrive right at the start of the auction – it wasn't going to make any difference.

"I brought the money," Betty said. "We have a grand total of $650. Charlie found a few more bucks in a bottom drawer he'd forgotten about."

Danny remembered the $85 he still had in his wallet but didn't mention it. No point getting Betty's hopes up. "I don't think you should count on bidding on anything. This is just to take a look like you said, okay?"

"Sure, Danny. Look, I know you mean well and want to convince me it's hopeless, but I just have to see for myself. Humour me, okay?"

"Okay, Betty."

When they got to the end of the bus route, they began ambling down the gravel road. Betty and Caroline walked in front while Charlie and Danny took up the rear. Danny figured it would take nearly half an hour to reach the auction at the rate they were going. Only one vehicle came from the opposite direction, all the other traffic was heading past them towards Malone's.

A station wagon slowed, then pulled over. The driver leaned out the window and called, "You folks heading to the auction?"

"We are," Betty yelled back.

The driver hopped out and opened the rear door. "Hop in, I'm going there myself."

"Thanks a lot," Betty said as she helped Caroline into the back. Charlie scrambled in beside them and Danny went around the car and got in the front.

"You folks looking to buy a car?" the driver asked.

"Well," Danny said. "Today we're really just looking."

"Have you been here before?"

"We've never been to an auction here," Danny said. "I just came this past week to look around."

"What price range are you looking at?" the driver asked.

"We're really just look –"

"Under a thousand bucks," Betty blurted, cutting off Danny.

"Under a thousand! Gee, that's not a lot."

Danny wondered how Betty had suddenly upped the figure to under $1000.

"I'm Frank Malone," the driver said. "I own the place with my brother, Larry. You won't find much going for under $1000. I have seen it happen, but they're mostly just bought for parts. Still, you never know."

He pulled up outside the metal building, then opened the rear door of the car and helped Caroline and Betty out. "You'll need an auction catalogue. There should be some on a table inside the door."

"Thanks a lot." Betty beamed.

"Good luck to ya," Malone said.

The building's large double doors were open, and people were streaming in. A microphone crackled and then, "Testing, testing, testing. Welcome to Malone's Auto Auctions, folks. We'll be getting started in about five minutes."

"Well, it doesn't sound completely hopeless," Betty said. "Mr. Malone did say he's seen the occasional bargain."

"Yeah," Danny said, "but I wouldn't hold your breath. I'm sure you won't see much at the price you're thinking."

They found the catalogues and Danny picked one up. A line of vehicles was forming outside, ready to be driven into the building. The auctioneer, seated behind a counter on a raised platform, was announcing the terms of the auction. "Remember, folks, we accept a maximum of $500 per vehicle on a credit card. Anything over that, please arrange for an alternate form of payment."

A second auctioneer was set up to the right of the first. Two sets of wooden bleachers faced the auctioneers, and the four of them found space on the front row. As they sat down the second auctioneer announced, "Okay folks, let's get started."

Two vehicles were immediately driven in and parked, one in front of each auctioneer.

"Jeez!" Danny muttered. "Are they gonna auction two vehicles at the same time? That'll be hard to follow."

"Okay folks, here we go," the auctioneer on the left called out. "Lot #15, the Dodge Cavalier. The reserve is eighteen-five; who'll give me $1800? Seventeen, sixteen, fifteen? I have fifteen. I have seventeen."

Now the second auctioneer started up. "Okay, folks, let's go on lot #14, the Chevy half-ton, reserve two thousand. Who'll give me $1900? I have seventeen-fifty, eighteen, eighteen, I have eighteen. Eighteen-five, I have eighteen-five."

Danny was having trouble keeping up. The auctioneer on the left banged his hammer. "Sold for $1900!" Meanwhile, the auctioneer on the right was still working on the Chevy. "I have $2100. Twenty-two, twenty-two. Come on sir, we've got a lot of vehicles to sell today. Twenty-one, going once, twenty-two... Thank you sir, twenty-three, twenty-three. Okay, sold for $2200. Thank you, sir."

Danny scribbled down the prices for the two vehicles as they were driven out through the exit doors on the right, then a couple of real clunkers were towed in. Despite having no reserves, they both sold for over $1000.

"I'm goin' to take Caroline to the bathroom," Betty said, helping Caroline to her feet.

"Okay," Danny replied. "Just watch yourselves going out. They're bringing in a couple more vehicles."

THE GRAND GETAWAY   55

As soon as they left, Danny turned to Charlie. "How long have we been here now, Charlie?"

"How would I know? Betty sold my watch, remember?" Charlie still sounded miffed.

"What's sold so far should convince Betty that buying a vehicle is just not possible," Danny said. "Look at that old camper. Sagging on one side. Needs new springs and probably a lot more work."

The auctioneer to the left banged down his hammer, "Sold for $1650!"

An old three-quarter ton Ford truck on their right went for $1275.

"Uh, those seats are taken." Danny turned to a couple of men who'd just sat down where Betty and Caroline had been sitting, but they ignored him. Betty and Caroline arrived just then.

Charlie motioned to the two men sitting beside him, but Betty said, "That's okay. I'll take Caroline up higher, I think the noise bothers her."

"How much longer do you want to stay?" Danny asked.

"Could we give it another half-hour?"

"Sure." Danny could tell from her voice that she was really disappointed with what she had seen.

Two more vehicles had been driven in and both microphones were going full tilt as Betty and Caroline made their way up the steps.

Danny was finding it hard to follow. He found his thoughts drifting. This was a bitter blow to Betty's dream – but on the other hand, he thought, she had to face reality. He hoped she'd treat this as just another outing.

A nondescript small bus rumbled in and stopped in front of them with the engine still running. It had once been blue and white, but someone had given it a bad yellow paint job, the words 'Park 'n' Ride' still showing through. Behind it, a green van with a badly cracked passenger window and a large dent in the side was towed in.

The auctioneer in front of them turned on his mike. "Who'll give me $400 on the Ford bus?"

The auctioneer on the left started asking for bids on the GMC van. "As you can see folks, this van is a little damaged. Who'll start at $500?"

Danny was surprised that there were three or four bids on the two vehicles and both auctioneers quickly brought the sales to a close, slamming down their hammers almost simultaneously.

"What did that wrecked GMC van sell for, Charlie?"

"I think it was $550."

"Ah, got it. But I missed the hammer price on that Park 'n' Ride heap."

Betty and Caroline joined them.

"You ready to leave?" Danny asked. "I'll treat you to lunch. There's a concession stand outside. You like hamburgers, Betty? My treat."

Betty didn't move. She stood looking at Danny with a mixture of panic and excitement on her face. Caroline was chattering to a little boy who was sitting with his parents on the front row. He was grinning at Caroline and his parents were smiling good-naturedly as Caroline gestured and smiled at him.

"What is it, Betty?" Danny laughed. "You didn't buy something, did you?"

"No. I didn't... Well... We... Oh Danny..." She was still holding Caroline's hand, but she put her other hand to her breast.

"Are you feeling okay? You're not having chest pains, are you, Betty?" Charlie asked.

"You didn't lose your money? Don't tell me you lost your money," Danny said.

"I didn't lose it. It was Caroline."

"You gave the money to Caroline? Holy shit!" Charlie gasped.

"No. I didn't give the money to Caroline," Betty snapped. "She... I had to blow my nose," Betty said softly. "When I let go of her hand Caroline made a bid. She bought us a vehicle." Betty's lip trembled. "I'm sorry."

Charlie looked like he was about to have a heart attack.

"Calm down, Charlie. Let's get outside. We'll get some food and coffee first. We'll be able to sort this out, it's just a mistake." Danny grabbed Charlie's arm and headed towards the door. Betty followed with Caroline. They ordered hamburgers and Betty asked for hot chocolate for herself and Caroline. There were some picnic tables nearby and Danny persuaded Charlie not to ask any questions before they were all sitting down eating.

Betty broke up Caroline's hamburger for her on the paper plates they were given and added a little ketchup. "I'm sorry. I screwed up. When I let go of Caroline's hand they were on the final bid and she saw a little boy and waved at him just before the auctioneer brought the hammer down."

"So, let's just take off," Charlie suggested.

"We can't do that now," Betty said. "I have a receipt."

"You already paid!" Charlie gasped.

"The deposit," Betty said. "As soon as I got Caroline down the steps the guy takin' the deposits was waitin' for us."

"You're sure the guy worked for Malone's?" Danny asked.

"Yes I'm sure. I have the receipt right here." Betty pulled the receipt from her pocket and gave it to Danny. It was an official receipt and was signed by a J. Henshaw for Malone's Auctions.

"I see they put Caroline's name on the receipt," Danny said. "Well, we'll go to the office and explain," Danny said. "It's no big deal. I know the girl who works there, and we've even met the owner. We'll get your money back. Which vehicle was it?"

"The last one before we came out," Betty replied.

"The wrecked van? The one they had to tow in there?" Charlie shook his head.

"No, the other one. The yellow bus," Betty replied.

"So how much was the bid?" Charlie asked.

THE GRAND GETAWAY   57

"It was $600. The receipt is for the $500 minimum deposit," Danny answered.

"Could we just go and look at the bus first, Danny?" Betty asked. "I'd like to see it before we ask for our money back. Then you can tell me how bad it is, and I'll give up this foolish idea. The vehicle we almost bought, our magic bus. I can still dream about it, anyway."

"Magic bus!" Charlie snorted. "I think the sooner we get our money back the better," he grunted.

"Come on Charlie, it'll only take a few minutes," Danny said. "It can't do any harm."

The bus wasn't hard to spot. Its smeared yellow paint job stood out in the back row of the lot.

"God, almighty." Charlie said.

Danny poked him and muttered, "Don't make Betty feel any worse. She feels bad enough."

"Park 'n' Ride," Charlie couldn't shut up. "More like Park 'n' Walk."

Danny walked around the bus, noting that the two front tires were almost worn out, though there was still a little wear left in the rear pair. The body had numerous scrapes and dents. Its previous owner must have thought that painting the bus yellow would somehow improve its looks. It hadn't.

He pushed open the entry door and climbed inside. There was a small second seat beside the driver's that must have been added later. He pulled the latch button for the hood and heard it pop open. He got out and lifted the hood as the others gathered round. He could see the worry and regret on Betty's face. Caroline had spotted the writing that still showed through the yellow paint and was repeating, "Park, park, park, ride, park, ride."

"Well?" Charlie asked. "How bad is it? It doesn't look like this wreck could even get us back to Cavandish and save us the bus fare. Let's just go and get the money back."

"It looks like it could do with a new fan belt and some tires, so far," Danny said. "That's all I can tell right now. I'll get in and see how it runs." He climbed in and turned the key. The engine turned a couple of times as he kicked the gas pedal, but it wouldn't catch. It just groaned and died. The battery was shot. If he couldn't get the engine started, he had no idea what kind of shape the bus was in.

"So... so far, new tires, new battery, and God knows what else," Charlie said. "Let's head to the office and get our money."

"Could we peek inside?" Betty asked. "Just take a look."

"Sure," Danny said.

"What for?" Charlie asked. "This is just a waste of time." Danny opened the door and Betty helped Caroline up the steps. As Danny climbed in, he heard Betty exclaim, "Oh, look! They turned it into a camper!"

Danny hadn't looked around himself when he'd first been inside. Behind the driver's and passenger seat was a small kitchen with a four-burner propane stove, a small aluminum sink, a tiny half fridge, a table with a fake leather u-shaped bench seat around it, and a small set of cupboards. The rear half of the bus was divided by a curtain and four bunks had been installed, two on each side. The top bunks could be folded up against the wall, allowing the bottom ones to be used as seats. Betty took Caroline and sat with her on the bench. The remains of what was once a curtain hung crookedly above one of the windows. A small closet completed the furnishings.

"It's lovely." Betty smiled.

"Lovely? You've got to be kidding," Charlie said. "Look at the dirt on the floor, and the dust!" He pounded on one of the bunks and a brown cloud rose into the air.

"We could clean it up." Betty sighed wistfully.

"What? And we all move in and live here, at Malone's?" Charlie snapped. "It won't even start. We'd be stuck here for the rest of our lives. Probably have to buy grave plots at the back of the property and be buried between another row of wrecks like this one."

"Danny, what do you think? Is it completely hopeless?" Betty asked.

"I knew this was a mistake," Charlie said. "We should have gone to the office and got our money back right away. Now Betty's gone back to being crazy."

"If the engine is good – and I can't tell that right now – but if it was..." Danny thought aloud. "Well, it would take quite a bit of money for tires, battery, fan belt, and I'm sure other repairs. Sorry, Betty but I think we should go to the office."

He felt like hell when he saw Betty's face fall, but he was only stating the facts. Putting something like this old bus on the road with no money was just an impossible dream.

CHAPTER 11

Charlie hurried ahead muttering about how Betty could have let such a thing happen. Every now and then he would stop and turn around, looking exasperated at the slow pace of the others. Danny stayed just a step or two ahead of Betty who was coaxing Caroline along.

Betty was stone-faced, angry with herself, while still thinking that the camper-bus would have been fine if only it was a bit better mechanically. But it wasn't, and that was that.

"I'm just an old fool," she muttered. She remembered how she had badgered Charlie into contributing his watch to the cause. She knew he didn't really want to give it up and, although he hardly ever looked at it and left it in a drawer, she knew deep down it had meant something to him, the only thing he had left from his years with the railway. Knowing that, she thought, I shouldn't have pestered him so much. *I'm a selfish old bitch. This was my dream – not Charlie's, not Danny's, and certainly not Caroline's. Oh God!* Tears sprang to her eyes thinking about it. She squeezed Caroline's hand and Caroline stopped her quiet jabbering and smiled at her.

Still, Betty thought, *if I'd seen the inside of the bus and known what it was like, I might have been tempted to take a chance and bid myself.* Sure it needed a good cleaning, but that was something that would only require soap and water. She thought about what it would have been like, all four of them setting out in the sparkling clean bus, fresh bedding on the bunks, new curtains on the windows, and the little fridge and cupboards stocked with food. She sighed. Stupid dream. Then for some reason her mind drifted to the doll's house she once had. It was given to her as a Christmas gift from Santa Claus when she was about five. She hadn't thought about it for years but now, somehow, the bus and its furnishings had taken her back. She remembered how much pleasure it had given her and how she'd loved to rearrange the furniture. Cleaning up the bus, maybe putting in new curtains, some cushions and knick-knacks, would have given her some of the same pleasure she'd had back then. But there was no Santa Claus anymore.

Danny walked slowly, allowing the two women to keep close to him. He was going over in his mind what he'd say when they got to the office. He took out the receipt that Betty had given him and read it again. The bottom lines caught his eye. *All vehicles are sold as is. It is the responsibility of the prospective bidder to inspect the vehicle prior to bidding. All sales are final.*

Well, Danny thought, we can prove that Caroline has dementia easily enough and her bidding on the vehicle was just accidental. It might, however, be harder to explain why Betty handed over the required deposit of $500, almost the full amount.

They arrived at the trailer that served as the office to find a crowd ahead of them, waiting to pay for their purchases. The line spilled out onto the steps in front of the door. They moved slowly, and it was probably 20 minutes before they got inside. Charlie had been hopping from one foot to the other, and had asked Danny more than once if he thought they'd get stuck with the bus. Danny shook his head and whispered reassurances. He could see how worried Betty was.

Now as they stood inside the door, Charlie hissed, "What are you gonna say, Danny?"

"I'll just tell them the truth. Tell 'em about Caroline."

"Yeah. But they'll wonder why Betty didn't say anything before she handed over the 500 bucks. It's gonna look like we bought it, then took a close look at the bus, decided it was useless and now we want our money back."

Betty heard this and Danny saw she was biting her lip.

"I'll think it'll be okay," Danny said, but the *All sales are final* tagline on the receipt worried him.

The last couple in front of them moved off and Danny found himself standing across the counter facing the woman he had met earlier in the week.

"Do you have your sales receipt?" the woman asked. He saw she was now wearing a name tag and her name was Gail.

Danny handed it to her and said, "There's been a mistake."

"Mistake?" Then she recognized him. "You were here this week checking out the vehicles, right?"

Danny nodded. "But we didn't intend to buy anything. This lady," he indicated Caroline behind him, "waved her hand by mistake."

Caroline, who had been jabbering and carrying on a conversation, was now silent and was giving the girl a friendly smile. "Gail, Gail. Gail, Snail, Mail." She'd caught sight of Gail's name-tag, read it out, and added some rhyming words as she often did.

Danny could see the doubt in Gail's face as she looked at the receipt.

"Which one of you is Caroline Gilchrist?" Gail asked.

Betty let go of Caroline's hand and indicated Caroline. "But she has – "

"Hey! Wait yer damn turn!" Charlie growled. Someone behind Charlie tried pushing ahead of him.

"Okay! Okay! Keep your hair on, you old fart! Are you in line or what? Haven't got all day."

"Up yours," Charlie snapped. He looked like he might throw a punch.

Danny moved quickly and grabbed his arm. "Calm down, Charlie. Let it go." The last thing they needed was a fist fight and the cops arriving.

"Next!" Another girl further down the counter called and the belligerent customer moved over to her, still throwing angry looks at Charlie.

"Next!" Danny turned to face Gail again. "Er, we're all together. Where's Caroline?"

THE GRAND GETAWAY

Betty looked around anxiously. "She was just here."

"You mean that other lady? The lady who bought the bus? She's in talking to Mr. Malone." Gail indicated the office door behind her. "Next!"

Danny stepped around the counter and Betty pushed after him.

"Hey!" Gail said. "You can't go in there!"

She tried to stop them but stepped back when she saw the determined look on Betty's face.

Danny pushed the door open. He heard Betty gasp. Mr. Malone and Caroline seemed to be hugging.

"I'm sorry, Frank! I couldn't stop them," Gail called out.

Malone broke away from Caroline and called, "It's okay, Gail. I know these people." He pulled a tissue from a box on his desk and handed it to Caroline who seemed to be whimpering. He turned to Danny, "Wasn't this lady with you when I gave you a ride in my car this morning?"

"She was," Danny answered.

Charlie had pushed his way into the office and with all five of them, the small office was crowded.

"This lady's upset," Frank Malone said. "When I asked her what the problem was, she started saying "Frankie, Frankie'. Then she started crying."

"She has dementia," Betty said.

"I kinda figured that out," Malone said.

Caroline was doing what she often did with a tissue and had smoothed it out on Malone's desk and was now busy folding it and refolding it.

Malone went behind his desk, lifted the chair from behind it and brought it around to the front. "Please sit down, ma'am", he said to Betty. "There's a couple more chairs there. So, what happened? I thought you said you were only going to look and you weren't going to bid."

"It was a mistake," Danny said.

Malone picked up the receipt from his desk and looked at it, then looked to Danny.

"So, tell me what happened."

"We were only coming to look, that's true. Betty took Caroline up to the back seats and Caroline waved at a little boy. The auctioneer thought she was bidding. Caroline loves little kids," Danny ended.

"I thought so," Frank Malone said. "But tell me why Caroline's name is on this receipt and why somebody paid the deposit of $500? I don't get it."

Danny was still trying to figure out what Frank Malone meant when he said, 'I thought so.' Why would he think that? Maybe people who had dementia liked little kids.

"Tell me. Who paid the 500 bucks?" Malone asked again.

"I did," Betty answered.

"But why? If it was a mistake, why would you pay the deposit? Something doesn't add up here."

"Like Danny said, it was all a big mistake and I made it bigger," Betty answered. "I didn't expect the fellow who was takin' deposits to be waitin' for us. I guess I just got flustered. He asked for Caroline's name and filled it in on the receipt. I had the money and I had this dream..."

"What's this dream?" Malone asked.

"Years ago, when I was quite young," Betty began, "I saw the Grand Canyon. I want to see it again before I die. We need a vehicle to get there and that's why we came here. When Caroline waved her hand and we accidentally bought that bus... well... I admit, in the heat of the moment I was terrified, and at the same time, full of hope. I should have said somethin' right away instead of handin' over the $500. Danny had told us there was no way we could get anythin' that was cheap and would be able to get us to the Grand Canyon."

"So you all want to go see the Grand Canyon?" Malone asked.

Danny noticed that Charlie also nodded when he and Betty said, "Yes."

"And Caroline?" Malone asked. "Her too?"

"We live in a long-term care home and none of us want to die there. If we leave Caroline behind, she'll have no one. Me and Charlie, and Danny, are all she has."

"Does she have no relatives, no husband?" Malone asked.

"Her husband died last year in a car accident comin' to visit her in a snowstorm. He came almost every day," Betty answered.

"Jeez." Malone paused. "Does she know?" he asked. "I mean about her husband."

"We're not sure. I don't think so. I think her memory is almost completely gone."

"Hmm. What's this home like?"

"Well, if home is where the heart is, mine left that home a long time ago. I was hopin' to follow it." Betty said. "Anyway, to make a long story short, that's the dream we had, it was my dream but the others... the others, I... convinced them. But it's over." Betty let out a sob and lapsed into silence.

Nobody said anything for a minute. Danny noticed Charlie patting Betty's hand. Betty took the tissue from Caroline who had folded it into a small rectangle and used it to dab her own eyes.

"Well, I've no problem giving you your money back. But you know that old bus is one of those exceptions I mentioned this morning when I picked you up."

"It doesn't even start," Charlie spoke up. "And Danny says it needs tires and we don't know what else. We'd sure appreciate it, Mr. Malone, if you could just give us our money back and we'll get out of here."

"Is that what you all want?" Malone asked. "To give up on your dream? Look, I won't give you any B.S. That old bus would get you there and back. Sure, it needs a few repairs. Let me tell you about it. It was one of those Park 'n' Ride buses that ferried people from the airport parking lots to the terminal. Back and forth, back and forth. Then, after about seven years, the company traded it in on a new one. I think the dealership that took it in sold it to some hippy and he turned it into a half-assed camper. When he quit making payments they took it back, but they couldn't resell it.

"They just wrote it off. It's been parked in the back of the lot ever since. Until today. Someone on my staff boosted it and drove it in. And you, well, Caroline bid on it. It's sound. I've got a set of booster cables in my car. I can boost it if you want to check it out, or I'll give you back your $500 right now."

There was silence for a minute, then Danny was surprised to hear Charlie clear his throat.

"Well, I know if we don't take another look and satisfy ourselves one way or the other, my friend Betty here is always going to wonder. I would not be able to live with myself if I didn't give Betty's dream every chance. And Betty would never forgive me, either. If I think living at Cavandish isn't great, living there with Betty calling me a traitor every damn day would be hell on earth. I say we take another look. I think the old gal deserves that."

Betty was trying to hold back tears.

"Thanks Charlie. But I hope you mean the bus and not me when you're talkin' about the old gal." Betty sniffled. "You old bugger. What do you think, Danny?"

"Okay, Betty. We can take another look. If it's not up to scratch, I've no idea how we could fix it up."

Frank said, "I'll get my car. I'll come and pick you up in a second."

They sat in silence for a moment after he left. Then Charlie said, "I hope we're doing the right thing."

"Oh Charlie, don't chicken out now," Betty said.

Danny looked at Betty. "Well, this is what they call crunch time. I think we have to decide one way or another. It's not just getting the vehicle. There's going to be a lot more to it. Registration, the license plates. Paying for tires, a battery and whatever other repairs are needed could cost way more than the price we pay for the bus. How do we get that done and where's the money coming from? Then there's gas, lots of stuff we haven't even talked about. If we decide to get it, then we're jumping in with both feet. And there's still the problem of crossing the border."

"Let's just look at it first. Please Danny," Betty pleaded.

Danny sighed. "I think you believe because I used to be a mechanic that I can somehow fix the bus. It's been an awful long time since I last looked under the hood of anything. I've got no tools. We have nowhere to keep it and parts cost a lot more nowadays."

"Yeah," Charlie said, "and I forgot that we don't have enough to pay the 100 bucks we still owe on it, plus the $60 for the buyer's fee."

"I'd hate to let you down, Betty," Danny said. "We could end up with your money gone, a bus we can't fix or drive, and that's as far as your dream will go. But at the moment I don't have a hell of a lot else on my plate, so I'll take another look."

Frank came in the back door of the office, "The car's out back, if you're ready."

CHAPTER 12

Frank gave Danny a thumb's up and Danny, sitting in the driver's seat of the bus, turned the ignition key. The engine roared to life with the booster cables attached to Frank's car. The others stood in a small group a few steps away, Betty holding Caroline's arm and looking anxious.

"Climb in folks and we'll take it for a spin." Frank followed them onto the bus and sat beside Danny as the others squeezed around the table in the small kitchen.

"I haven't driven anything in a hell of a long time," Danny said.

"That's okay," Frank said. "Just take it slow, down that aisle there between the vehicles, and then come around the other side."

The engine sounded smooth as Danny put it in gear, glad it was an automatic. When the bus reached the end of the line of vehicles, he steered it around the back of them and continued in the opposite direction. He tested the brakes. They felt pretty good.

"Take it around a couple of times," Frank said. "Try going a bit faster."

When they had completed three runs, he said, "Park it, keep it running and we'll take a look under the hood."

When Frank and Danny climbed back on board, Frank asked, "Okay Danny, what's the verdict?"

"Well, it sounds good. We know about the battery, fan belt and the tires, but otherwise I can't see anything major. It would need some good service too."

"Of course," Frank said. "Let me drive you all back to the office."

Betty was biting her lip and looking at Danny anxiously when he gave her a thumb's up.

"Wonderful!" Betty exclaimed. "I think we should take it."

"We can't take it anywhere right now," Charlie said. "We have nowhere to keep it."

They rode the rest of the way back to the office in silence, Betty smiling, but Danny and Charlie deep in thought. Caroline was busy looking at a credit application form she'd found on the floor of Frank's car and was reading softly, "Name, Name and add, address, please print, print, lint, mint."

When they'd settled themselves back in the office, Frank asked, "Could you clear up something for me? Do you know if Caroline was ever a teacher?"

"Yes, she was," Betty said. "Why do you ask?"

"Well, when Gail brought her into my office, I thought I recognized her from somewhere. When I asked her what the problem was, she started talking quite fast, but the words were all jumbled up. Then she suddenly stopped, looked at me – I mean really looked at me, and she started repeating my name, except she called me Frankie. She kept repeating it, 'Frankie, Frankie, Frankie,' like she recognized me, but I haven't been called Frankie since first grade.

"That really took me back, to my first day at school. At recess, one of the other kids pushed me off the slide and I hurt my arm. I started to cry, so he called me a baby. Then the bell rang for us to go in, but I was scared and I'd wet myself. I was mortified – I didn't dare go back inside with my pants wet. Everyone would have made fun of me and thought I really was a baby.

"Miss Hagerty found me crying in the corner of the playground. She took me by the hand and said, 'Frankie, everything's going to be okay.' She brought me inside and found me some dry clothes. And she was right – everything was okay. I loved being in her class, and the kid who pushed me off the slide later became my best friend. I think Miss Hagerty had something to do with that too. After Caroline called me Frankie, she started to cry, and I held her and that's when you all came in."

"I don't know if Hagerty is her maiden name," Betty said. "At the home she's known as Mrs. Gilchrist or Caroline Gilchrist."

"I'm positive this is her – calling me Frankie was the clincher." Frank paused. "All four of you are hoping to make it to the Grand Canyon. You're taking Caroline with you?"

"Yes," Betty said, "that's our plan."

Frank fell silent for a minute, looking down at his desk. "Here's what I'll do". He took out a stamp from his desk and marked their receipt *Paid in Full*. "We'll forget about the $100 and the buyer's fee. I owe Caroline that much anyway. Maybe you can use the money to buy the battery and fan belt. That's the best I can do."

"Oh, thank you, thank you, thank you," Betty said. "That's really wonderful. I could kiss you. And you too, Caroline." Betty squeezed her hand and Caroline smiled.

Frank laughed. "Look. We have an account with Select Auto Parts. We get 20% off and I'll get you the same deal. Okay?"

"Mmm," Danny interrupted. "I'd probably be the one to pick up the battery and fan belt, but I'd have a tough time lugging it here on the bus. Could we leave you the money we have and have the battery and fan belt delivered here?"

"Sure, that shouldn't be a problem. What's your last name, Danny?"

"Carroll," Danny answered.

"Another Irishman." Frank put on his best imitation of an Irish accent, "To be sure, did I not say dis marnin' that you could be havin' the luck of the Oirish here at Malone's? With Carroll, Malone and Hagerty, sure how could ya go wrong with the three of us in it. Sure you're all set for a grand getaway." He laughed and picked up the phone. "I'll call Select right now and they can deliver the battery and fan belt next week. What's your phone number Danny? Gail will give you a call when they come in."

"Er, I don't have a phone," Danny said. "Maybe I can call Gail?"

Once Frank got the price, Betty handed over the money for the parts and Frank scribbled out a receipt and said, "Look, it's been a long day. Why don't I give you all a ride back to the home?"

CHAPTER 13

When Danny next returned to Cavandish, he found Betty ecstatic and Charlie looking worriedly through the *Problems To Solve*.

Charlie shook his head at Danny. "Betty's been so hyper since we got the bus, they'll be putting her on Ritalin if she doesn't settle down. She's been going over that map you gave her and planning the route."

"Oh Charlie, don't be such a party pooper," Betty snapped. "He's been carryin' that list around with him and addin' so many new problems to it that he's worn out half a dozen pencils. I think we should just solve one thing at a time. Charlie's list is too depressin'."

"Depressing or not, we still have to figure out how to solve every one, and we won't be able to do that by dumb luck," Charlie retorted. "We can't count on Caroline having been *everyone's* grade one teacher."

"No, no smoking, smoking." Caroline was now repeating what the sign said on the door leading from the dining room into the kitchen.

"Look," Betty said, "the first two things we'll have to do, once we get the bus runnin', is get the license plate and another driver's license."

"Yeah," Charlie said. "Betty's got that last one all figured out."

"She's going to apply for a driver's license?" Danny looked at Charlie.

Betty was fiddling with her cookie. "No," Charlie replied. "You are."

"Me!"

Betty looked at Danny. "I'm sorry, to put such a big load on you. I know I'm expectin' a lot, but you're the key to makin' this thing work. My leg doesn't always work properly, and Charlie can't see his hand in front of his face."

"But I can't remember when I last had a license. I haven't driven anything in years."

"You did fine drivin' that bus up at Malone's."

"There's a hell of a difference puttering around at Malone's where there was no traffic, and driving on some freeway. The traffic isn't going to just park while I drive by, although that might be a good idea. I doubt if I could pass a test."

"Let's take it one step at a time. Look," Betty reached behind her and produced a booklet with the title, *Driver's Guide to Operation, Safety and Licensing – Cars and Light Trucks* and handed it to Danny. "First you do the written test. You can study this book and do it when you're sure of the answers. You get a learner's permit. You don't have to try the drivin' test for ages. And I don't remember any freeways when I went to the Grand Canyon with Arnie."

"Probably not," Danny said. "but that was then – this is now! And this guide says it's for cars and light trucks. We have a bus."

"It's not really a bus anymore. It's a camper. I'm sure it qualifies as a light truck. The rules should be pretty much the same."

Danny said nothing but started thumbing through the booklet. There was a lot of stuff on traffic signs, intersections and turns, highways and freeways, and lots more. "Where did you get this?" he asked.

"I found it on the book shelves here," Betty replied. "I have another one in my room. You could study and I could ask you questions next time you come."

"Why would driver's guides be in your library? I don't expect anyone in here is going to apply for a driver's license."

Charlie laughed. "The so-called library gets all sorts of stuff that people donate. It just gets dumped on the shelves. They think us old fogies are glad to read anything. I found a copy of the *Kama Sutra* once, and that was interesting. I only had it for a day before someone who works here ripped it off. Just when I was getting set to asking Betty to try out one of the positions."

Betty scoffed. "Let me know when you're ready Charlie, I'll be sure to put on my black negligee."

Danny tried to extend his bottle drive the next Thursday as he'd done before. He picked up a few extra bottles and cans, but nothing like the stack he'd found last time. They'd need every penny they could get their hands on if they were going to cover expenses and still have a little money left over when they headed off. If they headed off. He wondered how far they'd get, if that day ever came.

Next day, on the bus to Malone's, he spent some time reading the *Driver's Guide*. The conditions to get a regular license included having a learner's permit for a year. Now there's a problem, he thought. He'd have to discuss that with Betty and Charlie. He skipped to Chapter 2 on Traffic Control which he thought he understood okay and went on to Sign Shapes and Colours. Then he was into Designated Lane Signs, Permissive Signs and Warning Signs.

"God! There's a hell of a lot," he muttered.

When he reached Malone's, Gail handed over the tools he'd need. It didn't take long to replace the battery and fan belt. Then he started the bus and let it run. He listened to the motor and looked for oil leaks, but didn't find any. He checked the radiator and the oil. The radiator might need a flush, but the oil would definitely need a change. Danny turned off the motor and was sitting at the kitchen table with the *Driver's Guide* when there was a tap at the door. Gail was standing outside.

"Thought you might like a coffee," she said.

"Thanks. I'm studying for a driver's test." He indicated the *Driver's Guide*. "Never knew they had so many road signs."

"Yeah? Don't know if I could pass a driving test now," Gail said. "It's been a while. I didn't realize this was a camper. Sure a lot of dust and dirt." She touched a window and then looked at her hand disgustedly. "Would you like me to bring you a bucket of hot water and some soap? It would look a lot better if you could give it a wipe down."

"That'd be great. Betty wants to put up new curtains, but the windows could do with a clean first."

"Okay. I'll bring you some stuff," Gail said. "Back in a bit."

"Thanks, kindly."

When Gail returned, she brought a wheelbarrow with not only a bucket of hot water, but a whole array of cleaning supplies.

"I shoulda helped you with that," Danny said. "I didn't know you were bringing so much."

"That's okay," Gail said. "It gets me out of the office for a few minutes. If you want some more hot water just bring back the bucket."

Danny made two trips back to the office and by the time he was finished, the inside of the bus was sparkling.

As the local bus carried him back to town, Danny dozed off. It had been a busy day.

CHAPTER 14

"Okay Danny. What's this sign mean?" Betty held up a home-made flash card with a traffic sign that showed a black arrow curving around the right of a kind of black shield.

"Keep right?" Danny said, sipping his coffee.

"Wrong," Betty said. "It's Divider Ahead – Keep Right."

"That's what he said," Charlie objected.

"You have to be exact or they'll mark you wrong."

"That's dumb! If he didn't keep right, he'd hit the divider. He'd follow the direction of the arrow."

"Next one Danny," Betty waved Charlie's objection aside and held up another card with a black square, standing on end, inside a green circle.

"I haven't a clue," Danny said. "I don't remember seeing that before."

"It's permission to carry dangerous goods," Betty said. "Anythin' inside a green circle gives you permission."

"Permission to speak?" Charlie asked.

"What, Charlie?"

"What kind of dangerous goods are we going to be carrying, might I ask?"

"None, except for you. You'd be a danger to anyone. We have to help Danny practice because if you get more than five questions wrong you fail the test."

Danny got the next one right – don't pass bicycles.

"Jeez," Charlie said. "We'll never get to the Grand Canyon if we can't pass a bicycle. Let him finish his coffee."

"It's important to be prepared. There's no knowing' what they'll ask. I'd sure like to go and clean up that bus. Do you think we could all go up to Malone's another day?" Betty asked.

"I cleaned it after I changed the battery and fan belt. That girl, Gail, brought me cleaning supplies. I also ran it for a little while and it sounded good."

"That's really great, Danny," Betty said. "We're going to need some beddin', curtains for the windows, some pots, pans, plates. We all have our own comforters on our beds we could take, but I'm not sure how we could sneak out with those."

"I think those kind of things will have to wait," Danny said. "Whose name are we going to register it in? If not Caroline's, then we need a new bill of sale. We need an oil change, some new tires and..."

"Insurance," Charlie interjected. "I understand it can cost thousands these days."

"Insurance!" Danny groaned. "I forgot about that. God, that'll be a tough one."

"Yeah. I forgot about that too," Betty said, "but we need a licensed driver first."

"I don't know if you noticed, but that booklet says that you have to have a learner's permit for a year before you can get a regular license," Danny said.

"Yeah, I did notice that."

"So what do we do?" Danny asked.

"Well," Betty answered, "it does say that a driver with a learner's permit only has to be accompanied by a fully licensed driver over 18."

"Who's that?" Charlie asked.

"Caroline. As long as we don't do anythin' really dumb, we should be okay. Danny just has to pass the written test."

"You're serious?" Charlie asked. "We'll all end up in the slammer."

"That's where we are now!" Betty said. "We're makin' our break for freedom."

Caroline began repeating, "Freedom, freedom, freedom, see them, see them. There! Over there, over there."

Danny took the booklet with him when he visited the library and read it over and over again. He wondered how much time they gave you to do the test. His only experience on a computer was when a library worker had shown him how to look up the prices of vehicles. What if he accidentally switched off the computer in the middle of the test? Would he have to pay another fee to start over? The thought of taking the test at all terrified him. He saw one of those licensing offices and went in one day to ask a few questions.

The office wasn't very busy and he was called to the counter right away.

"How can I help you?" the young woman behind the counter asked.

"Er. I want to ask about licensing a camper," he started hesitantly.

"A camper? Like a tent trailer?"

"Um, no. It used to be a kind of bus but now it's a camper."

"Oh, you mean a mobile home?"

"Yeah. Sort of like that."

"If it was registered as a camper or mobile home before, it would be registered the same again. Is it single axle?" she asked.

"Yeah, single axle."

"Do you have a bill of sale?"

"Er, no. We're just, um... I'm just thinking of buying it. I just want to know how much the license plate would be."

"It would probably be around $80," the girl replied.

Danny jotted it down on his list of questions. "Er, how much does a learner's license cost?"

"The license is $20, but first you have to pass the written test. That costs another $17.60. If you don't pass the written test you have to pay each time you write it."

"So you have to pay $17.60 to take the test and another 20 bucks for the license?"

"You got it."

THE GRAND GETAWAY   73

"And the test is on a computer, right? What if you're not too good on a computer? Suppose you hit the wrong button and switch it off half-way through the test? Do you have to pay again?"

The girl looked puzzled. "I don't think that's ever happened."

Danny felt his time for questions was running out. "Do you have to have insurance on the vehicle before you get a license plate?"

"Yes. But we don't sell insurance. You have to go to an insurance agent."

"Yeah, okay. Thanks." He wasn't sure he could handle all this.

"When, or if, you buy the mobile home, bring in the vehicle information and we'll sort it out."

"Thanks." He would have liked to ask more questions about the test, but he figured he'd start to look suspicious.

The costs were adding up. The Shelter had an employment office that found work if you wanted it on a day to day basis. Maybe he could pick up a couple of days work to contribute some money. He hadn't worked in a long time. Looking after Pete and hanging out with him had been enough.

"Nobody answers their own phone anymore," Betty complained. "Even when you get someone to answer, they say they're transferrin' me to Deb, or Bill – or whoever – and then I get the same usual message, *away from my desk, lost at sea, missin' in action, dead and buried.*"

"Who were you calling?" Danny asked.

"Insurance agents. I finally got hold of some guy so I could ask my question."

"Which was?" Danny asked.

"What would be the approximate cost to insure our bus?"

"And?"

"Depends."

"Yeah, the answers are as crappy as what ends up in those diapers." Charlie chimed in.

"What diapers?" Danny asked.

"Depends! Depends! They advertise them on TV all the time." Charlie groaned.

"Forget Charlie and his dumb jokes," Betty said. "But the news isn't good. The cost would be more than $1000".

"Twice what we paid for the bus," Charlie said.

"That's crazy!" Danny said. "We don't want to insure the bus itself, it isn't worth anything. We just want insurance in case we run into somebody else. Did you tell them that, Betty?"

"I did. And that's the cost. It's really based on the driver. The guy asked who the driver would be, and I said an older man, sixtyish, with lots of experience and no accidents."

"What experience?" Danny asked. "They're never going to insure me if I only have a learner's license."

"Yeah. It might be a problem. I'm still workin' on it."

"So let's suppose we somehow convinced them to give us insurance, how do we come up with the money?"

"We sell the bus. Take the money and buy a 'First To Die' life insurance policy with all of us the beneficiaries. When one of us kicks off, the other three can collect the money and start over." Charlie laughed.

"Oh, piss off, Charlie," Betty snapped.

"Oh yes, piss off, piss off, piss off," Caroline repeated. "That's what she said, there, over there."

"Now you've got Caroline goin'," Betty said. "You really are a pain in the ass, Charlie. If you and I could just get our pensions to quit going to this place, we'd have lots of money. We'll have to talk to the bank. We need to cancel the automatic debits for Cavandish. I found an old debit card in one of my drawers, but it expired long ago. We'll ask for new cards. Then all we need, after we leave, are debit machines to withdraw our money. Once we're outta here we'll be home free."

"You got that right." Charlie laughed. "Free of this home, you mean. But what about Caroline? Will Cavandish keep grabbing whatever money she has coming in after we're gone? And are you sure we're doing the right thing, if we take her with us? Couldn't we be charged with kidnapping?"

Danny thought Charlie had a point. It wasn't as if Caroline was actually making the decision for herself.

"I don't have any guilty feelings about taking Caroline. You know damn well that if you and I abandon her here, she'll be really lost. We're all she has. What Cavandish does with her money after we're gone, I don't know, but even if we knew where her money comes in from, tryin' to divert it would have the cops on our tail for sure," Betty said.

"But they might accuse us of just using Caroline 'cause she has a driver's license. And when they find out that the bus was bought in Caroline's name, they'll sure as hell think we latched onto some of her money." Charlie sighed. "God, it's complicated."

"Even if we only got away for a month, and really did make it to the Grand Canyon, it would all be worth it. At Malone's, you said we'd all bought into the plan and that you'd never forgive yourself if you didn't give it a chance. Look, if you like, I'll sign a confession right now, sayin' it was all my idea and take full responsibility. I'll own up to being the gang leader."

"Okay, Betty, I'm still in. No need for any signed confessions," Charlie said, patting her hand.

"You still in, Danny?" Betty asked. "We really need you."

"I'm still in, too," Danny said.

"Still in, still in, still in. Me too, too, too," Caroline chanted.

"We won't leave you behind, Caroline. You have my word," Betty said.

Danny stayed at The Shelter overnight, grabbed a quick breakfast and headed for the Employment Services Office. To have any chance of a job, you had to draw a number. The numbers ran from 1 to 75 and were drawn from a ball-filled container like the ones they used for bingo. The lower the number you drew, the better chance you had of getting a job if any came in. There were already about a dozen men waiting at the counter to draw a number. Candace, a young volunteer was supervising the draw. When it came to his turn, Candace greeted him, "Haven't seen you for a while, Danny. Sorry to hear about Pete. How are ya doing?"

Danny kept quiet but flashed her a grin. Candace handed him the ball container and he turned the handle. A ball rolled out with the number 25 on it.

"Good luck, Danny." She moved on to the next person in line.

Number 25 wasn't bad, but from previous experience he knew it could be a long wait sitting on a bench in the lobby before he got a crack at any jobs that were phoned in. Some guys wouldn't bother to wait, and after a couple of hours they would just leave the building. This increased his chances, but depending on the job, some employers only wanted young strong guys and his age was against him. He took the *Driver's Guide* out of his knapsack and studied it some more. It was hard to concentrate. There was a lot of coming and going and a few loud voices raised in arguments or conversations being carried on across the lobby.

It was over two hours before Candace's voice came over the P.A. "There's a moving job for two, paying $15 an hour. Please come to the Employment Services Office if you're interested."

There were five of them at the counter including Danny, but Danny's number wasn't low enough.

Danny left to sit on the bench again. This was the hardest part, the waiting. You could wait all day and get nothing. A half hour later Danny's patience paid off. A call for two guys to help unload a couple of freightliners at a warehouse not far away came in. The pay was $12 an hour. A lot of the guys had left the building and Danny had one of the lower numbers. He and Eric, who had won the jobs, were driven to the warehouse. Three guys were already unloading. The freightliner was packed to its ceiling with heavy boxes. They were assigned to the second truck and instructed to stack boxes on empty pallets so that a fork-lift operator could haul them away. The two trucks were supposed to leave the city in four hours to pick up some shipments elsewhere, so they had to work fast.

Danny knew he was going to find his shoulders and arms aching before too long, but he was in better shape than Eric, who was puffing and panting the whole time despite being much younger.

They were 10 minutes behind schedule when they finally got the last of the boxes off the second truck, but the owner was pleased and feeling generous. He gave them each $60 and offered them a ride back to The Shelter.

Next day, Danny wasn't sure if he was lucky or not. He got a really low number and accepted a job with another guy digging a trench across a lawn to install an underground electrical line to hook up to a swimming pool. The pay was $15 an hour. It was another full day of back-breaking hard labour, but when Danny was handed $130 at the end of it, he figured it had been worth the effort.

He felt every one of his muscles aching the next day as he pushed his cart on his bottle collecting route in a cold drizzle. He was pleased with the two days' work and the bulge of the money in his jacket pocket. Thinking of the look he'd see on Betty's face when he handed over all that cash tomorrow made him smile and forget about his aches and pains for a while.

CHAPTER 15

"Here's a contribution to the cause, Betty." Danny passed her the bundle of bills as they sat at a table for the afternoon snack.

"What did you do, Danny?" Charlie asked. "Rob a bank?"

"Picked up a couple of day jobs through The Shelter. Tough going though — haven't worked that hard in a hell of a long time. I'm aching all over."

"Thanks, Danny." Betty pressed his hand. "How much is here?"

"Two hundred and sixty bucks."

"Two sixty! That's fantastic." Betty gasped. "Probably enough for two and a half months insurance. But, listen Danny. Please don't get hurt. We can't afford havin' you end up in hospital. Charlie and me'll have to put our heads together and come up with a few ideas to raise a few bucks from this end. Haven't thought of anythin' brilliant myself."

"You said we'd be okay once we're out of here," Danny said. "Once you and Charlie make arrangements with the bank and your pensions."

"We will be. But we can't do anythin' about that until the very last minute. It could be a bit tricky. We don't want to get into any deep conversations with a bank manager, and when Charlie and I go to the banks we have to have our stories straight. Can't have the bank worried that we're just old fogies maybe gettin' scammed by someone. You know how it is?"

"Not really," Danny said. "I can't say I do much banking. You said *banks*".

"Our pensions are deposited in separate banks, but I think that might be a good thing. If I went in with Charlie in tow, we'd make them suspicious for sure. They might think that old bugger's comin' in to try to scam this poor innocent lady out of her money."

"Poor innocent lady!" Charlie scoffed. "But it is our money. We should be able to do what we want with it."

"I just don't want the bank phonin' up Cavandish to ask if we're movin' out," Betty said. "We have to convince them that we're either movin' in with relatives or leavin' the country."

"Well we are," Charlie said. "Leaving the country, I mean. But we can't tell them anything about making a dash for the U.S. border in our Park 'n' Ride bus. And the border is as far as we'd get with no passports."

Betty ignored Charlie's last remark. "It's our money," she said. "Nobody has to sign anythin' for us. We're of sound mind. At least I know I am. I don't know about you, Charlie."

"Well you seem to know what you're doing, Betty," Danny said. "Have you got a date in mind when we might take off?"

"Off, off, off," Caroline swept the crumbs from her cookie into her hand and then looked around for somewhere to put them. When Charlie reached out to take them, she closed her hand.

"I was hopin' to get outta here in about six weeks," Betty said, "maybe a late afternoon on a Friday after shift change would be best. If we don't try to aim for a date to leave, we'll leave it too late. We'll just sit around here watchin' TV until one of us doesn't wake up. We may not raise all the money, but we need enough to get us on the road. We don't need $200 for gas to get us over the border. But it's the money we do need that's holdin' us up. The insurance money, the license plate, tire money, food and other stuff for the bus and your drivin' license. How's it goin' with that studyin', Danny?"

"Not bad," Danny replied. "But six weeks from now seems an awful short time to raise the cash we need."

"Well, that was my hope. That takes us into October. If we leave it much later than that we might be lookin' at buyin' snow tires to get outta here."

Behind them there was a loud crash that made Caroline flinch and startled Danny as an attendant flung a handful of dirty cutlery into a plastic container on a cart.

"It's okay," Betty touched Caroline's arm. "God, you'd think they'd try to fling the cutlery a little more gently. They scare the wits out of the likes of Caroline. And everyone else for that matter. Sometimes it's bedlam around here." Betty shook her head in disgust.

"What's the minimum amount you think we need?" Danny asked.

"About a thousand bucks to be on the safe side, if we can buy insurance on installments. With the money you brought today, we've got the gas money and some left over. We could get well into the U.S. Danny, why don't you try the learner's written test this week and see how you make out? Take some of this money and give it a try if you think you're ready. One step at a time."

CHAPTER 16

When Danny did his recyclables pick-up the following week, he tried scouting out a couple of licensing offices, looking for one with some older women. The one he picked was in a tiny strip mall. The next day he took the plunge.

"Can I help you?" the woman behind the counter asked. She looked to be about fifty.

"Er, yes. I'd like to write the driver's test for a learner's license."

"Okay. Do you have some identification?"

Danny dug his health care card out of his wallet and handed it over.

The woman tapped his name into the computer, then paused, "Address?"

"Mmm. The Shelter." He gave her the street address.

She tapped that in too after a brief glance at him. "If you get a more permanent address, you'll have to change the address on your license," she said helpfully.

"Thanks," Danny said.

"That'll be $17.60."

He handed her a twenty and she gave him a receipt and his change. "If you pass the test, we'll give you an eye test afterwards." She turned and looked over her shoulder. "Courtney, would you set up Mr. ..." she glanced at the form she had printed from the computer, "Mr. Carroll at a computer to do the Class 7 test."

Danny hadn't noticed the young girl sitting in a small alcove behind the woman at the counter. She got up from the desk, took his application form from the older woman and walked around the counter. She had part of her hair striped pink and had a cold sore on her bottom lip. As she came closer, he discovered it wasn't a cold sore, but some kind of piercing with a black stone centre. There was something hanging from her nose too. She snapped the gum she was chewing, startling him, and smiled.

"This way." She led him towards one of the computers set up at a small work station along one of the walls.

For a moment he thought of turning tail and running. But he was pretty sure he knew the stuff. Betty had given him a short review, and with an approximate date for their departure, he thought he shouldn't delay any longer.

As he sat down at the computer and the girl switched it on, he glanced at her nose again. The thing dangling there was some kind of ring that pierced one nostril. Danny felt himself shudder.

"The test is multiple choice. You can take your time. There's no rush," she said. "But if you get over five wrong out of the 30 questions it automatically shuts down. Okay?"

"Okay."

In front of him the screen lit up and he read the instructions which he knew already. The first question dealt with a no passing sign and gave alternatives:

A. No passing on the right.

B. No passing on the left.

C. No passing.

D. One lane closed ahead.

He clicked on C. No passing. A few more traffic sign questions followed.

He felt he was doing okay, but when a couple of tougher questions came up, he found himself mulling over the answers.

"Holy jeez," he muttered, "two wrong already." Betty's voice rang through his head. *You knew this stuff on Monday. Concentrate for God's sake, you stupid bugger! You know this.*

He tried, but now he felt flustered. He decided to skip the next question. He began to pick up confidence again when he was sure he got three right in a row.

Question 24.

Danny clicked on D.

No wait. Of course, it's C. Crap!

The screen changed suddenly showing a large red X and 'You have failed the test. Study the *Driver's Guide* before attempting the test again.'

"Holy crap! How the hell did that happen?" Danny muttered. "Betty will kill me!"

He scrolled through the answers and found he'd got six wrong out of the 26 he'd answered.

"I'm just not cut out for doing tests," he groaned. "Betty will be fighting mad."

Danny spent a good part of the next two days at the library practicing the test on the computer. By the second day he was passing the test almost every time he tried it so that afternoon, he went by the same licensing office, determined not to be thrown off by anyone with a ring in their nose.

This time Courtney wasn't there, and the woman who had taken his money last time set him up at a computer after he'd paid the $17.60. He passed and, after also taking the eye test, he paid the additional $20 and was issued his license.

Danny took his license out of his wallet and put it on the table in front of Betty.

"You passed!" Betty's eyes lit up. "That's great, Danny!" She reached for Danny's hand and gave it a squeeze. Charlie added his congratulations.

"Now if I can only figure out how to get our bus insured and registered. That's the next big hurdle," Betty said.

"Besides money," Charlie added.

"That too." Betty helped Caroline close her hand around a plastic glass of juice. "Do you think we might go out to Malone's one more time? Being cooped up here depresses me, but seein' the bus again would give me a lift."

"When did you want to go?"

"Maybe the end of next week. I'll think hard about the insurance in the next day or so. See if I can solve that problem."

"Okay," Danny said. "Let's aim for Friday. If I can pick up a couple of days working before then, plus my recyclables, we'll have a little more cash."

"Thanks, Danny," Betty said. "We'll have to have a talk about things next Friday and I'd rather do that in our bus than here. Make our final plans, so to speak."

CHAPTER 17

Danny stayed overnight at The Shelter that week so he would be available early for any work that was going. He picked up another half day with a moving company, and the next day, Roger – the owner of the landscape company Danny had worked for before – called The Shelter. Candace said that he had specifically asked for him. Danny was surprised to find himself back at the same location. The owner of the house, happy with the work Roger's company had done, had decided to extend electricity to a gazebo beyond the swimming pool. Danny put in a full day.

When Danny arrived at Cavandish on Friday to meet the others, he had just over $200 in his pocket. He met them outside and suggested saving time by splurging on a cab to drive them to Malone's.

Danny could see that Betty was bubbling with excitement, but whatever it was, she was keeping it to herself until they got to their bus at Malone's. Charlie, too, was keeping his mouth shut – no doubt on orders from Betty – and spent most of the cab ride humming to himself. He did try one joke, but Betty only harrumphed, and he went back to humming. Danny, glancing over his shoulder from the front seat beside the cab driver, saw that Betty had closed her eyes. Charlie winked at him but went on humming. Only Caroline really talked, reading and repeating the occasional word from a billboard, or the name of some store she noticed when they stopped at a traffic light. The cab driver asked Danny if they were going to buy a car at Malone's, and when Danny said they'd already bought one, the driver also lapsed into silence.

They reached Malone's and Danny directed the driver to the bus. As they pulled up beside it, the driver seemed surprised.

"This is it?"

"Yep. This is it," Danny replied. "Our home sweet home."

Danny paid the cab driver $42 and gulped at the cost, although his estimate had been pretty close. He didn't offer a tip.

As he opened the back doors and helped the others out of the cab he was sure the driver was going to ask, "You really live here?" but he seemed to change his mind and only muttered, "nice paint job!" before driving off.

Betty rummaged in the large shopping bag she was carrying, produced the keys, and they all climbed inside. Betty placed her bag on the table and looked around. "Nice cleanin' job, Danny." She ran a finger along a window ledge behind the table. "Just needs a bit of dustin'. We'll have to borrow a vacuum cleaner somewhere."

"Need power for that," Charlie said.

"We'll worry about that later." Betty replied. "Anyone for coffee?" She pulled a thermos out of the bag. "Cavandish coffee, the usual brown coloured water, but it's warm."

She produced four cups and a few sugar packets and got Caroline to sit at the table. She poured the coffees, added a packet of sugar to Caroline's, and then said, "Sit down! Sit down, everyone!"

Danny and Charlie squeezed in behind the table.

"That little stove, at least it's a four burner," Betty said. "We'll have to make do. And with no oven we won't be able to bake any cookies. I guess we can try makin' toast over a burner with a fork."

"It'll be like camping out." Charlie chuckled.

"Well we're gonna need a propane tank for it to cook anything," Danny said. "Okay Betty. There's something you're dying to tell us."

Betty sipped some coffee, but her eyes were shining over the rim of her cup. She put the cup down, smiled and pulled a license plate from her bag and placed it on the table.

"You registered the bus!" Danny laughed. "GCB - 469."

"GCB, GCB, GCB," Caroline repeated.

"How in hell?" Danny gasped. "Did you order that plate special? GCB – *Grand Canyon Betty*."

Betty laughed. "That's the plate they gave us. Next one in the pile. I thought maybe it was an omen."

"Like *God Crucifies Bullshitters*." Charlie cackled.

"Never mind, Charlie, Betty! Tell us the story," Danny said. "Is it in Caroline's name, then?"

"It is."

"But didn't you have to have the insurance first?"

"We did. We went to get that first."

"All three of you?"

"No. Just me and Caroline. We left Charlie at Cavandish to cover our tracks."

"Okay. Go on," Danny said.

"It was last Tuesday," Betty began, "and I got Caroline and myself out between breakfast shifts like before. I'd been lyin' in bed feelin' fed up just waitin' around and lettin' you do everything – bringin' in the money and all, and time is runnin' out. Well, I couldn't stand it any longer. You know I'm impulsive. Always have been.

"I filled Charlie in. I picked that insurance agent, the one who had answered the phone, the one who didn't make me listen to music or voice mail, and it was only a short bus ride away. I figured there's lots of insurance agents, and if we failed I'd look at it as a dry run and try some others."

"Didn't they ask Caroline any questions?" Danny asked. "I mean, how in hell did you convince them that Caroline will be the main driver? You have me on pins and needles."

"Yes, pins and needles, pins and needles," Caroline repeated.

"I'm comin' to that," Betty continued. "We got there early and I never did meet Mr. Marcoff, the guy who talked to me on the phone. A young girl, Diana, who said it was her first week on the job, looked after us, and she was real enthusiastic and friendly."

"God help her," Charlie muttered.

Betty ignored him. "She took our application."

"So how did Caroline answer her questions?" Danny asked. "Uh, sorry, go on."

"She didn't. She had laryngitis."

"Laryngitis?" Danny spluttered.

Charlie was laughing.

"I couldn't take the chance that Caroline might talk, and whoever we talked to might get suspicious. She was having a quiet day, anyway, and just before we went into the agency, I gave her a big toffee to suck on. As soon as we sat down with Diana, I told her Caroline was my daughter, but she had a bad case of laryngitis."

"Your daughter! And she believed that?" Danny laughed.

"Well the blonde wig that I borrowed from Cavandish's Halloween box helped, plus a little lipstick and make-up. I had the wig in my bag and put it on Caroline in a service station restroom just around the corner from the agency. I thought Caroline was going to pull it off. She kept tuggin' on it. But she got used to it in a few minutes and left it alone.

"I told Diana that Caroline was taking me on a short trip for a few weeks, a bit of sightseein' before winter really set in. I didn't mention the Grand Canyon. Said we might get as far as Vancouver to see my sister and stay there for the winter. Caroline concentrated on suckin' on the toffee and foldin' a road map I'd given her.

"I just handed over the proof of ownership from Malone's and Caroline's license and Diana copied down the details. Then she asked a few questions, like if Caroline was the only driver. I lied, of course. When she asked if Caroline had any accidents or convictions, I said no. I had no idea they could check your record instantly with your license number, but it turned out I was tellin' the truth! She went to another computer and came back smilin'. Said that Caroline's record was all clear.

"She printed up the pink card, proof of insurance." Betty took her wallet out of the bag and pulled out the card in Caroline's name. "I handed over $310 for three months insurance."

"What address did you give for Caroline?" Danny asked.

"I didn't mention Cavandish. I just gave them the street address. Diana already gave me the insurance policy. They won't be mailin' us anything until renewal time and we'll be long gone by then."

"But didn't Caroline have to sign the application?"

THE GRAND GETAWAY   85

"We got a break there. The phone had rung a couple of times, but the message machine must have picked it up because Diana ignored it. Then, when she handed Caroline the application to sign it, the phone rang again and Diana said she had to take it. While she was lookin' for something in her desk, I just huddled with Caroline and quickly scratched a signature. I put the application back before Diana finished the call.

She looked it over and said, 'You're all set to go. Have a great trip.' And then she noticed Caroline was still tryin' to fold the map and she said, 'Oh, let me help you. These road maps drive everyone crazy, trying to fold them again.' She folded it for Caroline and gave it back to her and I put it in my bag before she could unfold it again. She was very kind."

"God love her," Charlie said. "Let's hope we don't have an accident, or we'll really be in trouble."

"We'll be careful," Betty said. "Anyway, Danny is qualified to drive as long as we have Caroline along, our licensed driver with a clean record to boot. We'll keep to the speed limit, and nobody will bother us."

"So how did you get the license plate?" Danny asked.

"That was easier. Once we had the insurance, we just went to a license place and handed in the pink card, Caroline's license, and the proof of ownership. Everythin's done on computers nowadays. Hardly anyone talks to you. They just punch in the information without lookin' at you. That's it then. All we need now is to finish fixin' up this bus and we're set."

"I'd better start her up," Danny said. "I haven't had her running for a while. Even with a new battery, it's not good to let it sit."

Betty slid the keys across the table. Danny took them and slipped behind the driver's seat and turned on the ignition. The bus started right away.

"Sounds okay," Danny said. "I'll turn on the heater. Maybe it'll warm us up a bit."

Betty had come to stand beside him. "I forgot to look. Does it have a CD player?"

"No, just a tape deck," Danny replied.

"Well that's better than nothin'," Betty said. "It'd be nice to take some music along. I'll check out some of the tapes at Cavandish. There's a whole pile of them in a cupboard gatherin' dust. They never use them anymore, only CD's now."

"There's a radio here," Danny said. He switched it on. It sounded a bit crackly until he fiddled with it and a country station came on playing an oldie by Kitty Wells singing, *Don't Sell Daddy Anymore Whiskey*.

"Have we got enough gas for a short spin?" Betty asked.

"Not a lot, but enough, if it's short," Danny said. "The gauge shows a bit over a quarter tank. I guess it would take over fifty bucks to fill 'er up. Do we have any money left?"

"We do. You also said we need an oil change. Maybe we could get that at the gas station."

"Gas stations nowadays are just that," Danny said. "They don't do oil changes. They make more money from all the junk food they sell. I guess we could go as far as the gas station and back, but I'll have to put on the license plate. I've got a screwdriver in my knapsack."

When Danny climbed back into the bus, Charlie was spluttering and waving at a cloud of dust that rose from one of the bunks.

"Open a window for God's sake," Betty hollered, "before we all smother."

"What happened?" Danny gasped.

"Leave the door open, Danny, give us some more air. Charlie was decidin' which bunk he might like best and decided to shake up one of the mattresses."

"Sorry," Charlie said. "Didn't mean to cause a dust storm. Got a couple of windows open now, it shouldn't be too bad."

"We're gonna have to borrow a vacuum or get those mattresses outside and beat the dust outta them before we try sleepin' in here. Be nice if we could replace them, but they'll have to do for now. Maybe they have a vacuum at Frank's office we could borrow."

"I didn't do any vacuuming," Danny said. "I only scrubbed down the place."

"I think we need to make a new list," Betty said, as she pulled a pen and small notebook out of her purse. "We've got a lot done, but time is gettin' short and there's still a lot to do before we can take off. Let's check at the office and see if we can borrow a vacuum. Okay what else? Oh yeah, the oil change. What'll that cost, Danny?"

"Um, maybe $40 if we get it done at a Jiffy Lube."

"Okay. Oil change, $40." Betty wrote in her notebook.

"I don't know if the radiator needs a flush," Danny said. "We don't want it boiling over on the way. Let's guess $50 for now. I'm sure we need a new air filter. I could put that in myself, but I've no idea what it costs. We need a cylinder for the cook stove. They're 60 bucks."

"Hold on, I can't write that fast," Betty said. "We'll have to make a trip to a thrift shop and pick up the basics for the kitchen. I'll put down $70, no, better make that $100. Oh, and we're goin' to need groceries for a few days, say another $100. We're just over $400 now." Betty sighed.

"Four hundred now, now, now. Four hundred, that's what she said," Caroline repeated.

"Thanks Caroline. Anything else?" Betty asked.

"There's still the tires," Danny said. "I can't see us getting very far down the road on the ones we've got."

Betty sighed. "Let's see if we can borrow that vacuum. We'll worry about one thing at a time."

Gail was the only one at the office, but she had a vacuum they could use and there was an outside plug on the building.

THE GRAND GETAWAY   87

"I see you got the license plate, you nearly ready to take off?" she asked.

"Just a few more weeks," Betty answered. "If we can park the bus around back until we leave, we'd appreciate it."

"Sure thing," Gail replied. "Be sure to lock it up, otherwise you'll have people climbing in and out to take a look on auction day. I'll mark it *Not For Sale* but make sure you lock it anyway."

Betty got Charlie and Danny to haul out the mattresses. She borrowed a broom and directed Charlie to hang the mattresses over a hand rail on the ramp up to the office. Then she had Charlie beat most of the dust out of them. Danny, meanwhile, vacuumed the threadbare carpet and the bunks slots inside. When Charlie was finished beating the mattresses, she had him give them a vacuuming too.

"That'll have to do for now," Betty said. "You can put the mattresses back. I can only hope there's no bed bugs."

"If there were any," Charlie said, "with no one to feed off for such a long time, they've probably moved on."

"We'll, we'd better move on," Betty said. "Let's go get that gas and have our first ride in our bus."

Danny drove slowly out of Malone's yard with Charlie beside him and Betty and Caroline at the kitchen table. He turned right onto the gravel road.

"How does it feel?" Charlie asked.

"Pretty good. The steering seems fine. How does it feel back there?" Danny asked.

"Not bad," Charlie replied. "But I think I'd have to hold onto a coffee cup with both hands."

"We're not goin' to be eatin' or drinkin' while we're movin'." Betty said. "I can see I'm gonna have to draw up a list of rules."

"More rules! I thought we had enough at Cavandish," Charlie groaned.

"We have to have rules," Betty said. "We can't have Caroline gettin' scalded by hot coffee."

"Okay, but who's going to do the cooking?" Charlie asked.

"I'll start off," Betty said. "Nothin' fancy. But you and Danny can do a bit too. You two can do the dishes."

"You could barely wash a cup in that tiny sink," Charlie said

"It'll have to do. You can wash one cup at a time. Charlie, you can do the washin' too, the sheets, pillow cases."

"In that sink?"

"If you don't like it, then you can always go to the nearest stream and beat the washin' on a rock like all those women on your *National Geographic* shows."

They reached the end of the road and Danny waited until there was a big break in the traffic before turning onto the main highway. When they reached the gas station, he hopped out and filled the tank. There was a Speedy Muffler a few blocks away, and they had just enough money left for the oil change. Danny was happy to have that done in less than half an hour. Betty said they had just $25 left and the bus fare back to Cavandish would have to come out of that.

Danny suggested that he drop them off at the bus stop while he took their bus back to Malone's. He'd lock it up and make his own way back into town.

CHAPTER 18

Danny stayed at The Shelter again on the off chance there might be some work early Monday morning. They had spent all the money they'd had. If Betty was going to hold them to leaving in four weeks and they didn't come up with any more money, they'd have to postpone the departure. But Betty was stubborn. He thought she might insist on leaving, whether the bus was ready or not.

With no passports, the likelihood that they would make it across the border was probably zero percent, and they'd end up stuck in southern Alberta. Danny had nightmares about them camping with no heat, no groceries, no bedding, waiting for Charlie's and Betty's pension money to be deposited, while they got buried by an early winter blizzard.

He had read a guide book on the Grand Canyon which told him that access to the North Rim closes when the first major snowfall arrives. There was no camping after October 15th and it remained closed until the following spring. He hadn't mentioned that to Betty. He was almost certain they wouldn't get across the border anyway, so there was no point killing Betty's dream completely. It was the North Rim where Betty and Arnie Thorkleson had first made love, and Danny knew that Betty longed to be there again.

Danny was up early to draw numbers for any work that might be going, but he had no luck. The number he drew was high. Later on in the day he gave up and made his way to an auto parts place where he planned to check on the price of an air filter. Like the tires, he thought, it would have to wait until they got the pension money. They didn't even have dishes or pots. All they had was the four mugs Betty had lifted from Cavandish. *Yeah*, he thought, *this could be a total disaster*.

After leaving the auto parts place he walked a few blocks to the river and found a bench. It was a sunny day, but already the leaves were turning. He had no desire to go back to The Shelter with the constant racket. He'd wait until supper was served. He wasn't sure if he really wanted to stay there another night, and considered finding a place to bed down outside.

He stared at the river and his thoughts turned again to the trip. What would happen if they couldn't cross the border? And what did Betty have in mind if they got to the Grand Canyon? Just hang around there, living off Betty's and Charlie's pensions? The whole idea had just been something to keep Betty going. He didn't fancy driving around Canada with winter coming on. The bus probably wouldn't last, and neither would he. They really had to come up with a plan or forget about the whole thing. He dozed.

He woke with a start from the middle of a dream in which they were a bunch of geriatric hippies and they'd started up their own, what did they call those places, *conune*? "No that's not it," he muttered. "It's commune." He stood up, thinking it must be near supper-time, and headed for The Shelter. He vowed not to tell Betty about his dream just in case starting a commune became her next project.

When he got back to The Shelter, one of the residents named George called to him when he entered the lobby. "There was some guy looking for you."

"Who?" Danny asked. "Was it for work?"

"Dunno. He didn't say."

"Did he give a name? Was his name Roger?"

"Could've been. Don't know."

"What did he look like?"

"Mm...?" Danny could see George was thinking. "Say, would ya be able to lend me a couple of bucks?"

"No, George. I don't have any money."

George staggered against him and Danny was sure he was on something. His eyes looked glazed.

Danny went to the employment office to check with Candace in case it was Roger who had come by. He cursed himself for leaving and maybe missing out on a job.

Candace was gone for the afternoon and there was no one in the office. He checked for any notes on the notice board where she might have left a message but there was nothing. He thought he might go and question George again.

He found him sitting on a bench in the lobby, asleep.

Danny shook him.

George stirred, blinked his eyes a couple of times, then stared at Danny.

"What? You got the note, Danny?"

"What note?"

"The one your friend left for ya."

"Where is it?"

"I thought I gave it to ya."

"You didn't. Where the hell is it?"

George began to search his pockets.

"What did this guy look like?" Danny asked.

"What guy?"

"Jeez, George. The guy who gave you the note."

"Dunno. Think he said his name was... uh... Charlie. Yeah, Charlie."

Several scraps of paper, a half-eaten cheese sandwich, four prepaid bus tickets, two half pages torn from magazines, a crumpled piece of newspaper, a pencil and three cough drops now lay on the bench beside George.

Danny rummaged through the bits of paper, but they were mostly blank sheets from a pocket notebook. There was nothing written on them. Danny guessed the magazine pages and newspaper piece were probably George's emergency toilet paper.

George reached for the half-eaten cheese sandwich and unwrapped it, crumpling the paper and tossing it onto the floor.

"So where's the note?" Danny asked.

George shrugged, his mouth full of cheese sandwich. Danny glanced down at the crumpled paper on the floor. It was the note but, before he could read it, he had to peel off a partial slice of processed cheese and then the remains of a sucked cough drop which was gluing the paper together. It was from Charlie.

It read, *Danny, we have an emergency. Betty sent me to find you. George says he's a friend of yours and will give you this note. Come to Cavandish tomorrow morning for a meeting about nine. Betty really needs to talk to you. Make sure you show up. Charlie.*

Danny re-read the message. Had something happened to Betty or Caroline? Charlie was obviously okay because he'd been able to come to The Shelter. And Betty would be in hospital if she'd had another stroke.

George had fallen asleep again, the remains of the cheese sandwich still in his hand. Danny helped himself to one of the bus tickets from the debris on the bench beside him, then decided he'd better take two just in case he had to make a quick trip somewhere else after Betty's meeting. He picked up the remaining tickets and put them back into George's shirt pocket. If they were left on the bench they wouldn't be there for long. The rest of the stuff was just rubbish.

Danny decided to have supper at The Shelter, spend the night there, and get an early bus out to Cavandish in the morning. There was nothing else he could do until then. He wondered, had Betty finally realized the whole idea was impossible? Maybe the only trip they'd make would be back to Malone's to watch their bus go up for auction again. It would break Betty's heart.

CHAPTER 19

Charlie was pacing up and down the lobby at Cavandish and Danny could see the relief flood over his face as soon as he appeared at the front entrance.

"Thank God you're here! Betty has been laying into me. All last night before she went to bed, and again this mornin' all through breakfast because I couldn't find you yesterday. She wanted me to go back to The Shelter right away this morning to find you, and not to come back without you."

"So what's the emergency?" Danny asked. "Has Betty changed her mind or somethin'?"

"No. It's Caroline."

"Caroline! Caroline changed her mind? Caroline changes her mind every second." Danny almost laughed then caught himself. "Forget I said that. But, Caroline? What's..."

"Ssh," Charlie warned. They were just passing the front of the nurse's desk and a nurse was looking curiously at Charlie and Danny.

"For God's sake, Charlie! What's the emergency?"

"Betty wants to explain that to you herself. That guy, George, heard I was lookin' for you and said he'd be sure to give you a message. He seemed the reliable type and I was sure I could trust him. I gave him two bucks and four bus tickets. That's all I had."

Danny hadn't the heart to comment on Charlie's ability to judge reliability. "You did good, Charlie." Now he didn't feel the least bit guilty about lifting the two bus tickets from George.

"Here we are," Charlie said, as they reached his room. "I'll go get Betty."

Danny looked around the room while he waited. It looked like Charlie had a new roommate. There were some pictures on the wall, the bed was made up and pajamas were on the pillow. Danny poked his head out the door and noticed a new sign had been added to the wall. *William Wilkinson*, he read.

Charlie came back. "Betty's coming."

"See ya got a new roommate. When did he move in?"

"Two days ago. Snores like a bugger. Sits with Betty, me and Caroline for meals. He's gone on an outing somewhere – Dairy Queen, I think."

"Good to see you, Danny." Betty entered the room and sat in a chair. "I had a fit when Charlie came back last night without you."

"So what's the emergency? Charlie says it's something to do with Caroline."

Betty nodded. "Yeah. They're gonna move her."

"Who is? When? Where? And why? How do you know?"

"I overheard a conversation between that asshole Darlington, you know, the owner of this dump, and Alanna, the girl that replaced Brenda. It seems that

Caroline's money ran out a few weeks ago. I think her husband had made some bad investment, a **Ponzi** scheme or somethin', I don't know what. Caroline doesn't have enough money to cover her monthly keep here and Darlington wants her out of here. He's makin' Caroline a ward of the province, a charity case. This place doesn't handle charity cases or, at least, Darlington isn't willin' to keep her on here at a reduced price."

"So when is she moving?" Danny asked.

"As soon as an openin' comes up. And knowing Darlington he'll have her out of here *toot sweet* if he thinks Caroline is cuttin' into his profits."

"But where would they send her? It took ages for them to find a room-mate for Charlie here. How could they move Caroline so quick?"

"That's somethin' I didn't figure out until a day or two ago," Betty said. "I was keepin' my ears peeled hoping to hear more about Caroline. Alanna was askin' Darlington about a couple of discrepancies she'd found. It's a scam. Darlington was collectin' a big subsidy from the government for Charlie's long dead roommate, Jimmy, and another resident who died two months ago. I think Brenda must have been in on it, but when she left, it was too hard to cover up. That's all I heard, because Darlington noticed me and slammed the office door."

"But doesn't Cavandish have to report when someone dies? How could Darlington get away with it?" Danny asked.

"Who knows? Maybe they only have to report total numbers. The whole system is a mess. Look how long it took for Brenda to catch on that you weren't payin' anythin'. There was some sort of fiddle going on, I know that. Anyway, Caroline could be moved any day to any part of the city or even some town miles away. So we've gotta move fast. This week."

"This week! You have to be kidding! We haven't a hope in hell!"

"It's this week or never," Betty said, grimly.

Just then Caroline appeared in the doorway.

"Come on in love." Betty reached for Caroline's hand and Caroline smiled and sat on Charlie's bed.

"She'd be lost without us," Betty continued. "I can't bear the thought of her being hauled out of here, with no one to visit her, to some god-awful place worse than this. Probably locked away and left starin' at the walls somewhere." Betty's eyes welled up. "I was doin' this for me. But it's more than that now. I'm doin' it for Caroline too, and you, Charlie. And Danny... Oh Danny..."

Betty tried her best to choke back her tears, but she couldn't. Caroline looked concerned and patted Betty's hand.

"But we can't just take off in an empty bus, with no food, no way of cooking."

"Oh, I didn't tell you," Betty interrupted, wiping her eyes with the back of her hand. She gave Caroline a hug then turned back to Danny. "Yesterday mornin', me and Charlie slipped out to our banks. The banks don't send us statements anymore and I assumed that all my pension money was gobbled up by this place every month. It usually is. We pay by the day here, and most months have 31 days, but a few have only 30, and February, usually 28. So, when I went to my bank there was a small balance that had built up over the last few years. It was a surprise. There was 240 bucks in my account and I withdrew the cash right away. When we went to Charlie's bank, he had a balance too. There was $280 in his. So now we've got over $500. It's enough for all the things we still need to get. But we've got to do that now or it'll be too late for Caroline."

"I don't have anything to chip in," Danny said. "I was hoping to get a few hours work through The Shelter but I didn't have any luck. Won't the money for the next month at Cavandish come out of your accounts in a few days? That money will be wasted."

"Yeah," Charlie said. "It's too late to put a stop on our payments for next month. We'll end up paying for nearly a month and we won't even be here."

"But that's even better in a way," Betty said. "Darlington would be on to us. He'll be glad to pocket the money. Look, I hate giving the bastard money for nothin', but it'll give us more time. We'd be long gone before they know that the payments for me and Charlie are stopped. We could be at the Grand Canyon by then." Betty chuckled. "They won't do anythin' about findin' out where we've gone until they notice that there's no more money coming in from us."

"Jeez Betty," Danny said. "I don't know. You've been talking about getting away from here for so long, but I think we have to talk about what really happens when we leave. We still don't have any idea about how we'd cross the border."

"I know Danny, but now we have a crisis. If Caroline is moved before we can get away, well, I just couldn't go. It would be over for me too. I think we have to leave by Thursday. Labour Day weekend is comin' up. A lot of residents will be taken out by relatives, there'll be little or no recreation programmes goin' on here and there'll be reduced staff. Charlie says his room-mate is goin' to his daughter's on Thursday and won't be back until Monday night, so he won't know where Charlie has gone. I'm hoping like hell that nothin' happens to Caroline by then and we won't be missed until at least Monday night. That gives us nearly a four day head start. We have to go this week. It'll be too late after that. Please don't back out now, Danny."

CHAPTER 20

A half hour later Danny slipped out of Cavandish and caught a bus to Malone's. Betty had given Danny some cash so he could buy the supplies for the bus. Then he was to drive back to Cavandish and pick her up right after lunch. There was a thrift shop not far from the home where Betty was hoping to pick up some dishes, cutlery and bedding.

Betty, Charlie and Caroline had more than replaced his old buddy Pete. They'd taken him under their wing. But now he felt the roles had somehow been reversed, and it had given him a responsibility that he'd never had before. Without him, Betty's *Impossible Dream* couldn't even be attempted. He found himself humming the tune as he walked from the bus to Malone's.

He stopped off at the office to let Gail know he was taking the bus.

"We're off," he said. "Come hell or high water. I'm picking up a propane tank for the stove and some other stuff, then we're off to some thrift shop for bedding and things. First thing tomorrow it's groceries. Betty says that Caroline's going to be moved to another home somewhere soon. The owner at Cavandish found out what little money Caroline has won't cover her costs, so we have to leave this week."

"Jeez, that's a bummer. Poor Caroline," Gail said. "I'll walk you over to the bus and see you off. I sure admire you and your friends, heading off like this. It'll be quite an adventure. Would you send me a postcard if you make it all the way to the Grand Canyon?"

"I guess we could, but I wouldn't count on it. We might only make it as far as the city limits. Thanks for all your help, Gail, and thank Frank too. I wouldn't be surprised if you see us back here before long, asking you to sell the bus for us again. It's a hell of a dream Betty has. Hey! Look at that!"

Danny pointed to the back of an old school bus parked in a row in front of their bus. "I bet Betty would like a sticker like that." Fixed to the bumper of the bus was a sticker that read, *Fueled by Dreams*.

"I can give you one of those. I have one in the office over my desk. You can have it. Stop at the office and we'll put it on. Oh, and I almost forgot. Frank asked me to give you something for Caroline. He'd like her to have it."

Gail climbed into the bus behind Danny and sat in the passenger seat beside him as he started it up.

He pulled the bus up to the office and turned it off. Gail hopped out and came back with an envelope and the bumper sticker in her hands. She opened the envelope and pulled out a medium size photograph and handed it to Danny. "This is copy of Frank Malone's class photo from first grade. He searched for it for ages. His mother found it at her place in an old photo album. That's him, there, the second last kid on the right on the front bench, and there, standing at the back on the left is Miss Hagerty. Frank's teacher, your Caroline. I think he's right. It does look like her. She was real pretty. She still is. Anyway, Frank had me make a copy and he wants you to give this to Caroline."

Danny studied the photo. "I can sure see the resemblance. Thanks. We'll put it up in the bus. I doubt if Caroline will remember, but we'll have it with us and she'll see it every day. Betty will be pleased too. Probably see it as a good luck charm. And she'll love the bumper sticker. We'd better get that on the back bumper, and I'll get going. Betty will be waiting."

They put on the bumper sticker and Gail gave Danny a hug. "Good luck to all of you. I sure hope you make it. Oh, wait!"

Gail ran back into the office and came out with a small cardboard box filled with books of matches embossed with *Malone's Vehicle Auctions*. "You'll need matches to light your stove, and our address is on the matches so you can send me the postcard."

"Thanks, Gail." Danny climbed back into the bus, started it, and slowly pulled away, as Gail waved goodbye.

He drove slowly, familiarizing himself again with how the bus handled and when he reached the main road, he drove to the service station and bought a full propane tank for the stove. When he got back to the bus, he used a wrench to hook up the propane tank to the stove, and with the matches Gail had given him, he tested the four burners. He was pleased to find they all worked.

He was putting the book of matches back in the cardboard box with the others when something caught his eye. It was a $20 bill with a sticky note that read 'Good luck! For postage or whatever, Gail'. Danny put the $20 in his wallet and thought it could be their emergency fund when they ran out of money. He vowed he'd be sure to send a postcard to Gail from somewhere.

He made it safely back to Cavandish, although he had one anxious moment when he noticed a police car in his mirror in the lane behind him. He breathed a big sigh of relief when it pulled out, passed him, and kept going. On Betty's advice, he parked the bus around the corner from Cavandish beside a little park. She thought it best if no one connected them with the strangely painted vehicle.

Betty had saved him a couple of sandwiches from lunch for which he was grateful. He was hungry. He wolfed them down in the lobby while Betty got herself ready to go. Only she and Danny were going to the thrift shop and she had given Charlie strict instructions to stick close to Caroline until she got back. If anyone came to get Caroline, he was to somehow prevent her from being taken away. Charlie asked for suggestions, but Betty said, "Just make sure she's still here when we get back."

Betty and Danny slipped out quickly. No one was at the desk and she didn't bother signing out. When they reached the bus, Danny showed her the bumper sticker.

THE GRAND GETAWAY   97

"It's lovely. Thanks, Danny. *Fueled by Dreams*. Now if only gas was as cheap."
She laughed.

In the bus Danny gave Betty the bit of change he had left, then pulled out the
photo Gail had given him. Betty thought it was indeed Caroline in the photo.

"Caroline may not recognize herself, but she'll love all the little kids in the photo.
I'll pick up some masking tape from the office and tape it up over our table. We all
have a few photos. We'll bring them and tape them up too."

They pulled up at Value Village and Betty directed Danny to get a cart. Betty
grumbled, "We missed Senior's Day. It was yesterday. We would've got 10%
discount. Well, we'll have to really bargain hunt." Betty pulled a list from her purse.
"Let's go over there first." She pointed to a wall with a banner, *Kitchen Utensils*.

Attached to the wall were plastic bags filled with various kitchen utensils. Betty
immediately picked up a bag marked $4.99 containing teaspoons, tablespoons, a
selection of forks and a couple of knives.

"Not bad, but it's short on knives. I'll sneak a few more at Cavandish. They owe
us anyway." She placed the bag in the cart and Danny noticed she turned over her
list and under *Cavandish* she wrote, *knives*.

She selected a metal spatula, one sharp knife, a slotted spoon, a potato peeler
and a barbecue fork and added them to the cart. She noticed Danny raise his
eyebrows at the last item and she said, "Only way I know how to make toast over
the stove burners without burnin' your hand."

They collected a few cooking pots and a frying pan.

"We must have a tea-pot and some way to make coffee. Forget these cups and
saucers. Twenty-five bucks! We don't need a whole set of china. I saw a bag back on
that wall with plastic plates, for five bucks. We'll take those."

Some of the plates in the bag were kid's plates with dividers to separate the
different foods. "One of those will be good for Caroline," Betty said. "It'll help her
keep her food on the plate instead of fallin' over the edge. I think I'll use one myself.
I hate chasin' peas all around my plate. And look, Charlie will like this one." Betty
pointed through the plastic bag to a divided plate with pictures of Thomas the Tank
Engine and his friends.

"That's about all we can get here. Let's go check out the beddin' section then
we'll have to go."

Betty grumbled over the prices of sheets but found some twin sheets for $3.99.
"Caroline will like these pretty green floral ones and how about these dark blue ones
for you Danny? Hey! These Spider-Man sheets will be Charlie's and here's a matchin'
pillow case. He loved the Spider-Man movie. He already has Spider-Man pajamas.
Now for me ... jeez... $5.99 for these purple sheets. Well, they'll have to do, there's
no more $3.99 ones. We'll take our comforters from our own beds at Cavandish. You
have somethin' to throw on your bunk, Danny?"

"I'll be fine. I've got a zippered sleeping bag in my knapsack."

"Okay." Betty consulted her list. "We need a few towels."

Betty quickly picked out a couple of bath towels and a few hand-towels, then she found a plastic tablecloth. "Easy to keep clean," she muttered as she placed it in the shopping cart. She found a set of small curtains that she said she could fix up and sew by hand to cover the windows of the bus, replacing the remains of the tattered ones there now. The last item she decided on was a set of plastic place-mats with wildlife printed on them and four more cloth ones with bright floral designs.

"I think that's all we can get here. If you can drive me to the nearest Home Hardware, or Canadian Tire, we'll pick up a couple more things. Then we'd better hurry back. Charlie will be worryin' himself sick."

At Canadian Tire, Betty picked up a plastic bucket for water and a big plastic storage container they could use to store non-perishables. Then she decided on a second one to use for washing clothes. "It's deeper than a baby bath and we can stand in it and have a wash. We may not be able to find showers easily."

Danny spotted a small lantern on sale for half price. "That's a real good deal and we need some way of lighting the bus. This one has batteries good for sixty hours and there's no chance of it causing a fire."

Betty agreed, then found a can opener, which she said was something she'd forgotten to write down and was probably the most important thing. A pair of scissors was added – essential, Betty said, for any sewing, and cutting hard to open food packaging. Danny suggested a roll of duct-tape might be handy.

They checked out and Betty consulted the list again. "That'll have to do for now. We'll still need a few odds and sods, but maybe we can pick those up at the grocery store tomorrow. We've spent today..." Betty did a quick total of the two receipts from Value Village and Canadian Tire. "Not bad, $111.72. So, we've got some money for groceries and maybe enough for another tank of gas. We have no pillows, so we'll have to make do with rollin' up some sweaters or somethin' for a while."

Nearly two hours had passed by the time they made it back to Cavandish. Danny parked the bus around the side of the park by some trees where it was almost totally concealed. He planned to sleep in the bus during the night. He'd picked up a Subway sandwich on the way for supper and if he needed a bathroom, he could use the one at a service station a few blocks away. The others would slip out of Cavandish next morning after breakfast so they could buy the groceries.

Danny walked Betty back to the care home and they were just coming to the alleyway that ran behind it when an ambulance drove out of the alley and turned down the street.

Betty clutched Danny's arm. "Oh God! I hope that's not Caroline bein' taken away. Come on."

They walked as fast as Betty could go and when they reached the sidewalk to the front door Betty said, "I'll go in and find Charlie. If Caroline's gone, I don't know

THE GRAND GETAWAY   99

what we'll do. If she's still there I'll give you a thumb's up. If not, I'll wave you in. Pray she's still there, Danny."

Danny crossed the street and stood behind a large SUV out of sight of the front door, peeking round to watch Betty make her way back in. If Caroline was gone, the plan would be over.

Betty was taking a long time. Someone came to the door but it wasn't Betty, just one of the staff going home.

Danny watched the woman reach the main street and head towards the bus stop. *This waiting is killing me.*

He glanced back at the front door. There was a guy standing inside, peering across the street, looking his way. Danny ducked his head down behind the SUV, then peeked around the front. Charlie spotted him and raised his hand. He was giving Danny a very definite thumbs-up.

Danny felt a huge sense of relief surge through him as Charlie kept giving him the thumbs-up. He signalled a return thumbs-up then headed for the bus. He thought he'd better lie down. He was exhausted.

CHAPTER 21

Danny was awake early. The street had been quiet, and he'd slept well in one of the bunks at the back of the bus. He wasn't exactly sure what time it was. There was a clock mounted in the dash. It was running, and the time read 7:40 a.m. He had an hour to kill and he needed to use a bathroom. The gas station down the street that he'd used the night before had a Tim Hortons, so he put on his jacket and walked there. After using the bathroom and washing his face, he got himself a coffee and a doughnut and sat on one of the high stools looking out the window.

The plan was to buy groceries, and then take everyone back to Cavandish. Danny had suggested trying a food bank to save a few bucks. Betty had rejected that idea, saying, "No, we don't want to drive all over town for a couple of boxes of macaroni and I want to get back quick." They'd lie low that day and she and Charlie would do their best to gather up a few things they needed from Cavandish. Danny was to stay with the bus just in case there was any move on Caroline and they had to make a quick break for it. Thinking about that now made him finish his coffee fast and hurry back to the bus. He had put the things they'd bought the day before into the cupboards so there was nothing for him to do but wait.

He was sitting at the table getting anxious when he heard a tap on the door.

He opened it and Betty and Caroline stepped in. Charlie was carrying two plastic shopping bags which he put on the table.

"Here's some donations from Cavandish." Betty emptied one of the bags. There were four knives, a salt and pepper set and a glass carafe for coffee.

"We'll have to get a plastic cone somewhere and some filters. For now, we can make tea in it," Betty said. "We still need a kettle. Oh, and I brought you this alarm clock. And here's a bag of books from our library, in case you want to read somethin'. We had to wait ages before we could sneak out today. The darn nurse on duty was stickin' close to the front desk and I had to go into a room and set off an alarm to create a diversion. Even then, she took her own sweet time goin' to check. Good thing it was a false alarm. With all that, I nearly forgot to remove Caroline's alarm bracelet." Betty got Caroline settled behind the table and Charlie joined Danny beside him at the front.

"All set?" Danny asked as he started the bus. "Where are we headed?"

"Superstore," Betty called. "It's not far. Charlie knows the way."

Betty had her list ready when they got there. A case lot sale was on so Betty bought a case of baked beans and another of chili beans.

"Jeez, if we're gonna be eating all these beans we should've got a bus with air-conditioning."

"Shut up Charlie and just pick up that case," Betty said. "You'll be glad of beans on toast if we have nothin' else to eat and our money runs out."

THE GRAND GETAWAY   101

Using Betty's list, they picked up some vegetables and bananas. "You know how they're rationed at Cavandish," Betty said. "Charlie, go and get a bag of onions and some garlic. I'll need them for the soup and the chili." Then she added apples and oranges. "We should pick up some lettuce and stuff to make salads."

They found some sliced, day old, whole wheat bread for half price that Betty thought might last a week. A large jar of peanut butter, two dozen eggs and a bag of rice followed. "Rice goes a long way," Betty said.

They got some staples like tea, coffee, sugar, oatmeal for porridge and one container of milk. "We'll buy milk as we need it," Betty said. "We should get a bag of flour. I can make pancakes. We'll need a tub of margarine, and I guess we could splurge on a bottle of syrup."

"What about jam?" Charlie asked. "Caroline likes jam on her toast. Right, Caroline?"

"Yes, jam, jam, jam."

"Okay, Caroline," Betty said, "We'll get some blueberry, that's your favourite. Let's check the canned fish aisle, we need some tuna, the cheapest brand."

They picked up a large package of hand soap then went looking for a bottle of dish-washing soap. "A small bottle will do for now. You're in charge of the dish-washing' detail, Charlie, so make it last. Let's keep movin' and get out of here."

"Shit!" Betty said.

"That's what it's for all right," Charlie said. They were standing in the paper-products aisle.

"Oh, shut up Charlie. This toilet paper costs an arm and a leg. We'll be usin' public toilets in service stations and campgrounds mostly, but we'll still need some. Let's just get that package there, I'll bum a few more rolls from Cavandish." Betty laughed. "Is that what they call a pun? We'd have to get some pull-ups for Caroline. I'll grab a few from her room, but we'd better have some on hand."

When they checked out, they found out they'd spent $75. They got the groceries loaded in the bus and Charlie noticed the bumper sticker. He laughed, then said, "We'll have to come up with a name for this old bus."

"Yeah," Betty said. "Somethin' better than *Park 'n' Walk* like you called it – doesn't sound too hopeful. Let's come up with a more suitable name."

When they were settled and heading back to Cavandish, Betty carefully counted the money they had left. "We have exactly $220 left. I'm earmarkin' $155 of that for gas. So we're really down to $65. You may have to get by on beans for a few days, Charlie."

Charlie groaned.

They got back to Cavandish and avoided going past the front door. They parked near the park and Betty oversaw the stowing of their purchases.

"This is our last night at Cavandish," Betty said. "I'm excited about tomorrow. I see our darlin' Darlington is still here, I was hopin' he'd be gone."

"How do you know he's still here?" Danny asked.

"I caught a glimpse of his new red SUV in the parkin' lot."

"Probably doing the final paperwork on Caroline," Charlie said gloomily.

"Oh, quit that, Charlie. Don't keep worryin' me. Now about tonight ..." Betty gave Danny instructions about what she wanted him to do. If all went well, at midnight, Danny was to walk around the back alley, come into the garden behind the building and go to Charlie's window. Charlie's room-mate was supposed to be gone by then for the long weekend. Betty and Charlie planned to slip the clothes they were taking for all three of them out of Charlie's window, along with their comforters and whatever else Betty had gathered up and considered necessary.

"It could mean two trips," Betty warned. "We gotta go. Wish us luck. See you tonight at midnight. Set the alarm."

"Good luck," Danny said, surprising himself by whispering, as the three of them stepped out of the bus.

After making himself a peanut butter sandwich, Danny had a nap. When he woke up it was just after 4:00 p.m. He still had a lot of time to kill. He began to wonder how far they'd get the next day, if they made a clean getaway. He set the alarm clock and tested it to make sure it worked okay. He made himself another sandwich which made him wonder how long their food would last with four of them. Certainly not a month. Maybe they'd be getting by on the porridge or rice for the last few days until the pension money came in. He needed to get his mind off worrying about the trip. He looked through the bag of books Betty had pinched from Cavandish. He picked out *Losing Julia* by Jonathan Hull and *Cold Mountain* by Charles Frazier. He chose *Losing Julia*. *Cold Mountain* was definitely about a journey and even though it was set in the era of the civil war in the U.S. he was trying to shut journeys out of his mind. He read until it got too dark to see and then put the book away. A flashlight is something that would come in handy, he thought. They had the lantern, but he wasn't going to light it and draw attention to the bus. He fell asleep and only woke up when the alarm clock went off.

He found his pants and shoes in the dark and poked around until he found his jacket and slipped out of the bus. He made his way around the back of Cavandish, and quietly unlatched the gate into the back garden. There were one or two lights on. Charlie's window was in darkness.

He kept low and crouched below the window and listened. He heard nothing. He gave a light tap on the glass and the window slid open.

"That you Danny?" a hoarse voice asked loudly.

"Shut up, Charlie, you stupid bugger," he heard Betty hiss. "Who do you think it is? The Tooth Fairy?"

Betty's face appeared at the window. "Help me lift this Charlie, it's heavy."

THE GRAND GETAWAY   103

A pillowcase full of stuff was shoved out the window followed quickly by a second, landing on Danny's back as he bent to pick up the first. "Hurry back! There's lots more," Betty whispered, and then she slid the window shut. The two pillowcases were heavy, and Danny's arms were aching when he got to the bus. He dumped the two bundles on the floor of the bus and hurried back.

On the way back, he noticed the red SUV still parked down the street in the parking lot. He tapped on Charlie's window again and it was opened quickly and another bundle was pushed out. Danny grabbed the comforters which were tightly rolled and tied with belts from some robes.

"Wait, there's more," Betty instructed. There were a few bumps and clunks and Betty hissing, "Quiet!" Next came a huge plastic bag that they had trouble getting out the window until someone inside squeezed one side of the bag and changed its shape. It clunked onto the ground before Danny could catch it.

"Is that it?" Danny whispered. Then he heard Betty say, "Oh sh... sugar," and the window started closing as the room light came on. He heard a different voice. He crouched down, holding his breath, as a woman's muffled voice asked, "What's going on, Betty? How come you're in Charlie's room this time of night? Why aren't you in bed?"

"Um. I would've been, Wanda, but you just walked in. Me and Charlie were just gonna get it on."

"What!" Wanda gasped. "You and Charlie?"

"Yeah. 'Course me and Charlie. Mind you, he does need a little help sometimes."

"Help?"

"Yeah. You know, Wanda – an experienced woman like you. You know, with the old schlong."

"Schlong?"

"Jeez, I don't know what you young girls call it nowadays. A man's paraphernalia. His gizmo. I think the British call it the union-jack."

"Gee, Betty." Wanda laughed nervously. "I didn't know you had it in you."

"I didn't. We didn't have time." Betty started laughing.

Danny heard Charlie say something like, "Jeez, Betty, knock off the B.S. you..." then Wanda cut in, "Oh, Betty. You're terrible!"

Then he heard Betty say, "Wanda. I'm just kiddin'. Me and Charlie were just watchin' a late-night movie on Charlie's TV and we both fell asleep." Betty started laughing again.

"Betty," Wanda said sternly. "I think you'd better go to bed right now. I have to help Luis in the laundry room. He's waiting for me. I'll be back in fifteen minutes and when I come back, I want to find you in bed. Your own bed."

"I'll be there. Don't worry, Wanda. Good night."

A minute later the window slid open again. "You still there, Danny?" Betty whispered. "That was Wanda. Now that she knows me and Charlie are still up she'll be back. We'll have to get to bed right away."

"Is that it?" Danny whispered. "Is that all your stuff?"

Betty said, "I picked up a few extra things. Just one more bag and my walker. We'll shove them out now. See you after breakfast, Danny."

Danny hustled as quickly as he could. When he got back to the bus with the last bag and Betty's folded walker, he was sweating. The bag seemed really heavy and he couldn't imagine what Betty had put in it. There was no way he could empty the bags now, it was too dark. He stuffed everything onto the two lower bunks and was going to clamber onto one of the top ones to get back to sleep when he thought he'd better set the alarm again. By the light from a streetlight he set the alarm for 7:00 a.m. It was now 12:43 a.m.

He lay down on one of the top bunks and tried to sleep. It was no use. He shouldn't have had that nap this afternoon. He'd slept soundly until the alarm had woken him at midnight. He knew he wasn't going to get back to sleep now for ages. But what to do to kill the time? Something was bothering him. He thought about it and realized what it was. There was no way he could get to sleep if he didn't check it out. Then he'd be satisfied. He slipped out of the bunk.

CHAPTER 22

Danny was woken by a bright light flashing on and off. He rubbed his eyes and sat up. He looked at the clock. It was 6:25 a.m. A slight breeze was moving the branches of a tree at the edge of the park just beyond the bus, causing the light from a streetlight to appear to flash on and off. He'd set the alarm for 7:00 a.m. but he was wide awake now. He switched off the alarm and scrambled out of bed.

He would use the bathroom at the Tim Hortons and wash up, and he thought he'd shave too. He wanted to be all ready to go when the others arrived. This was the day and they couldn't have asked for nicer fall weather.

He bought himself a coffee and took it back to the bus, then sat at the table and began reading *Losing Julia* again. He had probably an hour and a half before the others would show up. He was enjoying the book.

He heard a noise at the door of the bus and scrambled to his feet.

"We made it!" Charlie was giggling with excitement.

"When Wanda walked in on you two," Danny said, "I was sure we'd get caught in the act."

"Yeah." Betty laughed. "And for a minute I had Wanda convinced she'd caught me and Charlie in the act, too. I embarrassed the hell out of Charlie." Betty handed Danny a heavy plastic shopping bag. "Here's a few more goodies." He took her arm and helped her in as Charlie assisted Caroline up the step.

Betty took Caroline's hand and was trying to get her to move to the table to sit down. She had her hand closed into a fist.

"What have you got in your hand, Caroline?" Betty asked. She tried to pry her fingers open, but she kept her hand closed.

"What is it?" she asked again. "Come and sit at the table, look, over here."

Caroline glanced at the table where Betty was pointing, and she opened her hand.

Betty picked the small piece of paper out of Caroline's hand and peered at it. She laughed.

"What is it?" Charlie asked.

Betty was still laughing. "It's one of the labels from the little plastic jam packets they give us at breakfast." Betty held it flat on her hand.

"Smucker," Caroline said, reading the label. "Smucker."

Charlie laughed uproariously. "I think we've got a name for our bus. 'The Smucker!'"

Betty smiled. "Would you like that Caroline? You chose this bus so I think you should name it."

"Smucker!" Caroline repeated.

"Okay we'll put the sticker right here on the dash." Betty placed the label on the centre of the dash and it still had enough stickiness to stay there. "I'll find the maskin' tape and stick it down properly later. I feel we should have a bottle of champagne to christen our bus, like a ship. Thanks, Caroline. The Smucker it is." She gave Caroline a kiss on the cheek.

Charlie slid onto the seat beside Danny and hollered, "Well, let's get this Smucker on the road!"

Danny glanced over his shoulder to check that Betty and Caroline were settled. Betty was smiling and crying at the same time. He started the bus and they pulled away.

He drove around the park to avoid going past the entrance to Cavandish and as they pulled onto the main street, Betty called, "There's Bill Darlington, the jerk. He looks mad about somethin'."

"He didn't see us, did he?" Danny asked.

"No, he wasn't lookin' this way. He was kickin' one of the back tires on his SUV. Maybe he had a flat."

"How come his SUV was there all night?" Danny called back. "Did he stay at Cavandish?"

"Hell no," Betty replied. "He goes out drinkin' with his buddies some nights, and he leaves his SUV at Cavandish so he doesn't get stopped by the cops. But let's forget him. And Cavandish! We're finally on our way and it's wonderful! Can we have some music?" Betty rummaged in the plastic shopping bag she'd carried into the bus. "Put this on. It's one of Caroline's favourites." She passed a cassette tape to Charlie. "Courtesy of Cavandish." Betty laughed

As Danny turned the bus onto Highway #2 south, the sound of Neil Diamond singing *Sweet Caroline* filled The Smucker.

CHAPTER 23

"Where are we now?" Betty asked.

"Just coming to the edge of the city limits," Charlie called back.

"We're still in the city! God! This place has sure spread out. I'd have thought we'd be well into the country by now. But then I don't think I've been down this highway for a real long time."

Betty was working on sewing, adjusting the new curtains, and Caroline was sitting beside her repeatedly smoothing out one of the pieces of material and talking to herself quietly.

"Oh Danny, I'm sorry. I completely forgot," Betty said. "I smuggled you out some breakfast. Toast and jam and a tub of yogurt, but in the excitement, I forgot all about it."

"I'm fine for now, thanks," Danny said. "I'll have a bite when we make a stop somewhere. I'd like to get the city well behind us. The traffic's still quite busy. Lots of cars heading south. It should thin out soon."

"Maybe," Charlie said. "But the Labour Day weekend's in full swing."

Danny kept in the right lane of the divided highway, keeping about 10 kilometres below the speed limit. The bus seemed to be handling well.

"We're just passing the High River turn-off," Charlie announced.

Betty glanced out the window. "Boy, this place must have really grown. There's a heck of a lot more buildin's along the highway. Maybe we should stop in about a half hour at some picnic spot. I brought a couple of those plastic milk jugs that we can fill with water and I'll try makin' us some fresh coffee."

When they reached a sign that told them they were coming into Nanton, Danny called out, "We're at Nanton. We just passed a sign that says there's a park here. Do you want to take a look Betty?"

"Sure, we'll give it a try." Betty had stopped sewing and was looking out the window. "Oh, look there's a big plane beside the road. I think I remember this place. I think the highway used to go past the front of these stores. I don't remember that plane."

"It's a WWII Lancaster bomber," Charlie said. "Too bad we can't borrow it to fly the rest of the way." Charlie was in a cheerful mood and as Danny made a right turn and they found the park and pulled over, he was softly singing the song, *Come Fly With Me*. The park was deserted.

"Looks like there's a tap for water and some picnic tables," Charlie said. "And I think there's washrooms over in the corner. We can all stretch our legs."

Betty stood up and rummaged in some of the stuff on the bunks and produced the plastic milk jugs. She handed them to Charlie. "Give these a good rinse and fill them. I'll see if I can figure out how to make coffee or tea on the stove when you come back. Come on Caroline, let's get out and take a little walk."

Danny unlocked The Smucker again. "Do you need any help?" he asked, as Betty climbed back in and Charlie handed in the water jugs.

"I think I'll be fine," Betty said. "It's such a nice day maybe we can sit at the picnic table and get some fresh air. I think we should go a bit further before we stop for lunch, if you're okay with that."

"That's fine with me," he replied. "The further we get from Cavandish the better. Oh, the matches for the stove are in the little drawer to the right. If you need any help, holler."

"I will," Betty said. "Just keep an eye on Caroline."

Danny went and sat with Charlie and Caroline. Charlie had closed his eyes and was sitting back with his face tilted towards the sun, soaking it in. Caroline was watching a magpie hopping about on the grass nearby. Her attention was drawn to a little dog that came scampering into the park followed by a small boy and girl.

About 10 minutes later Betty appeared in the doorway of the bus with a carafe of coffee and some mugs in her hand. Danny nudged Charlie who opened his eyes and the two went to the bus. Charlie took the coffee and mugs while Betty went back and returned with two more, the toast and yogurt she'd promised Danny, and a box of cookies.

"Darn, I forgot the milk. It's in the big plastic container on the bunk. Would you get it, Danny? We all take milk in our coffee."

Danny retrieved the milk and as he sat down he said, "I don't remember buying cookies."

"We didn't," Betty said. "A donation from Cavandish. Sorry there are some grounds in the coffee. My attempt at makin' a filter with a piece of paper towel to pour the water through wasn't too successful. The paper I used was too thick and when I tried pokin' at the paper, I poked too hard and made a hole."

Danny took a sip as he munched on a piece of toast. "Tastes pretty good to me."

"Well it's a little chewy. I think I should stick to tea until we get some proper filters," Betty said.

Charlie stared at the bus. "There's something different. I can't figure it out. Did you wash the bus or something?"

"Nope," Danny said.

"Well the front wheel hub looks real shiny," Charlie said. "I don't know why, but it looks different."

"Go take a look," Danny said.

Charlie strolled over to the bus, whistled softly to himself, then checked the other front wheel.

"Holy crap! How the hell...?" He walked back grinning. "We didn't have any extra money, did we?"

"Nope," Danny said.

"You didn't?"

"Did too."

"Holy! That beats all."

Betty had been helping Caroline with her coffee. "What? What are you two talking about?"

"The tires. The front tires," Charlie said. "The whole wheel. They look brand new."

"Almost," Danny said.

"My God! I thought The Smucker ran smoother." Betty whooped. "No wonder Bill Darlington was kickin' his tire when we left. You took the whole wheel? Two of them? When?"

"Last night. Couldn't sleep. When I went around the back to pick up the stuff from you and Charlie, something was bothering me. I think I must have seen Darlington's SUV the day before. I didn't know it was his until you mentioned it. The odds were against his bolts matching our hubs, so I took one wheel off just to be sure. They were a perfect fit. I couldn't believe it. Traded our two front wheels and tires for his two rear wheels. Took me a while, making sure I wasn't seen. Working in the dark, I could've done with a flashlight."

"I picked up one this mornin'," Betty said. "The maintenance guy was fixin' somethin' and left his maintenance room open. I thought about us not havin' one last night when Charlie and I were workin' in the dark too."

"Great," Danny said. "Anyway, I think I made a pretty fair trade with Darlington, seeing as how you are still paying for the next month at Cavandish. So it's not really stealing, is it?"

"Oh Danny! You're a wonder."

"Wonder, wonder, wonder, wanta, wanta, wanta," Caroline chimed in.

Danny laughed. "Well, now I won't be wondering if I could bring the bus to a safe stop if one of our front tires had blown."

"Good on ya, Danny," Charlie laughed.

"Well," Danny said, "let's put a bit more distance between us and Mr. Darlington. He may not entirely agree it was a fair trade and, when he finds you three missing, he may make us Canada's most wanted."

CHAPTER 24

An hour later they pulled over in the small town of Granum when Betty declared it was time for lunch and another bathroom break. Once again, they found a small park with some tables. Betty, with some help from Charlie, prepared tuna sandwiches and made tea in a saucepan with a couple of tea bags. Danny was sitting at the picnic table with Caroline, studying the map, when Betty and Charlie arrived with the food.

"I made some tea this time," Betty announced. "It won't be chewy like the coffee. My, don't the mountains look lovely." Betty pointed.

"Mmn," Danny mumbled as he bit into a sandwich. "We have to make a decision. Where are we gonna hole up for the night?" He gestured at the map.

"Well," Betty said. "How are you feelin? I think we're makin' good time. Are you gettin' tired yet, Danny?"

"I feel okay right now. I'm just looking at this map." He spread the map in front of Betty and Charlie slid over beside her.

"We're here at Granum," Danny said. "I'm not sure where you think we might try to cross the border, and have no idea how you think we can do that with no passports. As far as I can see there are five main crossings. Three are more or less straight south. One at Carway, south of Cardston, then south of Lethbridge is Del Bonita, and then there's Coutts. Coutts is the most direct way south if we were just driving through and we were legal, but I read that it's also the busiest."

"I'm sure it was Sweetgrass where Arnie and I crossed years ago. I don't remember it being that busy. I remember the name Sweetgrass." Betty ran her finger down the map. "Oh, I see. Coutts is on the Canadian side and Sweetgrass is the U.S. side. Do you think you could get us as far as Milk River by supper time? It's just north of Sweetgrass, and we might be able to drive down and take a quick look before dark. Scout it out, so to speak. Then maybe find a place to camp for the night and try for the border early in the mornin'."

"But what's the plan?" Charlie asked. "This isn't gonna be like getting into the zoo."

"Well," Betty said. "After we take a look at the border crossin' and see what it's like, couldn't we maybe see what other little roads might cross the border? It's supposed to be the longest undefended border in the world."

"I'd say that slogan is now as out of date as a ten cent chocolate bar." Charlie chuckled.

"Looking at this map, Betty," Danny pointed again, "no matter where we try to cross, there don't seem to be any roads heading south except for the proper border crossings. There might be some small farm service roads, but they're not on this map. Even if we found a little road or track heading south, it looks like we'd be driving for hours across fields, trying to get through fences, maybe even crossing rivers before we reached any road. The Smucker wouldn't last long driving over rough ground."

"I know it's not gonna be easy and maybe impossible," Betty said, "but we thought everythin' was impossible when I first mentioned it months ago. We have our little bus, we've escaped from Cavandish, and I'm not goin' back. Let's get to Milk River first. It's a little closer to the Grand Canyon, even if it is still in Canada."

"And then...?" Danny asked.

"We'll see."

"I think we'd have a better chance if we drive back to Nanton, buy a bit of gas and steal that Lancaster Bomber we saw to fly over the border," Charlie said.

"Come on," Betty snapped. "Don't be a smart-ass, Charlie. Finish your sandwich, Caroline, now, love."

Danny looked at the map again. "Looks like there's a campground at Milk River, probably have to pay if we stay overnight, though."

Betty said nothing as she gathered up the plates, cups and remains of the meal. Danny could tell she was mad at Charlie.

Charlie mumbled an apology and Betty nodded. "You can do the dishes after supper tonight. By yourself."

"Okay, Betty. No problem."

"It's been quite a day," Betty said, patting his arm. "I think I'll try makin' chili for supper. And maybe you can make a salad. Then we'll sort out the stuff we have and get set up for the night."

Before they left, Danny asked Betty if she'd like to hear more music and she handed him a few more tapes. As they moved on, Janis Joplin was singing *Me and Bobby McGee*.

Just before they reached Milk River, both Betty and Caroline, who had fallen asleep at the table, woke up.

"There's an old ruined farmhouse," Betty said. "Looks like it's been deserted for years. Where are we, Danny?"

"Just coming into Milk River," Danny called, and Charlie, whose head had fallen to his chest and was quietly snoring, snapped awake. Danny, too, was feeling drowsy and he thought they'd better stop and take a look at the campground. According to the map, it was about 20 km to the border crossing at Coutts-Sweetgrass.

When Betty discovered they'd have to pay $25 to camp overnight, she balked at that. Instead, she directed Danny back into Milk River to a service station. She'd spotted a rest stop by the side of the road and after spending $45 for gas and using the washrooms they headed back there. There was only one semi-trailer at the rest-stop and they pulled in behind it.

Betty got Charlie to make a salad while she set to work making a vegetarian chili. Danny climbed into one of the bunks that wasn't filled with their bags of stuff from Cavandish and tried to have a nap. Betty gave Caroline a few carrot sticks to munch on at the table.

It took about three quarters of an hour before the chili was ready and Betty got them to sit down around the table and start on their salads. Danny had only dozed for about 10 minutes. The rest of the time he'd been lying in the bunk wondering what tomorrow would bring. He didn't think they would be able to stay overnight at the rest stop with a campsite not far away. The cops would probably hassle them.

"This is pretty good chili, Betty," Danny said, as he spooned it out of the bowl. He suspected the bowls were **another gift** from Cavandish. A small plate of bread and margarine in the middle of the table completed the meal.

"After supper, we'll get everythin' sorted out, put all the stuff away and get our bunks made up," Betty said. "Then we'll drive down to the border just to take a look. Do you think we could come back here for the night?"

"I don't think that's a good idea," Danny said. "You're not supposed to camp here. The last thing we need is for the cops to come knocking on the door and ask us to move on, or worse, ask for I.D. We don't want to be drawing attention to ourselves. We're just too close to the road."

"Back up the road," Betty said, "I saw an old farmhouse with a little track into it. We could check it out. There were some trees around it too. Maybe we could park there overnight."

"We'll see," Danny said.

After supper, Betty organized the stowing away of all the gear. There were one or two surprises. A whole bag of oranges, a proper sugar bowl and cream jug, and a selection of knives, plus more of the cereal bowls which they'd just used for the chili. They hung up their clothes in the small closet and got the bedding set up on the bunks.

"We only brought some of our clothes," Betty said. "We wanted to leave the impression that we were comin' back. Maybe they won't look too closely, and they won't miss us for a while."

They still had no pillows, but they rolled up their coats and jackets instead. Charlie and Danny chose the upper bunks, leaving the lower ones for the two women. Charlie was delighted with the Spider-Man sheets and pillow case.

"I thought if you wore your Spider-Man pajamas and the border guys searched The Smucker," Betty said, "you'd only have to lie on your bunk and blend in and you wouldn't be noticed."

Betty got Charlie to hang up the one new curtain she'd finished and promised to get the other three finished in the next few days. She used some duct tape to temporarily hold the old ripped ones over the windows. She had heated some of their water and Charlie had most of the dishes done when she decided to help him dry them and put them away.

"Okay," Betty said, "Let's go down to the border. I want to take a look, see how things are."

The traffic was still quite heavy as they drove towards the border and as soon as buildings came in sight they pulled over onto the right shoulder. The U.S. Customs and Immigration entrance, a little further distant, was off-set on the right with separate lanes.

Betty came and stood at the front beside Charlie and Danny.

"There's not a lot to see," Danny said. "Looks like they have four lanes and the one on the right is for trucks only. Each lane has a booth with a border guy. Now what?"

"Just watch another minute," Betty said.

"If we go down there tomorrow," Charlie said, "when we go through one of the car lanes and they ask us for our passports, we're gonna end up in that office building at the back. They won't let us back up and drive off. We couldn't anyway. They're be another car behind us blocking us in."

"Okay," Betty said. "Let's head back to that old farmhouse before it gets too dark."

"You got a plan, yet, Betty?" Charlie asked.

"No. I'll have to sleep on it."

They used the washrooms one more time at the service station and found the ruined farmhouse just north of Milk River that Betty had seen. There was an old row of poplars that provided a shelter belt and some seedlings had sprung up across the front of the house which screened it even more from the road. The house was a wreck with old weathered clapboard, a roof with half the shingles missing and a sagging porch. Black space filled the gaping, glassless windows and front door.

Danny backed The Smucker along the driveway and pulled it up to the side of the house. They were practically out of sight from the road.

"Looks like there's an old outhouse just behind us, if we have an emergency," Betty said.

"Think I'll wait 'til morning," Charlie said. "I just saw a bat whiz past it. Let's hit the sack. I'm bushed."

CHAPTER 25

With Charlie carrying the broom as a weapon to ward off any wayward bats that might be lurking in the old outhouse, Betty ventured into it. Charlie stood by with Caroline and when Betty emerged, she pronounced that the outhouse was as good as any she'd seen when she'd worked up north.

"It's dry. Hasn't been used for years. And there's no smell. Come on in Caroline. It's fine."

Betty took Caroline in and when the two of them came out, all three headed back to the bus. Danny was inside supervising the heating of water for washing, shaving and coffee, using three different pots on the stove.

Betty prepared some scrambled eggs. Then she set up Charlie to stand by the stove with the barbecue fork, toasting bread over one of the burners.

"Now watch it doesn't burn, Charlie. When it's nicely browned, turn it over and do the other side. I'll try makin' some coffee in a pan. I found a small strainer I must have picked up from you know where. I can strain the grounds when we pour it into the cups. Okay?"

"Sure, give it a try," Charlie said.

Danny nodded as he finished shaving.

"Okay, Charlie, that toast is done," Betty said. "Slap some margarine on it and I'll put some of this scrambled egg on for Caroline." She placed the toast and egg in front of Caroline who was sitting at the table.

When Betty had the other three plates ready, she put them on the table. Then, using the strainer, she poured the coffee she'd been brewing in the saucepan into four cups. "Okay, everyone. Eat up."

As the four of them sat quietly eating, Charlie looked at the small alarm clock on the counter. "It's coming up to nine o'clock. What should we do first, Betty?"

"Finish our breakfast."

"No, I mean what we're planning to do."

"I know what you mean. If you're askin' if I have a plan, no. I think we should arrive at the border about ten o'clock."

"And?"

"And we'll drive up. We're just a bunch of old people who haven't been across the border in years. We're just four old dumb Canadians. We've never had to have a passport before. We didn't know we had to have one. Maybe we'll find someone with a sympathetic ear. I don't really know. Sometimes you get lucky."

"It's not gonna happen. Too much security, nowadays." Charlie said.

"What about that young kid who walked onto a plane in Minneapolis? He didn't even have a ticket and he got as far as Hawaii, you said."

"Yeah. Somebody screwed up there all right."

THE GRAND GETAWAY   115

"And then there was that guy at an airport in Canada. He had a home-made bomb in his carry-on luggage. And when they found it, they asked him if he wanted it back. He said he didn't, and they let him fly to the Dominican Republic. Do you think if I said we had a bomb, they'd let us go to the Grand Canyon?"

"For God's sake Betty," Charlie said. "Don't mention bombs or anything like that. These guys are armed. They don't mess around. They'd tear The Smucker apart."

"Well my one and only plan is to beg. If we get turned back, we'll maybe have to find some track goin' south, drive through some fields. Maybe we'll go somewhere else?"

"Where?" Charlie asked.

"I don't know. Eat your breakfast."

"Yes. Breakfast! Breakfast! Fast! Fast! Fast! Faster! Blaster! Blaster!" Caroline repeated, then concentrated on chasing a piece of scrambled egg with her spoon.

Danny was silently chewing a piece of toast and said nothing, but he thought for sure they'd wind up driving across Canada, east or west, and every time Betty got within driving distance of a border crossing, she'd want to try it.

"I bet the Indians go back and forth across the border all the time," Betty said. "Do you think they all have passports? Maybe we can find one to smuggle us across or somethin'."

"I think you'd better sit up front with me, Betty," Danny said. "I'll let you do the talking, but Charlie's right. You can't mess around. Some of these guys might shoot and ask questions later. I don't think we have a hope in hell of them letting us through. We'll soon find out, anyway."

Betty had them tidy up and put away the dishes. "We need everythin' ship-shape. We can't have dishes flyin' about if we get involved in a high-speed chase."

She looked at Charlie's and Danny's faces, then burst out laughing.

They crested a small rise and in front of them was the border with its lanes and booths and the traffic easing in. There were four lanes open now. Danny could feel sweat trickling under his armpits. He was really nervous. All the car-only lanes had at least two cars waiting ahead of them. He was heading for one in the centre when Betty cried out, "No. Go right! Go to the right!"

"What?" Danny braked, then swerved quickly to the right, hoping that he wasn't cutting anyone off or causing an accident.

"Right! Right! Right!" Betty said again.

Danny glanced in the side mirror this time and pulled the wheel right again. A huge freightliner was coasting behind him and, as he pulled into the lane to stop, he realized he had pulled into the truck lane. When he stopped, another freightliner was directly ahead of him and now the one following pulled up behind him, closing in on their rear bumper.

"Shit," Danny said. "I pulled into the truck lane. Why did you keep saying go right, Betty?"

"I didn't mean this lane. I meant the one that's on our left now."

"But I was going into that one and you kept yelling right! right! Why?"

"I liked the license plate on the car ahead of us. I thought it was a good omen. It said, Friendly Manitoba. When I said 'right' you said, 'What?' And I thought you didn't hear me, so I said it again."

"Holy sh..." Danny muttered.

One of the U.S. border agents was out of his booth talking to the truck driver ahead of them. He now stepped back, turned around and saw the bus in the truck lane. As he approached it, Danny rolled down the window.

CHAPTER 26

As Randel Fletcher approached the small bus, or whatever this thing with the weird yellow paint job was, he was still smarting from the telling off he'd just received from his supervisor, Hank Brinkerhoff. Brinkerhoff was an ex-marine who had served two tours of duty in what he called *Eye-rac*, and who made it obvious that he considered anyone who hadn't served in the military service of his country as low life. Randel had never felt the desire to put on a military uniform and as soon as he'd met Brinkerhoff, he was convinced he had made the right decision.

Nobody knew a lot about Brinkerhoff. He claimed to have previously worked with U.S. Customs and Border Protection – U.S. Department of Homeland Security along the U.S. – Mexico border and bragged that he'd been responsible for turning back and apprehending more wetbacks than any other border officer. To Brinkerhoff, all illegals trying to enter the U.S. were wetbacks, even if they were trying to enter the country from Canada. He still harboured the belief that there had been a Canadian connection with the 9/11 attack on New York. And Canada had refused to join in helping liberate *Eye-rac*. He claimed he was born in Phoenix, Arizona. Truth was, he'd never forgiven his mother for having given birth to him in a little town named Bagdad in western Arizona. Brinkerhoff told everyone he ran a tight ship. Regulations were there for a reason. He went by the book and he seemed out to prove it at every turn.

"On my watch," he'd warned, "there'll be no fuck-ups, no wetbacks, no terrorists. Canada is full of wetbacks, illegals, 'n' most are just usin' Canada as a steppin' stone to *Amurica*."

He had arrived at the Sweetgrass border crossing as a supervisor six months ago. Nobody knew whether it had been a promotion or demotion. Since his arrival, whenever they were on the same shift, it seemed that Brinkerhoff was determined to make Randel's life a living hell.

This morning Brinkerhoff didn't have to look for an excuse. Randel had been ten minutes late arriving for his shift and Brinkerhoff read him the riot act.

Brinkerhoff didn't ask why Randel has been late. "This is the busiest weekend of the year and you're layin' in bed, no doubt havin' a quickie. You're not a team player, Fletcher. I had to pull a man off passenger vehicles to help with the truck traffic. You were assigned that job today! You put a piece of pussy ahead of the security of your country! If you'd been in my unit in *Eye-rac*, and we were under attack by the *A-rabs*, and dependin' on you to bring up the ammo, and you showed up 10 minutes late, we'd a been fucked. I woulda had you court-martialled. I been watchin' you, Fletcher. You'll be in my report. Now get your sorry ass over to truck duty, pick up the slack 'n' relieve Wilson."

Now Randel had to go and find Brinkerhoff. The truck he'd just checked had a minor glitch with the paperwork. It was a refrigerated freightliner filled with pork bellies and there was one initial missing by a Canadian meat inspector. It was very minor and should have been caught by the trucking company or the driver. The proper inspection stamps were all there except for the initial, but Randel couldn't let the truck go without Brinkerhoff's okay. Brinkerhoff had given strict instructions that under no circumstances were any infractions of the rules to be overlooked. They were to be brought to his personal attention. He would either authorize the truck to go ahead or have it pulled aside for a thorough inspection. Randel hoped that wasn't going to happen or he might find himself scrambling around inside a refrigerated truck. With Brinkerhoff already pissed off at him, he had no doubt that it could happen. Brinkerhoff could punish him further and make an example of the trucker at the same time.

And now Randel had this crazy looking bus thing in his truck lane, right behind the freightliner and trapped by another that had pulled in. Brinkerhoff would no doubt blame him for that too. There was already a third freight truck pulling in behind the second and it wouldn't take long before there was a line-up.

Randel quickly walked back to the bus. *How the hell had they missed the truck lane signs?*

An old guy sitting in the driver's seat rolled down the window and Randel caught a glimpse of a elderly female with a blonde hairdo and a worried smile on her face.

"Sir. You're in the wrong lane," Randel said. "When the truck ahead of you pulls out, you're gonna have to follow the traffic cones and when you get to the end of them, make a u-turn. Come around again and get into one of the other lanes."

He looked around quickly trying to see if Brinkerhoff was still outside or had retreated to his office, and spotted him three lanes over with Wilson. When Randel arrived, Brinkerhoff was holding a passport and asking, "How do you say your name? Mahan- dra, Ma- han – dra Muk – her – jee. Mukkergee?"

Randel noticed the driver and the other occupants of the car looked like East Indians.

The driver stated his name.

Brinkerhoff repeated the name, mispronouncing it and then asked, "Is this your photo, sir?"

"Yes sir. My photo."

Brinkerhoff was peering at the passport then back at the driver when he noticed Randel. "What is it Fletcher?"

Randel noticed the irritation in Brinkerhoff's voice at being interrupted.

"Initial missing from meat inspector on shipment of pork bellies, sir."

"Well, glad you're noticing something, Fletcher. Everything else in order?"

"Yes sir."

"Who's the trucking company?"

"Briggs-Carlson Trucking, sir."

"Well we've had no trouble with them before." Brinkerhoff took the papers from Randel and signed the authorization. "Let him go. But warn him, next time we'll turn him back. The pork lobby are gettin' antsy about how much pork Canadians are shippin'."

"Yes sir." Randel took the papers and turned to hurry back, grateful that Brinkerhoff hadn't looked over to the truck lane and noticed the yellow bus. He'd turned back to the driver of the car. "This photo has no moustache," Randel heard Brinkerhoff say.

Randel stepped back into his booth, handed the trucker his papers and gave him Brinkerhoff's warning. The truck pulled ahead, and the yellow bus followed immediately. Randel turned his attention to the next freightliner pulling up to his booth with a hiss of airbrakes. Just then his cell phone rang in his pants pocket. He quickly looked over his shoulder, fearful that Brinkerhoff might have heard it. It was strictly against regulations to have a personal cell phone in your booth and Brinkerhoff had really raged at one of the female officers when he'd caught her on her cell phone. He usually left his phone in his locker but this morning in the rush, he'd stuffed it into the pocket of his uniform when he'd changed at work, and forgotten to turn it off.

Randel quickly looked at his phone. He didn't recognize the number. It couldn't be his wife. He'd warned her not to phone him at work and, anyway, she'd left without her cell phone. He'd seen it on the coffee table. "Shit!" Randel muttered as the trucker handed over his papers.

CHAPTER 27

When she reached the small town of Dutton, Amber decided to get off the bus. She'd been foolish. *I panicked,* she thought. The sun was hot, and she removed her jacket. The driver had retrieved the suitcase for the only other passenger who had got off and was about to close the baggage bay. He seemed surprised to see her. He was sure he'd had only one passenger getting out at Dutton.

"My bag," Amber said. "Could you get it for me please?"

"That's all that was tagged for Dutton," the driver said. "Are you sure you tagged it?"

"Yes. Yes, I did. But it was tagged for Great Falls."

"Great Falls! But this is Dutton."

"I know, I'm sorry. I changed my mind. I want to get off here."

The driver slammed the door of the bay and moved further along towards the rear of the bus, opening another. It was full of luggage and parcels and when Amber looked inside, she couldn't see her suitcase.

"What's it look like?" the driver asked.

"It's small and green, not leather, more like cardboard."

The driver hauled several bags and packages out onto the gravelled strip where they'd stopped, muttering to himself as he did so.

Amber could feel the other passengers on that side of the bus staring out at her through the windows.

"There it is." Amber pointed. "That one near the back."

The driver grunted and pulled out another large suitcase, then crawled into the bay to reach Amber's case.

"Thank you," she said as he handed it to her. "Would you happen to know when the next bus leaves for Shelby?"

"Shelby! Not for another four hours. We just met the Shelby bus a mile back, the next one's not until three."

"Thanks," she said.

"You'll need to buy a ticket inside if you don't have one." He nodded towards the small café.

"Thanks," she said again.

"You're welcome I'm sure." He slammed the baggage bay door, climbed back on the bus and drove off, leaving Amber standing in a cloud of dust and exhaust fumes. She carried her suitcase inside the café. It was a throwback to the 1950's or had been remodelled to look like that – a short counter with a metal edge, red topped leather stools, three small booths and a juke box. It was empty except for one girl standing behind the counter.

THE GRAND GETAWAY   121

Amber slid onto the red leather bench of one of the booths. She had to think. She'd had a ticket to Great Falls. *A waste of money. Money they could ill afford to spend.* She realized the waitress was standing beside her.

"I'll just have a coffee, thanks," Amber said, and when the waitress left, she rummaged in her purse for her cell phone. "Shit!" she mumbled. "Left it on the coffee table."

She noticed a phone booth outside. The waitress brought her the coffee and Amber asked for some change to make a phone call. She added some sugar to her coffee and took a few sips, then, leaving her suitcase on the bench, called to the girl, "I'll be back in a sec," and went outside to the phone booth.

It was stifling inside the booth and she propped the door open with her foot, dialed the number and inserted the required change when the automated voice told her to. The line was busy. Then she remembered she'd left the phone off the hook. She just wasn't thinking straight. It was no good trying him on his cell phone either. He would've been at work for a while now and he wasn't allowed to have his cell phone with him on duty.

As she walked back into the café, she thought about the busy phone. It was an old-fashioned cord phone. Why they'd kept it she didn't know. But now Randel was looking for a new job, it had come in handy. He was having a hard time with his new supervisor. He'd been happy working at the border crossing at Sweetgrass until Brinkerhoff's arrival. Now he was hoping to be taken on as a trainee investment advisor in Great Falls with Merrill Lynch, and he'd had an interview recently that he'd felt good about. Having the home phone number to give out to the interviewer meant Randel's supervisor wouldn't find out that Randel was thinking of leaving.

This morning Amber had grabbed up the grocery list and called out to him that she was going shopping and would be gone for a couple of hours. The car wouldn't start, and she'd come back in just as the phone rang. When she answered the phone and the person calling asked for Randel Fletcher, she was sure it was Merrill Lynch calling. She'd hurried outside to find Randel. He'd said something about going next door to check on their neighbours' house since the Johnsons were away on holiday.

Amber was hoping the call was good news. Her own job at the day-care didn't bring in enough to cover the mortgage on their little house, and then there was the monthly payment on the truck. Making ends meet was a bit of a strain and things would get more difficult now that she'd found out she was pregnant. She'd been delighted to learn yesterday that she was going to have a baby, but she hadn't been sure how Randel would accept the news. He'd wanted to wait a bit longer before they had children. Now with him trying to find a new job, he'd want to wait longer still. But the real reason she hadn't told him was because when she'd come home from work yesterday, she'd found him sleeping on the couch. He'd promised to pick and shell some peas for supper and re-stake the plants which were collapsing from their own weight. When she'd woken him and found he hadn't done it, they had argued. He'd been home for three hours from an early morning shift and said he was tired.

She was passing the Johnson's kitchen window when she saw a movement and was about to tap on the window to get Randel's attention when she froze.

It was Randel she saw, but there was someone else with him. She recognized Yvonne, the woman from the house on the other side of the Johnsons. Randel was sitting on a chair and Yvonne was bending over him, her blonde hair falling over his face as they kissed. Yvonne's blouse was unbuttoned, and Randel was caressing her breasts. Before Amber had stepped back from the window and fled, she saw Yvonne reach back to unclip her bra.

Forgetting all about the phone call, Amber had run back to her house sobbing, her heart pounding. She'd rushed into their bedroom, grabbed the small green suitcase from the closet and quickly stuffed in some clothes. She picked up her purse. There was only a $20 bill in it, but she had her bank card. She rushed out the front door and ran down the street. The bus station was eight blocks away and when she reached it, she hurried inside.

"When is the next bus leaving?" she'd asked at the ticket counter.

"To where?" the dark-haired, chubby woman behind the counter asked.

"Just anywhere."

"Are you all right?"

"Yes. Yes," she'd said. "Please give me a ticket. I just need a ticket."

The ticket seller had looked at her strangely and said, "Well there's a bus leaving for Great Falls now. They're already boarding at gate number five."

She went back inside the café and told the waitress she was going to the washroom. She noticed some pies in a glass case on the counter. "I'll have a piece of raisin pie when I come back, thanks."

In the small washroom she looked at herself in the mirror. Her thick, dark red, shoulder-length hair looked good. She'd been to the hairdresser a few days before. Her hair complimented her green eyes. She wiped off her smeared mascara and reapplied it. She looked younger than her 22 years, everybody said so. Her eyes brimmed with tears again as she thought of this morning. What had got into Randel? Yvonne was 30 years old or more and she certainly looked it. She dabbed her eyes once more and went back into the café. The girl had placed her pie on the table and was standing with a coffee pot in hand.

"Thought you might like a fresh cup."

As Amber stirred her coffee and sampled the pie, she thought again of what she'd seen. Now she wanted to go back to confront him but the more she thought about it, the angrier she got.

As soon as I said I was going for groceries, he must have phoned Yvonne. The bastard! I hope it was Merrill Lynch on the phone and they got fed up waiting for him and hung up. Maybe they gave the job to someone else. Serve the bastard right!

She decided she wouldn't wait around for the bus back to Shelby. It was still at least a three-hour wait. She would keep going south to Helena, where her friend Moira lived. Moira would put her up for a few days while she decided what to do, she was sure of it. She could still use the rest of her ticket to Great Falls. But before she left here, she'd phone that bastard, Randel, on his cell phone anyway, and give him an earful, even if she could only leave a message.

"What time does the next bus for Great Falls get here?" she asked the waitress.

"Not for another three and a half hours, at 3.30 p.m."

"Damn," Amber muttered. "It's three and a half hours whether I go on or go back."

"Thanks," she said to the waitress. She decided she might try hitchhiking to Great Falls. She'd get there a lot faster than waiting for the bus south. She picked up her suitcase and headed for the phone booth again, thinking of some choice words she wanted to leave for Randel on his cell phone.

CHAPTER 28

"Now we're really screwed, Betty," Danny said, as he followed the freightliner. "Keep a look out for the end of the traffic cones, I've got to make sure I don't ram someone coming out of another lane when I make the U-turn."

"Just keep followin' that truck," Betty said. "This is our chance. Just keep goin'."

"What! There'll be cop cars screaming after us in seconds. Here's the end of the cones."

A striped parking strip appeared on their left to allow vehicles to pull over safely and turn around when it was safe.

"Keep goin', Danny. Don't stop. Catch up with that truck!" Betty grabbed Danny's arm. "If we get stopped, we'll say we missed the place to turn back. We're confused old people. Speed up!"

Danny had eased off on the gas but, spurred on by Betty's urging and her grip on his arm, he eased his foot back down on the accelerator.

"What the hell are ya doing?" It was Charlie. "Holy shit!"

There was a scuffle behind Danny and Betty, but both were looking ahead, concentrating on the truck in front of them as they caught up to it. Danny glanced in his side mirror and saw the truck that had been behind them at the border crossing was now right on their tail.

Betty turned around. "What the hell are you doin', Charlie?"

Charlie was crouching underneath their little dining table and was holding Caroline's hand. He was doing his best to get her to duck under the table too, but she was resisting his efforts and was repeating the last words Charlie had spoken.

"Holy shit! Holy shit! Holy shit!"

"I'm trying to get Caroline to take cover," Charlie said. "You should get down too."

"Oh, for God's sake Charlie! Let her go! You've been watchin' too many cop shows on TV." Betty started laughing. "Leave poor Caroline alone. Get the hell out from under the table and sit down with her. Wrap yourself up in your Spider-Man sheet. You'll feel safer."

Charlie crawled out from under the table looking sheepish as Caroline sat down again at the table and he joined her. "You'll hear the cops or border patrol sirens any minute and we'd better pull over and surrender quietly," Charlie said.

"If they pull us over, we'll stop. But we'll wait until that happens. Meantime, we're headin' south. Now try and relax. You'll only upset Caroline," Betty said.

At the wheel of the bus, Danny too was waiting for the sirens to wail, but all he could hear was the truck following them and suddenly it was passing. He eased off the accelerator and the truck roared past. When Danny looked in the side mirror again, the road behind them was empty.

CHAPTER 29

Randel crouched down on the seat in his booth and answered his phone, while with his other hand he fumbled through the truck's manifest papers.

"Hello."

There was a hesitation then Amber's voice came on. "Randel? That you?"

"Yeah. It's me," he hissed. "What the hell are you phoning me at work for? You know I'm not supposed to answer my cell phone at work."

"Then why are you answering your phone, or do you only answer the phone for certain people? I thought you were supposed to keep your cell phone in your locker."

"What? Yeah, I am. But I was late getting to work and I forgot to put it in my locker. Brinkerhoff is on the war-path and I've got a line-up of trucks here. Is this important, Amber?"

"Yeah. I think it's damn important. In fact, I think it's fucking important!" Amber yelled. "And I know why you were late, you asshole!"

"What! What the hell are you talking about?"

"I'm talking about that bitch from two doors up. The one you were getting it on with this morning. And yesterday, you jerk! When I came home and found you sleeping on the couch, you said you were tired. You were home for hours, and only tired because you were shagging Yvonne!"

"That's not true! Honest. Can we talk about this at home, Am? I've got a truck right here at my window and a whole line-up." He could feel himself sweating as he stamped the trucker's papers and gave him a nod to go ahead.

"Well, if I were you, I'd stay away from windows," Amber snapped.

"Believe me nothing happened, Amber. I didn't let it happen."

"Oh yeah! Then if it wasn't you going at it hot and heavy it must have been your identical twin. And he was wearing *your* Denver Broncos sweats with the little white and orange horse-head logos, the ones I bought you over the internet for Christmas. Jeez! Randel! You're the only one I know that has a key to Johnson's house!

"I'd walked out the front door to go grocery shopping, but the god-damn car wouldn't start, and I came back in. You must have phoned up that bitch as soon as I left. Then the phone rang, and I thought it might be Merrill Lynch calling so like a good little wife I went looking for you."

"Look. Amber. Believe me. I didn't phone her. She saw me going in and I don't know what you think you saw. I was watering the Johnson's plants and she walked in the back door."

"Don't give me that. I've been in the Johnson's house lots of times and I've never seen any plants."

Another truck had pulled up and Randel was again doing his best to flip the papers over and check them with one hand.

"They have three little plants. Venus flytraps. I'd forgotten about them and they were drying up."

"Venus flytraps, my ass! I saw you! You prick! You were feeling her up. You liar! It was *her* Venus flytrap."

"Believe me, Am. It didn't go any further. I stopped it. Honest!"

As Randel stamped and handed back the trucker's papers, he knew what he said was true. But it was only true because just before he allowed things to progress much further with Yvonne, he'd caught a glimpse of the clock on the wall. It told him he had only half an hour to drive to work and he knew no matter how fast he drove, there was no way he could make it in 30 minutes.

He'd said, "I'm sorry, Yvonne. I'm late for work. I could lose my job. Gotta go." Randel had left Yvonne standing open mouthed in the middle of the kitchen.

In shock she'd gasped out, "What the hell!" She'd watched Randel rush out of the house, jump the low fence into his own back yard and dash for his truck parked at the back. Then, drawn by the sound of water, she'd walked to the sink to turn off the tap that was trickling water onto three tiny, funny looking plants.

Another truck had pulled up at Randel's booth.

"Let's talk about this when I get home, Am. Please."

They both heard the automatic voice come on the line and say, "Please insert another dollar and twenty-five cents."

Randel heard Amber say, "Shit! Not enough change," and he thought she said, "won't be home," as the phone beeped a couple of times and went dead.

CHAPTER 30

Amber had been hitchhiking at the edge of the highway for half an hour, but it seemed to her like forever. Car after car had passed her without any of them even slowing down. She'd glanced behind her at the café a few times and each time the waitress had been standing with her arms folded, staring out at her. Being stared at made Amber feel uncomfortable.

She took one more look over her shoulder and the waitress was still staring at her. *God! Doesn't she have anything better to do?*

Amber decided that she wasn't going to provide the only entertainment in Dutton any longer and walked a little further down the highway out of sight of the café.

As she stood there waiting hopefully for a ride, she thought about the conversation she'd had with Randel before it was cut off by a shortage of change. There wasn't a lot more she'd have said anyway. He knew now he'd been caught with his pants down. She'd thought they'd been happily married. They'd had their little arguments but nothing major until now. Now look at their marriage. Falling apart.

About another dozen cars had gone past without anyone really looking her way. You'd think someone might have stopped by now. She was tidy, not unattractive. Then she wondered, was this really safe? She'd never hitch-hiked before and had read all the stories about young women being picked up, raped and murdered. You'd think there'd be at least one decent guy in Montana who'd stop and pick her up, would welcome some company, even if all he'd get was a little conversation. *I'd bet if Randel drove by and didn't know me, he'd stop and pick me up, the horny bastard. What do I need to do here? Wave some panties?*

Amber's feet were beginning to ache from standing. She wondered if you got swollen ankles even if you were only eight weeks pregnant.

She flexed her shoulder muscles, which were a little achy too. While giving her suitcase a couple of swings back and forth to loosen her shoulders, the handle pulled away from the case. The case landed with a thump on the highway. It burst open and her belongings were strewn across the roadway. Without thinking, Amber dashed out after her things.

CHAPTER 31

Charlie had rejoined Danny at the front of The Smucker and Betty had gone back to sit with Caroline at the table. Charlie was still fearful that at any moment they'd be pulled over by a siren-screaming police or border control car. He couldn't believe how far south of the border they been allowed to drive without being stopped. He kept leaning back and forth from where he sat to check the side mirrors for any signs of pursuing cars. He half expected to see a road block appear in front of them.

Danny, too, couldn't believe they hadn't been stopped. Although he was tense, he concentrated on keeping their speed nearly 10 miles below the posted limit, ready to pull over at the first sound of sirens.

Betty had asked Charlie to keep her posted as to where they were and whenever they came to a sign for a small town, he called out the name. She was doing her best with their map at the table to follow where they were. Charlie had called out the names of places like Sunburst, Shelby, Conrad, Brady and Collins. Now he spotted a sign that announced they were approaching Dutton and he yelled that name to Betty.

"Okay I found it," Betty shouted back. "Maybe we should look for a picnic area, some washrooms soon, Danny."

"Okay," Danny called. "I'll keep an eye out. What the hell! Holy jeez!" He started braking and at the same time found the horn in the centre of the steering wheel and pressed it hard. "Brace yourselves, Betty," he called. "Hang onto Caroline." The Smucker shuddered as he pressed harder on the brakes.

"What in God's name!" Charlie gasped. "Doesn't she see us? Get off the god-damned road!" he yelled.

Right in their path, a woman was bent over with her back to them and appeared to be fumbling at something on the roadway. It looked like she was trying to pick it up. She got it awkwardly under one arm. Then she must have heard the horn and the squeal of brakes and turned around. She dropped the thing onto the roadway again, but she still had what looked like a red cloth in one hand. She threw up her hands and opened her mouth like she was screaming, but instead of running off the road, she froze, then covered her face with the red cloth.

Danny swerved The Smucker a bit to his left with the brake pedal pressed to the floor. There was the sound of a horn and he pulled right again as a car swerved around them on their left. He caught a glimpse of a face yelling, then an arm shot out the open passenger window as someone gave them the finger and the car sped off. The Smucker shuddered to a halt and he quickly unbuckled his seat belt and turned off the engine. At first he thought he heard screaming, but then it stopped. He stood and looked through the windshield after putting on The Smucker's flashers. Charlie stood too.

THE GRAND GETAWAY   129

Behind them, they could hear Betty mumbling, "Oh my God! Oh my God!" and Caroline mumbling along with her.

Danny looked down at a very young red-haired woman who was standing about a foot from the front of The Smucker. He thought her face was bleeding badly until he realized she had just put her hand over her mouth while holding something red that looked like a pair of lacy red panties.

The rest of the woman's face appeared as she lowered the panties. She looked at them in her hand for a moment, then quickly looked up through the windshield at Danny and Charlie who were staring down at her with anxious faces.

She gave a shaky smile as she caught sight of Betty, who had appeared beside the two men.

Charlie noticed the woman was holding a pair of panties. "My God! I've heard of hookers being aggressive, but these Montana hookers beat all! Waving her damn panties to get our attention."

Danny opened the door as the woman appeared to be mouthing and repeating the word, "Sorry." She raised her hand, gestured a small apologetic wave, then lowered her head and turned to walk towards the side of the road.

"Charlie, hop out and get her off the road," Danny said. "Make sure she's okay. I'm going to pull onto the shoulder before anyone hits us."

Charlie caught up to the girl, took her arm and got her safely to the shoulder as Danny started up The Smucker. He signalled to turn onto the shoulder, but Charlie held up his hand to stop him as he scrambled in front of the bus to grab something off the road and hurried back to the girl.

Charlie and the girl stood well back as Danny eased the bus past them onto the shoulder and stopped, leaving the emergency flashers on.

Betty said, "I'll get out and make sure that girl is all right. Keep an eye on Caroline, Danny."

Danny glanced back at Caroline who was still sitting at the table, peering at Betty's map and quietly reading some of the place names out loud.

"Great... Great... Falls... Hel... Hel... Hel... enna, enna... Miss... Miss... ou... ou... Miss... ou la.la. Miss—oo–la-la."

Charlie and Betty came to the door of the bus with the girl and Charlie was carrying a battered green suitcase. Charlie rolled his eyes at Danny.

"This is Amber, Danny," Betty said.

"Hi, Amber. You okay?"

"Yes, I'm fine. And I'm so sorry for being such an idiot."

"What were you doing in the middle of the road with your back to the traffic?" Danny asked. "You gave us quite a scare."

"I was trying to pick up my suitcase. I was hitch-hiking and I wasn't having much luck."

"You were using your suitcase to try to stop traffic? Can't see this little suitcase stopping much," Charlie said. He still had the bashed up looking suitcase in his hand.

"Thanks. I'll take that off you and I... Oh..." She suddenly seemed to realize she still had the panties in her hand and she quickly popped the lid of the case and threw them in, as she bit her bottom lip and blushed. "I was swinging my suitcase and the handle pulled off. The case landed on the road and burst open. I ran after it without looking and was trying to pick my clothes up off the road."

"That's enough questions for now," Betty said. "She's had a shock. We all have. Come and sit back here with Caroline and me. We're hopin' to find a picnic spot down the road. Which way are you headed?"

"I was trying to get to Great Falls. I'm sure there's a little picnic area about a mile and a half further down the road from here. I stopped at it once before."

"Great," Betty said. "We'll go there, have a quick lunch and we can get you to Great Falls. Come and sit down. Danny, take us to the picnic place."

Charlie and Danny buckled themselves back into their seats and when the three women were seated, Danny eased the bus back onto the road.

"She's a real good-looker," Charlie whispered to Danny.

"She is," Danny agreed.

"How old do you think she is?" Charlie asked.

"Don't ask me," Danny replied. "I'm no good at guessing any woman's age."

"I figure she's maybe 17. You think what she said was true?"

"What?"

"She was just picking up her clothes 'n' suitcase off the road?"

"Why would she lie about that?" Danny whispered.

"Beats me. You don't think she's suicidal or anything? Just ran out in front of us or maybe she's on drugs. Or throwing her suitcase into the middle of the road was the only way to get someone to stop. Maybe desperate for a ride."

"Jeez, Charlie. I thought you were a freight train conductor, not a detective. Give her a break."

It took them only 10 minutes to reach the picnic spot and as soon as they got there, Betty took Caroline to the washroom, leaving Amber at the table.

Danny and Charlie sat quietly for a minute then Charlie turned to ask, "You okay, Amber?"

"Yeah. I'm okay." She looked down at the table.

"Why were you hitching? Could be dangerous."

Amber looked a bit guarded. "I was ticked off and running away."

"From home?"

"Yeah. I guess."

"Does your Mom know?"

Danny gave Charlie an elbow in the ribs to shut him up.

"My Mom and Dad live in Texas."

"So why Great Falls?"

"I only decided on Great Falls because that's where the first bus leaving town was going to."

"But you weren't on a bus."

"I know. I got off the bus. I changed my mind."

"What were you running away from?"

"What?... uh, Randel."

"I think we passed through that earlier," Charlie said.

"What?"

"That town you mentioned. I think we passed through it earlier today... er, Randel."

"No. That's not my home town. Randel's my husband." Amber sniffed, started rummaging in her suitcase, then she was quietly sobbing.

Charlie left his seat and walked back to her. "Jeez Amber... I didn't mean to upset you." He found some napkins on the counter and handed her a couple.

"Thanks." She sniffed and wiped her eyes just as Betty arrived back with Caroline.

"Come on, Charlie," Danny said. "Let's hit the washroom."

"I'll make us a quick lunch," Betty said. "What's the matter, Amber? What's the matter, love?"

Amber started quietly sobbing again as Danny and Charlie exited the bus.

"Jeez! Charlie! You and your damn questions," Danny remarked.

"I was just trying to be helpful. Talking about problems sometimes helps. I thought she was just a kid. Maybe an orphan or something. She may as well be! Why would she be running away from that place, Randel? Why would a girl like that want to run away from home?"

"What the hell do you think we're doing?" Danny snapped. "Look, maybe we'd better take a little walk around this picnic area. Give Betty a chance to settle Amber down. She seemed pretty upset and I'd rather not walk in on Betty if she's in one of her moods and blaming us, you in particular, for upsetting the girl."

"Okay," Charlie said. "I was sure she was just a kid. Married already! Sheesh!"

Danny and Charlie circled the little picnic area a couple of times before approaching The Smucker. There was a picnic table beside where they'd parked.

Danny said, "You sit here for a minute. I'll go check how things are inside, just in case. Betty won't nearly be as mad at me as with you. I'll just stick my head in and see."

As Charlie sat down at the table, Danny walked to the bus, paused, then came back to Charlie. It was a warm day and Betty had opened a couple of windows. From the picnic table you could easily hear the conversation.

Amber was saying, "Just over two years. We were high school sweethearts."

"If you want to talk about it, it might help, but you don't have to," Betty said. "You don't know me from Adam."

Danny whispered to Charlie. "Maybe we should take another walk. I don't think we should go back in yet and we probably shouldn't be listening."

"How you gonna know when it's okay if we don't know what's happening?" Charlie whispered back. "Just hang on a sec."

Danny sat down and waited but felt a bit uncomfortable. He'd overheard lots of conversations at The Shelter he probably shouldn't have, or didn't want to, but there it was almost impossible to avoid them, with the people often having been drinking and talking in loud voices. This was different.

"We've had a few arguments but nothing major," Amber continued. "We were happy. At least I thought we were. 'Til I saw him with Yvonne."

"The neighbour?"

"Yeah."

"Sometimes these things happen," Betty said. "Do you still love him?"

"Yes."

"Do you think he loves you?"

"I thought he did. I think so."

"Do you think you might want to give him another chance? We all make mistakes, I know I have. Lots of them..." Betty trailed off, then continued. "What are you goin' to do when you get to Great Falls?"

"I thought I might go back and try to sort things out. I phoned Randel from Dutton and got mad at him all over again. So I decided to go on to Helena. I have a friend there, Moira, who might put me up. Give me time to think. It was a three hour wait for another bus, so I decided to hitch-hike."

"When you phoned Randel, what did he say?" Betty asked.

"Come on Charlie, let's go," Danny said quietly. "This is none of our business. If Betty catches us out here, we'll really be in shit. Let's take another walk. We can't go barging in now and I think we should give the kid a chance to talk to Betty."

"Yeah, you're right," Charlie whispered.

As they got up to walk away, Amber was saying, "and she came onto him. Randel says he stopped her and..."

Betty's voice faded as they moved out of earshot. "Here love, dry your eyes," and Caroline, "Oh No! Not cry, dry, dry, dry."

Danny and Charlie had taken another two turns of the picnic area before they heard Betty call for lunch.

They headed to The Smucker, both of them feeling a little self-conscious and guilty for having listened in. Caroline was sitting at the picnic table eating a bowl of green salad and salmon and Amber was helping Betty set things on the table. Amber smiled shyly at Charlie and Danny as they arrived.

"There you are. That's what she said," Caroline said.

"Yeah, a fat lot of good these two ne're-do-wells are, leavin' all the work to us," Betty chided, which made Danny and Charlie laugh and look at one another in relief.

THE GRAND GETAWAY   133

"They can do the dishes after lunch before we take off. We've made a green salad and there's canned salmon and a choice of tea and coffee. Bananas for dessert."

"What did Caroline do?" Charlie asked. "To help with lunch?"

"She found the salt shaker for us." Amber grinned.

"She sure did," Betty said. "She had it in her hand. But we didn't find it until she'd taken the cap off. Salt everywhere." Betty laughed.

"I'll just go to the washroom," Amber said, then headed for the bus.

"There's no washroom in..." Charlie was saying as Betty hushed him. Amber disappeared inside and came out quickly carrying her small make-up compact and headed for the washroom.

"She's a lovely girl," Betty said. "Been married just over two years."

"Two years!" Charlie said. "How old is she?"

"Twenty-two," Betty answered.

"She okay?" Charlie asked.

"I think so. I think she'll be fine. Just goin' through one of those, what's the word I want?... not gulch... what is it?... anyway, whatever, a problem in her marriage."

"I think it's glitch," Danny said. "I think that's the word."

"Glitch, glitch, glitch, bitch, bitch, bitty, bitty, bitty."

"Okay Caroline. Thanks love. Eat your salad," Betty said.

"Oh yes," Caroline said.

"Amber's decided not to go on to Great Falls," Betty said

"She's changed her mind again?" Charlie asked.

"Yes. She has," Betty said pointedly. "People sometimes do that."

"Yeah. Especially women." Charlie chuckled.

"Oh, shut up! Charlie," Betty said. "She's decided to go back."

"What about Yvonne?" Charlie asked.

Danny kicked him under the table and Charlie spluttered into the cup of coffee he was drinking.

"She told you about Yvonne?" Betty asked.

"Maybe her name came up. She didn't say much," Charlie said quickly.

"I think we should take her back," Betty said.

"To the bus station in that place, what was it?" Danny said.

"Dutton," Charlie said.

"No, take her home. To Shelby."

"What!" Danny and Charlie said in unison.

"It's not that far. I checked it on the map."

"You told her we'd take her back?" Charlie asked.

"I haven't yet. Now shut up both of you. Here she comes. Don't say anythin' about it to her. You hear? Both of you." Betty hissed.

Betty made room for Amber at the table. She had repaired her make-up and looked refreshed.

Betty dished her out some food and kept the talk to things like the food and the weather.

Danny did his best to help out with conversation, but Charlie stuck to eating silently, his thoughts racing about the idea of going back almost all the way they had come. He thought that Shelby hadn't been far south of the border at Sweetgrass. He could picture a line of police cars, maybe even motorcycles, all with their sirens screaming, escorting them back to the building where they'd be arrested and charged.

After lunch, Betty said, "I'm takin' Caroline to the washroom. You and Charlie gather up the dishes and give them a quick rinse. There's a tap over there. We'll give 'em a good wash tonight."

"Let me help," Amber said, getting up and collecting some of the plates.

Danny quietly had a word with Betty when she and Caroline returned. "If you haven't said anything to Amber about taking her all the way back to Shelby, I think we should talk about it first. We've got this far but we could risk getting caught if we head back near the border."

"Don't you think if they were lookin' for us, they'd have found us by now?" Betty asked. "But fine, I'll leave Caroline with Amber for a couple of minutes and we can discuss this with Charlie."

They left Amber and Caroline at the picnic table, Betty telling Amber that they needed to talk something over. Amber held Caroline's hand as they sat at the table, but she looked a bit anxious. When they were far enough from The Smucker, Danny asked, "Does Amber just expect us to take her back to the bus station at Dutton?"

"Probably. She decided not to go on to Great Falls, which is a lot further south. Dutton is just up the road. I don't feel good about dumpin' her off at that little place to wait hours for a bus. She's goin' through a bit of a crisis and I know she's anxious to get home. Do you know what it must be like when you have to be somewhere else and can't get there quickly? Worse than being stuck up a culvert, Danny. Look, she's had a terrible day and right now, I want to help her."

"If we go cruising back up near the border, someone may be on the look-out for us," Charlie said. "It's crazy to take that chance. We could get miles further south if we go on."

"Charlie's right, Betty," Danny said. "Showing up in our distinctive looking Smucker is maybe gonna trigger someone's memory."

"No. Amber's gonna have a baby," Betty said.

"Now?" Charlie let out a gasp. "Here?"

"No. Of course not. In about seven or eight months."

"Thank God!" Charlie breathed a sigh of relief. "I thought for a minute we were going to have to change our little bus into a delivery van."

"Amber needs to get home and tell her husband," Betty said. "He doesn't know yet. She loves him. I believe he loves her. I want to help and we're wastin' time!"

CHAPTER 32

When they walked back to The Smucker, they found Amber repeating rhymes with Caroline.

"James James
Morrison Morrison
Weatherby George Dupree
Took good care of his Mother,
Though he was only three."

She broke off as they approached. "I think Caroline might have known this. Her eyes lit up when I started reciting it."

"James, James, James, Morrison, Morrison, James," Caroline repeated.

"It's a poem by A.A. Milne who wrote *Winnie the Pooh*. It's called *Disobedience*." She smiled at the trio and said, "I work with little kids in a day-care, part-time. I know lots of kids' rhymes and songs. Caroline likes them too. Don't you, Caroline?"

Caroline smiled and repeated again, "James, James, James."

"Amber," Betty said, "you're sure you want to go back and not go on to Great Falls?"

"Yes, I'm sure. If you could drop me back at the little café, just near where you found me, I can catch the bus back from there." She stood up from the table.

"Yeah. We'd be glad..." Charlie was saying when Betty glared at him.

"But your bus is not for two more hours. We've decided we can do better than droppin' you off there. We've decided," Betty stressed the we "to drive you home, to Shelby. We'd like to see you safely home."

"But that's takin' you out of your way. Didn't you tell me you were driving all the way to the Grand Canyon? You'll have to drive all the way back here again. You don't have to do that."

"We do." Betty said. "We nearly ran over you and you've had a rough day and we'd like to do this. It would make us feel a lot better."

Amber ran quickly to Betty and hugged her. Then she burst into tears. "Oh, you're so kind. That would be wonderful. But are you really sure?"

"We're sure," Betty said, and when Amber hugged Danny he added, "Yeah, we're sure," and Charlie found himself agreeing when she hugged him and gave him a quick kiss on the cheek.

Amber wiped her tear-streaked cheeks with the back of her hand. "You're all so kind. Thank you. Oh, thank you. If we leave now, I could be home before Randel. I'd like that. To be there before he gets home."

"Well," Danny said. "Let's hit the road."

Danny pulled the bus back onto the road and headed north.

THE GRAND GETAWAY   137

They were just passing the café near where they'd almost hit Amber, when Charlie couldn't resist commenting to Danny, "This road looks vaguely familiar. I hope to God we're doing the right thing."

Behind them, Amber was telling Betty that she was pretty sure she could fix things with Randel. "He's always been kind. Oh! Would you like to see his picture? I have one in my wallet."

"Sure," Danny heard Betty say. "I'd like that. We all would. I don't think you told us what Randel does for a job."

"Didn't I? I'm sorry." Amber paused in fishing for the photo in her wallet and looked up. "He's with the USCBP, but he's not happy there."

U.S.C.B.P.U.S.C.B.P.U.S... B.P.... B.P... B.P. B.P." Caroline was smiling and repeating happily.

"Yes, it is kinda like a nursery rhyme, isn't it, Caroline? USCBP – USCBP," Amber repeated clapping her hands in time. She turned to Betty, "Randel's hoping to get a new job with Merrill Lynch. They're stock brokers. He had an interview with them recently and he's hoping to get taken on in Great Falls. I think that's what the phone call might have been about, you know, the one I told you about." She paused reflectively. "When I went to find him and found him with you know who..." She paused again, then recovered. "I left the phone off the hook. I hope it didn't mess up his chances. I'd like to move to Great Falls. It's much bigger than Shelby. And... we'd be away from Yvonne." She went back to looking in her wallet.

"Oh gosh! Here's my pay-cheque from the day-care. I'd folded it up in the back of my wallet and forgot about it. I was supposed to deposit it in our bank account so there'd be enough to make the payment on Randel's truck today. I used my bank card for my bus ticket so now there's probably not enough money in the account."

"Don't worry dear. You can fix that," Betty said. "But what is the USCBP?"

"Oh, I guess you wouldn't know that, seeing as how you're not from around here. He's with the U. S. Customs and Border Protection. Found it. Here's his photo."

There was silence for a moment then Betty let out a large gasp, startling Amber.

"Are you okay, Betty?" she asked.

"Yes love, I'm fine. Just sometimes I have a little problem with my breathin'. It's nothin' to worry about. My, he is handsome in his uniform."

"Should I pass the photo up to Charlie and Danny?" Amber asked.

"I'll take it to them," Betty said.

Charlie had only been partly listening to the conversation going on behind him. He'd been chattering away quietly to Danny about his worry that the closer they got to the border the more they'd need to be extra cautious about driving.

"See what I mean? Drive straight! For God's sake!"

Danny had veered over the centre line when he'd caught Amber's reference to Randel's job.

"It's crazy!" Charlie went on. "It's kinda like sticking your hand into a hornet's nest to see what happens. Did you hear what Amber said those letters stood for?"

"No," Danny lied, "wasn't listening."

"Well," Charlie continued. "I can never make head or tail of those, what do they call them, synonyms? No. Acronyms! Yeah that's they're called."

Betty stepped carefully forward, pressed her hand into Danny's shoulder and held Randel's photo in front of the two men.

Charlie gave a gasp when he saw Randel in the photo dressed in his work uniform. "Shit! Is that uniform what I think it is?" he whispered hoarsely.

Danny swerved over the centre lane again when he found himself looking at the same border guard who'd told them to go around again and get in the proper lane.

He glanced up at Betty without Charlie noticing. Charlie was still staring at the photo.

Betty waggled her finger at Danny and shook her head towards Charlie. Danny got the message which he understood to mean, *Don't, whatever you do, tell Charlie we know this border guard, and he knows us.*

Danny nodded his understanding to Betty, then called back to Amber, "He's a really good looking guy."

"Yeah," Charlie intoned. "Real good looking, especially in that uniform."

Betty took the picture from Charlie and walked back to Amber and Caroline.

"God!" Charlie whispered. "Do you think Betty knew Amber's husband was a border guard when she agreed to give her a ride back?"

"No, I doubt it. Don't worry. We're not going as far as the border. We'll have dropped Amber off and started back before he gets home anyway."

Danny pressed a little harder on the accelerator. He was sure if Charlie had known the border guard was the same one they'd encountered, he'd have had a heart attack right then or, at the very least, demanded that they stop The Smucker, and dump Amber off and head south again.

CHAPTER 33

The sign for the turn-off to Shelby came up faster than Danny had expected, and he called back to Betty and Amber, "We're coming up to Shelby turn-off now. After we turn off, we'll need some directions from Amber."

There was a conversation between Betty and Amber that Danny couldn't hear as he signalled and took the exit and, at that moment, Charlie's prediction of seeing more border patrol vehicles came true. Danny had just come onto what was called Highway 2 when, in his mirror, he spotted a border patrol vehicle. It had probably turned off Highway 15 from the north and was now following them into Shelby.

Danny held his breath, watching it in his mirror, expecting to see flashing lights at any minute but it signalled to pass them and pulled ahead.

"Jeez! I knew this would happen," Charlie said as soon as he caught sight of the vehicle pulling into the lane ahead of them. "Here's where our trip comes to an end."

Then as the vehicle sped up and pulled away from them, he muttered, "Probably going to get more reinforcements. There'll be dozens with all kinds of weapons pointing at us up the road. They've no idea what kind of desperados they're dealing with. Take it real slow, Danny. Get ready for the roadblock."

"Amber says just follow this road and it becomes Main Street. You can't miss it." Betty said. "Park half-way up Main Street. It's a one-way street. Amber just has to run into the bank."

"The bank!" Charlie whispered to Danny. "I thought we were just dropping her off and taking off. I sure hope she doesn't decide to go grocery shopping. I'd sure feel a lot better if we were outta here."

Danny said nothing. He was having a lot of second thoughts himself and hoped they could get out of Shelby quickly. Parking The Smucker on Main Street, he thought, was just asking for trouble.

The road they were on did become Main Street and Danny slowly drove along it until Amber called out, "Anywhere here is fine. The bank's right here."

There were two empty vehicle spaces directly opposite the bank and Danny easily pulled the bus into one of the spots and shut off the engine right outside the front door of the Shelby First Union Bank.

Amber walked to the front. "I'll just be a minute. I have to deposit a cheque, but with everything today... Thanks, Danny. Be right back."

Danny opened the door and she hopped out and disappeared into the bank. Charlie turned to Betty.

"Jeez. I hope we can get out of here quick. I'd feel a lot safer if we weren't hanging around this close to the border."

"Relax, Charlie. I hate to tell you this, but I think I need the bathroom and if I need it, Caroline probably does too. I drank too much tea. Could you help me get my walker? I've been sittin' too long and I'm a little stiff."

"God, Betty. Where are you going to find a washroom?" Charlie got up as Betty, carrying her large handbag, got Caroline to the door. He helped them onto the sidewalk and unfolded Betty's walker.

"There's a restaurant across the street but it's at the far end of the block," he said. "You going to be okay?"

"Yeah. We'll be fine. We'll find a place closer," Betty said.

"Okay. But be as quick as you can. We have to get outta here." He climbed back into the bus and sat down beside Danny. "This is a bummer, this waiting. Did you see which way Betty and Caroline went?"

"Not far," Danny said. "They went into the bank too."

"The bank!"

"Yeah," Danny said, but his attention was on the border patrol vehicle he could see in his mirror that had just pulled in on the opposite side of the one-way street. He wasn't sure if it was the same one they'd seen earlier. Charlie hadn't noticed it and Danny said nothing. He was feeling worried enough already and pointing it out to Charlie wouldn't help.

CHAPTER 34

Russell Hagen had only fired the gun on one occasion. He'd bought the small Smith and Wesson six months before in a gun shop in Bismarck, North Dakota, where they didn't ask too many questions. It was his first gun. He tested it the day he bought it. Soon after crossing back into Montana, he pulled over when he came to some scrubby brush land. He found a rusting tin can and set it on a stump, fired at it twice from ten paces, missing it both times. One of the two bullets did hit the stump. He had three bullets left and decided he'd better not use any more in case he needed them for real.

In the first five small banks he'd held up this past summer, it wasn't even necessary to show the gun. Usually just shoving the note across the counter in front of the teller was enough. All tellers had been instructed not to take any risks. They filled the canvas bag he handed them with cash while the other tellers stepped away from the counter, their hands on their heads as he instructed.

Hagen waited until the banks were virtually empty of customers. It wasn't until his sixth bank robbery that he'd drawn his gun when a customer had walked in behind him. She was an old lady, who cowered on the floor in front of the counter when he'd waved the gun and yelled at her to get down.

He disguised himself using a selection of wigs and beards he'd accumulated months before from thrift and costume shops with a different coloured baseball cap pulled low on his forehead. He'd been happy to grab whatever cash he got from only one teller, taking as little time in the bank as possible, getting in and out in about two minutes. The cash he got from robbing only one teller hadn't always been a lot, but it had helped to support his drug habit. But now his habit was coke.

This past summer he'd been working as part of a highway line-painting crew, painting the yellow lines on small secondary roads in Montana. The company set up a camp along the highway where they were working and provided some food. There was only a crew of five and two of them drove home almost every night, depending on where they were located. Hagen generally kept to himself most of the time.

On his days off he scouted out the small banks, the little independents, looking for ones that were usually about an hour to an hour and a half's drive away from where they were working. Of the six robberies he'd pulled off, three were in Montana, two in North Dakota and one in Idaho. For the past month they had been working along secondary highway 80 and the highway contract would soon be at an end. He thought he might try for more than one teller today. There was no knowing if he could pick up some more work when this job ended, and he didn't think he could risk knocking off banks more often. His luck might run out.

It was mid-afternoon when he pulled into Shelby, parking the car around the corner a half block from the bank he'd chosen. He pulled out the small snack tray with the coffee cup holder from the dash, took a quick look around and pulled the tinfoil packet from his pocket and laid down a line. It was the last of his coke. He had the dollar bill ready. He rolled it and snorted fast.

The coke hit his brain like a bolt of lightning, slamming him back in the seat. He sat there for five minutes feeling the rush. He shook his head. He felt ready.

Looking around, he waited for a woman pushing a kid in a stroller to pass on the sidewalk. He slipped on a blonde wig and beard and slapped on a baseball cap. He checked himself in the mirror, pulled the gun from the glove compartment and shoved it into his belt under his jacket. Then, checking once more that there was no one close, he grabbed two canvas bags off the passenger seat, stepped out of the car and turned the corner.

THE GRAND GETAWAY   143

CHAPTER 35

When Betty maneuvered herself, her walker and Caroline in the door of the Shelby First Union Bank, her reasoning was this – she needed a washroom, the bank must have one, and who'd turn down an old lady with a walker? Betty hadn't really needed the walker. She just felt it might be a useful prop.

There were three customers in the bank, a man and a woman at the counter being served by the two tellers on duty and Amber, a few paces behind waiting her turn.

The man finished his business with the teller and turned to leave. Amber was about to step to the counter when she was surprised to see that Betty and Caroline were just behind her.

"Betty, Caroline! Did you need something?"

"I was just wonderin' if me and Caroline could use the washroom," Betty whispered. "I drank a bit too much tea earlier."

"Oh," Amber said.

The teller who was free was Mrs. Muriel Crowley who had been with the bank for years and was now leaning forward, wondering how she could be of help. She was also a neighbour of Amber's, living just a few doors away. Muriel had occasionally chatted about gardening when Amber passed her house and had given her some hollyhock seeds one day after Amber had admired the outstanding hollyhocks that bloomed alongside Muriel's house.

"Can I help you, dear?" Muriel smiled.

"Oh Muriel, this is Betty and Caroline. They're friends of mine, tourists. They were wondering if they could use the washroom," Amber whispered. "A bit desperate."

"Oh. Welcome to Shelby. But we don't usually..." Muriel paused when she saw Betty shift uncomfortably with her walker and look a little downcast. "Oh, I'm sure it will be okay, just this once. Our manager is out at business meetings all day and... come with me."

Muriel took a key from a hook on the wall behind her and came around the end of the counter. "This way." She led Betty and Caroline across the floor to a door on the opposite wall beside the empty manager's office. She unlocked the door, pushed it open and switched on the light. "It's a little small, but there you go."

"Thank you very much," Betty said, easing Caroline and herself inside.

Muriel turned to Amber. "Now dear, how can I be of service?"

"I just have to deposit my cheque to cover our truck payment," Amber said. "I'm not sure there's enough in our account."

"Well, we'll soon look after that." She went back behind the counter and took up her position again as Amber took the cheque out of her wallet.

Muriel entered the account number and checked her computer. "Here's the balance and with your deposit you'll have..." she tapped the keys on her computer again, "a balance is $536.79."

"Oh, thank you. That's fine then." Amber breathed a sigh of relief. With the money she'd spent on the bus ticket there was still a little left over for the truck payment.

"I'll update your bank book," Muriel said.

The other customer, an elderly lady, had finished her banking and was carefully folding a receipt and taking her time getting it into her purse while she chatted about how lovely the weather was and how she was hoping the winter wouldn't be as long as last year's with so much snow. "You know I've lived in Shelby for over twenty years and I don't believe I remember so much snow – not since Harold, my husband, passed away, anyway, and that was fifteen years ago. Well, thank you dear."

"Thank you, Mrs. Berguson. Have a nice weekend," the teller, Lindy Jernigan said. She was dying to have a quick smoke out the back of the bank. She was twenty-one and had been with the bank just a year and was trying desperately to quit smoking. She was making progress, but she was still smoking four a day. She hadn't had a cigarette since 10:00 that morning and was now really edgy. She would have to get Muriel's attention and let her know she was going to slip outside for five minutes, but Muriel hated to be interrupted when dealing with a customer and disapproved of Lindy's smoking. She would have to wait until Muriel was finished with Amber Fletcher and hoped no one would come into the bank before she could escape.

Russell Hagen checked the street. There weren't many people along the sidewalk. He didn't see the border patrol car just across the street because his view was blocked by some kind of a strange looking yellow bus parked outside the bank. He reached the front door of the bank and walked slowly past, taking a quick look inside. He couldn't see much. An old lady was standing inside the door adjusting her handbag on her arm before pushing the door open. Hagen took a chance and stepped back to the door and held it open for her.

"Thank you, young man," Mrs. Berguson said as she stepped out.

He held the door open, taking a quick look inside. There was only one customer at the counter, a young red headed woman being served by a grey-haired elderly teller. Another female teller had no one at the counter in front of her. She was drumming her fingers on the counter looking bored. It couldn't be better. He stepped inside, letting the door swing closed behind him.

CHAPTER 36

"How far you think we can get today, once we get out of this place?" Charlie asked.

"Don't know." Danny replied, "I think we should be able to make it south of Great Falls, anyway. Then we should look for somewhere for the night and have some supper. That'd be enough driving for the day."

"Yeah. I hope those women get outta there fast," Charlie said. "It's getting on my nerves spending half the day this close to the border. We better make a rule that we're not going to pick up any more hitchhikers. We can't be running a taxi service up and down the whole of the U.S.A. going one step forward and one step back. We're chancing our luck. Tempting fate so to speak."

"Uh huh," Danny wasn't listening too carefully. He was concentrating on what was going on with the border patrol vehicle across the street. A white truck had parked ahead of it and one of the guards in the patrol car waved his hand. The driver of the truck was also a border guard and all three of them were now standing around talking.

"Holy shit!" he breathed, but he said nothing to Charlie.

Charlie had gone back and got the map and was now sitting beside Danny looking at it.

Danny sneaked another peek in the mirror. The three border guards were shaking hands. The two from the patrol vehicle hopped back into their vehicle and Danny watched it pull out from behind the truck and drive past them.

Charlie noticed the border patrol vehicle as it passed them. "Oh my God! We're about to be blocked in."

"It's just going past," Danny said. "They're not looking for us."

"Jeez. We have to get out of here."

Then Danny groaned inwardly. The guard who'd been in the white truck was crossing the road behind The Smucker. To Danny's surprise he walked past and turned into the bank without giving them a glance. He looked preoccupied and was carrying a bunch of flowers.

Danny was almost sure he recognized Randel, Amber's husband. What would happen if he ran into Betty inside the bank and Amber introduced them? And then there was The Smucker parked directly outside. Surely he'd put it all together. There was no way Betty would be able to talk them out of this mess.

CHAPTER 37

As Russell Hagen stepped up to the counter in front of the young teller with the pouty lips and the blonde pony-tail, he already had the note in his hand that said he had a gun.

Lindy looked a bit miffed for a moment then put on the 'friendly bank' smile and gave Hagen a "Welcome to Shelby First Union Bank. How may I help you?"

Hagen slapped the note down in front of Lindy and called out, "Put the money in the bag, fast. Keep your hands where I can see them." He tossed one of the bags to the young teller.

Muriel gasped, startled as she heard Hagen's demand and Lindy's stifled scream. Amber half turned towards Hagen.

"You!" Hagen yelled at Amber. "Face down on the floor. Now! And you won't get hurt! And you!" he flung the second canvas bag to Muriel as Amber gave a small cry and crouched on the floor. "Fill it fast, both of you! Keep your hands away from any alarms. Fill the bags! Nobody gets hurt if you do what I say!"

Amber was on her knees on the floor.

"Down! Face down! Now! Don't mess with me lady! Hands behind your head!" Hagen snarled. He glanced over his left shoulder to make sure nobody was coming through the front door.

Amber complied.

"You two tellers, faster! Get the cash in the bags, faster, faster!"

The young teller was trembling and sobbing as she stuffed the money from her drawer into the bag. A couple of bills fell to the floor and she was about to reach to pick them up.

"Leave them! Don't pick them up! I have to see your hands!" Hagen yelled. The old teller was white faced but was doing what he'd told her. *Things are going fine,* Hagen thought.

In a quavery voice, the old dame said, "That's it. There's no more." She pushed the bag across the counter towards him.

"Okay. Good! Hands on your head! Step away from the counter!" He glanced over his shoulder to check the front door again.

Muriel did as she was told as Hagen grabbed her bag.

"You too, shove the bag forward," he indicated to Lindy. "Now you step back too, like her. Hands on your head and nobody move!"

There was hardly enough room to move in the tiny bathroom. Betty desperately needed to go and needed some space. She pushed Caroline out, saying, "Just wait there, Caroline. I'll be right out."

THE GRAND GETAWAY   147

Hagen leaped almost a foot in the air when a woman he hadn't seen before, was suddenly standing just behind him to his right and saying, "Oh you! I know you." She was smiling at him.

Hagen grabbed the gun from his belt. *Where the hell had she come from? How the hell did she know him?*

He pointed the gun at the woman and yelled. "Down on the floor lady. Face down on the floor. Get down. Hands on the back of your head." He found himself trembling.

The slim woman with short grey hair and pretty face continued to smile at him and said, "Oh yes. That's what she said." But she made no attempt to get down on the floor. She didn't seem to be the least bit frightened.

He waved the gun at her again. "Get down on the floor, for Christ's sake! If you don't get down, I'll have to shoot you." He grabbed her arm and pulled her in front of him. He pressed the gun to her temple, thinking he might have to shoot her. Maybe he could just hit her over the head.

She frowned and simply said, "No. Cold. Cold."

The old lady teller gave a groan and collapsed in a faint while the younger one was crying and moaning, "Oh God no! Oh God no!" Lindy Jernigan suddenly realized she had wet herself.

As she adjusted her clothes and washed her hands in the tiny sink, Betty thought she heard some commotion outside and hoped that Caroline was not the cause of it. She hurried out and froze in horror at the scene in front of her. A strange looking man with a scraggly blonde beard and shaggy blonde hair under a red baseball cap was holding a gun to Caroline's temple. Betty shot a quick glance at the sobbing young teller. The older one who had let them use the bathroom was nowhere in sight. Amber was lying face down on the floor and Betty wasn't sure if she was alive or dead.

Betty felt a terrible tightness in her chest and thought she was having a heart attack until she realized she'd been holding her breath. She let her breath out quietly and slowly. *Do something! Now! Or Caroline's goin' to die!*

Betty pushed her walker quickly and quietly across the floor as the bearded man with the baseball cap yelled at Caroline, "On the floor! Now!"

To Betty's horror, Caroline suddenly reached her hand up and shoved the gun away from her head, saying, "Cold! Cold!" The man with the gun stepped back and stumbled over Betty's walker, and the gun was in Caroline's hand.

"What the hell!" another voice suddenly yelled. "Drop the gun! Drop the gun now! Lady!"

"Oh my God!" Betty turned to see a border guard holding a gun and pointing it at Caroline. He held a bunch of flowers wrapped in fancy paper in his other hand. She immediately recognized Randel, Amber's husband.

"Randel. Oh my God! It is you!" Amber staggered to her feet.

"Amber! What the hell are you doing here?"

Randel tried to keep his eyes on the gun that was in the woman's hand, but he couldn't help himself from looking at his wife. "Are you okay, Amber?"

"I'm fine! I'm fine!"

"Get behind me for God's sake." He quickly switched his gun to point it at the blonde old lady with the walker, who was gingerly prying the gun out of the other woman's hand. The first woman was saying, "Cold, Cold. Heavy."

Now, keeping his gun trained on the blonde old lady with the walker, Randel repeated, "Drop the gun! Drop the gun!"

"It's okay, Randel. They're my friends," Amber said.

"What! Holding up a bank?"

"No. He was. That guy." Amber pointed to the bearded man in the baseball cap.

Betty was nervously holding the gun flat in her hand, wanting to get it to Randel. "Please take the gun. We had nothing to do with this. We were just using the washroom."

Randel quickly grabbed the gun from Betty and trained his gun on the guy in the baseball cap. "Sit on the floor! Hands on your head and don't move! You two ladies move over there."

He pointed to the right and Betty took Caroline's hand and moved her away from the bank robber who was now sitting on the floor, his hands on his head.

Hagen couldn't understand how things had gone so wrong so fast. *Where had those women come from?* He was almost convinced he was having a bad trip, but he didn't want to take a chance that he was wrong. That gun the border guard was holding and pointing at him looked real.

"Okay Amber. What the hell's going on? What are you doing here? Fill me in quick. We've got to call the cops."

"I was depositing my day-care cheque to make sure we covered your truck payment. Why are you here? Why aren't you still at work?"

"I came to check to see if you made the deposit. I thought you were out of town some place when you phoned. I got a call from Merrill Lynch this afternoon. I start in two weeks. They left a message on my cell, said our home phone is out of order. I had to find you, so I booked off early. Brinkerhoff had gone for the day. I'm giving in my notice Monday. Jeez, Amber, I love you. Could you please call the police?" he called to the still sobbing teller. "Is there anyone hurt?"

Muriel suddenly stood up looking a little dazed, giving Randel a start.

"The police are on their way," Lindy said, then helped Muriel to a chair and found one for herself. Lindy was still sobbing quietly when she pulled a cigarette out of her pack and lit it. "To hell with it! I can't wait any longer," she muttered.

"Randel," Amber said, "just let Betty and Caroline leave. They brought me back here and only came in to use the washroom. They were in the washroom when this guy came in with the gun. Let them go. Their friends are waiting outside in their bus.

THE GRAND GETAWAY   149

I think you should let them go, before the police get here. Caroline, who got the gun away from that guy, has dementia. She doesn't understand anything."

"I think that blonde woman came through the border from Canada today in a funny yellow bus, in the wrong lane. Told them to go around. I'm not sure they're here legally. I didn't ask if anyone checked them through. The cops will want witnesses, so they need to stay."

"There's me, the tellers, and you for witnesses. I was leaving you, Randel, because of what happened today, but Betty persuaded me to give you another chance. Let them leave, okay? Caroline couldn't tell the cops anything. They're just old people on a holiday. If it wasn't for them, you'd have lost me. You owe them! Trust me."

"How do you know they're not some kind of illegals or something? That bus looked suspicious."

"Do you love me?"

"I do. I really do, Am. Here, take these, I didn't want to let them wilt in the truck." He handed Amber the flowers.

"Then do this for me! Don't mess these poor old people around. You can take all the credit. Do it for me! These flowers are a start. God! I hope you bought them for me. They're not for that bitch, Yvonne! Are they?"

"No! They're for you! I bought them for you."

"Thanks, Randel. But it's gonna take more than a few flowers. We'll have to talk. Now let Betty and Caroline leave! I mean it, Randel!"

The faint wail of a siren could now be heard.

"Okay." Randel still looked worried as Amber hugged him and waved to Betty and Caroline to go. Betty came over and gave Amber a hug.

"Have a safe trip, Betty," Amber said. "Look after Caroline and thank Danny and Charlie. I think Randel and I are gonna be okay. You'd better go now. Thanks for everything. Go now."

"God bless you, Amber. Have a long and happy marriage. Come on Caroline." Betty folded up her walker, grabbed Caroline's hand with the other and walked as fast as they could out the door of the bank.

As they clambered into The Smucker, Danny quickly turned on the engine. Charlie was saying, "I thought you two were never coming out of that bank. What took ya so long?"

"Oh, you know what it's like with us women. When we gotta go, we gotta go. Let's get out of here now. Amber says she'll walk home so we don't have to wait."

As they continued along Main Street, sirens, getting louder and louder, could be heard coming from behind them.

"Jeez," Charlie said. "I hope that's not for us."

"I wouldn't worry, Charlie," Betty said. "We only went into the bank for a pee. You might say we left a deposit. We didn't rob it or anythin', did we Caroline?"

CHAPTER 38

Danny stepped on the gas, going just a bit over the speed limit and keeping his fingers crossed that the police were otherwise occupied.

"I'm not sure where we're headed," Danny said to Charlie, "but I think we've got to turn around and head west to get back on the highway."

"Well, I wouldn't turn around on this road and go back. There seems to be all hell breaking loose back there. Do you think they're onto us?"

"I don't know what's going on. I'll see if we can go down a side street that might lead us back. I'll try this one coming up."

"We're now running parallel to Main," Charlie said as they made a second turn. "Sounds like we're heading right into those sirens."

"We'll give it a go, anyway. I'd like to get back to that highway as soon as we can."

Danny noticed that Betty was unusually quiet behind them and he took a quick glance over his shoulder. She was holding Caroline's hands at the table and had her head down.

Danny glanced at Charlie, who seemed to be holding his breath, then blew air out and said, "Whatever is going on must be happening near the bank on Main Street where we were. There's a sign for Highway 2 and 15, follow that."

They found themselves merging onto Highway 15 and seconds later they were heading south again.

There were no signs of any police or border patrol cars and Danny felt a huge sense of relief as they left Shelby behind. He eased off the gas again to keep within the speed limit. He sensed Betty stir behind them and took another quick glance at her and Caroline.

Betty caught his glance and gave him a weak smile then asked, "Do you think you could put on one of our tapes, Charlie? Somethin' happy, maybe?"

"I'll take a look," Charlie said. He did a quick search then said, "I'll try this. Some guy called Van Morrison. The first song is *Bright Side Of The Road*. That sounds happy."

"We're coming up to Dutton again, Charlie," Danny said.

Charlie looked back at Betty and Caroline. Both of them were nestled together asleep, Caroline's head on Betty's shoulder. Betty, her head resting against the wall behind them, had her arm around Caroline.

"They're both sound asleep," Charlie said. "Be a shame to wake them. Maybe we could go a little further. How are you doing?"

"I'm okay, but I think we'd better stop before we hit Great Falls and take a look at the map. I know we go through Yellowstone National Park, but that's way south.

THE GRAND GETAWAY   151

We'll just go a little further. Let the women sleep a little longer." He pressed the eject button on the tape player as Van Morrison had gone around again and was belting out *Brown Eyed Girl*.

The radio, crackly as usual, came on just as a song ended abruptly. "We bring you breaking news of an attempted bank robbery this afternoon. We now take you to our reporter Jay Zanzinger in Shelby."

"This is Jay Zanzinger reporting to you from Shelby. I'm standing on Main Street, just across the street from the Shelby First Union Bank."

"Jeez!" Danny gasped. "That's the name of the bank we were just at."

"My God!" Charlie said. "We just got outta there in time."

"Shush" Danny said. "Let's hear this."

"... has been cordoned off by police. There's a small crowd here and I've spoken to a couple of folks. There are few details as police are still questioning witnesses – but I understand that police have made an arrest. A man in the crowd said he saw a young man being taken away by police in handcuffs. A waitress who works at one of the local restaurants said she saw a uniformed border patrol officer and a young woman getting into a police car. Another couple of onlookers have told me that, as far as they know, no one was injured, but two female employees, who looked shaken, came out of the bank after police arrived. They were taken to hospital and are being treated for shock. We'll bring you further updates as soon as they become available."

The radio went back to playing music and Danny clicked it off.

"My God!" Charlie said. "The robbery musta happened only seconds after we left. That's why we heard all the sirens. Thank God Betty and Caroline didn't get caught up in that."

"Jeez!" Danny said again. His thoughts were racing. Had the sirens they'd heard started up before Betty and Caroline left the bank? He couldn't be sure now. He'd seen the border guard go in and he'd been sure it was Amber's husband, Randel. What in God's name had gone on in there? He hoped that Amber was okay. There seemed to be a lot of confusion from those witnesses on the street. Could Randel have tried to hold up the bank? He'd gone in just before Betty and Caroline came out.

He said nothing more to Charlie who was sitting beside him, holding the map and looking a bit dazed.

Danny glanced back and could see Betty stirring.

"You okay, Betty?" he called.

Charlie whipped his head around. "Betty, you awake? You shoulda heard what we heard..."

"Leave it for now, Charlie," Danny whispered. "Let's concentrate on where we're going next. Don't start pestering Betty about the bank."

They found a place to stop between Power and Vaughn. Caroline was her usual self, but Danny noticed Betty was looking preoccupied.

He said quietly to Charlie, "We're going to look over the map with Betty and decide which road to take from Great Falls. Don't mention the bank robbery to her. She'll only worry about Amber. I don't want her deciding we have to go back again to make sure Amber's okay or anything. I've had enough of driving up 'n' down this piece of road."

"No way! We sure as hell don't want that," Charlie said.

"Good," Danny said. "Let's concentrate on where we're heading."

Danny spread the map on a picnic table as the women returned from the washrooms. "Betty, we're just a little way from Great Falls. There's two ways we can go from there. We can stay on Highway 15 here," Danny pointed out the route, "or take number 89, south-east of Great Falls and go through White Sulphur Springs then Livingston. Looks like we'd go through Livingston whichever route we take."

Betty peered at the map. "What do you think? I remember I definitely went through Livingston with Arnie, but I don't remember White Sulphur Springs."

"It might be six of one or half a dozen of the other. There'd probably be more traffic on Highway 15, there's more towns, but it might be a bit faster. But Highway 89 is probably more scenic. I just thought you might like to go the exact way you and Arnie did."

Betty seemed to brighten as she looked at the map again. "Thanks, Danny. I can't really remember exactly where Arnie and I went, but I'm all in favour of goin' through White Sulphur Springs. I like the name. We're not in a real hurry and I like takin' the road less travelled. We've had enough excitement for one day. I'll make us a good supper when we stop for the night."

"Okay. Highway 89 it is. Maybe we should look for a place to stop near this little place called Monarch. Okay. All aboard!"

"Yes, a board, a board, a board, a board," Caroline repeated.

They found themselves alone in a small picnic area just off a narrow road east of tiny Monarch in the Lewis and Clark National Forest. Although the signs said, 'No Camping – No Fires', Betty declared that they would spend the night there. There were a couple of dry toilets and they had enough fresh water.

Next morning after breakfast, Betty suggested with the weather warm and the place they'd stopped being so nice that they take a breather. "No one's here. It's Saturday. I doubt if there are any Forest Rangers or whatever they're called comin' around to check on us. Let's spend the rest of the day here. We're doin' nothin' illegal here now, just picnickin'. And the woods smell so lovely. Let's have a nice relaxin' day. Caroline and I can go for a nature walk. Maybe see what birds we can find."

"Or Smokey the Bear," Charlie said. "Don't go too far."

THE GRAND GETAWAY   153

After lunch Betty had a lie down in The Smucker and was soon asleep. Danny sat at a picnic table and took up reading *Losing Julia* again and Caroline, at the same table, was busy rearranging a small collection of pine and spruce cones she and Betty had collected on their walk in the woods earlier.

"I'll take a walk into town," Charlie said. "See if I can pick up some milk. You okay here with Caroline?"

"Sure. Go ahead. I'm enjoyng this book and Caroline seems happy. You have a couple of bucks?"

"Yeah. A Canadian $5.00 bill," Charlie replied. "They should take that okay."

"Don't go wandering off. See if there's a gas pump where we can get gas in the morning, we're getting low."

"Okay. See ya later."

It took Charlie about 20 minutes to reach Monarch and find a store that sold some groceries. It had a couple of gas pumps outside. He was standing at the cash register waiting to pay for the carton of milk and was looking over a small tourist information leaflet he'd just picked up. The woman behind the counter chatted to the woman ahead of him who was buying some bread and eggs.

"Yea, Gladys. Over in Shelby. Union Bank. It's in the papers," the storekeeper indicated a small pile of newspapers on the counter.

"Things are getting worse every day. You're not safe anywhere. I'll take a *Tribune*," Gladys said.

"That's $5.75 altogether, Gladys."

As the woman paid for her purchases Charlie stared at a copy of the Great Falls *Tribune*. The headline, *Homeland Hero Foils Would-Be Bank Robber* jumped out at him. Beside the *Tribune*, a copy of the Bozeman *Daily Chronicle* had the headline, *Border Guard Bamboozles Bank Robber*.

"Can I help you?" the storekeeper asked.

"Er. Yeah. Thanks. This milk, and I'll take a couple of newspapers." Charlie picked up copies of both newspapers and offered his Canadian $5.00 bill.

"Canadian! That's $5.35 with the exchange. You have some more change?"

"Um…" Charlie fished in his jacket pocket and found a Canadian quarter. "That's all I have, sorry. I've got no U.S. money. I'll leave a paper."

"Ah that's okay. I'll cover it. Don't get many Canadian tourists stoppin' in Monarch. Just give me the 5 bucks. That'll be fine."

"Thanks," Charlie said.

"Welcome to Montana," the storekeeper called as Charlie left.

Charlie did his best to focus on the article on the front page of the *Tribune* but found it difficult as he hurried along the narrow road to the picnic site, while holding the carton of milk in one hand and keeping the other newspaper under his arm. He stopped walking a couple of times to squint at the fine print, but he had real difficulty as he'd left his reading glasses in The Smucker. He nearly stumbled into the small ditch at the edge of the road when he managed to decipher – *Yesterday, off-duty USCBP agent Randel Fletcher entered his local bank, Shelby First Union Bank, to find a robbery in progress. The quick-thinking Fletcher drew his gun and quickly disarmed the would-be robber and held him until police arrived.*

"Randel Fletcher!" Charlie groaned. "My God! Wasn't that the name of Amber's husband? Amber would have told him about her new Canadian friends. Us! And he couldn't have missed seeing The Smucker parked outside the bank."

Charlie practically jogged the rest of the way back to the picnic site, certain that the police were now on the look-out for The Smucker and four Canadians. How long, he wondered, would it take before that storekeeper in Monarch called police once she learned that the police were looking for Canadian fugitives. They'd get his fingerprints off the Canadian $5.00 bill. He was a wanted man.

CHAPTER 39

Danny sat at the picnic table, engrossed *Losing Julia*, chuckling to himself over the way the author described the main character's prolific growth of nose hairs. He suddenly felt the hairs rise on the back of his neck as he became aware of heavy panting and a scuffling sound approaching him from behind.

What was it you were supposed to do when a bear attacks? Play dead? Climb a tree? One was for black bears and the other for grizzlies, but which was which? Make a dash for The Smucker? Can't run 'n' leave Caroline sitting at the other end of the table playing with pine cones.

He took a quick look over his shoulder. "God! Charlie! You scared the shit outta me. What the hell are ya doing?"

A red-faced Charlie staggered to the table, wheezing for breath. He dropped a couple of newspapers on the table with a loud slap and let a small carton of milk fall onto the table top, where it bounced, toppled, and was headed for the ground had Danny not grabbed it.

Charlie bent over the table, propping himself on his elbows, trying to catch his breath.

"You okay?" Danny asked. "You're not having a heart attack are ya?"

Charlie shook his head.

Caroline grinned at Charlie. "Oh, there you are. Attack, attack, attack."

"I thought for sure you were a god-damn bear running up behind me." Danny looked back down the road. "Who's chasing you?"

"Betty..." Charlie gasped.

"Betty! What do ya mean Betty? She's still asleep in The Smucker. Sit down for God's sake. Take a breath."

Charlie eased himself onto the bench. "No. I meant... huh." He still panted but not as much as before and his face wasn't so red. "I meant where's, huh, hah... Betty?"

"I just told you, asleep in The Smucker."

"Nobody is chasing me. But they soon will be. Chasing all of us. Look at these newspapers. Remember on the radio...? It said a woman and a border guard were in the bank."

"Yeah, we knew Amber was in the bank. We took her there ourselves. So what?"

"The so what, is that the border guard turned out to be Amber's husband, Randel, for shit's sake. I don't know how he happened to show up." Charlie had almost recovered his breath but was still excited. "How the hell did he not notice The Smucker parked outside the bank? If Amber and Randel patch things up, it stands to reason all of us will be part of the conversation." Charlie took a couple more deep breaths. "And then the shit will really hit the fan. They'll be looking for us for sure. Now that woman in the store back there knows I'm Canadian. I paid for the milk and newspapers with a Canadian $5.00 bill. My fingerprints are all over it."

"Yeah," Danny said. "And probably a hundred other Canadian fingerprints. Maybe even the Prime Minister's." Danny laughed. "So, did ya read these newspaper accounts?"

"No. Just the headlines and a few bits and pieces. I didn't have my glasses. They're in The Smucker."

"Well. Why don't I get you a drink of water, get you calmed down and then I'll read what the newspapers say. Okay?"

"Okay. Fine. But we might not have much time. We'll probably have to high-tail it out of here, fast."

As Charlie sipped on the water, Danny quickly scanned the article in the Tribune.

"So, what does it say?" Charlie prodded.

"Okay. After the headline, *Homeland Hero Foils Would-be Robber*, which you read, it says – *Police are on the look-out for four other fugitives, believed to be led by Canadian gangster Charles Babyface Bannister.*"

"What the ff...?"

"Who recently broke out of Cavandish," Danny continued, *"Canada's maximum security prison."* Danny burst into laughter.

"Read what it says! "Charlie snapped. "Quit buggerin' around."

"Okay, okay. Sorry. Couldn't resist." Danny chuckled. "It says... *In Shelby, yesterday, off-duty USCBP agent Randel Fletcher entered his local bank to find that the bank was being robbed. A female customer was lying on the floor and the two tellers on duty were in the process of stuffing bags with cash while the gunman threatened all three of them with a pistol. The quick-thinking border agent pulled his own gun, disarmed the bank bandit and held him until police arrived. In a surprising twist, agent Fletcher discovered that the female customer on the floor was his wife, Amber.*

Police have charged Russell Hagen, formerly of Omaha, Nebraska, with attempted armed robbery, use of a lethal weapon, confinement and making threats. Hagen was working as part of a highway line-painting crew with a company under contract to Montana State Highways. Police are now looking into a string of bank robberies in Montana, North Dakota and Idaho, in which Hagen may have been involved. Hagen remains in custody while police continue their investigation.

Bank Manager Mr. Don Jordan, who was out of the bank at the time of the attempted hold-up, had high praise for Agent Fletcher. 'Thanks to the brave action of Agent Fletcher, the Shelby First Union Bank continues with its unblemished record of never having been a victim of a robbery.'

When asked how the two tellers were, Mr. Jordan said that both tellers were still somewhat shaken by the experience and were currently taking a few days sick leave from the bank. He preferred not to give their names.

In a brief interview with the Tribune, *Agent Fletcher was asked what went through his mind when he discovered it was his wife being held captive and lying on the floor.* 'I just reacted. I saw a man threatening the tellers behind the counter with a gun and a woman lying on the floor. My attention was on the gunman. I pulled my gun and caught him by surprise, and he turned over his weapon. You can imagine my shock, and then my relief, when my own wife, Amber, called out to let me know she was okay.'

Police expect to make a further statement in a day or two and Russell Hagen is expected to appear in court in Great Falls before the end of the week.

"There, that's the *Tribune*," Danny said. "It says nothing about us. Let's take a look at the other newspaper."

Danny read out loud. "*Border Guard Bamboozles Bank Robber* – Catchy headline. Okay – *Yesterday, USCBP agent Randel Fletcher had just booked off duty at the Sweetgrass border crossing and had driven to Shelby where he lives with his wife. Dropping by his local bank, (the Shelby First Union Bank), to make a payment on his truck loan, he got the surprise of his life.*" Danny stopped reading aloud and mumbled quickly to himself as he scanned the rest of the article.

"So, what's it say?" Charlie asked. "You quit reading."

"I didn't. I just finished and the rest of the stuff is pretty much the same as the first newspaper. It doesn't mention anything about any of us."

"But I don't get it," Charlie said. "Amber is in the bank and so are Betty and Caroline. Then Amber's husband arrives to find the bank being robbed. If Randel went into the bank when our Smucker was parked outside, he had to see Betty and Caroline inside."

"Not if Betty and Caroline came out before Randel went in," Danny said.

It was something that puzzled Danny too. He'd seen Randel go into the bank and knew for sure Betty and Caroline were still in there and would have been caught up in the whole thing.

He was certain Betty knew. He'd seen that in her face as they'd driven south from Shelby. He decided to keep his mouth shut. If Betty wanted to tell them anything it was up to her.

"What's happenin'? I sure had a good sleep." Betty was standing in the open door of The Smucker. "It's so peaceful here. It smells so good too, the woods 'n' everythin'."

"You should see the newspapers I picked up in the store in the village," Charlie said. "It looks like you and Caroline nearly got caught up in a bank robbery. It happened just minutes after you two got outta the bank. You were damn lucky. We all were. You won't believe it, but Amber's husband captured the bank robber while Amber was still in the bank."

Danny noticed Betty looked quite worried for a moment, but she recovered and said. "I'd better get Caroline to the bathroom. I hadn't realized I'd slept for so long. I'll read the papers later. I see ya got the milk anyway. Thanks, Charlie."

Betty took Caroline to the small outhouse and when they returned, she brought Caroline to the picnic table, where she began arranging the pine and spruce cones again.

Charlie said, "We may be in the woods here but the cops might be looking for us as witnesses, so we may not be outta the woods yet, so to speak."

When Charlie headed off to the outhouse, Danny looked at Betty. "You know there's not one mention in the newspapers of you and Caroline being in the bank, but I definitely saw Randel go into the bank when you and Caroline were still in there. I can tell you I was worried sick. Charlie didn't see him, and I said nothing. The papers say Randel somehow captured the hold-up guy.

"When Charlie saw the headlines this morning, he just about ran the whole way back here with these newspapers. I have him convinced that you and Caroline left the bank before the robbery. So what the hell happened?"

"Thanks Danny. You're a god-send. You know I have a soft spot for Charlie. He thinks he's lookin' after me, and Caroline too. I guess we're all lookin' out for each other. Charlie's been a good companion these last horrible years at Cavandish. In another time, another place, we might be what they call an item. I think if you'd told him Randel had gone into the bank, he might have come in after us and then we'd have really been in trouble. He means well. He just gets overprotective and panics sometimes.

"But if I was the cause of anything bad happenin' to Charlie or Caroline or you, Danny, I'd never forgive myself. And Caroline, yesterday... yesterday..." Betty broke off, tears springing to her eyes, "I nearly got poor Caroline killed." Betty wiped her eyes with the back of her hand.

"Caroline and I were in the washroom in the bank. The bank robber must have come in then. When we came out of the washroom this guy was wavin' a gun around and Amber was lyin' on the floor. Then Randel walked in and well... What does it say in the papers?"

"The same. Except, it's like you and Caroline weren't even in the bank. But why didn't Randel make you and Caroline stay there until the cops arrived?"

"That's thanks to Amber. She persuaded Randel to let us leave."

"You two talking about me again?" Charlie asked. "You read the papers, Betty?" He sat beside her.

"I did. We just got outta that bank in the nick of time. Sure glad Amber is okay and Randel turned out to be a hero. I think their marriage has a good chance. I'm glad we drove her back to Shelby.

THE GRAND GETAWAY   159

"You know, I've been thinkin'. We're not in a huge rush to get to the Grand Canyon. We're not goin' to have any money from our pensions for nearly a month and it's not costin' us anything to stay here."

"I think we should get as far away from here as quick as possible," Charlie said. "Someone's going to remember seeing The Smucker parked outside the bank."

"But we were just parked like any tourist," Danny said. "We didn't rob the bank. The guy who tried that is under arrest. The cops aren't looking for us, or for anyone else who happened to be parked in Shelby. I kinda agree with Betty. I think we should take our time getting to the Grand Canyon. The longer we take, the closer we'll be to getting your pension money when it comes into the bank."

"It's lovely here," Betty said. "I feel like we're on holiday now. If we were still back in Cavandish we'd be elbow to elbow sittin', starin' at that fake mural on the wall in the dinin' room. Here, we have real trees. God, you can even smell 'em. Real sunshine! And listen..." Betty held up her hand for silence and they all were quiet.

There was a whisper of a breeze through the trees and a chirping and whistle of birds. A squirrel chattered in the distance.

"There," Betty said. "Lovely."

"I agree," Charlie said. "It is peaceful. But we're still camping illegally."

"God! Charlie! I knew I was really missin' somethin'," Betty said.

"What's that?" Charlie asked.

"The constant whine of unhooked oxygen tanks."

Betty's face softened and she placed her arm across his shoulder and gave his arm a squeeze. Charlie turned to her and nodded and patted her hand.

"Relax, Charlie. Just kiddin'. Let's just enjoy this while we can. I'd like to do that."

"It's true we're not legally here," Danny said. "But it's not costing us anything to stay here for a day or so. Yeah, the more I think of it the better I like it. If we rush off now, we'll be in Yellowstone National Park in another day or so. Let me get the map and we'll take a look. If we get to the Canyon too soon, we'll run out of money long before your pensions come in."

Danny got the map and spread it on the table, standing behind Betty and Charlie. 'We're here." He pointed to Monarch. "The next little place just down the road is Neihart. I'm all for just moseyin' along slowly. Stay here for another few days and see where we can find to stay along the way, especially if it's free."

"You okay with that, Charlie?" Betty asked. "Come on! You're the one who claims to love nature. Always watchin' those nature shows."

"Yeah, I guess you're right. Too bad we can't light a fire. I used to love campfires. What can I do?"

"Well," Danny said. "As the naturalist in this party, you could try looking for edible plants to supplement our food."

"No, Caroline," Betty said. "Take that pine cone out of your mouth, it's not chocolate." She took away the small pine cone that Caroline was nibbling. "Guess we're all gettin' hungry. At least here we'll be able to smell the coffee. I'll go make some."

CHAPTER 40

"When we get our money," Betty said. "I'm goin' to buy us some fold-up lawn chairs. I don't know if my rear end will hold up if we have to sit on picnic-table benches for the next four weeks."

It was their second morning in the forest near Monarch and they had finished breakfast outside, as the weather had given them another pleasant day.

"What's on the agenda for today, Betty?" Charlie asked.

"Keepin' outta trouble mostly. Takin' it easy. Relaxin'. See if Danny needs a hand with the dishes, Charlie. But bring me some paddin' for this bench first. I think my bum is numb. It's nice not to be hustled out of this dinin' room and I like the quiet. No crashing and bashin' of cutlery and dishes. Right, Caroline?"

"Oh yes. Crashin' and bashin', crashin' and bashin', crashin', bashin', smashin', smashin', smashin'."

Charlie found Danny putting away the last of the dishes.

"How's it going? Betty's getting a pain in her arse sitting on the bench. Sent me in to get some sweaters to pad the bench and wants another coffee, if there's any left."

"There is, and I think it's still hot."

As Charlie got the coffee for Betty he asked, "What ya going to do today, Danny?"

"Finish my book. Maybe we could all go for a nice walk a little later, just take it easy. There's more books if you want to read something."

"Yeah. Maybe I'll do that."

A chickadee hopped onto the table beside Caroline, who was tearing a pine cone apart. The chickadee hopped about tentatively, quickly grabbed a piece of pine cone, and flew off. Caroline laughed and said, "Gone."

Charlie had been alternatively dozing and reading a copy of *The Girl Who Gave Birth To Rabbits* by Clifford A. Pickover. He'd chosen it from among the books Betty had purloined because he'd found the title intriguing. When he saw the chickadee fly off, he got up and went inside The Smucker. In the tiny kitchen he quietly found the oatmeal and put a handful into a cup, careful not to awaken Betty who had fallen asleep at the table, having retreated there to do more sewing on a curtain.

For the next hour Charlie, and then Caroline, had two chickadees eating the oatmeal out of their hands. Charlie was delighted with the pleasure Caroline showed on her face as the chickadees came and went and she talked quietly to them. Danny, sprawled against a nearby pine, looked up at Caroline's soft laughter. He was pleased to see Charlie engrossed in something that helped him relax.

As they sat at the picnic table eating lunch, Betty asked. "I see you've been readin', Charlie. The book any good?"

"Interesting, but not what I expected."

"Oh. What's it called?"

"*The Girl Who Gave Birth To Rabbits.*"

"Did she? I know rabbits have a reputation, but it sounds a bit creepy." Betty laughed.

"It turned out to be a hoax. Fooled some doctors at the time though, in England, back in the early 1700s."

"Sounds disgustin'," Betty said. "Wonder who donated that book to Cavandish? There's a few others you can try. I think I saw one called *Ladies Night At Finbar's Hotel*. It sounds it might be more up your alley. I was thinking of askin' you to go out lookin' for game for supper, but I think I just struck rabbits off my list."

They had another discussion on how much longer they should stay where they were. Betty suggested giving it two more days and they agreed. Charlie found the tourist brochure he'd picked up in the store in Monarch.

"We're on what they call Kings Hill Scenic Highway in the Little Belt Mountains. Most of the nearby towns are pretty small. There's a place called Neihart coming up next. Once a mining town, Neihart is called after some kind of reddish quartzite. There was some gold and even sapphires found in the area. Part of it's a ghost town now."

"Maybe you and Danny could do some gold-pannin'." Betty said. "Keep us goin' until our pensions come in."

"Then a little further on there's some campsites near a place called Showdown. Sounds a bit ominous. Hope there's no bank there. The only real town on this road until White Sulphur Springs is Neihart," Charlie went on. "There's a little place called Ringling after White Sulphur Springs."

"Ringling! Sounds like the circus," Danny said.

"You're right," Charlie said. "It used to be a place where Ringling Brothers Circus stayed over winter. Haven't been to a circus since I was a kid. Hey! There's a place called Pray just off this highway that was for sale for $1.4 million in 2012. Supposed to be a small town, privately owned."

"Hmn," Betty mused. "Maybe we'll buy it after you and Danny strike it rich in that minin' town. A handful of sapphires or a few gold nuggets might do it. Let's put the dirty dishes in the bus and go for a stroll. This picnic bench is puttin' a permanent crease across my bum. If I sit here much longer, I'll have a hot cross bun bum." Betty laughed.

The four meandered among the trees following narrow tracks. A couple of squirrels chasing each other skittered across their path, ran up a tree and scolded them from the safety of the branches.

Caroline tried to imitate their chittering, then put her finger to her lips telling them, "Shush."

THE GRAND GETAWAY   163

"Hey! Morels!" Charlie called out, pointing out a cluster group of brown mushrooms. "We can have these for supper or breakfast. They'd go good with eggs. Too bad we don't have any bacon."

"You're sure they're safe to eat?" Betty asked. "They look like sponges. I've only eaten real mushrooms."

"These are real mushrooms. I've eaten them lots of times. I used to collect them back in New Brunswick and any time I got stuck in the back woods travelling across the country by train. I think they grow after a forest fire. These would cost a fortune to buy. They taste good."

"You're absolutely sure?" Betty asked. "I'd hate to think of the headline in the papers. *Escapees From Nursing Home Die in Suicide Pact or, Elderly Hippies Mistakenly Eat Poisonous Mushrooms –Thought They Were Magic.*"

"I swear," Charlie said. "These are perfectly safe and they're nice and fresh."

Charlie's morel mushrooms were a great success, although the first time Betty only ate a small amount and would give none to Caroline. They cooked them for supper and had another feed of them next morning for breakfast. This time Betty, having seen the amount Charlie had wolfed down the night before without any obvious ill effects, tried a plateful.

They had half a day of rain and found The Smucker a little confining but got through the day okay. Betty did some more sewing on the curtains, Danny and Charlie read for a while and Caroline took an afternoon nap. With only the lantern for light they went to bed not long after dark each evening. Three days later in Neihart, with Charlie paranoid about encountering the storekeeper from Monarch again, Betty changed their Canadian money into U.S. dollars and they filled up The Smucker, as well as picking up some fresh lettuce and milk and a small bag of ice. Betty said they were doing okay so far with their food and might be able to stretch it to the end of the month if they only bought what they absolutely needed.

As they came out of the grocery store, Charlie found a day-old copy of *The Missoulian* on a bench and saw the headline, *Shelby Bank Hero Accepts New Job*.

"Hey! Look at this!" Charlie sat down on the bench, put on his glasses and, started reading aloud.

"Randel Fletcher, the border guard who foiled an attempted bank robbery this past Friday at Shelby First Union Bank, has accepted a job with Merrill Lynch, Bank of America's brokerage firm, at their branch in Great Falls."

"Oh," Betty said, "Amber will be thrilled. So will Randel, he wasn't happy as a border guard."

"Shush," Charlie said. "Let me read this. *In a telephone interview with The Missoulian, Fletcher said although he'd been happy with his job as a border control officer, he had been thinking of a change of career and when the offer from Merrill Lynch came up, he accepted the position as a trainee financial advisor."*

"Everyone says they were happy in their old job," Betty said, "when they are offered a better one."

Charlie waved his hand at Betty to quieten her and continued. *"He said he and his wife are thinking of starting a family and she is looking forward to the move to Great Falls.*

Hank Brinkerhoff, Fletcher's immediate superior officer with USCBP, said in a statement to The Missoulian *– I'm sorry that U.S. Customs and Border Protection are losing a good man like Fletcher. America needs men who put themselves on the line to stand in the way of criminals and terrorists and keep America safe for Americans. His training with USCBP probably saved lives in the bank. I wish him well in his new career."*

"Ha!" Betty said. "What a bullshitter! The hypocrite!"

"Hypocrite, hypocrite, hippo, hippo, hippopotamus, potamus, muss, fuss," Caroline added, and everyone laughed.

"Amber told me Brinkerhoff was always givin' Randel a bad time. Now Randel's the best border guard they ever had," Betty continued.

"Well, maybe we were lucky he wasn't," Charlie said. "Here it goes on about the tellers." Charlie pointed to a subheading *–Terrified Tellers Tell All.*

"We should get the ice in the bus before it melts," Betty said.

"Yeah," Danny said.

"Hang on. I'm just about finished," Charlie said. "It says *– We found Mrs. Muriel Crowley, senior teller at Shelby First Union Bank, tending her flower garden at her home and asked her to tell us what had occurred inside the bank. Mrs. Crowley was somewhat reluctant to say much, stating that she had been quite distressed by the whole affair. 'In my 25 years with the bank, never once was I confronted by anyone trying to rob the bank. I'm thinking of retiring and now is probably a good time. I was horrified when the man came in and suddenly ordered Amber to lie on the floor and for Lindy and I to fill bags with money.'*

(The Missoulian) *– Was the gun-man pointing a gun at you?*

(Mrs. Crowley) *– I think so. I'm not sure. I know Lindy dropped some money on the floor and he yelled at her to leave it when she tried to pick it up, so he probably was waving his gun at both of us.*

(The Missoulian)- *Were there any other people in the bank at the time?*

"Damn newspapers," Betty snapped. "Why don't they leave the poor woman alone? Come on, Charlie. The ice is melting."

"Wait! Wait!" Charlie said. "Just a couple of lines left. I'll be finished in a sec.

(Mrs. Crowley) *– I'm not sure. I think I fainted then.*

"There," Betty said. "Let's go."

"Go! Go! Go!" Caroline repeated.

Charlie got up but continued reading aloud as they all walked to The Smucker in the parking lot.

(The Missoulian) *– So you didn't actually see Mr. Fletcher disarm the gun-man?*

THE GRAND GETAWAY   165

(Mrs. Crowley) — *I don't think so. When I recovered, I was sitting on a chair and Lindy was giving me a glass of water. Mr. Fletcher had already arrested the gun-man. The day before our security camera had broken down and we hadn't been able to get it fixed, not that it would have done much good. The robber was wearing a disguise so he might still be robbing banks if Mr. Fletcher hadn't arrived when he did.*

When The Missoulian *contacted Ms Lindy Jernigan by phone, she did not wish to make a statement of her own. She said she was suffering from stress and would rather not speak to anyone in the media. When we read back to her what Mrs. Crowley had said, Ms Jernigan said that she'd been tending to Mrs. Crowley who had fainted and what Mrs. Crowley had said must have been the way things had happened. She said that Mrs. Crowley is a very experienced teller and, in the year she has worked with her at Shelby First Union Bank, she has never known Mrs. Crowley to make a mistake. Ms Jernigan said she hadn't been sleeping well and is reconsidering her career in banking. She said she might look into the possibility of becoming a hairdresser.*

No trial date has been set for Russell Hagen as police continue to look into links between Hagen and other bank hold-ups.

Betty gave Danny a quick look of relief then turned to Charlie as they clambered into The Smucker, "Okay, Charlie. That should be enough to convince you that we're not bein' hunted down by the cops. So you can cool down. Now, get that bag of ice in the fridge."

CHAPTER 41

Despite Charlie's earlier misgivings over the name Showdown, they found a place to tuck The Smucker into the bush. The place they chose to camp was not one of the designated campsites, although they could possibly have got away with camping there as there appeared to be no one around. It was only a very short drive from where they hid in the bush to the closest site, where they used the outhouses and picked up fresh water.

The next morning brought another rainy day and when they went to use the toilets, they found the campsite still deserted. They debated if they should move there, but decided they shouldn't risk it, not wanting to get into a confrontation with any kind of law-enforcement. Charlie argued that it was perfectly legal to camp in the designated site. There was just no one to take the fee.

"It's temptin'," Betty said, "parkin' in the proper campsite with the toilets right there, but if anyone official showed up we'd have to pay. It's not worth the risk."

When Betty was getting her sewing, she said, "Oh. I forgot all about this." She produced a plastic bag. "More Cavandish treasures. There's a deck of cards here and a crib board. It doesn't have any pegs. You'll have to use some matches if you two want to play. There's a jigsaw puzzle as well."

"You're full of surprises Betty," Danny said. "I haven't played crib for ages. Maybe Charlie and me can play and to make it interesting we'll bet on something."

"Like what?" Charlie asked.

"I dunno. Hey! It's my turn to do the dishes today. If I win, you do them. If you win, I'll do them again tomorrow when it's your turn."

"Okay. You're on."

Danny won the game, but Charlie said, "Let's make it a best of three."

Caroline watched and often repeated the numbers when the two counted their points. She distracted Charlie a couple of times when he was trying to add, and had Danny laughing.

"Fifteen two, two, two, six, eight, ten, ten, tenter," Caroline said as Charlie moved his peg.

"You only got eight," Danny said.

Charlie counted again. "Okay, eight."

Charlie eventually won the bet and got out of doing the dishes for the next day.

Betty produced the jigsaw and she sat down with Caroline, who began collecting pieces of the puzzle in her hand while Betty tried to find a few edge pieces to begin.

"What's the picture on the box?" Charlie asked.

"I believe it's somewhere in Venice. I'm just foolin' around. I never did have a lot of patience for jigsaws," Betty answered. "Remember that time we found a piece

THE GRAND GETAWAY   167

of jigsaw puzzle in Caroline's porridge at Cavandish? You wouldn't eat any porridge for nearly a week because you said that the porridge always tasted like old jigsaws pieces and now you had the evidence to prove it."

"It sure tasted like it," Charlie said. "The porridge you make tastes like real food. How did a piece of puzzle get in the Cavandish porridge anyhow?"

"I told you, Caroline brought it to breakfast in her hand and just dropped it into her bowl. She has a handful now, but I'll try to make sure she doesn't have any pieces in her hand when I serve the spaghetti I'm making for supper."

"I wonder if you could live on jigsaw puzzle pieces for a while if you were starving," Charlie mused.

"We can always find out. I'll start you on a diet of jigsaw tonight. There should be enough glue in the pieces to stick to your ribs, as they say. We'll save a lot on groceries. How would you like it cooked? Broiled or deep-fried?"

Charlie ignored that remark. "Do you think they've missed us yet at Cavandish?"

"Course they have. We left a week ago, today."

"Only a week? It seems like a lot longer."

"That's probably because we've been more or less doing somethin' different every day. We're coping on our own. It's kinda exciting. Nobody orderin' us about. We can do our own thing. No one calling for help every minute like poor old Mrs. Cripps. No one getting us outta bed so they can make it up again. We can sleep in if we like."

"Well so far I haven't felt any desire to sleep in," Charlie said. "I thought I would, but now I'm happy to rise early. I'm enjoying this camping out. So what do you think they're doing at Cavandish now that they know we're missing?"

"Probably not a lot. If anyone notifies Darlington, he won't care. First thing he'd check is whether we're paid up. And we are. So he's saving on food, has our money and is no doubt collecting the subsidy from the government. Sure, one or two will maybe worry about us, particularly about Caroline. What we scribbled in the sign-out book might have bought us a few days before anyone really thought about us."

"What did you write for you and Caroline?" Charlie asked.

"I wrote – *Away for two weeks visiting her sister* and printed a fake name for my made-up sister and for Caroline, I wrote –*Transferred*. I don't know if anyone would believe that, but remember they were gonna transfer her. The average worker won't check on the paperwork and just shrug it off. Anyway, we're long gone and I'm not worryin' about Cavandish. What did you write anyway?"

"I wrote – *Gone fishin'*." Charlie said.

"Jeez, that should really fool 'em." Betty laughed. "That's about as good as writing – *Called back by railway as full-time freight conductor*. I thought you were going to say – *Staying with son for a few days*. Somethin' like that."

"I think I just panicked the day we were leaving." Charlie sighed.

Betty laughed. "Charlie, you kill me. What's that book you're readin' now?"

"It's called, *Come Home Charlie And Face Them*."

"What!" Betty laughed. "It's not about you is it? Runnin' away from Cavandish and then goin' back to turn yourself in? Is it any good?"

"Pretty good. It's about a young kid in Wales who gets a job in a bank. Kind of a soft crime story. English writer, Delderfield. He's good. I think there's a bank robbery in it later. I haven't read that far yet."

"God Charlie! I shoulda left that one behind."

CHAPTER 42

Two days later they rolled into White Sulphur Springs.

"This is a pretty small place," Betty said. "I thought it would be bigger with such a fancy name."

"I think that was the hope of the first settlers," Charlie said. "Why don't we just park and have a look around?"

"We'll have to scout out the area if we plan to spend a night or two around here," Danny said. "You know if we wanted to, we could have driven all the way here from Great Falls in about two hours."

'Yeah," Betty said, "but we've been savin' money on campin' fees so maybe we could afford a night in Yellowstone National Park when we get there. Act like real tourists."

"Well we can act like real tourists here," Charlie said, "and it costs nothing. And it's a nice day for sight-seeing."

They parked and walked around the small town, stopping to read a tourist map about the town and area. The town was on the headwaters of the Smith River, one of the country's best trout streams. Gold had been discovered in the surrounding hills and there were hopes of the place becoming a premier tourist spot with the discovery of the warm sulphur spring.

"If that's it there down the street," Betty said, "it looks a bit like an Alberta slough."

"Hey!" Charlie said. "There was a railway running through here once. The White Sulphur Springs and Yellowstone Park Railway. Look, it connected at Ringling, just south of here to the Chicago, Milwaukee, St. Paul and Pacific Railway – known as the Milwaukee Road. Nearly abandoned in 1944 and finally shut down in 1980 when the Milwaukee Road closed the line through Ringling. What a shame. This place was cut off from a mainline cross-country railway. There's a station still here, restored for a movie, *Heartland*. I'd like to see that."

"We can't afford to see a movie," Betty said. "Anyway, it says it was made in 2000. Probably not playin' here now even if they have a movie theatre."

"I meant the station, not the movie," Charlie said.

"I know you did. Just pullin' your leg." Betty laughed.

They found the station not far away. Charlie walked up and down inspecting a Northern Pacific Railway sleeper car and a passenger car plus a couple of Milwaukee Road freight cars – a ballast car and a stock car.

Betty, Caroline and Danny sat on a bench giving Charlie as much time as he needed to look over the train cars.

"He still misses the railway," Betty said out loud, to no one in particular.

When Charlie came back to where they sat and said, "Let's go," they followed him along main street and came across a fishing tackle store where Charlie said, "Let's take a look inside."

The owner greeted them and asked if they needed help, but Charlie said, "Thanks, we're just browsing."

Charlie examined a few fishing rods, but they didn't spend long inside. They couldn't afford to buy luxuries like fishing rods and reels.

Further down the street they did find a junk store, and they browsed through that, too. Charlie found a small roll of fishing line and a couple of fishing flies, held them up and asked, "How much?"

The grizzled old man sitting behind a counter piled with all kinds of bits and pieces, said, "Ah, give me a buck."

Charlie looked at Betty and she nodded and handed over a dollar in change. Then Betty found an empty milk crate that she bought for 50 cents which she said could be used for storing their small supply of books, which were scattered in little piles inside The Smucker.

When they got outside, Betty said to Charlie, "You plannin' on fishin'? You might need a license."

"If we can't afford camping fees, we can't afford a license," Charlie said.

They spent another half hour exploring the town before Betty suggested they park down by the pond, and said she'd brew up some coffee. After that, they would see if they could find a place to hide out again.

"It's pretty country, and if we can hang around here for a day or two, I'll be happy."

"Let's go take a look at the map we saw earlier before we drive anywhere," Danny said. "No sense in using up any more gas than we have to."

Betty and Caroline climbed back into The Smucker while Charlie and Danny walked the short distance to the map.

"I guess seeing as how you bought some fishing line and flies, you'd like to be close to the river," Danny said.

"If we can," Charlie said. "I haven't fished in years. It'll give me something to do even if I don't catch anything. Keep me out of Betty's hair."

"What about a rod?" Danny asked.

"Maybe I can cut a willow out of the bush but without a reel it will only be something to tie the line to. I'm probably just fooling myself."

"Well the river's not far." Danny pointed to the map. "We'll have to lie low again and you'd better make sure you don't get seen fishing illegally by some game warden fella."

"Damn. I just wasted a dollar." Charlie let out a sigh. "I should've read all of this sign. I got distracted reading about the railway. Look." He pointed to a piece on the side of the sign about fishing on the Smith River. It informed them that most of the Smith River in the area ran through private property and to fish at the few access

THE GRAND GETAWAY   171

points on the map, they needed a permit from Montana Fish and Wildlife. It also warned that much of the river flowed through a canyon and even if they had a boat, they needed a special permit drawn by lottery.

"Seems almost like a private fishing river," Danny said. "Think you could float on your back and fish at the same time?"

"I was hoping to kinda sneak down to the river and hide in the bushes and try my luck with the fishing line and flies – fly-fishing would be the best way but with no rod 'n' reel I couldn't cast. I was going to jerk the line in the water and hope I could fool a fish. I don't think I would've had much luck anyway. I thought it'd be worth a try to contribute something towards our food supply, but it's hopeless with the river controlled so tight."

"Well let's move The Smucker down to that pond and have a coffee," Danny said. "Guess there's no fish in that water if it's hot and full of sulphur."

Later they tried a few narrow roads heading towards the river, but all had ended either in somebody's front yard or they were confronted by fences beyond which were grazing or crop-lands with prominent signs announcing, *Private Property – No Access To The River*.

After five attempts they'd pulled into a small clearing off a muddy laneway. Betty said they were just wasting gas and she was getting hungry. She would make lunch right there and later they could then decide if they should press on further south to Ringling. "It's quiet and we could at least spend a couple of hours here if no one comes along. There's not exactly a lot of traffic."

After lunch, Betty said she was tired and needed a nap and persuaded Caroline to lie down too. They could decide what to do when they woke up. Danny got the book, *Havana Bay* by Martin Cruz Smith, and sat outside on the milk crate they'd bought with a cushion on top of it and leaned against the side of The Smucker. Charlie sat at the table and spent a few minutes looking at the map. He felt restless, wishing they could have made it to the river. It would've been great to have been able to have some nice fresh trout for supper. He got up and went outside and found Danny had fallen asleep against the side of the bus, the book lying at his feet.

He felt in his pocket for the fishing line and the couple of flies and thought he'd just walk a little way further down the laneway. Maybe he'd be able to make his way to the river alone. He wouldn't stay long.

CHAPTER 43

Charlie started down the laneway carefully stepping over several water-filled ruts. He thought the river couldn't be far, judging by the map in town. He'd only gone a short distance when he rounded a bend and was confronted by a sign that read, *Private Driveway – Trespassers Shot – Survivors Prosecuted*. He hesitated, not sure if he dared go any further. Just beyond the sign he caught sight of a battered yellow mailbox on a post surrounded by a clump of tall thistles. The name M. Levinson was roughly painted in black lettering. He peered beyond a small cluster of pines and gasped. Was that a caboose? The trees swayed in the breeze revealing part of the faded white lettering just below the roof-line – *Northern Pacific – Milwaukee Road*. He took a couple more steps to try to get a better look and, as he did, the shriek of a train whistle and the rumble of a fast-approaching heavy freight made him leap into the narrow ditch beside the laneway.

If it weren't for the fact that there were no tracks, he would have been convinced the train was about to round the bend in front of him. It sounded like a steam engine rather than a diesel. The roar and rumble suddenly ceased as quickly as it had started, leaving only the breeze rustling the trees. He pressed on and the laneway opened to reveal the caboose standing in the middle of a rough patch of grass on a short section of rail. Smoke was rising from the narrow smokestack on the roof.

The caboose was different than the ones he'd ridden. It was a bay-window type. A side window jutted out from the middle of the caboose like a small bay-window on a house. He knew there'd be an exact copy on the opposite side. The ones he'd ridden on all those years had a cupola look-out at the back above the roof for surveying the train.

He was studying the outlines of it when he caught sight of a movement on the platform at the end of the car and a gruff voice yelled, "Hold it right there! Guess ya can't read or you don't hold your life in much regard. Whadda ya want?"

Charlie took a step back as he stared at a tall burly man who was pointing a shotgun at him.

"Take it easy," Charlie called nervously. "I don't want to bother you. I just couldn't resist taking a closer look at your *brainbox* when I caught sight of it through the trees." Charlie was hoping that the guy with the shotgun was an ex-railway man like himself and he'd used the term *brainbox* as a gamble. He was hoping this guy may have been a conductor. The conductor was supposed to be the brains of the train, smarter than the engineer. He could have used other terms, like clown wagon, doghouse, monkey wagon, glory wagon and others besides caboose. Those derogatory names for a caboose probably all came from engineers.

I hope to God he wasn't an engineer and I've just insulted him, he thought to himself. "I rode one of these for many years," he called out hastily, "but not the bay-window model."

"You sound like one of them damn easterners from Maine. Someplace like that. Where you from?"

"New Brunswick."

"That in Germany?"

"No. New Brunswick, Canada. East coast."

"You say you're a railroad man?"

"Yeah," Charlie replied.

"What railroad?"

"Canadian Pacific."

"Come on up." Charlie noted he lowered the shotgun but didn't put it down.

Charlie walked across the grass and climbed onto the platform as the man waved him to a battered chair, then quickly pushed the door of the caboose open. He snatched out another chair for himself with one hand, while holding firmly onto the shotgun. He sat with his back to the door and laid the shotgun across his knees, still eyeing Charlie suspiciously.

Charlie wasn't sure of his age, but guessed he was some years older than himself. He still had a full head of grey hair that almost reached his shoulders and a white, well-trimmed beard. Charlie noted his brown, remarkably clear, piercing eyes as the man studied him.

"You usually greet people with a shotgun?" Charlie asked tentatively.

"Them that pay no mind to my sign," he said gruffly.

"What in hell was that freight that I was sure was coming right at me? Steam engine. Maybe a 440."

"Close. A 460. You ever ride behind one of those?"

"Yeah. A few," Charlie replied. "All across Canada, 'til they introduced the diesels. Missed the steam for a long time afterwards."

"Me too. I spent most of my life ridin' this two-bit piece of railroad up and down this valley. It joined the Milwaukee Road at Ringling. Took a couple of rides cross the country as far as Chicago on that line. Just a visit, didn't stay long. Couldn't abide the city. Liked this valley, though. Grew up here, as did my folks goin' back to when this valley was first settled."

He took the rifle and propped it behind him against the door. "Retired just before they shut this line down in 1980. Got this little piece of land handed down from my auntie Jane. All that's left of the family's sheep and cattle farm. A good bit of land. Sold off piece by piece in hard times."

The door to the caboose creaked open with the breeze. Charlie jumped and held his breath when the shotgun clattered onto the floor.

The old man noticed Charlie's sudden start. "Not loaded. Just for show." He turned and picked it up again and rested it against the corner of the platform. "It's like my freight train. My alarm system. Forgot to turn it off this mornin'. I had some trouble with kids some time back. Spray painted my van. A fella in town rigged the alarm up for me. Haven't had any trouble since. You happen'd to snag my trip wire. Nearly scared the crap outta one of those Fish 'n' Wildlife fellas once when he did the same. Came to try to make me get a fishin' permit. Damn fools. My family have fished this river since Adam. Hell, I'm doin' all the jawin' here. I just made a fresh pot of coffee. You want a cup? Then I'll listen to yer excuse about not being able to understand my sign. And, dependin' on yer excuse, I'll decide whether I'm gonna have to shoot ya or not." He laughed. "But first we'll have a cup of coffee. Name's Magnus Levinson. Yours?"

"Charlie Bannister."

Levinson showed Charlie around his caboose and they debated the merits of the bay-window model versus the cupola style Charlie was familiar with.

"See for yourself," Levinson said. "You got a clear view all along the side of the train on both sides, easier to see shiftin' loads and hot boxes." He had Charlie sit on both sides of the caboose to test it out. He'd kept the original seats. The land in front of the caboose sloped gently and Charlie got a clear view of the river. "Milwaukee Road converted over nine-hundred cabooses in the '30s from cupola to bay-windows. Knew what they were doin'," Levinson continued.

The rest of the caboose had been outfitted with a comfortable living room and small kitchen with a decent electric cooking stove, although Levinson had also retained the original wood stove. Charlie was familiar with it. It had no legs and was bolted directly to the floor. It had a lip on its top surface to keep coffee pots from sliding off.

"I have a small electric heater, but this old stove keeps things nice and snug in winter. Was a wood stove originally, then they converted them to kerosene, but I couldn't abide the smell and switched 'er back to wood. Nothin' smells better 'n' wood, and lots of it around here."

The rest of the interior had been fitted with a tiny bathroom complete with shower and the bedroom, although compact, was well planned with a bunk bed and storage cupboards. Charlie admired everything.

"Yup. Sure glad that Milwaukee Road went over to the bay-windows," Levinson said. "I think I'd be none too happy scramblin' up those damn steps to the cupola to look down at the river. Nowadays, my old legs ain't as nimble as they used to be."

"It's damn nice," Charlie said. "Comfortable as all get-out. How did ya come by it?"

"Got a good deal when they were gettin' rid of the old cabooses. Modernization. Phaw! Just afore I retired. Had an old shack here then, but I got me a good crew to lay in the bit of rail and some Milwaukee Road boys with some heavy liftin' equipment and a truck. Yep. I just had to have some rail under her. Wouldn't have felt right. Keeps 'er out of the damp and mud. Cost me nuthin' to get 'er here, just had to come up with the money for the car itself. Another coffee?"

They reminisced about railways for a while then Levinson said, "You didn't say why you're out in this neck of the woods so far from New Brunswick."

"Travelling now." Charlie said. "Travelling with some friends. Heading south."

"Hmmf. That what they call snowbirds nowadays? Runnin' away for the winter?"

"Not exactly, but running away of sorts."

Charlie explained a little about their trip to the Grand Canyon and how three of them had been livin' in an old folks nursing home. "Got a small type of camper-bus. No real plans. Just want to make it as far as the Grand Canyon."

"Hate to be shut up in some nursin' home," Levinson said. "Hell, I'm eighty-eight now. Hope I die right here in my old caboose when the time comes. Think I'd shoot myself before I let them drag me off to some home. So you were thinkin' of fishin? Didn't see no rod or tackle. What were ya gonna do, tickle the fish to death?"

"No." Charlie laughed. "All I got is this." He pulled out the two flies and the spool of fishing line

"Holy crap! Ya might as well try ticklin' them for all the good that'd do. Come on. Let's go down to the river. I got a rod ya can try."

"I got no license," Charlie said.

"Me neither. Never have and never will."

They stood on the bank and Levinson tried a few casts before turning the rod over to Charlie. "Used to belong to my grandpappy. Fished all my life on this river. This little piece of land was part of the Levinson farm. Not much left of it as I was growin' up. The old homestead was pretty ramshackle, fallin' down around our ears. My daddy was a good man, but he was no real farmer and it was always a struggle. During the Depression, we couldn't get nuthin' for our sheep. Nobody had any money and before I finished school, my Daddy up and sold out.

"Only piece left was this piece my dad's sister had moved onto when she had some fallin' out with the family. She lived in an old log house, no more 'n' a shack. Same one I lived in when she passed the land onto me. Always had a soft spot for me, Aunt Jane did. Made sure she hung on here when the rest of the Levinson clan went their separate ways. We moved to St. Paul but there was little work, and when Dad died, just after I finished school, my mom, my older brother and me moved back here with Aunt Jane. Things got better and I got a job with the railroad. Eventually, when Mom and Aunt Jane passed on, I found myself alone here. Took a time, but I worked myself up to conductor. Did a spell in Korea, but got through that and came back here. Loved this valley. Railroadin' and fishin' was all I needed. Ya got one bitin'.

Gently now. Probably a brown trout. There. That's it. Let 'er run a little. Take yer time."

Charlie landed a nice size brown trout that Levinson declared was a good four pounder. Then he took the rod to have a turn and Charlie stepped away a little to play around with his fishing line and one of the flies. Levinson was reeling in a fish when Charlie felt a tug on his fishing line. With no reel he was forced to let some of the line out and play the fish as best he could. To his delight and to Levinson's surprise, Charlie eventually hauled in a good size rainbow.

"Nice fish. There's some eatin' on that," Levinson said.

"So you don't have to have a permit to fish from your own land?" Charlie asked.

"You do. Don't make no difference, you own yer land or not. Everyone around here supposed to have one. I'm a special case."

"How come?"

"Fish 'n' Wildlife boys tried to force me to get a permit. Took me to court up in Neihart 'bout 10 years ago. Judge was Ben Jackman. Passed on, now. But Ben and me went way back. Went to school together here and fished this very same piece of river. This is how it went.

When I showed up in court, Ben says, 'Magnus. How long you been livin' on that piece of land of yours?'

Pretty much since I was born, I say. 'Cept for a short spell in the Korean War, yer honour.

Judge says, 'I heard tell you got a Purple Heart in Korea and lost a brother.'

Yes sir, I says. My brother Conrad.

'And how long have the Levinson family lived on that piece of land you have?'

Since we first come into this country, yer honour, I say. Must be near 150 years ago. Maybe nearer 200.

'Why I heard tell you had a great-grandfather who fought with Custer at the Battle of the Little Bighorn.'

My grandpa, yer honour, Abe Levinson. That's what's wrote down in the family bible.

'Oh yes, your grandfather,' Ben Jackman says. 'And he fought with General Custer?'

Yes sir, I says."

"What year was that?" Charlie interrupted.

"It was June 25th, 1876," Levinson answered.

"But weren't all of Custer's men wiped out?"

"I reckon that's so. But let me finish my story.

Judge Ben asked me, 'How long is fishin' season for you, Magnus?'

I tell him – 'Bout six, seven months. River's frozen over 'bout three months and I don't usually fish 'til the ice is long gone and the weather improves. Gettin' too old to be standin' out there in cold weather.

'And how many fish would you say you usually catch in a week during those seven months of your fishin' season, Magnus?'

Well your honour... maybe three at the most.

'So that'd be some 90 fish in a year? That about right?'

I tell him that's probably pretty close.

'Well now,' Ben says, *'I don't think you're gonna fish out that old Smith River are you? You're not plannin' to start up one of those fishin' lodges or anythin'?'*

No siree, I say. Just me fishin'.

Then Ben turns to the Fish 'n' Wildlife fella and says, *'Well, I don't see a problem here. Here's a man whose family has been livin' on this land by the Smith River since before the river was the Smith River — Hell, his own grandfather fought with General George Custer at the Little Bighorn. He himself fought for this country in Korea and he was awarded the Purple Heart. Lost a brother there too. He and his family have done a lot for this country. I think the State of Montana can afford to let Magnus catch a few fish for his own use from the Smith River without havin' to buy a permit. With the powers vested in me, I hereby grant him permission to fish the Smith River where it borders his own property, for the rest of his life. Any objections?'*

There were none."

"That's a great story," Charlie said. "This grandfather of yours — where did he come from?"

"Born in these parts. I think his father might've come from Poland or Hungary, some place like that. My father swore he was Jewish. Jacob Levinson. Don't really know. Probably landed in the east and moved west sometime."

"Your grandfather really fought with General Custer?" Charlie asked.

"Well it's like this." Levinson scratched his beard. "I don't know how many people really knew the story. Probably a few. Ben Jackman might have heard part of it. When he asked if my grandpa fought with Custer, I had sworn to tell the truth. Ya see it depends on what ya mean when you say, 'fought with.' I fought with my brother lots when we were kids. So when Judge Jackman asked if my grandpa fought with General Custer, I said he did. It's just that he fought on the side of Sittin' Bull." Magnus burst into laughter.

"What! How?" Charlie asked.

Levinson was still chuckling. "The story, as us Levinsons knew it, was that my grandpa Levinson somehow got friendly with the Sioux — got hitched up to one of the Indian women. So you see I'm really part Indian. When Custer arrived, my grandpa was livin' with Sittin' Bull's people. So my grandpa did fight with Custer. And beat him."

"God! That's crazy."

"Crazy or not, that's the truth as I know it. Had enough fishin'? Soon be gettin' on for supper time."

"Jeez! What time is it?"

Levinson pulled out an old conductor's watch not unlike the one Charlie had owned. "Goin' on for four o'clock."

"Hell! The others don't know where I am. I didn't realize I'd been here nearly that long. I'd better go!"

"Where you got your camper?"

"Just a little further down the laneway."

"Bring 'em down here. It's a fine evenin'. I got a fire-pit out back. You're welcome to stay and cook up the fish. There should be enough here for a feed."

"Thanks, Magnus. I'll go get them and we'll take you up on your offer."

Charlie hadn't gone far when he ran into Danny.

"Thank God you're okay! Betty's been worried sick. So have I. We didn't know where the hell you'd gone. You've been gone so long, I thought you might've drowned."

"I caught some nice fish. They're down by the river"

"That'll make Betty happy. Maybe she won't give you hell nearly as bad."

"That's what I'm hoping," Charlie said.

"Oh thank God, Charlie!" Betty called out when she saw them approaching. She and Caroline were standing outside The Smucker when Danny and Charlie rounded the bend.

She gave Charlie a hug. "I was sick with worry, you bugger. Where the hell did you get to?"

"Catching fish for supper," he said, as Caroline said, "There you are, you."

"We're invited to come cook them just down the lane a ways. Met another old railway man. Lives in a caboose. Told him we'd be right back."

"Great," Danny said. "Let's drive The Smucker there. Hope we don't get stuck in the mud."

"What in tarnation do you call that?" Levinson asked when they pulled into his yard.

"We call it The Smucker," Charlie said, as he introduced the others.

"I thought my caboose was small but four of ya campin' in that! Must be the way sardines feel in one of those cans. Just gettin' the fire started. Come on."

They grilled the fish over the fire. There was plenty for everyone, and Levinson also added some fine potatoes to roast from his vegetable garden.

"Young fella comes to help me plant in the spring and get the last of it into my root cellar. I give him some of the crop."

After Levinson had proudly shown Betty, Danny and Caroline around his caboose, they sat around the fire until it started getting dark. They'd only been invited to cook their supper, but when Levinson had asked about them camping,

THE GRAND GETAWAY   179

Betty admitted they were mostly camping in the bush, being short of cash. They were relieved and grateful when he suggested they camp there overnight.

In spite of the initial welcome Charlie had received from him and Levinson's obvious aversion to strangers showing up on his property, it soon became clear that he had warmed to them, especially Caroline who had reached out and stroked his beard, and repeated, "Soft, soft," making him chuckle.

Before they all went off to bed, Levinson had heard about Betty's dream of seeing the Grand Canyon again, life at Cavandish, and how Caroline had named their little bus The Smucker.

CHAPTER 44

After Betty produced for breakfast what Magnus Levinson called the best damn potato-cakes he'd tasted in a long time, and they'd cooked up some bacon that he had on hand to go with them, they gratefully accepted his hospitality to stay one more night.

Levinson admitted he was not used to entertaining visitors. "However, I guess I could put up with you 'til tomorrow. Most people who wander down my lane are either busy-bodies or young kids up to no good. There's one or two who come here that I tolerate, besides the young fella who helps me with the garden. There's a lady named Martha, trying her damnedest to save my soul. Quotes me bits from the Bible. Brings her own herbal tea. Won't drink coffee. We sometimes argue a little. Keeps my brain alive. Tells me that Jesus and the disciples only drank unfermented grape juice. I got her riled up when I asked her if she thought that after a hard days fishin' on the Sea of Galilee, Mark or Peter said somethin' like, 'Can't wait to get ashore and have a few belts of that unfermented grape juice.' Still, I let 'er come. Mainly because she always brings me great chocolate chip cookies that she bakes. Never seems to get discouraged. But if there is a God, I guess you could say we've left each other alone. Maybe he read my sign." He chuckled.

"Then there's another lady. Social worker, I think she calls herself. Looks in on me now and again. Says people worry about me being out here all on my own. Tells me there's a nice rest home in Neihart I could move into if I wanted. Here's you all runnin' away from one of those places and this woman tryin' to talk me into one.

"I still drive into town about once a week for mail, groceries. I'm kinda worried now that Doc Wilson passed on two years ago and my license is due up in another six months. I bet the new doc in town, young whipper-snapper, won't prompt me on the eyesight test, same way Doc Wilson did. Well that's enough talkin' from me for now. You ready to go fishin' boys? I might have another old rod in my tool shed out back."

Betty said she'd tidy up and then she and Caroline were going to take a shower, seeing that Magnus had kindly shown her how to operate it. "Caroline and I will come down to the river and see how you're doin' a little later."

Charlie and Danny fished from the bank after Levinson had given Danny a few lessons on casting, and then he sat watching them from an old battered lawn chair he kept stashed in the bushes.

"How long ya plannin' on stayin' at the Grand Canyon, once ya get there?" he asked.

Danny and Charlie looked at each other.

"It's something we haven't talked about much," Danny said. "But we're going to have to."

"Yeah," Charlie agreed. "We didn't really think we'd ever get anywhere near the Grand Canyon. The whole thing more or less started as a bit of a gag. We were bored out of our minds at the home.

"Betty kept on pushin' us," Charlie continued, "and when we got the old bus and heard that Caroline might be shipped off to some other place, things steamrolled real fast. We couldn't have done it without Danny, here. Helped a lot on the outside. Gettin' The Smucker fixed up a bit, 'n' stuff like that. So here we are. But no real plans. Just want to make it to the Grand Canyon. Make Betty happy. After that? Who knows?"

"Hmm... but..." Levinson began. "Hey! I think you got a bite there Danny."

The fish took the fly and with Levinson coaching from the lawn chair, Danny landed a nice trout.

After the excitement of landing the fish, Levinson probed again. "None of my business, mind, but how long ya think ya can bum around the country in that tin can ya call The Smucker, especially as Betty says yer real short of cash?"

"We're hoping that problem might be solved soon," Charlie said. He explained how their pension money should be available in a couple of weeks. "We'll have enough for food and gas then, anyway."

"Well, ya sure as hell won't be able to hole up in a campground at the Grand Canyon for long. They won't let ya make any campground a permanent place t' live. You'll either have to keep movin' or find some place to bed down for the winter, anyway. Maybe rent a space in some RV park, someplace like that."

He stopped talking and they concentrated on fishing, but Danny knew that if they made it to the Grand Canyon, Betty, Charlie and himself were going to have to discuss what would happen after that.

They had caught three fish by the time Caroline and Betty joined them at the river and Levinson suggested they take a coffee and bathroom break. He also suggested that they try to catch some fish that evening to take with them, if they weren't sick of eating it. "I could put 'em in my fridge overnight and ya could pick up a bag of ice in town when ya leave tomorrow."

Levinson found a jar of Smucker's blackberry jam in his fridge to spread on the scones Betty had baked in his oven for breakfast, and he complemented Betty several times, eating five of them himself. They'd all had a good laugh when Caroline read the Smucker's label over and over as soon as she saw it.

Before they left, they studied their map and proposed going south as far as a tiny place called Emigrant. They'd look for a place to stop near there overnight and have a look around Livingston on the way. Levinson said it was a real touristy place nowadays. Betty said she remembered the name Livingston and thought she and Arnie Thorkleson might have stopped there for ice cream.

"If we can find a place near Emigrant, it's just a short distance across the border into Wyoming and then we reach Gardiner, the north entrance to Yellowstone National Park," Danny said.

"You're gonna have to pay a fee to go through the park," Levinson said. "Going around it would cost ya more in gas."

"Do you think maybe we could camp in Yellowstone just one night?" Betty asked. "Me and Arnie camped there and saw Old Faithful. I'd like to do that again."

"Let's see how much it costs," Charlie said.

They were well stocked up with fish, having caught another three the night before. Levinson insisted on topping up their vegetable supply by giving them some carrots and potatoes from his garden and a few of his tomatoes.

"You're goin' to be tired of eatin' fish."

Betty gave him a hug. "You're a good man, Magnus Levinson."

"Well, thanks Betty. I figure I've gone 'n' done enough jawin' to last me 'til at least spring. You get back this way, look me up, if I'm still here. I'll be 'bout ready for some more company by then. Hope things turn out for all of ya. Good luck to ya." He shook hands with Charlie and Danny and gave Caroline a quick hug. As they pulled away, Caroline was waving goodbye.

CHAPTER 45

"How much money do we have left, Betty?" Danny asked.

They had just bought ice and milk in White Sulphur Springs and needed to get some gas for The Smucker.

"We have exactly $104.10."

"That's not nearly enough money to get us all the way to the Grand Canyon," Danny said. "We're not likely to find too many people like Magnus Levinson willing to put us up and, after Yellowstone, it might get harder to find places to hide out without paying. It looks like there's more populated areas coming up once we get into Utah."

"We'll have to see how it goes," Betty said. "We have enough food right now anyway to keep us goin'. Every day that goes by gets us closer to gettin' our pensions. We'll just have to find places to stop. We can't go rushin' to the Grand Canyon and have no money to camp there. I was hopin' for a night in Yellowstone and maybe one in Bryce Canyon in Utah if we had enough money."

"It burns my ass," Charlie said, "that Bill Darlington has a whole month of our money right now. We would've even had enough money to stay in a couple of motels, maybe eat in a few restaurants."

"Well, it's no good eatin' your heart out or burnin' your ass, either," Betty said. "What's done is done. We've done pretty well up to now. Let's enjoy the journey. You had a great time with Magnus. Let's get some gas and see what this day brings."

Danny filled the tank to just half, telling Betty and Charlie that with less weight they might get a little better gas mileage. That brought their total cash on hand down to $89.10. He was still keeping quiet about the extra $20 that Gail had given him at Malone's, holding it back until they desperately needed it. He worried that they would need it real soon.

They had just passed through Ringling and Danny was coasting down any hills on his plan to save on gas. "This is pretty country," Betty said. "Magnus said they made a couple of movies down this way."

"I think I saw the movie *A River Runs Through It*, on TV," Charlie said, "about fly-fishing, but I didn't see that other one, *The Horse Whisperer*."

"Well if we run into a film company makin' another movie around here, maybe we'll get hired. We can provide them with a great cast of characters." Betty laughed. "Hey, put on some music."

Charlie, sitting up front with Danny, searched through their tape collection. He found a Barbra Streisand album and put it on. She was singing *People (Who Need*

People) when Betty started a discussion by saying that everybody needs people and Charlie asked, "What about Magnus?"

"Him too," Betty said. "We just happened along at the right time when he needed some company. The fact you were an old railway man helped. He just needed to talk, and after two days with us he was happy enough to have us move on. He also needs that woman who brings him cookies and talks about religion, and that social worker. He just doesn't need people as regular as some. Can you play that song again? I like it. She's a lovely singer."

Although they were going below the speed limit, they reached Livingston before noon. They found a park with picnic tables and Betty brewed up some coffee. They locked up The Smucker and decided to explore the town on foot.

"This town is sure nice," Betty said. "I'm sure it's changed since Arnie and I were here. It's a lovely day, not too hot. We'll find a bathroom and then play at being tourists."

Charlie was happy to find another restored railway station but disappointed to find that the museum inside, where he could have spent a couple of happy hours, had closed for the season just the week before. "Just my luck," Charlie said, "and it was free too."

In Sacajawea Park, alongside the Yellowstone River, they had lunch at a picnic table, making sandwiches with some of the tomatoes Magnus had given them and the last of their bread.

They hung around the riverside park for a couple more hours and found a large statue of an Indian woman on horseback that explained the park's name. Sacajawea was a guide for the Lewis and Clark expedition which had passed through the area in 1805-1806.

Betty took Caroline to watch some ducks swimming on the river but eventually, all agreed they should move on as they were getting restless.

They drove slowly south on highway 89 again, everyone quiet as they listened to Willie Nelson singing *Always On My Mind*.

Betty said, "I love this song. God, this scenery is beautiful."

What was on Danny's mind was the talk they'd have to have about what would happen after they reached the Grand Canyon, and he was determined to have that conversation soon.

They drove through what Charlie said was called Paradise Valley, according to the tourist information brochure he'd picked up in Livingston. They stopped often, just to admire the scenery, but when they reached Emigrant and drove slowly through, they began seriously looking for somewhere to stop.

"I think we'll need to find somewhere for at least a couple of nights," Charlie suggested. "Once we reach Yellowstone Park, we're gonna have to shell out some money just to drive through it."

THE GRAND GETAWAY   185

They had passed a picnic and campsite area where they would have had to pay to camp, and they were anxiously scanning the terrain looking for someplace free, when Betty said, "This place we're passin' has a real estate sign. One hundred-fifty acres. And there's an old farm-house just comin' up. Let's turn in and take a look."

They coasted down a small hill and came to a tree-lined driveway on their right. The house they'd seen from the top of the hill couldn't be seen from where they were now.

Danny braked and turned slowly into the driveway.

"Let's hope there's no one like Magnus Levinson waiting for us with a shot-gun," Charlie said.

"There won't be," Betty said. "If they expect to sell the place, they got to expect visitors comin' to look at it."

"Maybe the real estate company phones ahead to warn them," Charlie said. "What are we gonna say when we get to the house and someone comes out and asks what we want?"

"We'll ask for directions," Betty said. "Tell 'em we're lost."

They turned a bend in the drive-way that opened into a large farm yard. The house, a long, rambling, two-storey white clap-board with peeling paint was angled to give it the best view of the range of mountains to the west. A narrow veranda ran along the front and the side of the house. Set behind it were a few unpainted out-buildings and a large barn. Danny stopped The Smucker and turned off the engine.

"Looks like it was a nice house in its day," Charlie said.

"Still is," Betty said. She had come forward to stand behind Danny and Charlie to get a better look. "It just needs a good coat of paint."

"You think it's empty?" Charlie asked.

"Most likely," Betty said. "There's nobody comin' out to see who we are. They would've heard us. And there's no dogs. Every farm has a dog. And a few chickens scratchin' around. Let's get out and just walk around. If anyone comes out, we'll say we're lost. Where are we tryin' to get to again?"

"Gardiner, then Yellowstone," Danny said.

They all climbed out and stood in the yard. "God what a great view," Betty said. "Wonder what they're askin' for the place?"

"You thinking of buying" Charlie asked.

"It's as good a reason as askin' for directions," Betty said. "We're just takin' a look."

"Think we should knock?" Charlie asked. "We can't just go nosing around. If someone is inside, they might think we're casing the place 'n' call the cops. Or maybe they're just in town and they'll be back at any minute. Maybe the dog died, or they took it to the vet."

"Oh, Charlie!" Betty said. "We're just lookin' at this place that's for sale. And it's empty."

"I think Betty's right," Danny said. "Someone would've come out by now. But the right thing to do would be to knock on the door. I'll try that."

He stepped onto the veranda and approached the front door as the others waited. He knocked loudly with his fist, then listened. There were no sounds, so he tried once more, then turned to the others. "Guess there's no one home. And there's a good layer of dust on this old rocker here, nobody's sat in that for a while." He indicated an old rocking chair to the right of the door. "Why don't you wait here and I'll check out the other farm buildings."

Danny walked across the yard at the rear of the house and poked his head into a couple of sheds. The doors were unlocked and all the sheds were empty. He checked the barn last, but all he found were a few old bales of hay. He found a narrow flight of stairs along one wall leading to the loft and went up. He stepped to the opening at the front of the loft where an old pulley with a frayed rope running through it hung from a boom. He called to the others who were watching from the corner of the house.

"Nothing here. No machinery. Nothing. Looks like whoever lived here has moved away." He rejoined the others. "Let's move The Smucker beside the barn. We'll probably be okay for the night. There's an old outhouse out back. Hasn't been used in years. If anyone does show up, we'll use one of Betty's excuses, ask for directions or say we saw the real estate sign and just came to take a look."

They moved the bus and Danny hauled a bale of hay out of the barn to sit on and got out his book while Betty busied herself getting some fish cooked for supper. Caroline sat beside Danny on the bale while Charlie checked out the outhouse, then ambled down a small track leading to a hay field and a small wooded area.

When he came back, he went inside The Smucker to get something and then disappeared down the track again. Betty looked at him questioningly but Charlie said nothing. After supper they sat outside, using a couple more bales for seats and watched the sun go down behind the mountain range.

The next morning, right after breakfast, Charlie had disappeared again, but then returned quickly, stepping past Danny who was sitting in the doorway of The Smucker finishing a coffee.

Betty was heating some water for herself and Caroline to have a wash while Charlie rummaged in a drawer in the kitchen.

"What are you up to Charlie?" she asked.

"Not much," he replied. "Too bad we're not near a river. I could try fishing again."

"You'll be sick of eatin' fish," Betty said, "by the time we get through what we have. We've got enough for two more days at least. The ice has held up well and the fish will be fine."

"Sounds good," Charlie said, slipping a sharp knife into his pocket when Betty turned her back.

Betty, Danny and Caroline were sitting on the bales of hay, enjoying the sunshine when Charlie returned carrying something.

"What on earth have you got there?" Betty gasped. "Don't tell me that's road kill! There's no way I'm cookin' road kill!"

"It's not road kill!" Charlie laughed.

"It's chicken? You found a chicken. I thought there weren't any on this farm," Betty said.

"It's rabbit. It's fresh. It'll be great roasted."

"Rabbit! How in hell did you catch that? Poor thing. Although I have eaten roasted rabbit once on our farm years ago. It was good. You skinned and cleaned it?"

"I did. Saw a few rabbits last night running around the back of those woods. Figured I'd try making a couple of snares with that fishing line I had. Did it years ago when I was a kid. Didn't know if I could remember how, but it worked. And I found a fire pit at the back of the house with an old grill. We can roast it over that for tonight's supper. Make a change from fish."

"We'll tell Caroline it's chicken," Betty said.

Charlie's rabbit was a great success and they sat around the fire-pit long into the evening.

Danny said, "Our excuse that we're just looking for directions isn't going to be too believable with us sitting here on bales of hay from the barn, Caroline sitting in the rocking chair and us feasting on the wildlife."

Danny was going to bring up the topic of the plan for beyond Grand Canyon, but he didn't want to spoil the mood. Betty was pleased with Charlie's success, and Charlie was basking in the glow.

It was about two hours after lunch on their third day. They had eaten the last of the fish. Charlie had managed to snare another rabbit and they were looking forward to roasting it for supper. They had cleaned up and were sitting outside The Smucker when Danny said, "Sounds like someone's coming."

They listened and heard a vehicle coming fast and, almost at the same time, noticed a cloud of dust filtering through the trees on the driveway.

"Quick," Charlie said, jumping to his feet. "Let's try to make it look like we've just arrived."

"Too late now," Danny said. "Sit down. Best not to panic. They're here."

The vehicle, a fairly old brown camper-van with large side windows, had slowed as soon as it had appeared around the bend in the driveway. It hesitated for a moment, then moved ahead, coming to a stop before it reached the house. The engine was switched off but no one got out.

"Who do you think it is?" Betty asked.

"No idea," Danny said, "but I think they're surprised to see us here. Probably have no more right to be here than we have."

As he finished speaking, the front passenger door opened and a slim long-haired blonde girl wearing a short red dress stepped out, and was quickly joined by the driver who came around the front of the van. He was a tall muscular guy wearing jeans and a blue shirt. He had a blue bandana tied on his head.

"Pirates," muttered Charlie.

Two other figures, another man and woman, stepped out from the camper-van and all four, led by the bandana wearing guy, walked towards where they sat.

They were all young. The other girl had long dark hair and was wearing some kind of a raggedy, purple garment that looked like something that had gone through a shredder. She was taller than the other girl and was showing a lot more leg. The fourth member of the group was a slim man with long, dark hair and about a four-day growth of beard.

They stopped a few feet away and the young fellow with the bandana smiled and said, "Hi. You caretakers? Keeping an eye on this place?"

"In a manner of speaking," Betty said cautiously. "Who are you?"

"We're *Cockatoo*."

"Cock – a – what?" Charlie asked.

"*Cockatoo*. We're an Indie band."

"An Indian band? Charlie asked. "This isn't Indian land, is it?" he muttered to Danny who was sitting next to him. "They don't look Indian," he whispered.

The blonde in the red dress heard, and chuckled. "We play music. He's Dax." She indicated the blue bandana-clad guy. "I'm Alexa and this is Sapphire and Reuben." She indicated the two behind her, who nodded.

Betty introduced their group.

"So what kind of music do you play?" Charlie asked. "East Indian music?"

Alexa chuckled again. "No. We'd call it soft rock. We're an Indie band, as in independent. We produced our first album ourselves."

"Actually," Dax interjected. "We were hoping to make a video for one of our songs right here, if we won't be disturbing you, that is. It's a great location. We checked it out last week."

"A video. You mean like a movie?" Betty asked.

"Yeah," Dax said. "Only real short. Just as long as the song. We pre-recorded the music, so we'll just be kinda miming we're playing our guitars and singing."

"Like air guitar," Danny said.

"Exactly."

"Sure," Betty said. "Go ahead. We'll watch if that's okay and we'll stay out of your way. Do you want us to move our bus behind the barn?"

"No," Dax said. "It's okay where it is right now. We're gonna film outside the house with the mountains in the background. Say, that's a great looking bus. Would you mind if we took a few shots of it? It would look great on the album cover." He turned to the others. "What do you guys think?"

"Yeah," Alexa said. "Totally. Great idea."

"Real cool," Reuben agreed.

"What's the name of the album gonna be?" Danny asked.

"*Runnin' on Empty*," Dax answered.

Charlie guffawed. "Yeah, our bus fits the bill."

"We have to wait 'til Luke gets here," Alexa explained. "He should've been here by now. He's gonna operate the camera. Hope he didn't get lost. We don't want to lose this light. Anyway, we'll get set up on the veranda, try out a few moves."

Dax walked back to their camper-van and drove it close to the house. The others followed, and Reuben started unloading a drum set while the girls pulled out guitars and slipped the straps over their shoulders. When Reuben had the drums set up on one corner of the veranda, Dax moved the van back from the house, then pulled out a large CD player and set it on a rack on top of the van and hooked up a couple of speakers to it, facing the house. An electrical cord ran from the CD player back to the van's dashboard. Dax walked back to the house carrying a guitar and consulted with the others who arranged themselves on the veranda, Reuben sitting on a stool behind the drums.

After a bit more discussion and with Alexa climbing up onto the veranda rail at one point, Dax walked over to the foursome at The Smucker.

"This is just a rough run-through but could one of you do us a favour? Luke hasn't shown up yet and we all have to be in position on the veranda when the music starts. We need someone to just press play on the CD player."

Danny volunteered and followed Dax back to the van. Dax had Danny stand with his feet inside the open door of the van so he could reach the CD player on the roof. He returned to the veranda and after a nod to everyone, gave Danny a thumb's up.

The music was loud, and Caroline jumped, then held her hands to her ears.

The lead was sung by one of the girls, while the others sang harmony and the chorus. The story, as far as they could make out, was about a girl leaving home to make her name as a singer in the city, being successful, but then realizing that was not the life she wanted and deciding to go home where her heart really was.

After about five run-throughs, with Danny resetting the CD each time and Dax and the others consulting on the action on the veranda, they stopped. Dax, looking frustrated, walked over to Danny and the two of them walked back to where Betty, Charlie and Caroline were sitting. The other members of the band followed.

"Luke hasn't shown up and we can't get hold of him on our cell-phone. Without him, we've no one to do the video-taping, so we'll probably pack it in."

"It's a bummer," Sapphire said. "We probably won't get another great day like this."

"Yeah," Alexa said. "What did you think of the song, anyway?"

"It sounded pretty good," Betty said. "I don't think I got all the words until I heard it the third time. That was you singin', Alexa? You have a great voice. All of you are good singers."

"Yeah," Danny said. "And all of you can sure play."

"Can I ask a question?" Betty asked. "Are you just gonna prance around on the veranda there for the whole song? How are you gonna show the whole story?"

"Well," Dax said. "We're going to have Alexa's name up in lights, and we're going to film that, plus a huge audience cheering as she sings alone, some big city shots, then maybe a shot of this house with no one in front of it, just the house and the mountains, and then, of course, us singing the song. Luke was supposed to help us with the parts at the house."

"The bit about the name in lights and the audience and everythin' in the city sounds fine. When Alexa is singin', *I had to get away, I had to find my place*, is that where you'd show the farmhouse and the mountains?"

"Yeah," Dax said. "Something like that."

"Aren't you gonna show her leavin' home? Do you have the lyrics handy?"

Dax pulled a print-out of the lyrics from his back pocket and handed it to Betty. Danny and Charlie peered over her shoulder.

"What about someone waving goodbye? Your camper-van maybe pullin' up outside the house and Alexa climbin' into the van with her guitar on her shoulder?" Betty asked.

"When she's thinking of the boy she's left behind, are you gonna show him? When she sings, *And now I'm comin' home, And I'm hopin' he's still there?*" Danny added.

Sapphire said, "Hey! All that sounds really good. To hell with Luke. Let's figure it out ourselves. We'll save his fee. We have the camera here. We can do it ourselves."

"Who's gonna operate the camera?" Dax asked.

"It's not that hard," Reuben said. "I bet Danny could do that, too."

"Hang on," Dax said. "Let's figure out some of the scenes, to fit them into four and a half minutes."

By the time they finished, everyone including Caroline was involved. The girl, played by Alexa, left the farmhouse, suitcase in hand and guitar on her back, and climbed into the camper-van with the others hanging out the windows, and drove away from the house to the opening verse of the song. Caroline, wearing a blonde wig that Sapphire had in a costume box in their van, played her mother, and Betty coached her from the sidelines. She got Caroline to wave goodbye, but it took three takes because in the first two, Caroline was smiling and looking too happy.

Betty and Charlie played Alexa's grandma and grandpa, Betty sitting in the rocking chair on the veranda and Charlie standing beside her. Dax said they would fit the boyfriend in as a side-bar later as Alexa sang about him and they would film Alexa stepping off a Greyhound bus. After Reuben took over the camera and filmed

THE GRAND GETAWAY   191

the empty house and the empty rocking chair, they all walked down the driveway to watch Dax, minus his bandana, appear on the roadway to greet Alexa as she supposedly stepped off the bus and the two of them then wrestled the For-Sale sign out of the ground and threw it in the ditch.

Danny took the camera back again as *Cockatoo* did one more run-through of the song with all four playing on the veranda. As they watched the replays on the camera, Dax said, "We've got some great stuff here and with some good editing, and the few scenes we have to film later, I think it's a winner. You guys have been a great help."

Before they left, they took some photos of Betty, Caroline, Danny and Charlie and The Smucker on their cell phones. "We'll give you all credit on the album cover," Alexa said. "I guess you wouldn't happen to have an e-mail address? You're all just camping here, right?"

"Yeah we are," Betty agreed. "We're a bit short of cash right now, savin' on gas and campin' fees for a couple of days."

"Where are you headed?" Reuben asked.

"We're hoping to make it as far as the Grand Canyon," Danny said.

Alexa drew the other band members aside and they had a whispered conversation.

When they walked back Alexa said, "We're not exactly flush with cash ourselves, but we've come up with a few bucks. It's all the cash we have right now. We'd like you to take it. And here's a copy of our first CD. I hope you like it. We all autographed it." She hugged everyone and they said their goodbyes.

As they climbed into the van, Dax said, "I guess we'd better put the For Sale sign up again before we leave. Thanks again."

After they left, Betty said, "They were nice kids. I hope they're a big success. I hadn't the heart to tell them we don't have a CD player after they'd all autographed their CD for us. Maybe we'll buy one when we get our money. Those kids gave us 60 bucks. That should be enough for the entrance fee at Yellowstone, and a night's campin'. Maybe even a shower."

CHAPTER 46

"I remember that archway," Betty said. "Arnie and I rode under it on the motorcycle."

"It says here that Teddy Roosevelt laid the foundation stone for that archway in 1903 and its named after him, but Yellowstone Park was actually founded by Ulysses S. Grant way back in 1872." Charlie was reading from the brochure they'd just picked up at the park entrance.

Just a short distance inside the park they stopped for half an hour to view Mammoth Hot Springs, fascinated by the coloured terraces, trickling water and the rising steam.

"Did you know," Charlie said, "that Mammoth Hot Springs produce more than two tons of calcium carbonate every day? I guess that's the white stuff at the edges of the pools. I think they make toothpaste from calcium carbonate."

"Jeez Charlie! Is there gonna be a test on this? Let's just enjoy the place. I feel like you're makin' us all cram for some kind of exam," Betty said.

"Holy Crap!"

"What now, Charlie?"

"According to this bit about camping here, it seems we should've booked a spot online about six months ago. They fill up awful fast, even at this time of year, and we don't have enough money to be staying in a hotel. The Mammoth Springs Hotel just over there is over a hundred bucks a night or you could go for a luxury suite for near $500."

"That's a bummer," Danny said. "There's no way we're going to be able to hide out in the park. There's too many people and no doubt the rangers patrol this place day and night."

"Wait," Charlie said. "It does say that at Norris Campground they don't take reservations," Charlie said. "It's straight down the road we're on. It has flush toilets."

"I like the sound of that," Betty said. "Is it anywhere near Old Faithful? I want to see that again."

"Not too far," Charlie said.

"Let's have a look at the map. I think Charlie's right," Danny said. "Let's check out this Norris campsite and see if we can get a spot, then decide what we're gonna look at."

"Okay," Betty said. "But first I think Caroline and I should check out the flush toilets in the hotel here."

The campsite at Norris only had five spaces left when they got there. They checked in, paid a $14 fee for the night and found a spot.

"Arnie and I had no trouble pitching our little tent when we camped and I don't even remember havin' to pay," Betty said. "If we did, I bet it wasn't more than two

THE GRAND GETAWAY   193

bucks. I'll make us some coffee and we can plan out our little touristy trip. I hope we can see Old Faithful blow. I remember seein' it with Arnie. We only saw it once, but it was sure excitin'.'"

While they drank their coffee, they discussed whether they should continue round the circular road they were on. It would take them through Canyon Village, and they could view the canyon and the waterfalls on the Yellowstone River.

"If we go around this circle, we'll go through Mammoth Hot Springs again and come back down the road we just came in on. Let's see," Danny studied the map, "it's about 70 miles around to get back here and then Old Faithful is 30 miles south of us."

"Do you think we could make it around and still see Old Faithful before dark?" Betty asked.

"We should be able to, it's only eleven o'clock, but the traffic will be slow and we'll be stopping lots," Danny said. "Or we could head straight south to Old Faithful now and go round the next circle south by Yellowstone Lake. Tomorrow we have to head south through Grand Teton Park and find some place to stay, maybe south of Jackson. We won't be able to afford another night's camping here if we want to have some money for gas. We'd pass Old Faithful again on our way."

"That sounds like a plan," Betty said. "I think I remember some waterfalls, and if we can see Old Faithful again tomorrow that'd be great. We still have some of the money Cockatoo gave us, plus some of our savin's, so we're doing okay. I was hopin' we might have showers tonight, but maybe we shouldn't splurge. We'll be spendin' more on gas seeing the sights."

It was nearly 4:00 p.m. when they returned to Norris, and they had enjoyed the trip. They had seen both the Lower and Upper Falls and several viewpoints of the canyon, enough to satisfy everyone. Charlie had suggested that if they took the trail down to the Lower Falls, they could get a free shower from the spray, but Betty was quite happy with the views from above. Nobody had any intention of taking the Lower Falls trail for a real close-up view, although the trail was short. Even if they'd managed to get down, they weren't certain they'd be able to climb back up. Charlie, acting as travel guide, told them that the Lower Falls were twice as high as Niagara.

The noise of the falls, too, had been a bit scary for Caroline. Everyone had found the viewpoints dizzying enough, standing well back, all of them clinging tightly to each other.

They found out the expected times for the eruptions of Old Faithful and had a light supper in The Smucker before heading out for an early evening viewing. They passed several geysers on the way. They had to get to Old Faithful before it erupted or there'd be a lengthy wait until the next time. There was a huge crowd waiting but they found a spot, getting there just 10 minutes before the eruption. A couple gave up their seats on a bench to Betty and Caroline. Old Faithful didn't disappoint, and Caroline was repeating, "Whoosh, Whoosh, Whoosh," long after the geyser subsided.

"There's so much to see here, we could spend a whole week," Charlie said. "Couldn't we stop at Fountain Paint Pot? It's along the way. We just passed Grand Prismatic Spring. I'm hopin' to see that tomorrow. It's another must see." Charlie had made a list of the most important sights.

"What do you think, Danny?" Betty asked.

"Sure," Danny said. "It's still light out. We just won't be able to stop at everything on the way south tomorrow. We can take a quick look now if it's close to the road."

The sign for Fountain Paint Pot came up quickly and they pulled into the parking lot. They followed the boardwalk passing Silex Spring, full of all kinds of coloured algae and, just a few steps further on found Fountain Paint Pot. They stood with a small crowd watching gobs of coloured mud being thrown high into the air. Caroline clapped her hands and laughed at the sight.

Danny found a bench nearby and he and Caroline sat down on it while Charlie and Betty ambled on a little further. Caroline was talking quietly to herself. Danny was feeling a little tired from the long day. He expected they all were, but everyone seemed happy.

His thoughts turned to what had been gnawing at him. In the last few months his life had changed so much he could hardly believe it. Pete's death, and the day he'd wandered into Cavandish, now seemed like an eternity away. He couldn't have imagined in his wildest dreams that he'd be seeing some of the wonders of the world in the company of what you could say were really three other homeless people. Unless you considered The Smucker a home. It was really just a place to bed down with a few more comforts than a culvert. A culvert on wheels. He chuckled at the thought.

Back in Calgary he'd still be collecting bottles and cans, sleeping outside, or at The Shelter. Now he was seeing some great scenery, relaxing when he wasn't driving, reading some good books, and the food hadn't been half bad. He was certainly enjoying the company.

But what astounded him the most was the responsibility he'd taken on. Admittedly, before he'd met Charlie and the others, he'd felt responsible for Pete, looking after him as best he could, particularly when Pete was drinking. But this was different. Now he was, in a way, responsible for three other people. Just a short time ago, no one would have considered him a responsible person. He was homeless, had a drinking problem, kept company with people like himself, vagrants. He'd suffered from trauma that had often overwhelmed him, and his best friend had been a drunk.

But Betty, Charlie, and even Caroline had taken him in, made him feel part of a family. He realized some would say that Betty had taken him in in more ways than one. He was well aware that she had used him to implement her plan. He was a key, a cog that had made it all work so far. But he didn't mind. He was grateful she had. The whole thing was unbelievable. Even after they got The Smucker, it had seemed impossible.

He had taken on the task of doing his best to get them to the Grand Canyon. He'd see that through. He'd pretty well given his word on that. But if they made it, what then? Where did his responsibility end? He'd mentioned before that they could only stay at the canyon until the first snowfall, and then they'd be forced to move on. Betty was counting on their pension money seeing them through and improving things. But what then? They had to consider what happened after that. He could hardly believe he was worrying about the future when before all this had happened, he hadn't had much of one to worry about.

"There, there, over there," Caroline was pointing at some geyser spouting water and steam in the distance.

And then there was Caroline. How long could they go on looking after her properly? With everyone in an apparent good mood he thought that tonight would be a good time to hash things over.

His thoughts were interrupted by a loud yelp and he saw Charlie scamper out of sight round a bend in the boardwalk. He jumped to his feet as he heard him yell, "I'm coming! I'm coming, Betty! Danny! Danny! Come quick!"

He wanted to dash after Charlie and see what had happened, but he couldn't leave Caroline on the bench by herself. He grabbed her hands and pulled her to her feet. She smiled at him.

"Come on, Caroline. We have to go fast. Quick! Quick!"

He walked as quickly as he could, pulling Caroline along with him. There were no other people in sight on the boardwalk and it seemed to take a long time to get to the bend where he'd last seen Charlie.

They rounded the bend and Danny heard Betty and Charlie's voices before he spotted them. He thought they were arguing. Then he caught sight of Charlie kneeling down on the boardwalk reaching for something. It took him a second before he realized it was Betty. She was almost up to her shoulders in one of those bubbling mud-pots.

"Oh my God!" Danny muttered. "She'll be scalded. Come on Caroline, run." He dragged Caroline into a trot as he looked ahead, and, to his horror, saw Charlie suddenly jump into the mud beside Betty.

"Jeez, Charlie, I'm coming! I'm coming!"

When he got to where they were, he stopped and held Caroline back. Betty and Charlie were both facing him, up to their armpits in light-brown mud, and they were arguing. There was mud plastered in Betty's hair and on her face. Charlie didn't look much different. There were little eruptions of mud bubbling all around them.

"What the hell did you jump in for, you old fool?" Betty spluttered.

"I thought you were going under," Charlie said.

"I told you I was standin' on the bottom, but you didn't listen."

"I was sure you were going under. I was going to hold you up 'til Danny got here."

"And you didn't worry about being scalded by the boilin' mud?"

"You'd told me this mud was just warm, not scalding hot."

"Listen," Danny interrupted, still trying to catch his breath from running and with the adrenaline pumping through him. He was kneeling on the boardwalk holding Caroline's hand. "Stop arguing and listen! Charlie, try to move Betty a little closer to me so I can reach her hand."

Charlie pushed Betty forward but it was a struggle in the thick bubbling mud and they splashed a lot of mud about.

Betty reached a hand towards Danny, but it was just out of his reach.

"Try getting her a bit closer, Charlie." Danny said.

Charlie got behind Betty and pushed her forward.

"Jeez, Charlie! Do you have to put your hand there?"

"Sorry, Betty. Keep your mouth shut. I think this mud is poisonous. Don't swallow any."

"Too late now, Charlie. I already have."

"God! How bad is it?"

"Tastes just like Cavandish porridge." Betty started to laugh as Danny grabbed her hand and pulled her close to the boardwalk.

"Okay, Betty. Give me your other hand." He let go of Caroline and cautioned her not to move. "Charlie. I've got hold of Betty. You're gonna have to boost her up so I can drag her onto the boardwalk. Ready?"

"Yeah," Charlie spluttered, spitting some mud from his mouth.

With Danny pulling and Charlie heaving, Betty suddenly shot up out of the mud. Danny dragged her upper body onto the surface of the boardwalk.

"Charlie! I'm out! I'm out! Quit coppin' a feel of my ass, you dirty old bugger."

One more heave from Danny and she was completely onto the boardwalk.

"Jeez, I feel like a damn walrus or a beached whale you see on one of those nature shows you watch, Charlie." Betty laughed.

Danny helped her to her feet and she started scraping mud off her clothes in great gobs and flinging it off the boardwalk.

"Just watch Caroline, Betty, while I get hold of Charlie," Danny said.

Charlie pushed himself through the mud towards Danny and when Danny started to heave on Charlie, Betty bent and grabbed Charlie's elbow and lent a little more leverage. Charlie flopped up onto the boardwalk.

"God! We look a sight," Betty said. "Let's get the hell outta here before someone with one of those damn cellphones comes and takes our picture. We don't want to become the latest hit or whatever they call it on YouTube. Thanks, Charlie, for tryin' to rescue me. I'm an old fool stumblin' off the boardwalk like that." She gave Charlie a muddy kiss on his cheek.

Danny noticed that Charlie looked shaken, but Betty was laughing the whole thing off. He had to admit he was a bit stressed himself.

"Thanks, Danny. I won't kiss you. This stuff stinks." Betty giggled. "I'm sorry, but I think Charlie and I are gonna have to splurge and have showers. Otherwise we'll stink you out of The Smucker. Where are the nearest ones from here?"

Charlie knew. "There are public showers at Old Faithful Lodge, but I don't fancy walking into that place smelling like rotting eggs. There's some at Canyon Creek Campground, but we have to go through Norris again. That's the next closest place."

"Well, I think we'll keep the windows open while we drive there, and you two should get those muddy clothes off as quick as you can," Danny said. "Come on Caroline. Don't get too close to these two. They stink."

"Stinky, Stinky, Stinky," Caroline said, holding her nose.

CHAPTER 47

Danny jerked awake suddenly, a scream dying on his lips, Mick's headless body and Kenny's face grinning at him, blood squirting and pumping until Danny was struggling to keep from drowning in the waves of blood that engulfed him. He gasped for air as the nightmare faded and he recognized the roof of The Smucker just above his bunk. He lay there panting. He'd hadn't had that nightmare for months, and he wondered why no one was asking why he'd been screaming. He listened. Everything was quiet except for Caroline's soft murmurs as she talked to herself. He could hear Betty's raspy breathing and Charlie gently snoring. He guessed he'd been only screaming in his head.

The nightmare must have been triggered by what had happened the night before. They'd all seen the warning signs about keeping on the pathways and the dangers of the hot-steaming pools, mud pots and geysers. Charlie had mentioned that a number of people had been killed or injured falling into mud-pots or boiling hot springs. Even bison and elk died from the hydrogen sulfide fumes when they hung around the pools and mud-pots. *Yeah,* he thought, *Betty and Charlie had been damn lucky that the mud-pot they had fallen into was only warm and not boiling.*

It was getting quite dark when they'd got to bed after Charlie and Betty had showers at Canyon Creek and they'd driven back to Norris. They dumped their mud-covered clothes into a garbage container on the way to Canyon Creek but, even now, the stench of rotten eggs still lingered in The Smucker.

He slipped out of bed and quickly pulled on some clothes. Caroline smiled at him as he passed her, then continued talking quietly. He headed for the washrooms.

When he got back, Betty was up and on her way to the washrooms with Caroline.

"I'll get the coffee on," Danny said.

"Good," Betty said. "Charlie's still asleep. When Caroline and I get back I'll make some pancakes for breakfast."

The bustle of making breakfast, or the smell of the pancakes and coffee, roused Charlie and they all sat down to eat.

"You okay, Betty?" Charlie asked.

'I'm fine, Charlie. How 'bout yourself?"

"Fine. Fine."

"I'm sorry about last night," Betty said. "I turned too quick to look at somethin' and next thing I knew I was fallin' into the mud. I shouldn't have got mad at you. I know you jumped in to try to pull me out. Thanks." Betty patted Charlie's hand. "And thanks, Danny. Sorry we had to splurge for showers. I was hopin' to keep any money we could for gas."

THE GRAND GETAWAY   199

"That's okay, Betty," Danny said.

"God, we must've looked a sight." Betty chuckled. "How come that mud wasn't boilin'?"

"Don't know," Charlie said. "I guess the temperature varies a lot, or maybe that particular mud-pot was nearing the end of its time, maybe dying out. We were lucky. Otherwise we'd have been boiled like a couple of lobsters." Betty nodded.

There was silence around the table except for Caroline repeating, "Lucky, Lucky, Mucky, Smucky, Smucky," as she chased a piece of pancake round her plate. Betty helped her spear it.

Danny interrupted the silence. "That was a good breakfast, Betty. Thanks. I think we should get on the road as soon as we can. We have to be out of here by tonight unless we pay to camp again. Our entrance fee covered Grand Teton Park too, so we've got all day. We can stop along the way, see Old Faithful again."

Neither Charlie nor Betty wanted to stop at any more mud-pots as they headed south to Old Faithful, although they did stop briefly at Grand Prismatic Spring.

"This is Yellowstone's largest hot spring," Charlie announced. "I read that the temperature is 170 degrees Fahrenheit."

Betty shuddered. "I don't want to even think about it."

They admired the steaming pool with its red and yellow algae, and the brilliant blue of the pool, but they all stood well back, holding onto each other, the misadventures of the previous night still fresh in their minds.

They arrived at Old Faithful and viewed the geyser from a very safe distance. After watching it erupt once more and strolling through the massive lobby of the Old Faithful Inn with its enormous stone fireplace, they bought some more gas and headed south again.

Their mood seemed to lighten as they got on the road when Charlie put on the Van Morrison tape with *Bright Side Of The Road*.

They picked up a copy of the *Grand Teton Park Guide* at the north entrance to the park, and it wasn't long before they were skirting along the edge of Jackson Lake with great views of the Tetons. They stopped a few times to admire them. It didn't take long to reach Colter Bay on the shore of Jackson Lake, where they stopped briefly.

"We have to decide which road we want to take before we get to Moran Junction," Charlie said as he studied the brochure and map. "We can turn down the road to cross Jackson Dam to Jenny Lake, which is one of the highlights, and rejoin the main road at Moose Junction."

"Okay," Betty said. "Let's do that."

By the time they reached Jenny Lake, Charlie had given them a run-down on the history of the place. "The lake was named after the wife of Beaver Dick Leigh…"

"Beaver Dick, Beaver Dick, Beaver Dick," Caroline chanted.

"He was born in England and Jenny was a… was a Shoshone." Charlie snorted and started to chuckle and then burst into a loud guffaw and was joined by Betty as Caroline repeated again, "Beaver Dick, Beaver Dick." Danny's shoulders shook as he tried to control himself and The Smucker.

"Oh God. What a terrible name." Betty giggled.

"He was the first white man to live around here in about 1863," Charlie spluttered, "as he… scraped a living by trapping, hunting and… as a guide." He couldn't control another burst of laughter.

"Beaver Dick," Caroline said again.

"Okay Caroline," Betty attempted to get herself under control. "I think we've heard that joke before."

"Beaver Dick."

"Oh Caroline. Stop now. If you make me laugh any more, I think I might wet myself. That's enough, love. I hope you didn't use words like that when you were teachin'. You'd have been thrown out of the school."

Charlie finally managed to stop laughing. "Anyway, his wife, Jenny, and their five kids all died from smallpox."

"This is a lovely place but that's real sad," Betty said. "And here we are laughin' our heads off. Imagine living here in the middle of nowhere and your whole family dies."

"It does say he remarried and raised another family," Charlie said. "Says he met Theodore Roosevelt on one of Roosevelt's hunting trips."

Just south of Jenny Lake village they parked beside the lake and had a coffee break. They sat around the kitchen table and Danny took another look at their map. "It won't take us long to get to Jackson. We're well into Wyoming now. But I think if we make it somewhere near this place called Montpelier tonight, we'd be doing well. From there we'd only be maybe a half-hour or so drive from the Utah border. Or, we could bypass Montpelier on another road that goes on to a place called Cokeville back in Wyoming."

"Sounds like it's a toss-up," Charlie said. "How are we for money, Betty?"

"Well," she said, "it's not great. We have $85.10 left. We're okay for food, lots of potatoes, carrots, some rice and some canned beans but, what's the date again?"

"September 14th," Charlie said.

"Well, that still leaves a few weeks before our money hits the bank," Betty said. "We'll have to scrimp every bit we have left for gas."

"We'd better count on staying a few days in one or two places without spending any money," Danny said. "If we're all finished our coffee, let's get on to Jackson, anyway."

THE GRAND GETAWAY   201

They hadn't gone far when a sign told them they had entered the valley of Jackson Hole.

"It's sure pretty country," Danny said. "Look at those mountains. A hell of a name, though, for such a pretty place."

"Well, it used to be worse," Charlie said. "It was called Jackson's Hole, but they tried to make it sound a bit more polite by dropping the apostrophe and the s. Mountain men called a large valley surrounded by mountains a hole. I don't know why they just didn't go whole hog and change the name to Jackson Valley."

About 30 minutes later they drove into the town of Jackson itself.

"Now I'm sure I remember this place," Betty said. "I recognized the name, Danny, when you brought that map to Cavandish. It's sure a busy place though. Let's find somewhere to park and eat lunch."

After a cold lunch of the last two cans of salmon and rice, they took a close-up look at one of the four huge arches made of elk antlers in the corners of Town Square.

"I hope they didn't shoot all those elk just to make these arches," Betty said. "There must be hundreds of antlers."

"I expect some may have been shot and donated by hunters, but some would have been collected in the bush," Charlie said.

"If the economy of Jackson is dependin' on tourists like us," Betty said, "I think they'd be disappointed. We won't be buying any souvenirs."

They strolled around a few blocks, but with no money to spend they decided they should really move on. As they headed south again, Danny said, "It looks like we might be in for a little rain. What's the next place, Charlie?"

Charlie studied the map. "Er, here it is. Hoback. Then a place called Alpine, then Etna, then Freedom, then Afton. They look like real small places just a few miles apart. Yea, we're going right along the western edge of Wyoming. You want me to put on a tape, Betty?"

"Sure Charlie. Might as well."

"Hey! What's this? Looks home-made."

"What is it?" Betty asked.

"Looks like some kind of tape. It says *Snow Poems*, on the front. Don't know what it's about."

"Put it on. Let's find out," Betty said.

Charlie slipped the tape into the slot. As it began, there was faint Christmassy music in the background, then –

Sing, Ho for the snow! White stars and feathers,
Winter is one of my favourite weathers.

"Turn it up, Charlie! That's Caroline!" Betty called.

"Caroline! What?" He cranked up the dial.

They listened in silence as Caroline read some poems about snow. Even Caroline was quiet. None of them had heard Caroline speak in complete sentences before.

Danny had slowed The Smucker to a crawl. There was very little traffic, and in the quiet that followed there was only the hiss of the rain, the wheels running on the wet surface of the road, and the steady beat of the windshield wipers. The tape lasted about four minutes.

Danny looked quickly at Charlie who was staring ahead and biting his lip. Danny felt a lump in his own throat and when he glanced back at Betty, he saw she was hugging Caroline and wiping tears from her own eyes.

"God that was beautiful," Betty said, her voice snuffly. "She was a wonderful reader."

"Yeah," Charlie said. "She musta been a great teacher. Too bad we didn't have a chance to play it for Frank Malone. I think he'd have liked it."

"Had to be something she'd put together for school years ago." Danny said.

"How did that end up at Cavandish?" Danny asked.

"I bet Caroline's husband found it at their home and brought it for her to listen to and it just got mixed up with the other tapes," Betty said. "I'd like to hear it again, Charlie. It was lovely."

Charlie replayed the tape, and they all seemed to be holding their breath as it reached the final poem again and Caroline's expressive voice filled The Smucker.

In the winter time we go
Walking in the fields of snow
Where there is no grass at all
Where the top of every wall
Every fence and every tree
Is as white as white can be
Pointing out the way we came
Everyone of them the same
All across the fields there be
Prints, of silver filigree
And our mothers always know
By the footprints in the snow
Where it is the children go.

They drove in silence for a few more miles and the rain was coming down hard. They found themselves in a grassy valley surrounded by forested mountains, although the mountains were becoming hard to see with the falling rain. Danny was driving more slowly because of the rain, and when they drove under a *Welcome To Afton* sign on an arch that stretched across Afton's wide main street, Charlie called out, "Take a look at that!"

THE GRAND GETAWAY   203

The arch was made with elk antlers and had two large, stuffed elk butting heads in the centre.

"The elk must take a beating around here," Charlie said, "or they must be as prolific as rabbits considering all the elk arches around this area."

Danny checked the gas gauge. "We should get a little more gas here, we're getting low."

The rain eased off as they left Afton and shortly after they came to another small place called Smoot.

"I don't remember any of these places," Betty said.

"Well they're all really small," Danny said. "And don't forget you and Arnie were belting along on a motorbike back then and we're crawling along. You and Arnie would have passed through these towns in seconds. I can't even remember some of the places we passed today."

"I read that these were Mormon settlements," Charlie said. "Seems Idaho and Wyoming had different laws and the Mormons found Wyoming a bit more easy going about having a whole bunch of wives. Hey, it says here that in Montpelier, part of Butch Cassidy's gang held up a bank to try to raise bail for one of the gang members who was in jail. They robbed trains and banks in this country and in Bolivia."

Danny pulled The Smucker over to the side of the road. "I'd like to take another look at the map."

"Some of the roads further south go through some mountainy country and one here says, 'Closed in Winter.' Maybe we'd better play it safe with this weather. Stay on 89. Go through Montpelier and stay in Idaho. We go through lots of little towns. Let's see, Ovid, Paris, then through Garden City in Utah."

"I've always wanted to visit Paris," Betty said, laughing. "Think they have an Eiffel Tower there?"

"I doubt it," Charlie said. "And no *Folies Bergere* either. I've always wanted to see that."

Montpelier was a larger town than all the others they'd come through since Jackson. They stopped briefly when Charlie spotted an information sign that included a piece about the Butch Cassidy gang. The sign explained that the town was named by Brigham Young, the Mormon leader, after his own birthplace in Vermont. The sign went on to confirm Charlie's information about the bank robbery.

"Wonder how that would've worked?" Charlie said. "Do you think they just picked up the money from the bank 'n' walked down the street to the jail to pay the bail?"

They headed south again, and the rain came down in earnest.

Charlie announced, "We just went through Paris."

"I missed it," Betty said.

"Time to look out for a place to pull over. I can hardly see a thing," Danny said. "With all this rain and dark clouds, we're losing visibility. If we can find a safe place, I'd like to get off the road altogether."

A couple of miles further on, Charlie said, "Just there, ahead on this side of the road. There. See that old barn. Let's take a look."

They came to a track leading into the field with the barn.

Danny put the headlights on high beam as the rain pelted down and rattled on the roof of The Smucker. He eased the bus through the gap as the headlights lit up a weathered, unpainted barn, sagging on one corner. He drove cautiously along the side of the barn to the rear and found a wide opening high enough to drive The Smucker inside.

"What do you think?" Danny asked.

Betty came forward and stood behind the two men. "It looks spooky." Betty said. "But it's spooky out here too." A gust of wind sent the rain drumming on the roof, making The Smucker sway. "The roof leaks in there," Betty said, "but the rain's not nearly as heavy as it is out here. Just pull inside the door and we'll get some shelter and see if the rain eases off. We're safer off the road."

"Yeah," Charlie said. "Providing the rest of the barn roof doesn't come crashing down on our heads."

CHAPTER 48

The rain didn't ease off. It seemed even heavier to Danny an hour later as he stood in the open door of the barn looking out. The roof of the barn dripped water in several places and there was a steady gush of water in the far left corner where the roof sagged badly. Underfoot, the floor was coated with layers of old hay, much of it going moldy, but it was mostly dry. Danny took a quick walk around the barn. There were a few small bales of hay, a collection of old boards leaning up along the side of the barn, an old hay-fork with half its handle broken off and a couple of old plastic twenty-gallon white pails. There was evidence that a few cattle had been housed in the barn as Danny noticed a few lumps of very old, hard and dried-up dung.

He went back inside The Smucker. The others were sitting round the table. They'd finished the coffee that Betty had made, and they had the lantern on.

"I'd say we're here for at least the night," Danny said. "The rain's not letting up but we've come about as far as I thought we'd get today, and this place is as good as any."

"Yeah," Betty said. "It's cozy enough in here. That rain was sure heavy and we're okay here for now, except for a washroom. Caroline and me will need to go soon."

"I don't know if we could rig up something," Danny said. "Charlie, you want to give me a hand? I have an idea that might work."

Charlie followed Danny out into the barn.

"What I thought we might do is run a couple of boards across the top of one of these pails and leave a gap between them to make a seat so it's a little easier for all of us," Danny said.

They grabbed a couple of the hay bales and stood them on edge to give them enough height to clear the top of one of the pails. They spaced two boards apart and, using the hay-fork, Danny scraped a shallow hole in the hay floor to help support the pail.

"Let's put a little water in the bottom," Charlie said. "That'll keep it from falling over and it'll be easier to dump out if we're going to be here for a couple of days."

"Good idea," Danny said. He took the pail to where the rainwater was coming in though the sag in the roof, catching enough water to give it some weight and set it back in the space they'd made between the boards.

"What do you think, Charlie?"

"I think it'll work. Don't know if we've got the boards spaced right for the women. Betty will figure it out. Maybe we could stack these last three bales along this end to give them a bit more privacy."

When they finished, Charlie sat on the planks. "Feels like it might work. Let's get Betty to take a look."

"It's nothing fancy," Charlie said. "But it should do in a pinch."

"We'll try not to pinch our bums on those planks," Betty said. "Thanks, guys. I think we should get a bowl of water, a towel and a bar of soap and set it on these hay-bales so we could wash our hands right here. If you and Danny could get those for us, oh, and a toilet roll, we'll give it a try."

"We're not sure if we have the spacin' right on the boards but you can slide them closer or further apart, if you need to," Danny said.

"I wouldn't shift around much on the boards, Betty. They're not real smooth. Could get slivers," Charlie said.

"Just bring the stuff, Charlie. I gotta go!"

"And there's your shower right there," Charlie said, pointing to the water running in a steady stream from the roof hole. "I already turned it on for you."

"Just go, Charlie, before I wet myself."

Betty declared the home-made toilet a success, apart from the mouse that startled her when it ran over her foot. "We'll have to think about supper. We're all goin' to have to become vegetarians. Here's what we've got. Rice, potatoes, carrots, three cans of soup, four cans of baked beans, two cans of chili beans, six eggs, and some sugar and flour. I think that's about it." Betty had been going through the food cupboard as she spoke. "And we have some tea and coffee."

They settled on rice and beans, the rice being quite plentiful.

After supper, Danny and Charlie played a couple games of crib while Betty and Caroline watched, then Charlie thought he'd get ready for bed. He took the flashlight and headed for the toilet while Caroline quietly played with the cards.

"There's something been botherin' you, Danny," Betty said. "What is it?"

"I thought we'd just about lost you, the other night. Charlie too," Danny said. "And I've been thinking about what happens when we get to the Grand Canyon."

"I'll make sure I won't fall into the Grand Canyon," Betty said. "But we haven't got there yet."

"I know that. But we have to talk about what we do if, and when, we get there. I mean, you know we can only stay there until the snow comes and that may not be long from now. Everyone has to leave the North Rim once it snows. It's just, where we go from there? Once we get there, we'll have a couple of weeks at best."

Betty said, "You know how much I wanted to see the Grand Canyon one more time. When our money gets into the bank, things will be easier. I thought you were okay with that."

"I've got no idea how we're going to make it to the Grand Canyon before your money kicks in. We have to hang around in places like this until that happens. We're pretty well out of money for gas and we'll need some more food."

THE GRAND GETAWAY   207

"Hell, Danny, don't start worryin' about everything now. You've slept in worse places than this – you said so yourself. Look how far we've come! Don't start chickenin' out now. When our money comes in, we'll have enough for food and gas and other stuff. We can go anywhere we want. But, damn it! If you're gettin' cold feet, I'll buy you a Greyhound bus ticket back to Calgary! But let's get to the Grand Canyon first. Anyway, if you did go back, what would you do? Go back to sleepin' in culverts? You bought into this plan to get to the Grand Canyon. Let's stick to that."

"I'm not backing out," Danny said, stung by Betty's accusation that he was thinking of quitting. "I gave you my word on that. But if I did leave after the Grand Canyon what would you and Charlie do? And what about Caroline?"

"Hell! We'd have enough money to hire someone to drive The Smucker."

"A chauffeur!"

"Yeah, a chauffeur."

"Jeez, Betty. You're goin' to find someone to drive you around for pay? I don't think that'd be easy."

"We found you and you're doin' it for nothin'."

Danny said nothing.

"I thought you were enjoyin' this trip. Most of it anyway," Betty said.

"I was. I am. You've been the brains of this whole thing, Betty. You must've thought about what happens next."

"Oh, don't patronize me, Danny. All I could think about was getting' out of Cavandish. Maybe me and Charlie have lived too long. But I think it's better to be dead than miserable. And me and Charlie were miserable. Hell, sometimes the only social event was someone's funeral."

"Was it really that bad? The food was half decent and it was filling. Charlie didn't seem that unhappy."

"Hah! You ever heard that misery loves company? You hadn't been listenin' to him moan about everythin' for years, every day, before you showed up. And I was the same. You showin' up made a difference to both of us."

"And Caroline?"

"She's happy. Aren't you Caroline?" Betty turned to her, patted her hand and Caroline smiled. "We couldn't have left her behind. She had no one."

"I thought she was going to be moved? That was true, wasn't it, Betty?"

"As far as I'd heard, yeah it was. You're not accusin' me of making that up are ya? Of rushin' out of Cavandish and usin' her just to get goin'? But I'm damn glad we got out of there fast. This is the best thing that could've happened to us. We've had more excitement, met more interestin' people in the last couple of weeks than we'd ever met in Cavandish.

"I admit I haven't given what happens after the Grand Canyon a lot of thought. Once our money comes in, we can find some spot. Maybe in one of those trailer park places. Hell, maybe we could even find a cabin some place, a permanent place. Raise a few chickens."

Charlie came in then. "It's still raining hard outside." He noticed the tension between Danny and Betty. "What's up?"

"Danny's been wonderin' if we weren't better off at Cavandish."

"What!"

"That's not what I said, Betty."

"What was that about raising chickens?" Charlie asked.

"Oh, Danny's been worryin' about what happens when we reach the Grand Canyon."

"And you told him we're gonna raise chickens? I don't think they'd allow that in a national park. Anyway, there's lots of vultures. Be cheaper just to buy our own eggs." Charlie laughed. "Well. I'm off to bed."

"I think that's a good idea," Betty said. "We'd better try the bathroom one more time, Caroline. You want to show us the way with the flashlight, Danny?"

Danny shone the way to the make-shift toilet for Caroline and Betty, handing Betty the flashlight when they got there.

Betty said, "I will think about what happens once we get there. But there's no way we're goin' back to Cavandish. Look how happy Charlie is. Me too. And Caroline. Let's get there, okay, Danny?"

"Yeah, okay."

Danny stepped back to the centre of the barn and waited while the women used the toilet. He had no option but to go on. He'd never thought about quitting.

He heard Caroline say, "Cold, cold," as Betty got her to sit down.

"I know darlin'. I'm sorry. I should have gone first and warmed up the plank. We'll complain to the management when we go back."

There was silence for a couple of minutes. Then, "God you're right Caroline. These planks are givin' me frostbite." He heard Betty laugh.

The flashlight moved again as Betty placed it on a hay bale. "Let's wash our hands in the bowl, Caroline. No, here use the soap. Stop – don't slop the water out. Holy–!"

"What!" Danny called.

He ran towards them as he heard the splash of water and the bowl hitting the floor of the barn. Betty yelled, "Yikes!"

Danny reached the women as Betty grabbed the flashlight.

"What the hell happened?" Danny asked. "You two okay?"

"Oh." Betty panted. "There was a mouse swimmin' in the bowl of water. Caroline was tryin' to scoop him out 'til I grabbed the bowl and dumped it. Let's stay at least one night in a motel when we get our money. One with a real bathroom, without the hot and cold runnin' mice."

Danny laughed. "Sounds like a plan. Like you said, life is more exciting now."

CHAPTER 49

It was still raining next morning and there was no point in rushing on. They had some coffee and baked beans for breakfast. Betty busied herself making a list of possible meals they could make with the food they had. She had put all the food they had left on the table.

"Here's what I've come up with. Rice and baked beans – three suppers. We have lots of rice and I'm only using one can of baked beans each time." She took three cans of baked beans off the table and set them on the floor. "I could make a sort of stew with a can of soup, by addin' some of the carrots Magnus gave us and some potatoes. I could throw in more rice if needed for filler. That would make two batches.

"We could have chili beans with potatoes maybe once or the chili beans with more rice and stretch it to two suppers. That gives us a total of, let's see, seven suppers, a week of suppers from tonight. Okay?"

Danny and Charlie nodded.

"For a change I could try potato cakes with the last few potatoes and the last egg, then it's just rice. We really don't have anythin' for lunches."

"Well the Chinese and the Japanese eat rice about three times a day," Charlie said, "and they seem pretty healthy. I heard about a Japanese woman who lived to a 110."

"Well," Betty said. "I don't think she quit eatin' after a week. That's about how long we've got food for."

'We might find a soup kitchen in a city like Salt Lake to give us a couple of meals," Danny said, "but we still can't keep driving with no gas money." He felt a bit guilty for not mentioning the $20 he still had in his wallet, but he reasoned they'd be okay for a few more days. "Let's give it a couple more days here, anyway."

"Okay," Betty said. "We'll have to amuse ourselves though, or we'll go crazy cooped up in here. Maybe you could see if you could snare another rabbit, Charlie."

"Maybe," Charlie said. "I'll scout around after the rain lets up. See if I can see any evidence of rabbits around here. Give me something to do."

The rain had stopped completely the next afternoon and they had ventured out for a short walk. They didn't go far, just a short distance along highway 89 and back to the barn, having been sprayed by rainwater from the road by a couple of speeding freightliners. Despite the heavy rain, the land here looked decidedly drier than what they'd seen before. The sun was warm and steam rose from the roadway. The countryside was more open and the hills were covered with scatterings of sagebrush.

Everyone tried to find something to keep busy as the time dragged on. Charlie set up a couple of snares in the field. He and Danny played several games of crib, but they packed that in after a while, becoming bored. Danny found another book to begin reading by an American author, Andre Dubus, called *House Of Sand and Fog* and Charlie went back to finishing *Come Home Charlie and Face Them*. He dozed off after about half an hour and went out again to check his snares when he woke up. Danny had taken on the task of looking after the toilet pail, digging a hole at the back of the barn to dump it and making sure their primitive toilet was kept clean. Betty and Caroline looked through an old magazine together then Betty got out the jigsaw puzzle and sat, half-heartedly, trying to find a few pieces to fit, while Caroline gathered little handfuls of the pieces. When Betty gave up on that, she took down the school picture Frank Malone had given them where it had been taped to the wall of The Smucker and looked at it with Caroline. Caroline spent a long time staring at it and talking quietly.

They stuck it out in the barn for five nights altogether. Meal times marked the passing of time and became a relief. They went for a few walks in the field, staying away from the road, and ate their meals outside the barn in the sunshine, sitting on the old hay bales. They had collected rainwater and Betty heated up some on the stove to wash some of their clothes. Caroline had fun helping Betty, laughing as she slopped the clothes around in the tub, and repeating, "Sploosh, Sploosh, Sploosh." Charlie, using some of the fishing line, rigged up a clothesline.

Danny studied the map again. They were just south of Paris, Idaho, not far from the Utah border when the rain had forced them to stop.

"It's still quite a distance to Salt Lake and then Bryce Canyon. So, what's the decision? Stay here or go on?"

"I say we go on," Betty said. "We're all gettin' on each other's nerves sittin' here. Let's make a fresh start."

Next morning, another bright sunny one, they were up early, eager to get on the road again. They quickly passed through little places like Bloomington, and St. Charles as they drove along the shores of Bear Lake. They crossed into Utah shortly after and drove through Garden City on the same lake. It turned out to be even smaller than Danny had thought despite being called a city. As they followed highway 89 westward, the road twisted and turned through gullies and up and down sagebrush covered hills with forested peaks.

By mid-morning they had just barely entered the small city of Logan, set in a valley flanked by mountains, when they found themselves in a long line of slowly moving traffic.

"What's going on?" Charlie asked. "Maybe construction up ahead? But I haven't seen any signs."

They rounded a bend and found themselves in a line-up in the left lane as other traffic started passing them on their right.

THE GRAND GETAWAY   211

The line of traffic sped up a little and they soon came upon a cop directing the vehicles in the left lane into a large parking lot.

"I guess I should have got in the right lane sooner," Danny said. "I hope this isn't some kind of a police check or we're screwed. What is this place?"

"Holy crap! It's a funeral home," Charlie said. "Jepson's Funeral Home. Everyone's going to a funeral."

Danny pulled The Smucker into the space indicated by the parking attendant and turned off the engine.

Betty said. "I just saw a sign that said, 'Funeral – All Welcome.' Let's get out."

"What! What are we gonna do then?" Charlie asked

"We'll go in," Betty replied. "Look. We didn't do this on purpose, but we're here. Funerals are similar to weddin's. They serve food afterwards. Anyway, they'll have washrooms here, and Caroline and I need to go."

Charlie looked at Danny who shrugged.

"But we don't even know who it is that died," Charlie argued.

"That's okay," Betty said. "We can still pay our respects. Come on. Let's get out. Half the people at funerals don't know who the other half are. It's the same at a weddin'. Let's use the washroom anyway."

They climbed out of The Smucker and followed the people ahead of them. As they stepped into the carpeted lobby of Jepson's Funeral Home, a female attendant nodded to them and said, "Thank you for coming. Would you please sign the book before going in?" She indicated an open hard cover book on a stand which a couple just ahead of them had signed.

Betty stepped forward holding Caroline's hand, took the pen beside the book and signed for both of them. She indicated to the attendant that she and Caroline needed the washroom which she had spotted just across the lobby. The attendant smiled and nodded as Danny and Charlie signed the book in turn. The crowd coming in had dwindled to a few last stragglers as Betty and Caroline returned and the attendant ushered them inside the large chapel where they found some vacant seats in a back row. The room was crowded and up on a small stage at the front, on a table covered in gold cloth, was a large photo of an elderly man wearing a cowboy hat. Two large vases filled with flowers stood on both sides of the photo. Quiet organ music faded as a man in a dark suit stepped onto the stage and stood behind a lectern with a microphone attached.

"Welcome friends. It's wonderful to see such a great turn-out for the celebration of the life of Alvin Welcome or, as he was known to everyone, Al or *Big Al*. As all of you know, Al wasn't just called *Big Al* because he was a large man, but because of his big heart. He was as big-hearted as any man that walked this earth."

"*Al Welcome*," Charlie hissed at Betty who was sitting beside him. "That's the guy's name. The sign didn't say All Welcome."

Betty gave Charlie an elbow.

"I'm not going to take a lot of time talking about Al because I'm following Al's wishes. When I visited him at his home just before he died, this is what he said to me. 'Pastor Paxton, promise me you won't have people doing a lot of jawing about me after I'm gone. I don't want no long-winded boring speeches or eulogies or whatever they call them, making those poor people squirm in their seats. If they have a funeral service for me it's not to go more than 15 minutes. Fifteen minutes is plenty of time to say anything that needs to be said. I've had a good life and a long one, and I'd rather you have a good time at my funeral. I want everyone to have a little party, so forget the jawing and give them a good feed and a little music.'

"Well I could go on half the afternoon talking but I'd only make Al mad at me, so I'm doing exactly what he asked. I gave him my word.

"Al grew up here in this valley just north of Logan on the Bar 5 W Ranch which his own daddy had started more than a hundred years ago, and Al took over the running of the ranch when his daddy retired. He raised a fine family with his lovely wife, Joleen, who predeceased Al four years ago, and was a fine upstanding citizen. He was always a charitable man, never wanting to see anyone go hungry. Al passed away last week at the age of ninety-four and was laid to rest two days ago in the family plot on his beloved ranch. He will be sorely missed. Now I've used up five minutes of my time and keeping Al's wishes in mind, we have 10 minutes left to see a few small pieces of *Big Al's* life. Then folks, Al wanted everyone to join the family outside in our picnic area. There's some fine food and the hamburgers are made from the finest beef provided by the Bar 5 W Ranch itself. After this short presentation please join Al's two sons, Jim and Roy and their families and celebrate Al's life as he'd like us to do."

The lights were dimmed and a screen rolled down from the ceiling at the front of the room. A black and white photo of Al, as a very young boy wearing a cowboy hat and sitting on a horse being led by his father, appeared on the screen. The captions beneath the photos told the story. Several coloured pictures of ranch life, herding cattle, branding and scenes which included Al and his two sons and the grandchildren on the ranch followed, with soft organ music playing.

As the pictures of Al's life ended, and the lights came on, Pastor Paxton stepped to the mic again. "Now folks let's bow our heads in prayer. Let us pray to thank God for giving Al his life on earth to share with us and for showing us how we should go through life, an example to us all. You are in God's hands now Al. God bless you and bless your family here on earth." The pastor looked up at the congregation. "And now folks, as we file out the side doors to the picnic area, we end this service as Jeff Ashburn sings Al's favourite song, *Don't Fence Me In*. The barbecues have been fired-up and the food is all ready, so in honour of Al's wishes let's quit jawing and use our jaws to eat. I know you all have stories to tell about Al and you can tell them as you enjoy your food."

A man dressed in cowboy gear moved onto the stage with a guitar in hand and began to sing *Don't Fence Me In* as the crowd moved slowly through the double doors leading out to a large grassy area set with picnic tables. The smell of sizzling burgers filled the air and a large number of servers stood ready to dish them up.

As Betty spooned some salad onto Caroline's plate, the woman ahead of them turned to Betty and said, "*Big Al* will surely be missed in this valley. A great man."

"Yes. That's true," Betty agreed, as she accepted a scoop of baked beans onto her plate. "Never wanted to see anyone go hungry."

CHAPTER 50

As they left the city of Logan, Charlie said, "That was a great feed, but I hope to God we're not going to follow hearses from here all the way to the Grand Canyon. Gives me the creeps."

They had stopped to buy a few groceries, and Danny had confessed to having the $20 in his wallet, saying he'd held it back in case of an emergency, but as they were low on food and needed gas, maybe this was the time to use it.

He was surprised when Betty said, "Let's hang onto to it, Danny. We'll spend about $10 for food as we planned, and get a half tank of gas as usual. We'll be sure to send a card to Gail when we make it to the Grand Canyon and thank her."

Betty said it was a good time to go grocery shopping because she'd read that you should never go grocery shopping when you were hungry and all of them had eaten all they could at *Big Al's* funeral, Danny and Charlie managing a second burger when they were offered.

They scoured the grocery store for deals. Charlie had commented that a roasting chicken in the supermarket sure smelled and looked good, but Betty had scolded him that he couldn't possibly be hungry already, and said to Danny, "It was a mistake to tell Charlie about the 20 bucks from Gail. He'll bug us now all the way to the Grand Canyon every time he smells something good to eat. We'll have a slap-up meal the day our pensions kick in, Charlie, but I think we'll leave you in The Smucker next time we go grocery shoppin'."

After driving through Wellsville and Mantua on Highway 89 they joined Interstate 15 and headed directly south again. The places they were passing were much bigger now than any they had come across since leaving Calgary, and as they passed through Ogden, Roy and Layton, the highway became busier with the flow of vehicles leaving and joining the highway. Danny kept their speed low and they were continually being passed. It wasn't long before he was longing for a back road, but the map had shown him that this was really the only route to follow. Just north of Salt Lake City, at Bountiful, the traffic was bumper to bumper. The countryside was getting drier and drier and the hills had a decidedly desert look. Clumps of trees were coated in the yellows of fall.

"We're just about in Salt Lake City," Danny said "but I don't think we should try stopping there. We're getting into rush hour, and finding a place to park would be a nightmare. If we get stuck in traffic and run out of gas, we'll have a big problem. Take a look at the map, Charlie. What's coming up after Salt Lake?"

"It looks like we'll be passing the outskirts of Salt Lake City for a little while," Charlie said." If we make it to a place called Spanish Fork, we could get onto Highway 89 again going south which would eventually take us to Bryce Canyon."

"How far is Spanish Fork?"

THE GRAND GETAWAY   215

Charlie looked at the map again.

"Probably at least three-quarters of an hour drive from here, maybe more, but I'm just guessing."

Twenty minutes later they had passed Salt Lake City and when Danny checked on Betty and Caroline, they had both fallen asleep. The gas gauge was down to less than a quarter. It was time to take a break.

He pulled off at an exit looking for a service station or public park that might have a washroom. Ahead, he spotted a shopping centre with a Walmart and turned in, found a parking spot and turned off the motor. Charlie snapped awake and Betty and Caroline stirred behind them.

After using the bathrooms, they spent a little time wandering the aisles of Walmart. Finding the air conditioning colder than they thought it should be in contrast to the heat outside, Betty complained that they should have worn sweaters. Charlie pointed out a bulletin board that he discovered near the information centre. It was a welcome to tourists, particularly owners of recreational vehicles who were touring the area. The bulletin board stated that owners of such vehicles were welcome to stay for one night only, using a particular area of Walmart's parking lot. There were some other conditions but as soon as Betty saw it, she said, "That's us. We can stay here overnight free."

Danny read the information. "I think it means those really big buggers with their own bathrooms and everything, you know the ones like a complete house on wheels. I don't think The Smucker qualifies."

"What do you mean we don't qualify?" Betty asked. "The Smucker is *our* house on wheels."

"Well, we don't have a bathroom," Charlie said.

"Oh for goodness sake!" Betty said. "We're not going to empty a chamber pot on their parkin' lot or anything. Come on, I'm freezin' in here. Let's go back to The Smucker before we catch pneumonia and I'll make us all a coffee."

Over coffee, Betty took up her argument for a free night of camping. "Look, we can't really drive any further. Danny's exhausted. We don't have any money and we can use Walmart's bathroom up until nine tonight before we go to bed."

"They might have a security guard patrolling the parkin' lot at night who might make us move on," Danny said.

"Maybe we could ask at the information desk," Charlie said.

"I don't think that's a good idea," Betty said. "That'd just put them on their guard. They'd be sure to say no if we ask. Point out the fine print or somethin' like that. It's all just interpretation. Look at those signs out there that say, 'Parking for expectant mothers only.' Whose gonna give anyone a pregnancy test in the parkin' lot to see if they qualify? Maybe the woman only had sex a half hour before she parked there. She could still qualify. If we're asked to move on, we'll just say we misinterpreted the information on the sign. Let's just stay here until dark and see how it goes. If some security guard wakes us up in the middle of the night, I'll talk to him. I don't think Walmart would like the bad publicity if they saw somethin' in the papers like, 'Walmart forces crippled woman and woman with dementia out on the highway. Killed in highway crash.'"

"But you're not crippled," Charlie said.

"I still have my walker and Caroline does have dementia."

"Well we're not planning on getting killed on the highway," Charlie said.

"I know we're not! That's just an example. These big outfits don't like bad publicity or law-suits. Nobody will bother us if we leave next mornin'. It's only one night for God's sake. Let's have a late afternoon snooze before we have supper, anyway."

They decided to look for a park where they could have their supper and sit outside. They found one not far off and had a light supper. About a half hour before closing time at Walmart they headed back. They found two large bus-like RVs parked behind each other in the designated area. Danny pulled into the space on the right side of the RVs which screened them from the store. All four of them paid a quick visit to the washroom inside. Betty came back with the news that there were also Walmarts at Orem and Provo which were just to the south.

Charlie and Danny were awake early, and Walmart wasn't yet open but both of them needed a bathroom. Another RV had pulled in behind them during the night.

Danny slipped on some clothes and whispered to Charlie that he had to find a bathroom. They found a service station and Danny suggested they spend another ten bucks for gas as they were low again and couldn't afford to find themselves stalled later on busy Interstate 15.

They headed back to the park they'd found the night before and Betty cooked up some scrambled eggs and toast.

Danny was looking at the map again and pointed out that Orem and Provo were only a very short drive down the highway and, as it was still early, rush hour would be in full swing.

They decided to wait a couple of hours and killed time by strolling a few times around the park. Danny was reading his book again when Betty interrupted.

"We've still got about nine days left until our money comes in. We can kill off two more if we stay at the Walmarts at Orem and Provo."

"We could," Danny agreed. "Those places are just down the road. But when we get to Spanish Fork, just past Provo, I'd like to get back on Highway 89. I'm not comfortable driving on Interstate 15, too busy, and we'll probably have a much better chance of finding somewhere to stop overnight on 89.

"We'll just take it one day at a time. One day at a time," Betty said.

CHAPTER 51

Once they got on their way, it only took them about 15 minutes to reach Orem. They found a Walmart but decided to look for a public park where they could possibly find some shade and sit outside. It was an exceptionally warm day and it dragged by, punctuated by coffee breaks and meal times. It seemed that the evening would never come. When they finally returned to Walmart, it was 8:00 p.m. and they spent a long hour meandering the aisles, trying out lawn chairs and other furniture with Betty renewing her vow to buy some good, fold-up lawn chairs as soon as they got their money. They made a final trip to the bathrooms before finding their spot beside five monster RVs. They tucked The Smucker into the lee of one of their looming shadows.

The couple who owned the RV closest to where they'd parked were out checking their tires when Danny emerged the next morning to check the oil and the water in The Smucker's radiator. They did a double-take when Charlie stepped out and then Caroline and Betty appeared in the doorway.

"You folks came all the way from Canada in that little bus?" The tanned grey-haired elderly man pointed to their license plate. "All four of ya? Hiram Brady." He thrust out his hand to Danny. "And this is my wife Margo." He indicated a short, chunky, smiling woman with blonde-streaked dyed hair.

Danny shook the proffered hands and acknowledged that all four of them had indeed come from Canada in their little bus.

From The Smucker's doorway Danny caught Betty's eye and she mouthed the words 'park' and 'bathroom' and he nodded.

"Margo and I drove all the way to Canada five years ago," Hiram went on. "Went to Calgary, then drove up through Banff and Jasper. Great scenery, friendly people. Love Canadians. A couple drove us miles when we ran out of gas somewhere between Lake Louise and a place called *Sask- ca- chewing River Crossin'* and back again. Wouldn't accept a cent."

Danny heard Betty hiss, "Bathroom," behind him.

"How far you, going?" Hiram went on.

"Grand Canyon," Danny replied, "but..."

"Hiram, honey," Margo Brady interjected. "I think the lady said they've got to find a bathroom. Sorry, Hiram's a little hard of hearin'. They don't have a bathroom in their little bus, honey."

"No bathroom, jeez! Hell, we've got a fine bathroom in the Gypsy Clipper. Come on over. Margo here was just about to cook us a breakfast of pancakes and bacon.

Why don't you join us? Maybe we can repay that favour from your fellow Canadians."

"Sure. Come join us. We'd like that," Margo said. "But let's get these two ladies to the bathroom first. Come along ladies, these men will gab all morning and I know what it's like when you gotta go. We can talk over coffee while I cook breakfast."

Hiram and Margo were from Houston, Texas, and Hiram had made his money in the oilfields. They were on their way to Santa Barbara, California, taking a long way round, to stay with their daughter and son-in-law for the winter.

After everyone was sitting down for coffee, Danny introduced all of them. Betty explained about Caroline, but gave no hint that Caroline, Charlie and herself were escapees from a care-home. In fact, she said all four of them had been friends for years and were thinking of retiring to Arizona or, at least spending a winter there. It was understood that Betty and Charlie and Danny and Caroline were partners.

The Bradys didn't probe too much and Danny was thankful for that because he was sure they must be wondering why all four were travelling in such a small, beat-up bus, if they had the means of spending the winter or longer in Arizona. Hiram did ask about air-conditioning in their bus and they all had a good laugh when Charlie said, "We just open a window."

Betty said they'd be looking for either a permanent place or something like the Brady's RV to spend the winter in and had only set out in their bus as a sort of an adventure, a kind of old-time camping trip from their youthful past.

"Sounds really fun," Hiram said, "and I bet it's real easy on gas. Not like our outfit. But Margo and I like our comfort." This led to Hiram showing them all the features of their RV, including a large TV mounted behind a panel for viewing when they were sitting outside.

"Hiram loves his football. Can't bear to miss watchin' his Houston Texans," Margo said.

They had a great breakfast and Caroline tucked into the food without much prompting from Betty.

It was nearly two hours before they said their good-byes. The Bradys were heading west to spend a day or two in Reno. Hiram said it was still a fair ways to Bryce Canyon, but the foursome should easily make it there before nightfall.

As they headed south feeling well fed, nobody felt like stopping when they reached the city of Provo just a few minutes down the road.

"Those people were really nice," Betty said.

"I'm not sure they believed everything you told them, Betty," Charlie said. "I don't think they bought the bit about us being well-off Canadians just going to check out Arizona in our crappy-looking bus. Maybe Hiram being a bit deaf helped, but Margo wasn't fooled."

THE GRAND GETAWAY   219

"Well, you tellin' them our air-conditionin' was just to roll down the window didn't help. But no matter. Some Canadians had done them a good turn once and they were happy to repay it. Let's go on to this Spanish Fork place. We've been lucky so far. Let's check it out."

"Well here we are, already," Charlie said as Danny took a turn off from Interstate 15 and found a service station.

"We're gonna need some more gas and we're burning a little oil," Danny said. "Better add a quart and I should top up the water in the radiator too. From here on its desert and more desert, and I figure we've got to take it easy with The Smucker. She's served us well up to now, but it's still pretty hot here and we'd better baby her along."

They spent another $28 for gas and oil, bringing their remaining balance to a grand total of $17.75.

"Things are looking a bit grim in the finance department," Charlie said. "Maybe we'd better spend the money on a big bag of oatmeal to keep us alive."

"You might be right, Charlie," Betty said. "We'll be using the last of our rice tonight and then we might have about one more days' worth of food. Let's see what this place holds before we go rushin' off."

They found a small park and pulled The Smucker under a tree. They sat at a picnic table to consider the situation. They just didn't have enough money for food or gas to go much further.

"We probably should stay here," Danny said. "Maybe hide out in some park. If we go down Highway 89, the places are few and far between and at least here we might have a chance of getting some food."

"From where?" Charlie asked. "Panhandling or what?"

"Can you sing?" Betty asked.

"Can I, hell." Charlie laughed.

"Well we might try for a food bank. Maybe a Salvation Army soup kitchen," Danny said. "Then there's also dumpster diving."

"What! Scrambling into dumpsters behind supermarkets." Charlie snorted. "You've done that? Jeez. What about food poisoning?"

"My old partner Pete did it a few times. Mostly looking for something to sell for booze. I had to help haul him out a few times when he couldn't climb out but once he found a whole case of Kraft salad dressing and another time quite a few cans of some kind of beef stew. It tasted fine to me but dumpster diving would be a last resort."

"Let's go for a walk," Betty said. "I'm gettin' depressed listenin' to this. Come on Caroline. On your feet. It's a nice day. Come on you two. We've had a good breakfast. Maybe we can scrounge a lunch somewhere without rootin' through garbage cans."

They found themselves on a busy street with a fair amount of traffic. They walked a couple of blocks and when Betty spotted a bench near a shade tree down a narrow street she said, "Let's take that bench down there, we're just wanderin' and it's not that interesting, mostly auto-body shops and warehouses."

Just before they reached the bench, they came to a small restaurant and a hand-printed sign in the window caught Betty's attention. "Look." She pointed, then read the sign out loud, "Help wanted."

"Forkin' spoon," Charlie muttered.

"Oh, Charlie," Betty snapped. "There's no need to swear."

"I'm not swearing. That's the name of this restaurant. Look." He pointed to the red painted sign hanging at right angles above the doorway.

"It's Fork 'n' Spoon," Betty read out loud. "Not what you said."

"What? I just read it faster," Charlie protested.

Danny laughed.

Charlie was peering in the window. "It's empty."

"Let's go in," Betty said.

"Betty, we've hardly any money," Danny said.

"Maybe we can earn some."

"What? What do you think we could do? The place is empty," Charlie protested. "I doubt if any of us would be hired to wait on tables. There's no customers. No hope in hell of even getting a tip and there sure as hell wouldn't be any dishes to wash. You're crazy, Betty. Is the place even open?"

"It is," Danny said. "There's a guy behind the counter staring back at us."

"Probably hoping we're gonna be the biggest sale of the day. Boy is he gonna be disappointed. Come on. Let's go," Charlie said.

"Wait!" Betty said. "Let's go in anyway. See what the job is. It's a pizza joint." Betty pointed to a picture of a pizza on the front door. "Maybe he wants a few pizzas delivered or somethin'."

"Jeez, Betty... " Charlie said, but Betty was already opening the door and a bell above it jangled.

The others hesitated but followed when Betty looked over her shoulder and tossed her head to signal them to follow.

The restaurant was bigger than it looked from the outside and the empty tables were covered with red and white checkered tablecloths. Danny noticed there was enough seating for about thirty people.

"Welcome. Welcome." The dark haired, fiftyish-looking man bustled from behind the counter, ready to show them to a table. A woman, whose face they could just see over the shelf of a serving hatch behind the counter peered at them anxiously.

"Where you like to sit?" The man asked, waving his hand expansively round the room, showing them the large choice of tables.

THE GRAND GETAWAY   221

"Er, what's the job?" Betty asked.

"Job? What?... Job? You like pizza? We have *ver* good pizza." He put his fingers to his lips making a lip-smacking sound, and added, "*Delicioso.* Marie-Angela's *mather*, God rest her soul, her own recipe."

"Your sign..." Betty said, "in the window. It says, 'Help Wanted'. What sort of help do you need?"

"Help?"

"Yea, the job? You have a job? Your sign?"

"You lookin' for job? Four peoples?" The man stared at them for a moment then seemed to recover. "Customers is what we need. I forget sign in window. You *doan wanna* pizza?" His dark eyes looked mournful and he glanced over his shoulder at the woman looking through the serving hatch and he shook his head. She muttered something as the man went to the window and removed the sign.

"My name Giovani. I hire young kid. One day. He say he bring customers. I pay for special sign. He stand on corner with sign. He spin, do tricks. But no customers come. I go find. He sit, play video game or something. I get mad. But no customers. When I go back again, he asleep. I fire him."

The woman from the kitchen had now joined them. "And now we soon *haf* to close. Only open one week. No business. Sell only three pizzas in two days. I ask Giovani what we do? We come from Italy six months. Work hard. Save money. Dream to open restaurant. But now *haf* to close. Pizza very good, but no one come to try."

"My wife, Marie-Angela," Giovani said.

Marie-Angela smiled. "You taste. You like. I have some pizza ready." She hurried back to the kitchen and quickly returned with a platter with four large slices of pizza, sizzling hot. "Sit. Sit. You taste."

"But... We don't..." Betty said.

"No money. Free. You try. You tell me if good." Marie-Angela placed the pizza on a table as Giovani urged them to sit.

Betty helped Caroline to sit and she, Charlie and Danny took seats too as Giovani placed four small plates on the table in front of them.

"It smells great," Charlie said. "Lovely thin crust."

Betty took a piece from the platter onto her plate and slid another onto Caroline's, warning her, "Hot, Hot."

"Yes. Hot, hot, hot," Caroline repeated.

Giovani and Marie-Angela hovered over them, anxiously awaiting their opinion as they tasted the pizza.

"Italian sausage. Italian spices," Giovani said. "Marie-Angela. Her *mather*. Recipe from her *mather*."

Danny and Betty were biting into their pizza slices and Charlie was already chomping on his third mouthful and making appreciative noises.

"My God! That's good!" Betty exclaimed. "Hmm. I don't think I've ever tasted pizza so good."

"It's fantastic," Danny said.

Charlie swallowed and managed to blurt out, "I could eat this for breakfast, lunch and dinner and then have it for dessert."

"You like?" Giovani asked.

"Like it? I love it." Charlie licked his lips and then took another huge bite.

Giovani and Marie-Angela beamed.

When they were finished, Betty said, "I'm sure you would do very well sellin' great pizza like this. But maybe nobody knows about you. You need to advertise."

Giovani shook his head. "No money. All our money gone... rent, printing menus. We want to change name to Mama Mia's Pizza, get new sign, but no money left."

"Maybe we could do somethin'," Betty said. "Do you have the sign you paid for, Giovani?"

"Si. Is in back... But..."

"Can we see it?" Betty asked.

Marie-Angela had retreated to the kitchen and when Giovani went to get the sign there was a muffled conversation.

"Betty, what have you got in mind?" Charlie asked.

"I don't know yet," Betty said. "But maybe we could give them a couple of hours on the corner with the sign. We just scrounged some of the best pizza any of us have ever tasted. I feel sorry for Giovani and Marie-Angela. It seems like they've sunk all their money into this place and they're goin' to lose it. They make fantastic pizza. People need to know about it."

Danny said, "They have to be discovered. Sometimes that takes a lot of time and sometimes never happens. It's probably like a writer with a great novel who can't find a publisher. I'll bet there's quite a few really great ones that never get the chance."

"Hmm," Betty said. "There's an awful lot of fast food places, like McDonalds, Kentucky Fried Chicken, and so on. Americans and Canadians eat at a lot of those places, pizza joints too. There's a lot of competition, but that pizza... it would sell like mad if it got that chance."

Giovani returned with the sign, looking a little sheepish. "Here sign." Giovani read the writing as he held the board in his arms. "Fork 'n' Spoon – Real Italian Pizza."

"Isn't that a surfboard?" Charlie asked.

"This is sign kid used. Do tricks, Spin, throw in air, point to restaurant. He call himself sign-spinner or, he say, human billboard. He show me tricks he do but nobody come and he sleep. But you. I don't think you could..."

"Do tricks?" Betty laughed. "Probably not. But let's borrow the sign anyway. We've nothin' else to do at the moment. Why don't we give it a try? We'll go back to the corner where there's more traffic and see if we can get you any business for lunch time. It can't hurt."

THE GRAND GETAWAY   223

Giovani laughed. "You fill my restaurant, I pay one dollar for every customer. But you get tired. You all…"

"Old," Charlie said. "Yeah, you got that right."

"Let's give it a try, Charlie," Danny said. "We can take turns. Maybe two at a time. We can do shifts."

"You ever see those guys do the tricks with these boards?" Charlie asked. "They flip them in the air, throw them up high and catch them. I've even seen a guy do a backward flip and come up and catch it. We try throwing that thing in the air it'll probably go through the windshield of a passing car."

Danny laughed. "Maybe the four of us can do a comedy act."

Charlie and Danny carried the board between them to the corner although it was quite light. Betty got Caroline to wave at every passing car which she did enthusiastically, especially any that she saw were carrying small children. A few cars honked as Charlie and Danny held the sign up, pointing in the direction of the restaurant but none turned down the street or came back to check out the restaurant. One car did pull over and stop when they did a Charlie Chaplin act, pretending to be struggling under the weight of the sign. The driver hurried up and said, "Here, let me give you a hand with that," then seemed a bit embarrassed when he found out they were only fooling around and were trying to publicize the restaurant. Betty did tell him about the great pizza available there, but he said, "Maybe next time. I got a dental appointment."

After half an hour Betty took Caroline back to sit on the bench while Danny and Charlie did a sort of strong man act, pretending they were heaving the very heavy sign above their heads.

Betty appeared a short while later carrying two boxes of pizza. "Look after Caroline for a few minutes. Don't let her wander into the road. I got Marie-Angela to slice up two pizzas and I'm goin' to give out free samples to people who work around here. I figure once people taste this stuff they'll be convinced. Giovani looked a bit suspicious, like I was just lookin' for more free food but I think Marie-Angela believed me." Betty turned the corner and went into an auto parts dealership. As she came back and passed them again she said, "If this doesn't work nothing will." She began working down the street where the restaurant was, going into a body shop, a paint store and a few small warehouses on both sides of the street.

She rejoined them at the corner about twenty minutes later. "Just after eleven o'clock. Look, someone just went into the restaurant."

"I didn't see anyone," Charlie said.

A bus with the name Jubilee Retirement Home drove slowly by and they waved frantically. It pulled to the curb and stopped, and the driver got out and walked back to where they stood. "Hi, there. I've got a load of oldies, um… twenty-five seniors," he corrected, noting that the four standing in front of him also fell into the category of oldies. "We just drove down from Orem and we're looking for the Oasis Grill. I guess I took a wrong turn somewhere and the um... the seniors in the bus are getting fed up driving around. You wouldn't happen to know where that restaurant is, would you?"

"No," Betty said. "But just down this street there's a restaurant called the Fork 'n' Spoon which has the best pizza in the whole State of Utah, maybe the world. We just had some ourselves. We're seniors, and know for a fact that seniors in a retirement home rarely get pizza that doesn't taste like old cardboard. So you want to keep them happy, take 'em there. We guarantee it's the best."

"Thanks. I'll go ask them," the driver said.

"I'll come with you, in case they need convincin'," Betty said.

The driver looked a bit startled as Betty followed him onto the bus.

"Listen up folks," the driver said. "This is, er..."

"I'm Betty," Betty called out as the noise in the bus subsided. "You folks want to taste the best pizza you ever had?"

"I thought we were going to the Oasis Grill," an old lady hollered. "They serve pizza? We get pizza at the home once a week and it's damned horrible."

"I know how that is," Betty said. "I got pizza like that in the home I was in. It was so hard and tasteless, they used it to replace the broken tiles in our dinin' room." There was a chorus of laughter.

"I don't got my teeth with me," an old fellow near the back called out.

"It's okay, Jasper, don't worry," a young female attendant sitting near the back replied, "I've got them in a plastic bag in my purse."

"Jasper," Betty said. "The pizza at this restaurant is so tender, it'll melt in your mouth, teeth or no teeth."

"Well let's get to it," someone hollered.

"Yeah, let's go! Let's go!" someone else yelled and the chant was taken up.

"Where's this place?" the driver asked as he scrambled into the driver's seat.

"Down the street you just passed in the middle of the block. Turn right at the next street and take another right. I'll show ya."

"I hope this is good," the driver said, "or I'll be listening to the complaints all the way back."

"It is. I promise," Betty said.

When they pulled up across the street from the Fork 'n' Spoon, Betty hurried into the restaurant.

Giovani greeted her, beaming. "We sell two pizzas already and we got phone calls for two more from places where you give samples. Coming to pick up." A smiling Marie-Angela waved at her from behind the serving hatch.

"Well, get ready for a lot more. There's a bus-load comin' in right behind me." Betty was panting. "Fire up the oven or whatever you do. They're hungry and they might be a bit grumpy. When they get in here, give everyone a slice as quick as you can to keep them happy. Here they come."

THE GRAND GETAWAY   225

The first of the seniors were just pushing through the door. When Betty looked outside, the rest were crossing the street while the driver and the attendant, using a lift at the back of the bus, were unloading the last four passengers who were in wheel chairs.

"You're gonna need some help," Betty yelled at Giovani. She scrambled through the crush at the door and hurried down the street to where Charlie, Danny and Caroline were still waving at traffic and holding up the surf-board sign.

"Come on," Betty yelled before she reached them. "We need help in the restaurant."

"What?" Charlie called, then he and Danny noticed the bus parked down the street and the crush at the door of the restaurant.

Danny grabbed Caroline's hand and Charlie carried the board as they caught up with Betty.

"What are we supposed to do?" Charlie asked, as he hurried along beside Betty. "When Danny and I saw you take off in that bus we thought maybe you had decided to become a tour guide." He laughed.

"No time for jokes, Charlie. When we get inside, you and Danny help get everyone seated. I'll run into the kitchen to see if I can help Marie-Angela and Giovani. Then you two will probably have to act as waiters."

Danny and Charlie were taken aback at the hubbub in the restaurant. Several of the seniors were already seated and the attendant, the driver, and Giovani were doing their best to get the rest of them settled. Betty took Caroline's hand and pulled her along into the kitchen, where Marie-Angela was looking anxious as she frantically spread toppings on the raw dough bases for four pizzas. "I phone my niece. She coming soon to help. Giovani say we make two kinds pizza first, prosciutto ham and sausage. Serve small slices to *everone* fast."

"Now, what can I do?" Betty asked.

Marie-Angela gave her a hair-net and got Betty to wash her hands. "You sprinkle spices." She handed Betty a large jar with a perforated lid.

Betty grabbed a chair and sat Caroline down and found a small pile of red paper napkins and gave her a few. Caroline immediately started to fold them, as Betty, under Maria-Angela's direction, sprinkled the seasonings on the pizzas.

Giovani bustled in and said, "*Everone* sitting. We make pizzas fast. Danny and Charlie pouring water. Lady and driver say they help too. I explain to lady, we serve *everone* slice of pizza quick, like taste, then we maybe catch-up. She think good idea. Keep *everone* happy."

The phone rang and Giovani grabbed it as Marie-Angela slid four pizzas into an oven. "Si. Si. Half an hour. Prosciutto ham and pineapple and one Italian sausage with peppers. Si, Audrey. From paint store. Si. You pick up. Si." He grabbed some dough and pummelled it for a few minutes and then tossed it into the air, whirling it around as he caught it on the backs of his hands. "Marie-Angela. Cut pineapple and more prosciutto. Ah Francesca, bueno." A young, pretty, dark-haired girl entered the kitchen and quickly pulled a hair net over her hair and went to a sink to scrub her hands. "Our niece," Giovani indicated to Betty. "You look after phone if ring, Francesca, for pick-up orders. Two coming. Look after till. I arrange special price with old people from bus. Then maybe you serve tables with Danny and Charlie."

Somehow everything worked out, although Caroline folded a few more napkins before Betty was able to grab the unfolded ones. Marie-Angela had Betty slice up lots of Italian sausage. "I think you work in restaurant before," she said.

"I did, but it was a hell of a long time ago," Betty replied.

Danny and Charlie scurried back and forth from the serving hatch to the tables, plonking down a slice of pizza in front of everyone as quickly as possible and serving glasses of non-alcoholic drinks with some help from the driver and attendant. The attendant then took orders for whole pizzas and arranged with Giovani to put a variety of slices on platters so everyone got a taste of the four different kinds they were making. The seniors were mostly quiet apart from appreciative comments as they wolfed down the pizzas. When Betty came out of the kitchen, Jasper grinned at Betty and she noticed he had his teeth in when he called out to her, "You were right! This pizza does almost melt in your mouth. I think I could even eat it faster without my teeth. It's great!"

Betty, Danny and Charlie helped tidy up the dirty dishes and took them back to the kitchen as the attendant settled up the bill with Giovani. Marie-Angela quickly loaded the dishes into the dishwasher and set it running. She then had to prepare two more pizzas that someone from one of the nearby warehouses had come in and ordered.

"Listen up everyone." It was Jasper from the bus scrambling to his feet. "Wasn't the pizza here just great?"

There was a chorus of agreement from around the room and the crowd broke into applause. "We'll be back. You can count on that," someone yelled. Then there was a bit of a line-up for the washroom and the attendant got that organized. Danny noticed that the driver and Giovani were now sitting at a table engrossed in conversation.

When the last of the seniors from the bus had filed out the door, Giovani sat Betty, Danny, Charlie and Caroline down at a table.

"You work hard. You make me and Marie-Angela ver happy. Now you eat."

Marie-Angela brought out another selection of pizza slices and set it before them. "Eat, eat," Marie-Angela urged. The foursome didn't hesitate.

"I think we be okay, now," Giovani said. "Lots orders comin' from neighbourhood and Joe, bus driver, he say he drive for four other old-people's homes. Take people out once a month. He say he come here, every Wednesday. I give you this money

THE GRAND GETAWAY   227

like I promise. Someone say they put on internet, Facebook, Twitter. Already we get calls for tomorrow. You big help." He slid five $10 bills across the table to Betty.

"You're sure you want to give us that much?" Betty asked. "It seems like a lot."

"Si. Si. You take. You earn. You make me and Marie-Angela ver happy. I forget to ask. You live in Spanish Fork?"

"No, we're just passing through," Charlie said. "Heading south."

"You come back any time. We give you free pizza. You take box pizza now. I make special. Take for supper."

As they left the Fork 'n' Spoon carrying a large box of pizza, there was a middle-age man sitting on the bench tapping away on some kind of tablet. Beside him was a box with three partly eaten slices of pizza.

"Well he wasn't exactly bolting down his pizza," Charlie said after they were out of earshot. "More interested in checking his e-mails or his Facebook or whatever it is they stare at all the time these days."

"Yeah," Danny said. "Nowadays they spend as much time taking photos of what's on their plates as they do eating it."

"At least I don't have to cook supper," Betty said. "I hope you're not sick of pizza. My feet are killin' me. Let's get back to The Smucker so I can put my feet up."

CHAPTER 52

They all had a long nap after they reached The Smucker at the park, and it was nearly four o'clock when they finally roused themselves.

Danny said, "We'd better find a supermarket and stock up on a couple of things. What's our total cash situation, Betty?"

"We have $67.75 but I just realized there's one more important item we need, desperately."

"What's that?" Charlie asked.

"Toilet paper," Betty replied. "We're down to our last roll. We've been lucky so far but if we're gonna hide in the bush we may not be always able to scoot into a washroom at a service station or a Walmart."

"There won't be any Walmarts down Highway 89," Danny said, "and maybe not a lot of bush either. I think there will be more sage than trees."

They still had $55 left after buying some bulk oatmeal, toilet paper, a box of pancake mix, another carton of milk and two cans of tuna. With some daylight left, they decided to head down the much less populated two-lane Highway 89.

They passed by the tiny settlement of Birdseye, and when they reached the next little place, Indianola, just a little way from the highway, they stopped there at a service station for a bathroom break. As they were leaving, Caroline sat in the front seat when she climbed back into The Smucker.

"Let her sit there, Charlie," Betty said. "We won't be going too far. Just make sure you buckle up her seat belt. That okay with you, Danny?"

"Sure, that's fine. You can help me find a place to camp, Caroline. We need to try to find a place with some trees."

"Oh, yes. Trees, trees, trees."

The land was now open, dry, scrubby grassland with some distant treed hills, but the sage brush was becoming ever more prevalent. Just south of Indianola it clouded over and was just coming onto dusk. Danny turned on the headlights. A car heading in the opposite direction passed them, slowed, and then made a u-turn. Danny noticed it in his side mirror.

"Uh, oh," Danny said.

"What?" Betty called.

Flashing red and blue lights came on behind them and there was a short wail of a siren.

"Cops," Danny called out as he pulled The Smucker to the side of the road and stopped. The police car pulled in behind them, its lights still flashing.

"Shit!" Charlie said. "You want me to come up front, Danny?"

"No. Stay here, Charlie," Betty said. "Let's see what he wants. We certainly weren't speedin'. Anyway, I think Caroline is supposed to sit up there with Danny.

She's the one with the driving license. Try and handle it, Danny. I'll come up and help if I'm needed." She glanced out the side window. "There's one cop comin'. Hmmf! He looks like a cowboy."

"But what if..."

"Shssh, Charlie," Betty said.

Danny rolled down his window, his heart pounding.

The cop, wearing a tan, Stetson type hat and a dark brown shirt with a gold star and a yellow, beehive-shaped shoulder patch with the words *Utah Highway Patrol*, appeared at the window.

"Evenin' folks. One of your headlights is burned out. 'Fraid I have to give you a ticket. Can I see your license and registration, please, sir?"

Danny reached inside the glove compartment and pulled out the documents and passed them through the window.

The cop looked at Danny's and Caroline's licenses and examined the registration.

"I see this vehicle is registered in the name of Caroline Gilchrist. Is that you, ma'am?"

"Yes," Danny said quietly. Caroline was silent. The police officer examined the photo on the license and was now studying Danny's.

"This is a learner's permit."

"Yes, that's right, officer," Danny replied.

The cop grunted. "You all Canadians? What are you all doin' in Utah?"

"Just a vacation," Danny replied.

The cop pulled out a ticket book and started writing the ticket. "I have to make this ticket out to the registered owner." He was copying down Caroline's name and the license plate number from the registration onto the ticket when the radio receiver on his shoulder squawked, startling Caroline.

"Smucker!" Caroline said. "Smucker!"

Danny realized she'd spotted the Smucker jam label still stuck on the dash and was reading it out loud. The cop stepped away from the door of The Smucker but was frowning as he answered the call on his radio.

"Be on my way in a sec," the cop said as he clicked off the radio and stepped to The Smucker's window again. Danny patted Caroline's hand as she repeated, "Smucker!" once more.

The cop scowled. "What did you say, lady?"

"Nothing," Danny said, "She was only reading that jam label."

"Huh?" The cop's radio squawked again as he thrust the ticket and a pen in the window. "Here, sign that, lady. It's a $50 ticket but I can make it a lot more if you like." He stepped away to talk on his radio again as Danny quickly scribbled what he hoped was a believable Caroline Gilchrist signature.

The cop finished speaking on the radio as he came back to the window. Danny passed him the signed ticket and the cop ripped the ticket and a duplicate off the pad and handed them back. "There's an auto-parts dealer in Mount Pleasant, the next town just down the road. It'll be closing now. You'd better stay there overnight and get that headlight fixed. You have forty-eight hours to get it fixed and report to a police station to prove it. You have three days to pay the ticket. You can mail in the payment or pay at the police station. There's one in Mount Pleasant. Don't drive at night. We have your license plate number and will be lookin' out for you. I have to attend to somethin' or I'd be givin' this vehicle a good lookin' over." He handed back the licenses, registration and proof of insurance.

"Thanks, officer," Danny said as he took the papers and began to roll up the window.

"Smucker!" Caroline said again but the cop was now out of earshot and walking back to his patrol car.

Danny waited until the cop made a quick u-turn and, with its lights flashing and siren wailing, the patrol car disappeared.

As Danny started The Smucker, Charlie called from the back. "Jerk! You got that right, Caroline. He was a smucker. But what now? That's just about all our money gone for that damned ticket. We don't even have enough left for a new light bulb."

Betty laughed as Danny drove on. "He was goin' to give us the ticket, no matter what," Betty said. "Caroline just added a bit of comedy. I nearly burst out laughin'."

"Jeez. That would have really helped," Charlie said.

"I think we'd better find a place to camp right away," Danny said. "We've got two days to figure things out."

"Holy crap!" Charlie said. "What would have happened if he'd asked for our passports? Lucky he didn't. But maybe we're buggered anyway."

A short distance further down the two-lane highway they came to a gravel road running south-east, with a sign pointing to a place called Fountain Green. Danny slowed The Smucker. "We could go a little ways down this road and pull over if we can find a little tree cover. I'd feel a little better if we're off this highway, just in case that cop comes this way again."

They drove about a mile and came to a hollow with a dry creek-bed at the bottom. They crossed a small bridge and pulled off the road into a copse of stunted trees with a tumble-down wooden shack beside the creek-bed.

"This will have to do," Danny said. "The trees will give us a bit of cover and some privacy if any of us need a bathroom."

"It'll do, Danny," Betty said. "We'll make an early night of it. I'll heat some pizza in our pan and make us some coffee or tea."

Danny climbed out of The Smucker, leaving it running. He thought he might pull a little further into the trees, but he wanted to check the ground first and he also needed to pee. He looked at the headlights. It was the one on the passenger side that was out. He decided The Smucker was fine where it was. He stood beside a tree

THE GRAND GETAWAY   231

and had just started to pee when Charlie flicked the headlights to high beam. Danny heard him laugh and called, "Okay, Charlie, shut 'er off."

Charlie switched off the headlights just before he switched off the engine.

As Danny zipped up his pants, he noticed that the running-lights had come on just before Charlie turned off the motor. "Hey, Charlie," he called. "Turn on the motor again."

"Okay," Charlie called. The engine fired and both running-lights lit up.

"Now, switch the headlights on."

Charlie did but only one light came on.

"Leave it running, but switch off the headlights."

Charlie followed Danny's instructions and both running-lights were now on. "Now, flick the high beam lever," Danny yelled. Both lights came on brighter. "Right, shut 'er off again."

Charlie turned off the motor and stepped out. "What's happening?"

"You watch and tell me what you see." Danny climbed into the driver's seat and started The Smucker again. "How many lights on?" he yelled to Charlie.

"Two," Charlie yelled back.

Danny flicked the high-beam lever. "What do you see now?"

"Two lights on, only brighter," Charlie answered.

"And now?" Danny switched on the regular headlights.

"One light out."

Danny turned everything off as Charlie climbed back into The Smucker. "I don't get it," Charlie said.

"Let's have a coffee," Danny said. "I need to think. I have an idea that might work."

"But... "

"Coffee first. Gotta think," Danny said.

"What are you two doin', wastin' gas turnin' the engine on and off?" Betty asked.

"Danny will enlighten us, pardon the pun, but only after he has a coffee," Charlie said. "I thought I'd be sick of eating pizza, but it sure smells great."

"Okay. Here's what I think is happening," Danny said. "Headlights have two filaments, one for low beam and one for high beam. Unlike the USA, in Canada, pretty near all vehicles have running lights that run off the high beam filament but at a lower intensity or power level because we use 'em in the day time. You can flick the running lights to high beam though. As you probably noticed, they're not as bright as the headlight high beams but both light bulbs were on."

"Sooo...? How is that gonna help us?" Charlie asked.

"Well, here's what I'm thinking." Danny said. "The cop said we have to show we've fixed the headlight."

"But we haven't," Charlie said. "So how...?"

"Here's how. I'm not guaranteeing it'll work, but it might. As I said, here in the States, most cars don't have running lights."

"How come?" Charlie asked.

"Hell, I dunno," Danny said. "Maybe a constitutional right, like the right to bear arms or something. Maybe Americans feel it's an invasion of privacy. They don't want other Americans to see them coming down the road. Whatever!"

"But won't they want to see a receipt for getting' it fixed?" Charlie asked.

"Maybe we can convince them it's working. We leave the vehicle running outside the police station. One of us goes in and pays the ticket. Our running lights will be on. They work. When a cop comes to look, he might want to see our high beams go on. One of us in the driver's seat can flick the lever to high beam and hold it on. That might fool them."

"And if they aren't?" Charlie asked.

"We're buggered," Danny said. "And right now I am too, so I'm off to bed. We'll practice it in the morning after breakfast."

CHAPTER 53

As Charlie was having his morning pee in the trees, he noticed he was hitting a small clump of prickly cactus. He looked around and noticed several other cactus protruding from the rough, dry grass. He'd warn Betty that she and Caroline better not squat too low. He was hoping he'd be able to hold out until they reached Mount Pleasant before he had to do any other business. In fact, now that he'd seen the cactus he was determined to wait until they reached a service station. He'd have to go easy on the porridge this morning.

When they finished breakfast, Danny went over how things might work at the police station if all went well.

"What if the same cop is there?" Charlie asked. "He might not be very accommodating after what Caroline called him last night."

"Well," Betty said. "I could go in to pay the ticket. I don't think he really had a good look at me. You sit with Caroline at the back, Charlie, and keep her busy so she doesn't bring on the riot squad with their tear gas." Betty laughed.

Charlie was relieved he wasn't going to be called upon to go into the police station and that Danny would be sitting in the driver's seat. The thought of things going wrong were making his stomach rumble and he was relieved when they reached Mount Pleasant and he got to a service station washroom.

"Okay," Danny said. "Let's find the local police station. You're sure you want to go for it, Betty?"

"Yeah. Nothing ventured, nothing gained, as they say."

It wasn't hard to find. Danny pulled The Smucker up to the front of the small police station, keeping the motor running. Betty stepped out of The Smucker with her purse containing the ticket and the money to pay for it and Charlie passed her walker out the door. Betty insisted that the cops wouldn't hassle her if she had it with her. Charlie wasn't so sure about that if she came upon the same cop from the night before.

Charlie went and sat with Caroline at the table as they watched Betty reach the door of the police station. She pulled on the door and a young blonde officer, not the one from the previous night, appeared at the door and held it open for her.

"So far so good," Danny said.

"God. This is nerve-wracking," Charlie said. "I think I'll need a bathroom again soon."

"Relax, Charlie," Danny said. "If anyone can bluff her way through paying a ticket, it's Betty."

Inside the police-station there were two Utah State Highway Patrol officers, the one who had helped Betty in the door, and another seated at a desk working on a computer. The cop from the previous day wasn't there, much to Betty's relief.

"How can we help you, ma'am?" the officer asked.

"I've just come in to pay this ticket," Betty said.

"You weren't speedin' were you ma'am?" the cop said, light-heartedly.

"No. Danny, my husband is a real slow-poke. Can't get anythin' up to speed, these days."

The two cops chuckled as Betty pulled the ticket from her purse along with the five ten-dollar bills. She sighed as she handed over their Fork 'n' Spoon earnings.

"Ah. A headlight. Sorry about that ma'am. But it is a violation. Safety hazard."

"Hedley?" the cop at the computer asked.

"Uh huh," the blonde cop confirmed, speaking over his shoulder to his partner. "Near the end of the month. Must be nearing his quota," then he turned back to Betty. "Where you from, ma'am?"

"Canada, havin' a little vacation," Betty replied.

"Sorry about that, ma'am. Hope your welcome to Utah hasn't been spoiled too bad."

"Oh no," Betty said. "It's a lovely place. We're headin' for Bryce Canyon."

"Now there's a real scenic wonder." The cop stamped the ticket 'Paid' with a rubber stamp and handed back the duplicate copy to Betty. "Have you had the headlight fixed yet, ma'am?"

"Yes, we did."

"Good. Is your vehicle outside?"

"It is."

"Great. I've just got to take a look," the officer said.

"Thanks, kindly," Betty said.

"Here, let me help you with the door."

"I really appreciate that," Betty said. "Gettin' a walker through some of these doors isn't always the easiest. Nice to meet a real gentleman, even if you have to pay a ticket to meet him."

"Thanks ma'am. Sorry about the ticket, but it's the law." The cop helped Betty through the door then stared at The Smucker which Danny had running. "That's quite a camper," he said to Betty. "I see your headlights seem to be working fine but I have to check the high beams." He walked her to The Smucker, helped her in and handed in her walker. "Have a good trip, ma'am. You too sir," he called to Danny who gave him a salute. "If you'd just show me your high beams are working then you can be on your way." The cop walked back towards the door of the police station, turned and faced The Smucker giving Danny a thumbs up, then called, "Switch on the high beams, sir."

Danny pulled down on the headlight lever and held it down.

THE GRAND GETAWAY   235

The cop gave him another thumbs-up and called, "Have a safe trip, you all." He waved and disappeared back into the police station.

Charlie gave a whoop, slapping Danny on the back as he reversed The Smucker out of the parking space. "You're a damn fine mechanic, Danny Carroll."

As they left Mount Pleasant and headed south again, Betty said, "Let's have some music, Charlie. Anythin' we haven't played yet?"

"Let's see. I think we've played most of them." Charlie rummaged through their tapes. "Oh. We have a Bob Dylan tape. You want that one?"

"Sure, Charlie. Play it."

The tape came on with Dylan singing *Lay, Lady, Lay* and Charlie said, "Hey that's kinda sexy, Betty."

"It's mellow. I like it. Let's listen."

Charlie picked up the map again and looked at it. They were passing a place to the west of the highway called Spring City. "That sign says it's one of the prettiest towns in America," Charlie said.

"Yeah, but to drive in there means we use more gas," Danny said.

"What ya think we should do, Danny?" Charlie asked, quietly tapping the gas gauge.

"I know our bumper sticker says *Fueled by Dreams,* but without money for gas our dream dies with the motor. Once the gauge gets close to a quarter tank, we're gonna have to start looking seriously for a place to hang out for a few days. So you see any really good places, call out."

They passed through Ephraim, a fair sized place about another ten miles further south, and then Manti where Danny pulled over to take a look at the map.

The land around them was a dry, open plain with low mountains in the distance. A large temple dominated the skyline in the town.

"I thought maybe it was too dry around here for tornados, but I guess not, according to that sign. It was September too." Charlie pointed out an information sign about a tornado that had struck the town on September 8th, 2002. It caused about two million dollars worth of damage, but no one was killed. Dylan was singing *Blowing In The Wind.*

"We'll go as far as we can without running out of gas," Danny said. "If we're lucky we might make it as far as this place called Joseph." He pointed it out to Charlie. "Maybe there, near the Big Rock Candy Mountain. That'll be about it. We'll have to find a place by then, I figure."

A couple of minutes later Charlie called out. "Hey! Take a look at that sign!" They were passing a small church in the middle of nowhere with a sign that read, *Save On Gas. Walk With God.*

"Now that's *really* helpful," Betty called out.

Charlie snorted. "Yeah. If we see God hitchin' along this road we'll pick him up. I have a few questions I'd like to ask him."

They had just passed Axtell, so small they hardly noticed it, when Danny said, "We can't go much further. We're not as far as I thought we'd get and we're down to a quarter tank. Time to find our next hideout."

"What's that up ahead?" Charlie asked. "That white thing?" The land was quite flat, and in the distance, close to the road, a white rectangular shape stood out.

As they drove closer, Danny said. "It looks like a big tent."

"Couldn't be a circus," Charlie said. "Tent's too small."

Betty was now peering ahead. "It looks like one of those tents they hold weddin' receptions in," Betty said. "Funny place, though, for a weddin'."

As they came up to the tent, Danny slowed The Smucker and they read a sign beside the road that said, *Salvation! Meet God Tonight! – Pastor Leroy DeVille. The Liberty Church Of America. Supper Following Service. Free Chicken Dinner For All Who Attend. Church Service At 6:00 p.m.*

"Now there's a better sign than the last one," Betty called out. "A free chicken dinner sounds great. We haven't had chicken in ages."

"Well right now we need to find a place to spend a few nights," Danny said. "I'm looking for a grove of trees off the road." He was driving slowly and about half a mile further on Danny turned onto a small gravel road on their left with a few trees running into a gully.

The land was rough, unfenced, with low sage and a few bushes. Danny eased The Smucker off the road, driving very slowly. "Watch the ground, Charlie, keep a look out for any big rocks. We don't want to rip off our oil pan or the exhaust or anything."

He drove The Smucker parallel and close to the trees, down into the gully. There were gaps between the trees, and he found a fairly level spot before the gully dropped off sharply. He pulled into the gap and looked around before shutting off the motor. They were out of sight of the gravel road.

"This is it," Danny said. "We're gonna have to make the best of it, here. We can't risk going on and not find some place to stop and run out of gas. We're out of sight here and we should be okay. Sorry, there's no bathroom. We'll have to rough it."

"Do you think we could take in that free chicken dinner that's on offer?" Betty asked. "It's just a little way back up the road."

Danny said, "Sure. I've been to a few mission services back in Calgary, sang along with the hymns, and got a few hot meals out of it. We won't use much gas going back up the road and I'll eat chicken any time."

"Me too," Charlie said. "Maybe we could have a little snack in the meantime, Betty. I'm hungry, and we didn't have any lunch today."

"Okay. But first, I'll take Caroline to our outside 'bathroom'. Then I'll see what I can rustle up."

Betty served potato-cakes to the other three sitting at the table and sat down herself. "Caroline has something in her hands. I couldn't get her to open them when I went to wash them, and I gave up. I'll cut your potato-cakes, Caroline. There you go. What have you got in your hands? Come on now, eat your food while it's still warm. Pick up your fork. Here, take your fork."

She sighed as Caroline sat there, her hands cupped together, talking quietly.

"What have you got in your hands, Caroline? Give it to me so you can eat." Betty reached out to Caroline, but she withdrew her cupped hands.

"It's lunchtime, Caroline," Charlie said. "These potato-cakes are yummy."

Betty took Caroline's fork and speared a piece of potato-cake and put it to Caroline's mouth. "Open, Caroline. Open your mouth. Take a bite."

Caroline began chewing the potato-cake, but she still had her hands cupped.

Betty reached for her hands. "Let me see. Have you got jig-saw pieces again?"

Betty tried to gently pry Caroline's hands apart but Caroline said, "No." She withdrew her hands further away. She parted them momentarily and took a quick look and cupped them closed again. Betty speared another piece of potato-cake on Caroline's fork and handed it to her. This time Caroline took the fork in her left hand, keeping her right hand gently cupped. She lowered her head and said softly, "There, there," to her partially cupped hand.

"There ya go, Caroline," Charlie said, "that's right, eat yer..."

Betty's scream stopped him mid-sentence, and he and Danny jerked back as Betty tried to extricate herself from the table bench. Caroline dropped her fork and she quickly cupped her hands together again.

"What's wrong?" Danny asked, as he tried to rise from the bench. He was on the inside and impeded by the table.

"She has a spider!" Betty had managed to get herself free from the bench. She gave a shudder. "Oh God! I saw it move."

Charlie scrambled out quickly beside her.

Caroline was now talking quietly again to her cupped hands.

"Charlie get it off of her for God's sake," Betty said. "Where did she get it?"

"Take it easy," Charlie said. "She won't give it up easily. Caroline never would kill any kind of bug at Cavandish. Can we see the spider, Caroline? Can we see it?"

"Spider, spider," Caroline repeated. She slowly removed her top hand to reveal a dark grey, hairy spider covering most of the palm of her hand.

"It's a tarantula," Charlie whispered. "It's not fully grown, probably a young one."

"Oh my God!" Betty gasped. "Is it poisonous? Oh God. What'll we do if it bites her?"

"It hasn't yet," Charlie said. "Their bites are not usually fatal but they can be quite painful. Some people keep them for pets. You see them in pet stores. They get much bigger than the one Caroline has."

"Oh jeez, Charlie. Don't give us a science lesson, now," Betty whispered "Get her to open her hand again and maybe we could knock it out of her hand?"

"That might make it bite her. Maybe we could get Caroline to let it crawl onto a plate and we could put a pot lid over it. We can't startle it, or Caroline for that matter." Betty handed him a clean plastic plate and a pot lid.

He sat down beside Caroline as Danny eased himself from behind the table.

"Can I see the spider again, Caroline? Let me see the pretty spider." Charlie said quietly.

"Yes, spider," Caroline said. She slowly took her top hand away. The spider still sat on her other hand.

"Danny," Charlie said, "can you take the pot lid? I'm going to take Caroline's hand so she can't cover the spider again and try to tilt her other hand towards the plate. I'm hoping the spider might crawl onto it. If it does you'll have to be quick with the lid to cover it. It might jump, so you'll have to be fast. God I'm sweatin'."

Charlie took Caroline's left hand in his and reached slowly around her back to take the wrist of her right hand where the spider sat. He felt Caroline tense. "It's okay Caroline," he said quietly. "We're just going to move the spider. We'll put him on the plate and take him outside. That's where he lives. He wants to go home." He had no idea if she understood anything he said. He could sense Danny and Betty holding their breath.

Slowly he tried turning Caroline's hand. He had to make sure she didn't try to jerk her hand away, but it was hard to turn her hand sideways. He eased his fingers further along to the back of her hand and pushed gently. Her hand tilted slightly towards the plate, but the spider didn't move. Charlie was afraid to shake her hand. She might get bitten.

The spider moved and slowly slid two of its legs onto the plate. "Tickles," Caroline said quietly. Then the spider moved onto the plate and stopped. Charlie pulled Caroline's hand away as Danny slapped the saucepan lid over it. A piece of the plastic plate broke off, but the spider remained covered.

Charlie got up, taking the plate with the pot lid and the spider outside. He could see a couple of legs protruding from the broken edge, but he steeled himself to walk a good distance from The Smucker. With a quick motion, he flung the lid and plate into some sage. He'd get the pot lid back later. His heart pounding, he hurried back to The Smucker.

Betty was standing inside the door but Danny was sitting down again finishing his meal and opposite him Caroline was quietly using her fork to finish hers.

"Did you kill it?" Betty asked quietly.

"No." Charlie said. "Caroline wouldn't have wanted that. She was protecting the bugger."

THE GRAND GETAWAY   239

"I know. But I hate spiders. They give me the creeps. God, you were brave Charlie. Thanks." She gave him a big hug. "It's goin' to be hard to sleep here tonight. Do you think there's any more in here?"

"No. Caroline probably brought it in with her."

"When we went to the bathroom? God, how are we goin' to go outside to the bathroom again with those damn spiders out there?"

"I'll hold yer hand," Charlie laughed. "But they usually don't bother anyone. Look how long Caroline had it in her hand."

"Do me a favour, Charlie while it's still light," Betty said. "Could you and Danny go through our bus and make sure there are no more spiders and make sure the windows are closed tight? What's a fear of spiders called?"

"Arachnophobia."

"That **even** *sounds* creepy. Caroline was never scared of spiders or anything. I used to squish them if I saw one, but Caroline wouldn't hurt a fly. Not even to feed a spider."

"I think spiders prefer them alive," Charlie said.

"Oh gross." Betty shuddered.

CHAPTER 54

Five years ago, Pastor Leroy DeVille had founded The Liberty Church of America. He had been flicking through TV channels one morning looking for something to take his mind off his troubles. He was struggling to keep his roast chicken outlet, DeVille's *(Devilishly Delicious)* Roasted Chicken, located in Gunnison, from going under. When he'd paused to pour himself a bourbon and get some ice from the fridge, his channel surfing had landed on one of the religious category channels and he watched in awe as he saw the amount of donations streaming across the bottom of his TV screen from telephone callers. His chicken outlet could do with sponsors like that. As he sipped his drink, he watched the pastor encourage those on the telephone lines to give generously to help spread the word of the Lord.

The religious programmes reminded him of some of those weight loss programmes Lavinia, his wife of ten years, used to watch. Still 40 pounds overweight, she had deserted him a year ago, taking the last bit of their savings. She'd run away with a wrestler from the WWE circuit who promised her a more exciting life than filling cardboard boxes with roasted chicken, French fries and gravy. Leroy was stuck with several hundred dollars' worth of diet food and slimming potions which Lavinia had run up on his credit card.

He spent the rest of the day fascinated with the world of television evangelism. He marvelled at the huge crowds that flocked to massive arenas in search of God, miracles, or the hope of improving their lives. As far as Leroy could see, an endless supply of money was flowing in, money that obviously more than paid for the hours and hours of television time. He studied the techniques of the various preachers and, then and there, decided he had no desire to continue struggling to keep his lowly chicken outlet afloat. His head cook had quit, unwilling to put up with his wages being late for the third month in a row. But with the bank clamouring for payments on the loan he'd taken out and with chicken sales stalled, he needed time. Leroy had inherited DeVille's chicken outlet from his late father before the proliferation of the big nation-wide chicken chains and it had provided an adequate living. The chicken outlet was all he had. He had to keep it going and had to improve sales so he could unload it, if he wasn't going to walk away from it with nothing.

He got lucky the very next day when an itinerant cook walked into Leroy's chicken outlet and applied for the job advertised in the window. He called himself Sonny, and claimed to have been born in Paraguay, although he sounded like a New Yorker. Sonny said he was travelling the world. He proved to be an adequate cook and he brought with him a recipe of spices and a technique that infused the chicken with a taste that lifted Leroy's *ho-hum* chicken to a new level. Locally, sales of DeVille's chicken took off as word spread, and Leroy was forced to hire two more part-timers to handle the demand. Sonny moved on a month and a half later, following his own compass but leaving his recipe with Leroy, who immediately applied for a patent.

Meanwhile, Leroy pursued his plan to enrich himself. He found a college on the internet located somewhere on Grand Cayman which offered a divinity degree in one year and he enrolled, obtaining his graduate certificate just over a year later. He concentrated particularly on studying the Old Testament, thinking it gave him more scope for interpretation, and he took copious notes from the various preachers he watched on television, practicing their gestures in front of the bathroom mirror until he had them perfected, learning by heart many of their catch phrases about the need to always send money.

When he felt ready, he purchased a couple of new business suits and a small portable marquee that could be assembled quickly and transported in a pick-up truck. He began his own ministry, setting up his tent with the help of a couple of employees from DeVille's Chicken who were happy with a few extra bucks. When Leroy first pitched his tent, his services didn't draw big crowds, but when he offered a free chicken dinner after each service, more people stopped by. Nobody had ever complained, happy to leave clutching a cardboard box of piping hot, mouth-watering chicken.

Leroy found he had a gift for acting and was quite charismatic when he delivered his messages of hope, salvation and the possibility of a miracle or two. He was more than pleased with the way people generously threw handfuls of money onto the collection plate and even more surprised when he received testimonials from a few who had attended his services, claiming to have been cured of some illness shortly afterwards. Leroy reread these at subsequent tent services and found he was even beginning to believe in his own healing powers.

Before long he purchased a larger tent to hold the crowds, setting it up between small towns on wasteland or, for a small fee, in some farmer's field. He retained four attractive ladies with good singing voices to belt out some gospel hymns and bought a small generator to power the lights inside the tent. His chicken business was taking off too, and he was now negotiating with a couple of business people interested in purchasing franchises. He'd managed to cook up his own miracle, indeed!

"Well, we certainly won't be the only ones coming for the chicken dinner," Charlie said. "Looks like there's quite a crowd."

The tent was surrounded on all sides by vehicles, and Danny had trouble finding a place to park The Smucker. Light shone from inside the large tent and gospel music and clapping filled the air.

"Let me have my walker, Charlie," Betty said. "I find it useful to give myself a little space in crowds. We're not late, are we?"

"Maybe just a few minutes. They're probably just warming up," Danny said.

When they reached the entrance, the gospel song was just ending and, as the rhythmic clapping ceased, a few in the crowd called out, "Hallelujah."

The entrance flaps were folded back, and they found themselves standing at the end of a centre aisle. The tent, lit by a number of hanging lamps, was jam-packed, the congregation filling fold-up chairs on both sides of the aisle. There were no vacant seats in sight.

"Welcome, welcome, brothers and sisters," a voice boomed from the front. "Come forward. There are four seats right here in the front row. I'm Pastor Leroy DeVille and we welcome you to The Liberty Church of America."

There was a chorus of 'Welcome and Amen', throughout the tent.

Standing on a raised dais, Pastor DeVille, a burly man in his forties with long, dark hair, was dressed in a grey suit, white shirt and red tie and he called out again as he saw the foursome still hesitating at the end of the aisle. "Come forward friends. These four empty seats are a sign. You see, God wants you to sit here in front and hear His word. God knew you were coming and He saved these seats for you, brothers and sisters. You came last and as God said in the Holy Scriptures, 'The last shall be first.' Come forward, friends. The Lord has reserved a place for you."

The tent was filled with another chorus of 'Praise the Lord' and a few 'Amens'.

"I guess we are late," Betty muttered and pushed her walker down the aisle towards the front as the others followed.

There were two seats at the front on each side of the aisle. Betty and Caroline took the two on the right side, leaving Charlie and Danny to sit on the left. They found gospel hymn books on the seats and Betty picked up the one on Caroline's before helping her to sit.

Pastor DeVille beamed down at them. "Welcome friends, welcome." He now spoke to the whole congregation. "My friends, we are gathered here to praise the Lord. Tonight is your night to surrender your life to become a radical child of God. All over America, friends, people are looking for hope, for a better life. But they don't know where or how to seek it. They have despair in their hearts until they find the path to God. Still, my friends, many have doubts in their hearts. Once, I too had such doubts. You know friends, when I was a younger man, the Devil was messin' with my head. He said, 'You and I got a lot in common. Why your name sounds much the same as mine.' And in my drug crazed mind, yes friends, as many of you know, I was hurtin' my body, killin' my brain cells, craving that next fix, and in my head, I remember asking myself- the Devil's name is Leroy?"

The congregation guffawed.

"That's how confused I was, my friends. That's what went through my head until I realized He was talking about my last name, DeVille. It's a fine name, a French name handed down to me from my ancestors, but I had dragged that fine name through the mud. My ancestors would have been ashamed that one of their kin had brought that name so low.

"When God laid his hand on me and lifted me up, He told me He wanted me to believe and to spread His word. My first thought was that I should change my name. People would joke and laugh at a name like Pastor DeVille. When I was a child in school, I was sometimes picked on and the kids called me Leroy Devil. But then I prayed to God and He lifted me out of that pit of despair. He told me to keep my name, be proud of my name and to shake off those negative thoughts. Today, my friends, I am proud of my family name. And I thank God that I can come before you and spread His word. Now friends let us sing that fine old gospel hymn, *God Called My Name*, on page five of our gospel booklet."

Four ladies, who had been sitting in the front row stepped up onto the dais, one of them carrying a guitar, and led the congregation in a rousing rendition of the gospel hymn. The congregation clapped in time to the singing and Caroline began swaying to the rhythm. The lead singer held the last rising notes of each verse much longer than the rest of the choir and waved her hands high above her head, seeming to be almost in a trance.

Leroy liked Roxanne's enthusiasm. He had known her in high school when she was a cheerleader and she had always been able to jump higher and yell louder. She had fallen on hard times of late and was now a single mother raising four kids. Leroy often slipped her an extra $20 from the collection plate.

Now Pastor DeVille took up the calls of 'Praise the Lord,' that followed the end of the hymn and added his own, "Yes, praise the Lord. For the Lord has called my name. You know friends, the Lord calls many, but few are listening. Few are listening. We must learn to listen, for the Lord is calling out to us. When things go wrong, everybody asks, where's God?

"You know friends, we sometimes have to be patient. We have to be patient. Sometimes God waits until the time is right. Abram was 99 years old before God gave him a son. Think about that. Ninety-nine years old. In Genesis 15, God spoke to Abram and said, 'Look now toward heaven, and tell the stars, if thou be able to number them: and He said unto him, 'So shall thy seed be.' Abram had faith in God and at age 99 was given a son."

Charlie lost track of most of the things Pastor DeVille was saying, thinking about what it would be like to have a son at age 99. It would certainly be in the *Guinness Book of World's Records*, and he was sure sperm banks didn't exist back then.

"God said, in Genesis 17, 'And I will make my covenant between me and thee and will multiply thee exceedingly.' "And Abram fell on his face: and God talked with him, saying, 'As for me, behold, my covenant is with thee, and thou shalt be a father of many nations.'"

Danny found himself thinking about the number of times he'd fallen on his face when he was dead drunk. It wasn't too painful at the time, but hurt like hell whenever he regained consciousness.

Pastor DeVille continued, quoting God, "Neither shall thy name any more be called Abram, but thy name shall be Abraham; for a father of many nations have I made thee." So God told Abram to change his name to Abraham. Why? We'll leave that as a mystery of the Bible. God called my name too, but He told me not to change it. Preachin' God's word with a name spelled nearly the same as the Devil's own, God knew that would rile up the Devil real good.

"You know sometimes we find it hard to believe God's word. The children of Israel were scared and found it hard to believe God's word when Moses told them to follow him. And Moses, in Exodus 14, 'stretched out his hand over the sea: and the Lord caused the sea to go back by a strong east wind all that night, and made the sea dry land, and the waters were divided.' The children of Israel were afraid. Of course they were fearful. I very much doubt that many of them knew how to swim. It was highly unlikely that the Egyptians provided their captives with any kind of recreational swimming programme."

There were a few chuckles, but Leroy decided he'd have to find a new joke. That one was getting tired.

"Of course they were afraid," he continued. "But, my friends, Moses believed, and his people found their courage and walked through that parted sea without a drop of water touching their feet."

Loud calls of 'Praise the Lord,' rose from the crowd as Caroline mumbled quietly, "Yes, feet, feet, feet, feetie, feetie," as Betty patted her hand and wondered how long it would take until they got the chicken dinner. She was getting hungry.

"Now friends, let's rise and sing, *God Will Part The Water*," Pastor DeVille intoned. "You'll find it on page nine of our hymnal."

The hymn ended with an even more spirited performance from the choir, especially Roxanne, so much so that Leroy wouldn't have been much surprised if she'd concluded with a cart-wheel from her cheer-leading days.

Pastor DeVille stilled the hallelujahs and amens of the congregation with a calming motion of his hands and bowed his head as if in silent prayer as the crowd quieted.

He raised his head. "Friends, I have here a letter from a lady called Bernice who wrote to me from Tabiona, Utah. She writes, 'Me and my husband were passing through Twelve Mile Flat a month ago and we saw your church tent and went in. You were preaching about how the Lord can work wonders for those who believe. Pastor DeVille, that day, my left arm was aching so bad with my arthritis. I'm left handed and I've suffered terrible pain for over five years, and I could barely lift that arm. I listened to what you said, and as my husband and I drove away on our journey, you know Pastor, the pain in my arm started to fade. Now two months later, my arm is completely healed. I have no pain. I can raise my arm above my head and just this past week, I want you to know, I won the left-handed tennis championship of our little town.'"

Shouts of 'Praise the Lord' echoed through the tent.

THE GRAND GETAWAY   245

"Now I know there's people here tonight who are lookin' for a miracle," Paster DeVille continued. "I know you didn't all come out this way just for some of DeVille's chicken – wonderful as it may be. I myself can't make any promises. I can promise you the chicken – that is comin', but it's God who makes miracles, not Pastor Deville. Some of you will leave here tonight and you'll never be the same again. You're not goin' to walk out the way you walked in. Some of you are lookin' for relief from pain, to be set free from the curse of alcohol, for success in business, success in your marriage. God wants you to succeed. God wants you to prosper. Don't give up.

"My friends, tonight you may not receive a miracle. God has his own timetable. But you may get a miracle later. Your business may begin to prosper soon. Your finances may improve. If you gave everything away tomorrow, God would provide. The power of God is here tonight. What He's done for so many others, He'll do for you. God will break every yoke of the enemy." Leroy threw in a hodge-podge of platitudes he'd memorized from his TV viewing.

"Let us all stand. My friends, whatever your prayer, whatever your needs. Come quickly now! Come forward! Come runnin'! Come down here!" Leroy's voice rose, passionately, and he stepped down from the dais to the front of the crowd.

About twenty-five people hurried forward and clustered at the front of the centre aisle, many of them elbowing their way as close to Leroy as they could get. Betty got an elbow in her ribs and clutched her walker more tightly with one hand and held Caroline's hand with the other.

"Close your eyes, friends. Raise your right hand and let us pray." Pastor DeVille raised his hands and bowed his head. "Oh Lord, grant the prayers of those that truly believe and have faith, help to relieve their pain, their suffering, grant them success, help them to prosper, save their relationships." He opened one eye and caught sight of a woman struggling with her walker in the front row. "Help the lame to walk, let them throw away their walkers, their canes. Let them come running to you, Lord." He felt himself being carried away with his own words and was in danger of being knocked over by the crush around him. He backed up onto the dais. Some kind of struggle seemed to be going on in the front row.

Betty was sure someone was trying to wrench her walker from her hand and someone else had squeezed in between herself and Caroline. She still had hold of Caroline's hand but could no longer see her. She heard Caroline's voice rise, talking rapidly, probably distressed by the hubbub going on around her.

"Walkers, walkers, walkers, talkers, talkers, talkers, running, running, running, Lord, Lord, Lord."

Leroy was feeling inspired. The crush of people around him were crying out, 'Hallelujah, hallelujah,' and some were yelling, 'I believe, I believe.' The woman in the front row with the walker seemed to be working herself into a bit of a frenzy and a woman near her was now jabbering, speaking words he didn't understand. Was that what they called speaking in tongues? He wasn't sure if he was the cause, and couldn't remember if speaking in tongues was a miracle or an affliction. But Leroy was convinced something was happening and called out again, figuring that it couldn't do any harm, "Help the lame to walk, oh Lord let them throw away their walkers, their canes, their crutches and let them come runnin,' Lord."

The woman with the walker gave a loud grunt and suddenly her walker was sailing towards his head. He ducked just in time and saw it land and bounce harmlessly against the back wall of the tent.

The crowd in front roared, 'Glory to God, Hallelujah' and 'Praise the Lord' and broke into applause. Leroy, afraid things were getting out of hand, signalled Roxanne and the rest of the choir and bellowed out, "Let us sing together that fine old gospel hymn, *Lay Your Hands On Me, Lord, Let Me Walk With You*."

The choir led the singing as those who had assembled at the front slowly made their way back to their chairs, clapping and singing along. The woman who had taken his call literally, to let the lame throw their walkers away, gave Leroy a small wave of apology and appeared to mouth 'Sorry', for nearly taking his head off. She and the woman beside her began prancing about in time to the gospel hymn.

Leroy was convinced that by the enthusiasm of the congregation, most were sure a miracle had occurred. He had become so caught up the in the role he might have played in possibly producing a miracle that he'd almost forgotten the most important part of the service, the collection of donations. Tonight's crowd should provide in abundance, he thought, after what they had witnessed. In the inner pocket of his suit, he felt his phone vibrate to signal that DeVille's Roast Chicken delivery truck had arrived.

As soon as *Lay Your Hands On Me, Lord* ended, Pastor Leroy called out, "Before we leave friends, to partake of our roast chicken dinners, I must remind you how important it is to give to the Lord. It is through your offerings that we can continue with the Lord's work."

Leroy relied solely on his congregation's offerings. There was little overhead, except for the slip of paper in each box of Deville's *(Devilishly Delicious)* Roast Chicken with some text from the Bible so Leroy could rightfully claim he was spreading the word of God.

Leroy had given the assignment of typing up the slips to one of his part-timers at DeVille's chicken, a lapsed Mormon who, when business was slow, revelled in churning them out on a computer in a back room of the chicken outlet. Although she often hadn't a clue as to their meaning, if anyone had questioned the quotes she printed, she would probably have said something like, "What the hell! It's the word of God."

"My friends," Pastor DeVille's voice rose, "your giving is crucial to spread God's word. The more you give the more God blesses you. Help to save more souls with your donations, whatever you can give. Now, as we pass the collection plates, let us sing together that wonderful gospel hymn, *Doing The Work of God - Investin' In The*

Lord, page 15 of our hymnals. What you sow, you shall reap, so give generously my friends, and you shall be blessed."

As the choir led the congregation in the singing of the gospel song, a favourite of Leroy's, four trustworthy women moved through the congregation passing collection plates along the rows. Leroy vowed that he must talk to the woman who'd thrown away her walker to get her name and her story for future use. In fact, he thought, hanging that walker from the ceiling of the tent would be a constant reminder of what had occurred tonight. The walker could become a religious relic. There were churches all over the world filled with them. He beamed down at the woman now as she bobbed and swayed to the beat of the gospel hymn.

The collection over, and the plates delivered into Pastor Leroy's hands, he bowed his head and gave the congregation his blessing. Then he called out, "Go forth, my friends. Enjoy the DeVille's chicken that awaits."

As Leroy was about to step down and talk to the woman in the front row, he was suddenly accosted by two of his faithful followers who rushed forward, one of them crying out, "Pastor DeVille, Pastor DeVille, tonight you've inspired us. What a magnificent service. We are both overcome."

Before he could politely extricate himself, the two women in the front row had disappeared. By the time he got outside, through the number of well-wishers shaking his hand to congratulate him on his perceived miracle, they were nowhere to be seen. He hurried back into the tent, intent on retrieving the woman's walker, but it was gone too.

The Smucker was filled with the delicious smell of roast chicken as they drove back to their camping area.

"My, that chicken smells great," Charlie said. "What were you thinking, Betty, when you flung your walker at that preacher's head? I thought for sure we'd see no chicken tonight. Why did you do that?"

"I didn't fling it at his head. Someone grabbed it in the crush and I was only tryin' to get it back. I was almost fallin' over when whoever was yankin' on it let go. I lost my grip and it sailed away. The pastor seemed to be happy anyway, I'm sure he thought he'd witnessed a miracle. So did that crowd. Did you hear how many kept saying, 'Praise the Lord,' and pointin' at me when we were getting the chicken? Glad you got my walker back for me, Charlie. I don't use it much, but I think I'd miss it if we'd left it there."

Charlie put four plates on the table after he'd washed, then popped open a box of chicken. "This isn't Chinese food, is it? There's a slip of paper like the ones you get in fortune cookies, only bigger. It says, 'Brought to you by The Liberty Church of America – Leroy DeVille, Pastor. *It shall be health to thy navel, and marrow to thy* bones – *Proverbs Chapter 2 Verse 8*. I don't know if that's a comment on the chicken or what."

"Okay, Caroline," Betty said. "Let's wash your hands. Oh my God! Not again! Charlie, she's done it again!"

"What?" Charlie mumbled. He was already sinking his mouth into a piece of chicken.

"Picked up another one of those spiders. Musta grabbed it when we went to have a pee. Oh heaven help us! Quick, Charlie, do your Spider-Man thing again." Betty backed cautiously away as Charlie picked up a plate and looked for a pot lid.

"Let's see, Caroline," Charlie said quietly. "What's in your hand?"

Charlie jumped back as Caroline opened her hand. He hadn't expected her to open her hand so fast. Something fell to floor, and he recovered quickly and stamped on it.

Betty screamed, "Did you kill it?" She'd fled to the front of The Smucker.

Charlie burst out laughing. "I don't think you can kill a $50 bill by stamping on it. Good God! She's got two of them!"

"Oh my God!" Betty whooped. "She musta lifted them off the collection plate. I closed my eyes when the collection plate came round, pretendin' I was carried away by that gospel number. We'll all burn in hell!" Betty burst out laughing.

"Yeah, we might," Danny said, "but before that, maybe we could afford to camp a couple of days at Bryce Canyon."

CHAPTER 55

"Oh Caroline, let me give you a big hug," Betty said. "You really got us out of a jam last night."

"Smucker, Smuckers," Caroline said.

Betty laughed as she gave her a kiss on the cheek. "Yes, that's a jam too. And today we can go on, thanks to you, darlin'. Let's get those chicken boxes tidied up, Charlie, and we'll have breakfast."

"That chicken sure was good," Charlie said, as he began flattening the empty boxes.

Caroline picked up the slip of paper with the biblical text from her chicken box and Betty looked at it and laughed. "Look what it says on Caroline's paper."

"And the Lord shall bless all the work of thine hand," Danny read, *"Deuteronomy 28, Verse 12."* He chuckled. "He sure did, Caroline."

"Doesn't that beat all?" Charlie said. "Yep. God does work in mysterious ways." He laughed. "Caroline takes some money and is given forgiveness at the same time, according to that text."

"Where are the slips from our boxes, Danny?" Betty asked. "I'd like to read them."

Danny rummaged around on the table, then found a slip on the floor. "Oh, here's the one I got but I couldn't make head or tail of it. It sounded like an ad for razor blades to me. It says, *And Jacob said to Rebecca his mother, Behold, Esau my brother is a hairy man, and I am a smooth man. Genesis 27, Verse 11.* I guess he's saying Esau has a beard and he doesn't, but I expect their mother might have noticed that."

"Hmmf, so what happened to the one from my box?" Betty asked.

"Here it is," Charlie said. "You want me to read it out?"

"Yeah, go ahead."

"It sounds a bit gloomy. *But as for you, turn you and take your journey into the wilderness by the way of the Red Sea.* That's it. It says it's from *Deuteronomy 1, Verse 40.*"

"Well we are goin' to Bryce Canyon. It's red but I don't recall any Red Sea on the way. We still have about a week to wait for our pension money, so we'll have to hang around in the wilderness like that Bible bit says. Here, the coffee's ready." Betty poured Danny a cup and passed it to him. "Let's move on somewhere else. Stickin' around here in **Spiderville** gives me the creeps."

"I'll hang onto the newspaper pages they wrapped the chicken in," Charlie said, beginning to fold them up. "Keep it for emergencies in case we're in the wilderness for forty days and nights and our toilet paper runs out. Hey, look at this! Here's a review from some guy about the Fork 'n' Spoon pizza place in Spanish Fork. Listen to this. It's written by some guy called Denton Myers. He says, *'Brianna, one of the followers of my column and blog, tweeted to tell me that a great new pizza place just opened on Rodney Way, in the warehouse district of Spanish Fork. I happened to be in the area when I got her tweet and checked it out. The place was jam-packed and I ate my pizza sitting on a bench outside the front door.'*

"Hey, that musta been the guy we saw when we were leaving," Danny said.

"It goes on," Charlie said. *'It has a terrible name, Fork 'n' Spoon, but the owners are planning to change the name to Mama Mia's Pizza. I saw a couple of elderly waiters serving the tables. As soon as the owners gauge the clientele over the next week, they said they will be looking to hire some new staff, no doubt some younger and more agile waiters.'*

Betty laughed.

"He ends," Charlie said, "with, *'I'll be back. The pizza is certainly a winner and I'm giving it 8 out of 10 stars.'"*

"Giovani and Marie-Angela must be very happy," Betty said.

"It was all your doing, Betty," Charlie said.

"It was all of us, Charlie. We all worked hard and made it happen. But I guess you and Danny weren't agile enough, so you got laid off." Betty laughed. "And you didn't get any tips."

They filled The Smucker with gas in Salina, the next town south of where they'd camped. Danny thought the full tank would get them into Bryce Canyon. With Betty hoping to spend a couple of days in Bryce, and a few more days left until Pension Day, Danny suggested they might want to spend at least one more day camping out. "We don't want to blow all our money and then find we can't make it to the Grand Canyon."

"Nothing's goin' to go wrong," Betty said. "The banks said our cards are ready to go as soon as there's any money in our accounts."

"Yeah," Charlie said. "And we can always take Caroline to church if we run short. We've got one last music tape left, Gordon Lightfoot. Want me to put it on?"

"How come you're only tellin' me now we have Gordon Lightfoot? You know I like him," Betty said.

"I could say I was saving the best for last," Charlie said, "or admit I never did sort out what we had in the bag."

"Play it!" Betty said. "But don't ask me for a reference if you ever apply for a job as a DJ. That Bob Dylan tape you played before was beginnin' to get me depressed. I like him, but he sometimes sounds a bit too mournful."

Danny and Charlie both laughed as Lightfoot sang *Early Morning Rain.*

"Oh shut up you two," Betty said. "We've got more than $100 in our hand, thanks to Caroline here."

"Yes. More. More. More," Caroline repeated.

THE GRAND GETAWAY   251

They skirted the fairly large town of Richfield and passed through the much smaller towns of Elsinore and Joseph. There was some greenery, but beyond the towns the desert appeared to have taken over and the vegetation was for the most part sparse and low growing. The surrounding and distant hills appeared similar. Shortly after Joseph, as they headed straight south on Highway 89, the Big Rock Candy Mountain loomed up in front of them, its yellow rock shining brightly in the sun.

"I remember this mountain," Betty said excitedly. "Let's take a break here, Danny. It looks like there's a service station ahead and probably washrooms. I don't think there was anythin' here when I came by with Arnie, just the road and the mountain."

There were gas pumps and a small convenience store and motel, and they managed to make use of the washrooms without spending any more money. They retreated to a parking area and took a morning coffee break.

Danny was looking at the map, trying to figure out where they might stop. It was still early and the terrain they had passed hadn't looked too inviting for an overnight stay.

They went on, not in any rush, and passed by Marysvale, Junction and Circleville. Danny pulled over to look at the map again. "Panguitch is the last town before Bryce Canyon, and when we get there it's only 23 miles to Bryce, so I think we'd better find something, if we can, between here and there."

Nothing they saw appealed to them. There were only a few driveways with houses visible from the road and the continuing low vegetation offered no cover. They found themselves entering the town of Panguitch sooner than they expected and decided to stop, take a look around and get some information on Bryce Canyon. They parked on the main street.

"This looks like an interesting place," Charlie said. "Kind of wild west, cowboy country. Look at the store fronts."

They had parked across from Cowboy's Café, and Betty and Charlie went in. They picked up a couple of Bryce Canyon brochures from the counter and Betty confirmed that there was no Walmart in Panguitch. Just a couple of doors up the street they came upon Cowboy's Collectibles and between that store and the next they found an empty lot with picnic tables.

"Why don't I make us some sandwiches for lunch and we can eat right here. I'll boil some water and make some tea for a change."

"I'll come and give you a hand, Betty," Charlie said.

Ten minutes later, they came back carrying a plateful of tuna sandwiches and a pot of tea and some mugs.

"We're havin' a picnic, Caroline," Betty said as she and Charlie sat down at the picnic table.

"It says here that entry to the park costs $25 per vehicle for up to seven days but camping costs $15 per night." Danny was reading one of the brochures. "So, say two nights camping in Bryce, that's $55 total."

"Do you think we could afford one shower for everyone?" Betty asked.

"Possibly. But we have to find somewhere for tonight."

"Just think," Betty said "in a few more days, we'll be able to shower every day when our pension money arrives. Even twice a day. Maybe we'll check into a motel and I can have a real bath."

"And I'll scrub your back," Charlie said.

Betty laughed. "Not unless you brought your rubber ducky, you won't."

Just before they reached Highway 12 where they'd have to turn off, Danny slowed The Smucker to a crawl.

"Here's a place with some trees further in. What do you think, Charlie?"

"There's a cattle-guard across the drive entrance. Could be a ranch, or maybe just a private house and the guard is to keep cattle out, not in. Let's take a look."

Danny turned into the driveway and they rumbled over the cattle-guard and followed a dirt track that twisted and turned between stocky pines and scrub. After about a quarter mile, with no sign of any dwelling, they came to a cluster of pines.

"This looks promising," Danny said. "Let's see if we can hide ourselves in these trees."

Danny eased The Smucker between the trees and stopped when he was satisfied that they were out of the view of anyone driving in or out of the property.

It was getting late in the afternoon and Betty suggested they should have an early supper and get to bed. "We're so close to Bryce Canyon, we should be able to get a prime camping spot there tomorrow. And I'm looking forward to that hot shower."

Danny sat up reading a bit more of *House Of Sand And Fog* after the others had turned in, until he started nodding off and the book slipped out of his hands. As he climbed into his bunk, the only sound was a slight breeze sifting through the pines outside and the breathing of the others as they slept.

Some kind of groaning noise woke Betty, but when she was fully awake, she lay there, listening, convinced she must have just been dreaming. In the bunk opposite hers, Caroline was peacefully sleeping. Through the windshield, the piece of sky Betty could get a glimpse of was beginning to lighten. It's still early, she thought, time for a few more minutes of sleep. She'd just closed her eyes when the low moan started up again, only much louder this time. Her eyes flew open. Across from her, Caroline was still asleep and Danny, in his bunk above Caroline's, was breathing softly. The moan had come from her side of The Smucker.

What the heck was it? Was it the wind? The moan sounded again. It had to be Charlie in his bunk above her. "Oh for God's sake, Charlie. Stop that god-awful

THE GRAND GETAWAY   253

moanin' or snorin' or whatever it is you're doin'." Betty slapped at the edge of the bunk above her. She heard Charlie snort and another low moan followed.

"Jeez, Murphy, Charlie! Surely you're not playin' with yourself, you dirty old bugger!"

Suddenly The Smucker rocked and Betty sat bolt upright. "Charlie, what the hell are you doin'?"

Danny was now sitting up and Betty could see Caroline stirring as The Smucker heaved and rocked violently again.

"Oh my God!" Betty yelled. "Danny, is it an earthquake?"

Danny was untangling himself from his bedding and making his way to the front as The Smucker gave another lurch and a series of bellows came from outside.

"What's happening?" Charlie was sitting up in his bunk. "How come we're rocking?"

Danny reached the door and pushed it open as Betty scrambled out of her bunk to the window. She saw Danny jump out and disappear around the front of The Smucker, then heard him yell as about ten cows suddenly shuffled into view, bellowing.

Betty started to laugh as a bare-footed Danny, arms raised above his head, herded the cattle away from their bus, then came back, joining in Betty's laughter when he saw her in the window.

He was still laughing when he came in. "One of those cows was using The Smucker as a scratching post. There's no damage done. I scared the hell out of them. Don't think they'll be back."

"When I heard the first moos, I thought it was you, Charlie." Betty let out another peal of laughter. "For an ex-farm girl, you'd think I'd know the difference between a cow's moo and a Charlie moo."

"Gee! Thanks a lot Betty."

"Sorry, Charlie. I guess I wasn't fully awake and then I thought..." Betty burst out laughing again.

All through breakfast, Betty's giggling threatened to break into full fits of laughter.

Danny persuaded them to stay where they were for one more night before going on to Bryce Canyon. He pointed out that it was best to be on the safe side and not get trapped somewhere between Bryce and the Grand Canyon with few places to hide and no money.

"It's quiet here and the weather is nice and I haven't seen any spiders."

Charlie laughed. "Probably all trampled to death by the cattle."

"Okay," Betty said. "We'll stay one more night here, but we're definitely gonna have showers as soon as we get to Bryce Canyon."

"This looks like a nice campin' spot. We'll have a great view from here. Isn't this place just fantastic?" Betty swept her arm around to point out the glowing reds and oranges of Bryce Canyon opposite where they'd parked The Smucker.

They had clambered out to take in the view and examine the camping spot where they would spend the next couple of days. Caroline was dozing inside at the kitchen table.

"It's perfect," Betty said. "It could even be the same spot where Arnie and I pitched our little tent. We'll be on our own here and it's not too far back to the showers. Let's camp here."

Danny bent down to move a rock from the space where he intended to back in The Smucker.

"Oh my God!" It was Charlie. "The Smucker!"

Betty and Danny whirled around. The Smucker was gone.

Betty gasped. "How? Oh no!"

Danny was already running down the road which sloped away and around a bend close to the edge of the canyon. His heart was racing. *I had turned off The Smucker, I had, I'm sure of that.* He felt for the keys in his pocket. They were there. *Had I left it in park? I must have, I always do. I know I hadn't put on the hand brake, I hardly ever use it. Somehow The Smucker had rolled away. Oh God... Please... Caroline had been sound asleep at the table.*

Behind him he could hear Charlie's panting and the sound of his feet crunching on the gravel as they both ran.

CHAPTER 56

Danny urged his body on, his legs rubbery and beginning to ache. He couldn't remember the last time he'd run like this! He gulped air through his open mouth, his nose incapable of grabbing nearly enough oxygen. He had to get round the bend ahead but dreaded that The Smucker would have already disappeared, plunging off the road into the canyon.

He rounded the bend. The bus was still on the road about 100 metres ahead, rolling slowly down the slope. There was another bend ahead of The Smucker, much sharper that the first, and Danny was certain it wouldn't make that bend. He tried to put on a burst of speed in the hope of catching up, but he was near collapsing. Charlie was even further behind.

What was poor Caroline doing? Was she still blissfully sleeping at the table? If she was awake, would she even know she was in danger or was she just sitting there talking quietly to herself? I helped Mick and Kenny get into that sports car and they'd died and now it's about to happen all over again.

Now he was really gasping for air, his vision blurring, but he forced his feet to keep moving. As he stumbled on, he saw flashes of Caroline's face in his head – smiling with pleasure as a butterfly landed on her hand that day at the zoo. Her soft voice saying, "tickles" and then "gone," laughing as it flew away. Sitting beside him at Cavandish at coffee time as she innocently helped herself to his cookie, having already eaten her own. Swaying in time to the music at Pastor DeVille's church service – talking to the baby tarantula in her hand, protecting it. She seemed to enjoy to the full every little pleasure life gave her. What had happened to her was so damned unfair. Neil Diamond's Sweet Caroline began repeating in his brain with every faltering step.

He brushed the sweat from his eyes as he stumbled on. Two figures appeared on the edge of the gravel road, not far from the bend, where they must have been admiring the view. The sound of tires crunching on the gravel made them stop and turn to watch the silently approaching vehicle. Danny wanted to yell out, "Stop that bus!" but he had no breath.

Somehow he kept his aching legs churning, but his heart sank when The Smucker hit a small bump and suddenly veered left towards the canyon. Danny saw the man throw up his hands, then grab the arm of the woman beside him as The Smucker, still rolling along slowly, passed them. Then The Smucker took a definite turn to the right, coasting a few more metres downhill before stopping and rocking gently, its progress halted by the one and only large bush at the edge of the road.

Ahead of him the couple scampered after The Smucker. With a new surge of adrenaline, Danny pushed himself forward.

The couple had scrambled into the shallow ditch and were approaching the door, but paused as Danny staggered around the front of The Smucker.

"God! Is this your bus?" the man asked. He was dressed in shorts, as was the woman with him. They wore hiking boots and both of them carried hiking poles.

Danny, gasping for breath, could only nod. He was almost doubled over, his hands resting on his knees.

There was a shuffling sound behind The Smucker and then Charlie tottered into view, trying to say something but unable to catch his breath. All that came out were gasps.

"I thought when it suddenly swerved in front of us that it was going to send us into the canyon," the man said. "There was no one at the wheel, but then that woman appeared at the front, grabbed the steering wheel and steered it into this bush."

Danny raised his head and looked through the windshield where Caroline sat in the driver's seat, looking anxious until she saw Danny looking up at her. A smile broke out on her face and she waved to Danny.

"Don't know where she came from," the man went on. "Say, are you okay? Here, have some water." He handed Danny a flask of water and he gulped it greedily, making him splutter as he stood there grinning up at Caroline and then gasping, "Thank God. Oh thank God."

The woman handed a similar flask to Charlie, who was leaning heavily against the side of The Smucker, puffing and panting. He could only nod his thanks before he swallowed some water and then sloshed some over the back of his head and neck.

Danny waved to Caroline and handed back the water-flask to the man.

"Glad yer okay, thanks... thanks... for the water," Danny panted. "We were picking out... a campsite... just up the road... when The Smu... our bus... rolled away... Caroline, that's Caroline..." he pointed and his voice almost broke, "was asleep at the kitchen table." Danny was beginning to breathe easier now. "I guess I didn't put it in park properly when I stopped... Damn stupid of me. God! We left Betty up the road. She'll be worried sick. We've got to get back there quick. Thanks... thanks for your help, folks. Come on Charlie."

"'Kay," Charlie gasped. "Better... look for... a spot to turn."

"No. I'm gonna back up real slow. We might have to go a long way for a turning spot. I don't want to try a U-turn either with the edge of the canyon so close. Betty will be frantic. Come on! Get in! You folks want a ride?"

"No thanks, we'll walk. We're going the other way anyway. Glad you're all okay."

"Thanks again," Danny said as he shook hands with the couple and Charlie did the same.

"Come on Charlie, let's get our bus back to Betty before she calls out the Parks Service and has helicopters sweeping over the canyon." He tried to put on a brave face and make light of it, but his stomach was churning.

THE GRAND GETAWAY   257

He opened the door of The Smucker and climbed in. He reached back to help haul an exhausted Charlie in, then he bent and gave Caroline a long hug.

"I'm sorry, Caroline. I'm a dumb old fool. You were great. Thanks love, thanks."

Caroline patted Danny on the back as he held her and he found it hard to hold back his tears.

Charlie hugged Caroline too and took her back to sit at the table with him. Danny assured him that he'd be okay backing up using The Smucker's side mirrors. He flicked on the flashers and started reversing.

Charlie positioned himself in the centre of the bus so he could see out the rear window to warn Danny of any oncoming traffic. The road was clear as Danny sounded the horn and cautiously backed round the bend.

"Betty's just ahead," Charlie called out. "I can see her."

"Has she seen us?" Danny called.

"Not yet. She's sitting on a rock with her head in her hands. Honk the horn again."

Danny did, leaning on it.

"She's standing up," Charlie said.

"I can see her now in the mirror," Danny said. "Take Caroline out so Betty can see she's all right. Hurry."

Danny watched Betty in the side mirror as she walked towards The Smucker, then saw her throw up her hands in joy as she caught sight of Charlie and Caroline. He saw all three of them hug. He turned off the motor, made sure The Smucker was in park and pulled on the hand brake. He waited a couple more minutes before he climbed out and started walking towards them.

CHAPTER 57

Before Danny reached the others, he paused and stood for a moment, looking into the canyon as a fragment of white cloud floated overhead, casting a small shadow on the canyon face opposite. As the cloud drifted on, its moving shadow caused the glowing reds, oranges, whites and browns of the rock formations to appear to pulse and flicker as if tiny fires were breaking out. He was awed by the spectacular scene before him.

In the past, Danny had never needed an excuse to drink but he thought right now, in this moment, if he ever needed one, this would be it. Caroline, miraculously, hadn't been injured or killed. She was okay. And he could not think of a better reason to celebrate. He knew, once he started, he could never have stopped at one. If Caroline had died... then the urge to drink would have been undeniable and nothing could have staved off his plunge back into that bottomless pit. But Caroline was alive. Caroline was fine.

"If you're really out there somewhere God, thanks, thanks a lot. I owe you one," he said softly. Then Betty was calling to him, telling him that she and Caroline were going to walk back up the road to save the camping spot.

When Charlie reached him, he asked, "How's Betty? What did she say?"

"She was sure Caroline was a gonner along with The Smucker. She blames herself for leaving Caroline in it while we checked out the site. I told Betty that Caroline was behind the wheel when we caught up with The Smucker. She must've somehow taken it out of park and it rolled away."

"It was my fault, not Caroline's," Danny said. "I didn't put it in park properly. Didn't you hear that guy? He said that when they first saw the bus there was no one at the wheel and then Caroline appeared and grabbed the steering wheel. She saved The Smucker and herself. I guess she woke up just in time. Betty thinks that Caroline made the bus roll away and that you and I are such great athletes that we managed to catch up with The Smucker, get into it while it was still rolling, and bring it to a stop. She thinks you and I are heroes! Well, not for long. I'll tell her what really happened. It was Caroline who saved the day."

"Then Betty will be mad at you. Right now she's happy everything turned out okay."

"Well, I'm gonna tell her. It's Caroline who deserves a medal."

They had just reached The Smucker when a shuttle bus pulled past them and stopped.

A young female driver in a parks uniform got out and walked back to them. "You fellows having trouble with your bus?" she asked. "I can call on my radio if you need a tow."

"No, we're fine, thanks," Danny said.

THE GRAND GETAWAY   259

"Well you realize you shouldn't park here? This road is narrow and you're a traffic hazard. You don't want to be the cause of an accident. You have to move on or a Park Ranger will give you a ticket."

"Sorry miss," Danny said. "Charlie here was feeling a little queasy and I just stopped to let him get a breath of air. He's okay now. We're going right now, thanks."

"Okay." She looked at Charlie. "Next time you feel car-sick you're gonna have to throw up in your..." she paused, "bus." She stared at it like she couldn't believe the paint job, "or hold on until you get to a view-point. You could get a pill like Gravol. You can get some at the Park Headquarters. I gotta go. I've got a bus load of people waiting to view the canyon."

"Thanks kindly," Danny said. "I'll be sure we get some pills for Charlie here as soon as possible. Come on Charlie, let's get going."

As soon as the shuttle-bus had disappeared around the bend, Danny started backing up again.

"Jeez, you made me sound like a real wimp," Charlie said. "What the hell are you doing?"

"Backing up. The campsite is only just behind us. We'll be there in seconds." Danny laughed. "If I drive too far you might throw up before we get you some of those Gravol pills. Wimp! And I beat you in the race after The Smucker."

"Jerk!" Charlie laughed. "You had a head start."

"Keep an eye out. We're nearly there," Danny said. "You can get out in a minute and help me back in so I don't run over Caroline or Betty."

When they were safely in the camping spot, not only did Danny make absolutely sure The Smucker was in park and the hand-brake was on, but he also found the rock he'd moved earlier and wedged it under one of the back wheels.

Betty came to him and gave him a hug. "I'm sorry Danny, I shouldn't have left Caroline alone, but she was asleep. From now on we can't leave her alone in the bus. I was never so relieved as when I saw The Smucker back-up around that corner..."

"It was my fault," Danny interrupted. "Make us some coffee. I'll tell you the real story. I need to sit down. I feel like I've run a marathon."

Betty was still hugging Caroline long after Danny had explained what had happened. They were all sitting around the table, sipping their coffee.

"Thank God everythin' worked out okay. Don't blame yourself, Danny. We just won't leave Caroline on her own in here again." She gave Caroline another kiss on the cheek as Caroline grinned. "If we had more money, we'd have a party. Let's do that in a few days, anyway. Caroline's birthday isn't until May, but we can have an early birthday party for her at the Grand Canyon and celebrate our arrival there, too. I think we're gonna make it now. In the meantime, let's put what happened this mornin' behind us and enjoy this place. It's beautiful. We'll just be careful not to fall into the canyon."

"It does say that the most common mishaps are sprained or broken ankles, usually on the trails." Charlie was reading the safety section of the information leaflet they'd got at the entrance. "It recommends good hiking boots. I guess we won't be doing any hiking."

"No, Charlie, we won't be doin' any hikin'," Betty scoffed.

"Hang on," Charlie said. "It says here another concern is bubonic plague."

"What? How can you get that?" Betty asked.

"It says it's found on fleas in prairie dog colonies, so we should..."

"Isn't bubonic plague that plague they got in London a few hundred years ago. How in hell did they have any prairie dogs in London?"

"It was fleas on rats in London," Danny said.

"So what's a prairie dog?" Betty asked.

"Probably the same as gophers in Canada," Charlie said, "but it says here, avoid contact with wild animals, in particular prairie dogs, chipmunks, ground squirrels and other rodents. You should dust any pets you bring into the park with flea powder."

"We don't have any pets," Betty said. "And we'll make sure Caroline won't make a pet out of any of those creatures, right, Caroline?"

"Oh yes," Caroline replied.

"I think you mean no, Caroline." Betty laughed. "Anyway, no pickin' up any prairie dogs, chipmunks or squirrels. Now I feel itchy and we don't have any flea powder. Danny, do you think you feel up to drivin' us to the showers? I really would like to wash my hair and Caroline's and I'm sure you and Charlie could do with a shower too, after all that runnin'."

"That'd feel real good right now," Danny said.

"I didn't mention that the park is also home to mule deer and mountain lions," Charlie added.

"Well, Charlie, if I find Caroline with a mountain lion under her arm, I'll tell her to put it down," Betty said. "Let's hit those showers."

CHAPTER 58

Danny sighed with pleasure as the hot water coursed over him, soothing his aching muscles and easing the tension in his shoulders. The run after The Smucker had taken a lot out of him. His legs would probably be stiff and aching tomorrow, he thought. The day before, Danny had come to the last few chapters of *House Of Sand And Fog*, and it had dramatically illustrated how a small thing – in the case of the book, a bureaucratic error which should have easily been fixed – had caused things to spiral out of control. He didn't know why that had come into his head, but then he realized why. He tried to shake it off. Most of the books he'd read recently had unhappy endings. They were fiction. But what had nearly happened was real.

The thought of what could have happened had badly shaken him and, for once, he was grateful that Caroline's dementia had blocked out any memory of the event. Caroline was her usual self, chatting and smiling, living just in that moment.

"Boy that feels good!" Charlie whooped from another shower stall. They were the only two in the shower-room. "How are ya feeling, Danny?"

"This hot water's making me feel better. My legs might be killing me tomorrow. I haven't run like that since I was a kid."

"Me neither. My legs feel like cooked spaghetti. But Caroline's fine – she's as happy as a lark. Betty too. She's really determined to enjoy our stay here. We've gotta enjoy ourselves now. Let's put what's happened behind us and when we make it to the Grand Canyon we'll really celebrate.

"You know it's amazing how things have worked out," Charlie continued. "Getting all the way down here. Sometimes it blows me away. Sort of like I've been waiting to go on this trip all my life after spending most of my years running across Canada in freight trains. You ever think we might have been, you know, put on this earth for a purpose? I don't mean religion, really... just thinking, ya know, how we choose to do the things we do?"

"You mean like fate. That sort of thing? Like you sticking to the straight and narrow and me going off the rails, so to speak with the booze." Danny laughed and Charlie joined in.

"Hey, that's a good one, Danny. I guess maybe I do mean... Fate. Or, maybe more than that."

"Are you talking about the meaning of life, Charlie?"

"Yeah. Maybe that's it. Yeah, the meaning of life."

"Can't say I've given it a lot of thought." Danny chuckled. "You have any more coins?"

"No. Why? You want me to pay you a penny for your thoughts?"

262   THE GRAND GETAWAY

"No. But I don't think I can decide on the meaning of life in such a short time. These showers only run for six minutes and I'd say we're about on the last minute."

"Crap! I'm still covered in soap. Gotta rinse off quick."

Danny was thankful and somewhat relieved when Betty suggested they take the free shuttle to see the sights of the canyon. They could leave The Smucker at their camping spot and catch the shuttle in the campground just around the corner from where they'd parked.

"We still have another whole day here tomorrow," Betty said, "and we can look around on our own and take our time. Today, Danny, you take a break. We can really feel like tourists."

When they discovered that there was a great picnic spot at Rainbow Point with tables and washrooms, Betty decided they should take a picnic lunch. They boarded the shuttle with another 15 passengers.

At Rainbow Point as they sat in the warm sunshine eating their lunch, Charlie pointed out that from there, they were looking at, "According to this guide-brochure, views of Utah, Arizona and sometimes New Mexico."

Next morning they were back again at Rainbow Point breakfasting on Betty's pancakes at 8:00 a.m. Charlie had read that the best time to make the drive with little or no traffic was early morning. After breakfast they drove very slowly back towards their camping spot, catching the early morning light at the various viewpoints. At Bryce Point they all squeezed onto the same bench, staring in awe at what was called Bryce Amphitheatre. Charlie pointed out a view of the Black Mountains to the northeast and the Navajo Mountain to the south. Even Caroline was silent as the four of them drank in the view.

Betty finally broke the spell when she said, "I think I'm beginnin' to feel like a tourist. You know we have $42 left. Let's stay one more night. Tomorrow is Saturday, September 27th. We hung around with those cattle for an extra night, and we didn't even have an outhouse. Here we've got toilets and showers. If we all have a shower on Sunday mornin' we'll have, let's see, about $34 left. Would that be enough gas money to get us to Grand Canyon, Danny?"

"Maybe. We still have about a quarter tank left."

"Let's splurge. How about an early supper and we'll just drive a little way to catch some of the sunset colours. All right?"

"All right." Danny laughed. "Why not?"

"Thanks, Danny," Betty said, giving him a hug.

On Sunday morning they all had showers and said their goodbyes to Bryce Canyon.

As Danny drove The Smucker out of the park and turned onto the highway, he glanced back at Betty. She was sitting as usual with Caroline. Charlie had put on their Barbra Streisand tape and Barbra was belting out *Happy Days Are Here Again*. Danny could see Betty looking through the window. She had a sad, wistful look. *Probably thinking back to her visit here, years ago, with Arnie Thorkleson*. Then Caroline said something to her and she smiled and gave her a hug.

If all went well, this should be their last day on the road before they reached their destination.

For some reason Danny wasn't really sure how he felt about that.

CHAPTER 59

"We're coming into Kanab," Danny said. "I believe it's the last town in Utah before we cross over the Arizona border." They were travelling along a dry plateau with tall sagebrush and some kind of shorter bushes covered in bright yellow blooms. To the south loomed a high, bright red ridge of cliffs.

"Wonder if we've committed crimes each time we crossed a state border?" Charlie asked.

"Whadda ya mean?" Danny asked.

"Well you know, in those FBI movies they're always charging bad guys with crossing state lines. Like kidnapping someone and crossing from one state into another."

"How does that make it worse, if you kidnap someone?" Danny asked.

"Beats me. But they always seem to tack that charge on, if they kidnap someone or rob a bank. It's like you're supposed to stay in that state and not try to get too far away, like you're not playing fair or something. Maybe kinda like cheating in Monopoly, passing Go when you shouldn't and collecting the $200."

"Hmm," Danny said. "So how many crimes do you think we've committed by crossing state lines?"

"Well let's see. We've crossed into Montana, Wyoming, Idaho, then Utah, and when we cross into Arizona, that's how many states?"

"Five," Danny said.

"So every time we committed a crime it would be multiplied by five times."

"Crimes such as?"

"Driving into the country illegally to begin with. Violating all kinds of motor vehicle laws, like not properly licensed. We never asked Caroline if she wanted to come with us, so they might call that kidnapping. Stealing Darlington's wheels."

"Do they count crossing the Canadian border?" Danny asked. "It's not a state line."

"The Montana border is."

"Okay. Any more crimes?"

"Let's see. Fooling that cop over the headlight."

"What's that crime called?"

"Um? Probably perjury."

"Don't you have to swear on a Bible and lie in court to be charged with that?" Danny laughed.

"Then maybe false pretenses. And that cop was sure Caroline swore at him."

"You're gonna count that?"

"Well, no."

"Anymore?"

THE GRAND GETAWAY   265

"Trespassing?"

"We trespassed about 10 times. We caught those fish with Magnus Levinson illegally, and we ate those in Montana and Wyoming. What about those rabbits you snared? Might've been a protected species."

Charlie laughed. "You never know."

"Is that it? You think we'd get life if they added them all up?"

"Then there was the 100 bucks Caroline lifted at that church service."

"You forgot working illegally at the pizza place, and we probably broke all kinds of sanitation laws. I saw you wipe your nose on the back of your sleeve. I think you're supposed to wash your hands after that. I'm sure you and Betty broke environment laws in a National Park when the two of you jumped into and polluted that mud-pot at Yellowstone, or maybe you'd be charged with swimming in a prohibited area. And you forgot vandalism and littering."

"Vandalism?"

"Yeah, we ripped up boards to make that toilet seat in that barn and we crapped in private outhouses."

Charlie laughed again. "I think they'd call that defecation of character. And the littering?"

"I'm sure I saw you throw an apple core on the highway somewhere near the Montana-Wyoming border. We were close enough that it probably rolled across. Anyhow, here's Kanab. Let's see what this place looks like before we spend the next 10 years fighting extradition charges from each state after we've served our time in prison in Utah."

"Look at that! It's called Little Hollywood." Charlie pointed to a sign as they reached the top end of the main street.

As Danny drove down main street, he slowed so they could read the signs listing the movies made in Kanab and the nearby area.

"Some of these go way back," Charlie said. "Looks like as far back as 1929. Hey there's *The Lone Ranger* – 1956 with Jay Silverheels. I probably saw that. And *Planet of The Apes*, made at Lake Powell, I guess that's near here. *Bandelero* with Jimmy Stewart. *The Outlaw Josey Wales*. Clint Eastwood was in that. *The Apple Dumpling Gang Rides Again* – Tim Conway and Don Knotts. I remember Don Knotts from TV with Andy Griffiths. *The Man Who Loved Cat Dancing* with Burt Reynolds, Sarah Miles and Lee J. Cobb. Wonder what that was about. *The Desperados* –"

"See if you can find a bathroom, Danny," Betty called. "Caroline and I are nearly dancing back here, getting a bit desperado ourselves."

Danny sped up as Charlie asked, "You think after we leave the Grand Canyon we should maybe head to Hollywood? See if we can get jobs as extras?"

"Jeez, Charlie," Danny said. "What's next?"

"Next better be a bathroom," Betty called.

"There's a service station coming up on the left. Just turning in," Danny called. "We need gas, we're running on empty."

As Danny pulled up to the pumps and stopped, he turned to Betty. "It's 80 miles from here to the North Rim. We're gonna use up most of the money we have for gas to get there and we'll have no money to pay to camp."

"We'll talk about that when we come back from the bathroom," Betty said. "That's priority number one right now. Don't fill up until Caroline and I get back."

Danny removed the gas cap, unhooked the pump nozzle and inserted it into the tank. "We're gonna have to get a little gas now anyway or we won't make it more than a few blocks. I didn't realize we were so low, you distracted me with all those crimes that we might have committed. Is it tomorrow your pension money comes in? What's today's date?"

"Er, the 28th, Sunday," Charlie said.

"Was Betty figuring on the money coming in tomorrow?"

"Maybe. But it could be the 30th."

"Jeez, that's two more days," Danny said.

When they'd all reassembled at the pumps, Betty agreed that they'd have to buy some gas. "I think there's a chance our money might come in tonight," she said.

"But it's a Sunday," Charlie said. "Bankers work bankers' hours. Who's gonna put the money in our accounts?"

"No one actually puts the money in, it's done automatically on computers. There's no one behind those bank machine's stuffing the cash out through a window at us." Betty laughed. "Officially, I think our pension money is supposed to come in on the 30th of each month but the teller I was dealin' with said it sometimes comes earlier if there's a weekend."

"I know there's no one stuffing money in the bank machine," Charlie growled. "How come you never said before about our money getting in earlier? I didn't ask anything at my bank, I was too nervous. I wanted to get out of there fast."

"Well right now," Danny said, "I've only put in ten bucks worth of gas and we're being studied by someone through the window, we're taking so long. Probably wondering if we're ever going in to pay."

"Uh sorry," Betty said. "Put in about another $10 worth. Will that take us to the Grand Canyon, Danny?"

"Maybe, maybe not," Danny replied.

"Why not fill up?" Charlie asked. "If our money is already in our accounts, we'll have lots. How much will we have left after we buy the gas?"

"About $14," Betty said. "Let's hang onto it for now, just in case."

"In case of what?" Charlie persisted.

"Dunno. Let's find a bank machine and try it."

Danny sensed that Betty was suddenly nervous about the money being in the accounts, but he said nothing. It was unlike her. She was usually ready to ride rough-

THE GRAND GETAWAY   267

shod over all difficulties that might face them. They were so close now it would be a real disaster if the money didn't show up as planned.

"Welcome to the Grand Canyon State," Danny, Charlie and Betty all called out when they caught sight of the sign as they crossed into Arizona. Their shouts got Caroline smiling and repeating, "Welcome, welcome, welcome."

"We're gonna make it," Betty called out. "Oh, I can't wait to see the canyon again." She hugged Caroline.

A few minutes later they passed through the tiny town of Fredonia and Betty suggested a coffee break. As they were looking for a place to pull over, they passed a small house on the edge of the town with Garage Sale signs and Betty said, "Look they have some fold-up lawn chairs for sale. Let's stop."

"But we've only got 14 bucks," Charlie said.

"Let's stop anyway. We can take a look." Betty said. "It's a garage sale. People expect you to bargain."

A bearded, grizzled, late-sixtyish man wearing faded blue coveralls and a red, ragged, Arizona Diamondbacks baseball cap came out of the house as the four of them crossed the street from The Smucker and entered the front yard. A label stitched to the left shoulder of his coveralls proclaimed his name was Virgil.

"Howdy, folks. Come and have a look. Got ya some real good deals here."

"Thanks," Betty said.

"Got a great set of golf clubs over there. Almost brand new. Only used 'em twice. That was enough for me to find out that golfin' wasn't for me. Couldn't see the sense of it, walkin' all that way beatin' the hell outta a little white ball and gettin' frustrated. Packed it in after my second game. Never used them again. Terrific deal."

Betty shook her head.

"Golfin' not your thing either?" He looked hopefully at Danny and Charlie, who shook their heads. "Darn good price. Probably get $100 at a second-hand store if you took 'em into the city. Well then, what about a whole box of *National Geographics*? Complete set from 1971 – 1976. Great reading, terrific pictures. Only $10 for the lot. Seventy-two magazines altogether. Why that's only, let's see, about... 15 cents a magazine. Ya can't beat that! And we got lots of useful kitchen stuff on that table there, meat grinder, cherry pitter, couple of fondu outfits."

As Caroline picked up a fat, white, smiling stuffed-toy monkey with a $2 price tag, Charlie asked, "What ya askin' for the lawn chairs?"

"I'll take 20 bucks for the four." Virgil replied. "They're in great shape. Fold up real easy."

As Virgil demonstrated how easily one of the chairs folded, Betty gave Charlie a glare, then sat in one of the other chairs.

"We'll give ya $10," Betty said.

Caroline started chanting, "Ten, ten, ten, ten."

THE GRAND GETAWAY

"No. Couldn't let 'em go for that, probably worth $10 apiece. It's early in the day yet. Give me $18 and I'll throw in the monkey."

"Ten, ten, ten, ten," Caroline chanted.

"Thanks, anyway," Betty said. "We gotta get goin'."

Betty took Caroline's arm and nodded to Charlie and Danny.

"Okay sixteen," Virgil said. "That's as low as I can go."

"Ten, ten, ten," Caroline repeated.

They were almost out to the sidewalk when Virgil called, after them, "Come on make me an offer. Fifteen then."

"Twelve," Betty said.

"Ten, ten, ten," Caroline continued

"Okay, okay. God you drive a hard bargain. You're robbin' me."

"Ten, ten, ten." Caroline couldn't seem to stop.

Virgil thought his wife Ethel was sure stubborn but he'd never before encountered a woman like this. He was so distracted by her chanting 'ten' that he overlooked Betty's higher bid of $12 and just wanted it finished.

"Okay, damn it! Give me ten."

Betty slapped a $10 bill into his hand and quickly folded up one of the chairs, gesturing to Danny and Charlie to grab the other three.

As they headed across the street to The Smucker, a woman stepped out onto the veranda of the house. She had a sharp high-pitched voice and they could hear her calling, "Sell anything Virgil?"

"Just the lawn chairs, Ethel."

"Whatcha get for 'em? You get $20?"

"Um. No. Best I could get was $15."

"Fifteen! God ya give the stuff away."

"People never give ya the askin' price, Ethel. You know that. They expect a bargain."

"They got that all right. Where'd they come from? That bus looks strange."

"License plate was Canadian. I think they thought it was an auction. One of the women kept bidding. Maybe they don't have garage sales in Canada."

"Well I hope ya at least got real American bills. Not that funny coloured stuff Canadians call money."

"It's American money, Ethel. I'm not that dumb." He thought, *I'm not gonna tell her I only got $10 for the chairs. Hell! I got nothin' for that damned stuffed monkey. Did I say I'd throw that in?*

Danny checked that everyone was buckled in, then started The Smucker as he rolled up the driver's window, cutting off whatever Ethel was saying. Behind him Betty was hugging Caroline, and Caroline was hugging the toy monkey.

"Thanks Caroline," Betty said. "Now I can sit in comfort when we get to the Grand Canyon. I won't get a pain in my rear end sittin' on a picnic bench."

Charlie laughed. "We shoulda got Caroline bidding at Malone's for The Smucker. We'd have got a better deal. Hey, see the sign in that corner store? There's a bank machine inside. We're down to $4. Let's see if our money's arrived."

Betty said, "But it's still early. It may not get in until later tonight."

"Hell," Charlie said. "Let's give it a try."

"Okay," Betty said.

As Danny pulled up in front of the store, Charlie asked, "If the money is there, how much should we take out?"

"Both our bank cards have a limit of $500 per day or a $1000 a week. If we both take out $200, that'll be plenty."

"Jeez. We'll have almost as much as the day we started out," Charlie whooped as he hopped out of The Smucker.

"Wait up Charlie," Betty called as she began helping Caroline out of her seat. As Danny came to give Betty and Caroline a hand, Charlie disappeared into the store.

When they got inside, they found Charlie staring at a Bank of America machine. He'd already inserted his bank card and the screen was flashing *P.I.N. Verify Failed*.

"It didn't work," Charlie muttered.

"What did you do?" Betty asked. "Did you remember your code number?"

"Yeah. I think so. It's 86, aah... 34."

"You sure?"

"No. It's 8643." He quickly punched in that number.

The screen flashed again, *P.I.N. Verify Failed*.

"Shit!" Charlie said. "Oh, I got it! I got it!"

"Wait up, you stupid bugger. I've got your code number in my purse. If you put in the wrong number again, the machine will keep your card. Wait! Wait!" Betty was rummaging in her purse, but Charlie had already punched in a number.

"It's 6843. God! What did you put in this time?" Betty asked as the machine clunked and the screen began flashing again.

"Er. I think it was..."

"What? Let me see?"

Charlie moved over and Betty looked at the screen. It read, *Please Select A Transaction*.

"Thank God! You got it right this time," Betty said. "You crazy bugger."

"You press the buttons, Betty. I'm too nervous now. I'll crap my pants if I lose my card."

"Okay. I'll try withdrawin' $200 and see what happens."

Betty slowly and carefully pressed the buttons as Charlie and Danny watched nervously. Caroline was repeating, "Crazy bugger, crazy bugger."

The machine gurgled again and there was another clunk and then it asked *Do You Want To Make Another Transaction?*

Betty looked at the buttons and punched *No*.

The machine rumbled and Charlie's card appeared in the slot. A bundle of $20's appeared in another slot and the screen flashed, *Please Remove Your Cash* and, *Do You Want A Receipt?* Betty pressed *Yes*.

Betty removed the cash and Charlie's card. Charlie let out a huge sigh of relief. Then she plucked the receipt out as it finished printing and looked at it. "They charged you a $5 fee because it's not a machine from your bank."

"Damn bank robbers," Charlie said. "Thanks, Betty. Supper's on me tonight."

CHAPTER 60

"You look beautiful in that dress, Betty," Charlie said. "I can't remember you wearing a dress much in Cavandish. You look taller too."

"I'm wearin' the one and only pair of high heels I brought. Haven't worn 'em in years. Afraid I'd fall over. They're a bit tight and I'll probably regret wearin' them, but this is a special occasion. You can hang onto me and keep me upright, Charlie."

"It'll be my pleasure." Charlie grinned.

"Caroline, you look lovely in that pink blouse. I'll just put a little of this lipstick on you and we'll be ready. There you go." Betty dabbed Caroline's lips with a napkin to take off the excess lipstick. "Now you're really pretty, Caroline."

"Really pretty, really pretty," Caroline repeated.

Danny said, "We're all cleaned up, ready to have supper to celebrate our arrival and stare at the canyon. And I'm gonna look for a post-card to send to Gail back at Malone's. I promised her I would if we made it."

They drove the short distance to The Grand Canyon Lodge and pulled in beside a one-ton truck with its hood raised and a horse-box hitched behind. Charlie helped Betty out first.

"Oh crap," Betty said. She was staring down at her feet.

"What's the matter?" Charlie asked.

"Horse shit."

"Huh?"

"You're no great escort for a lady, Charlie. How come you didn't notice?"

"Oh, shit! Sorry. I was reading the writing on that truck."

Betty had both feet right in the middle of a very large, steaming pile of horse manure.

Danny called out, "What's the matter?"

"I just stepped into the biggest pile of horse dung ever," Betty said. "Bring some paper towels."

Danny was helping Betty balance herself as Charlie took off one of her shoes and wiped it clean. A man wearing a black headband with feathers, and his face painted in red and black streaks, stepped out from behind the horse trailer. Betty gave a high-pitched yelp and Danny did a double-take. The North American Indian was bare-chested, apart from a small breastplate of porcupine quills. His straight greying hair reached his shoulders and he was carrying a scoop-shovel.

"Oh hell," the Indian muttered then called out, "I'm real sorry folks. Sorry to startle you ma'am. I was just about to clean up that mess my ponies made. Let me help you with that. I'll grab some water and a rag. Let me clean those shoes for you."

272 THE GRAND GETAWAY

As he took Betty's shoe from Charlie, he unhitched a water bag from the front of his vehicle and pulled a rag from a pocket in his buckskin pants.

"Sorry about this, ma'am. I was going to grab a quick coffee and be on my way, but for some reason my truck won't start. There, I think that shoe is clean. Let me have the other one. I'm Winston Whatoname, by the way." He gestured towards his truck which had his name painted across the side and the words *Canyon Trail Rides – Hualapai Indian – Shaman*.

Charlie was staring dubiously at him. "You a real Indian?" he asked.

"That I am. Honest *Injin*." He chuckled.

"What kind of an Indian name is that? Winston Whatoname?" Charlie asked.

Winston grinned. "You were expecting Charging Elk, Running Buffalo or maybe Little Eagle, something like that? Whatoname is a fairly common name around here. No doubt we got it from the white man who couldn't say our Hualapai names." He pronounced it *Wal–lah-pie*. "It means people of the tall pines. The Hualapai have lived around here for thousands of years. There, ma'am. I hope those shoes are okay now."

"Thanks," Betty said. "I'm a farm girl from way back. Stepped in lots of manure in my time. Mind you, I usually wore rubber boots." She laughed.

"Glad you're taking it so well. I'd better get that pony poop cleaned up quick before someone else steps in it. They don't take kindly to having manure left outside The Lodge. Then I'll see if I can get my truck started, but I'm no mechanic."

"Danny's a mechanic," Charlie volunteered.

"Haven't been for a long time," Danny said. "I could take a look, but I've got no tools. Is your battery dead? Hop in and turn it over."

Winston slid into the driver's seat and turned on the ignition as Danny stuck his head under the hood. There were just a couple of clicks but no sound from the engine.

"Could be the solenoid," Danny said. "You got a hammer or wrench or something?"

Winston brought him a wrench and a hammer.

Danny took the hammer, leaned over the engine and banged on something. "Give it a try now."

Winston turned the key and the engine fired.

He came back to Danny and Charlie, beaming. "Show me what you did."

Danny showed him where the solenoid was and explained that he'd hit it a couple of times. "It wasn't sending the electrical charge to the engine. You'll probably have to replace it soon, but a couple of raps with the hammer sometimes works."

"Thanks. Thanks a lot. I see from your plate that you're from Alberta, Canada. How long are you staying here?"

"We were hoping to stay a few weeks, but we just got here today and we only got a camping spot for four nights," Betty answered. "Everything's booked solid."

THE GRAND GETAWAY   273

"Betty here – I'm Danny by the way, and this is Charlie and Caroline – well, Betty was here at the Canyon 'bout 50 years ago, and all this time she's dreamed of coming back. We left Canada over a month ago. We weren't sure when we'd get here and didn't book ahead. If we don't get lucky and there's no more cancellations, we'll have to move outta here early Thursday morning."

"Yeah. There's only the one campsite here. There's a few other spots but you need a special overnight permit, and they are usually full this time of year. The North Rim here shuts down here for camping October 15. There are more campgrounds on the South Rim but it's quite a drive and there are even more tourists. I guess you passed the campgrounds north of here, outside the park at DeMotte and Jacob Lake.

"We did," Danny replied.

As Winston had been talking, Caroline had become fascinated by the breastplate that Winston was wearing as part of his costume and was now running her fingers over its tactile surface.

Winston studied her face and smiled and she smiled back at him. He was quiet for a moment and Betty was about to stop her when Winston shook his head. "It's okay. Let her be."

Everyone was quiet for a few more moments until Caroline stopped touching the breast-plate and then just stood quietly looking down as if she was deep in thought.

Winston touched her hand and she raised her head and smiled.

"Look," Winston said, "I have to take off to Peach Springs. My wife works in a clinic there. Have to pick up some feed for my ponies and get that solenoid fixed too. I've held you up enough. You'll want to get to supper if that's where you're heading." He nodded towards the lodge. "Sorry about messing up your shoes, Betty. You'll probably have to wait for a table, but I'd be glad to buy you all a coffee and we can wait in the lounge area. Great view of the canyon and they'll call you when your table is ready."

"That'd be real nice," Betty said, "but you don't have to do that. Charlie is payin' for supper and he can afford the coffee, yours too."

"No," Winston said. "Let me pay for that, my treat. I have a soft spot for Canadians. Lived in your country for a while a few years back. Vancouver. Let's grab that coffee and see about getting you a table for dinner. If I turn off the truck, you think we can start it again, Danny?"

"Yeah. Shouldn't be a problem."

They were told they'd only have to wait 20 minutes before getting a table. As they waited, they had the chance to stare in awe at the changing colours of the canyon through the massive windows of the lodge, which sat on the very rim. They were quiet for a moment as they took in the stunning view laid out before them. Betty had a peaceful and happy look on her face, drinking it all in.

274   THE GRAND GETAWAY

As Winston ordered the coffee Charlie chuckled, and said to Danny and Betty, "I guess they don't enforce a dress code here." He nodded towards Winston as Betty gave him an elbow in the ribs.

Winston overheard and laughed. "Oh, I did get thrown out once. Made the mistake of coming in with a couple of fresh scalps on my belt and the blood was still dripping. Got some blood on the carpet in front of the fireplace and they were a bit upset about that. Put up a sign for a while that said, *'No shoes, No socks, No service, And Please Check All Scalps At The Reservation Desk.'*

Charlie gulped and looked a bit embarrassed and mumbled, "Sorry," as Betty glared at him.

"It's okay." Winston grinned. "Tourists don't expect to see Indians. They usually make special trips to our reservations so we can pose for photos. I'm about the only one still hanging around here."

As they waited for their table, sipping their coffees and staring at the canyon right in front of them, Charlie said, "You said you lived in Vancouver for a while. What were you doing there?"

"That was a long time ago. There was a small war going on in Vietnam that I didn't exactly agree with. You Canadians welcomed people like me. I really appreciated that. Sometimes you have to stand up for something you strongly believe in. Governments aren't always right. Me being here now is because I'm making another stand."

"What kind of stand are you making?" Charlie asked. "Aren't you just camping here and giving people trail rides in the canyon? Are you camping illegally?"

"The government thinks so. The Hualapai and Havasupai once roamed over five million acres of these canyon lands. Miners and settlers moved in, and then soldiers arrived to force us out, and we fought back. A peace treaty was signed, but then the army was ordered to move us to a small reservation 150 miles south. We considered that a betrayal because we had provided scouts to the army in their fight against Geronimo, chief of the Apaches, who weren't exactly friends of ours either."

"Yeah." Charlie nodded. "I think I saw a movie or two with Geronimo and the Apaches. Never saw any with *Hoola Pie*, though."

"*Wal-lah-pie*," Winston gave the pronunciation of the tribe's name again. "When we were forced onto the small reservation, the usual starvation and sickness wiped a lot of us out and the Havasupai too. The remaining Havasupai were eventually granted land on the South Rim of the park area. In 1883, the Hualapai were granted a new reservation further west, about a million acres along what's now known as Route 66. Ah, your table is ready, and I'd better get going. I've got a bit of a drive."

"So if you've got a million acres, why do you still have a beef?" Charlie asked.

"A long story. Let's say a matter of principle. I gotta go, but I'll be back Wednesday evening. I come here about three or four days a week when school's out. I sometimes hang out at Uncle Jim Trail doing pony trips, so I'll look you up

THE GRAND GETAWAY   275

when I get back." He shook hands with all four of them and Charlie couldn't resist saying, "Hey Ho, Silver."

Winston laughed. "See you soon, Kimo Sabi." He clapped Charlie on the shoulder.

"I'll come out with you," Danny said, "to make sure your truck starts."

When Danny returned, he found the three seated at a table and Charlie asked, "You think he was a real Indian?"

"Yeah. For sure. He gave me his card."

"What's his card say?" Charlie asked.

"Says, Dr. Winston Whatoname. Gives a number at Peach Springs, Arizona. Says, *Hooalapie*. Indian Trail Rides, Legends, and a website."

"A doctor? Why would a doctor be doing trail rides?" Charlie asked.

"No idea," Danny said. "He said he only comes here a few days a week. Maybe he works as a doctor the rest of the time."

"Jeez. He'd scare the hell out of you if you were waiting to see a doctor and he walked in dressed like that."

"Why the hell did you say 'Hey Ho Silver' to him? What was that all about?" Betty asked.

"Ah." Charlie laughed." I was just pretending I was the Lone Ranger. That's what he always said at the end of a movie as he galloped off on his horse, Silver, with his Indian buddy Tonto."

Betty shook her head. "Look at the menu. I'm hungry and remember you're buyin,' Charlie."

CHAPTER 61

As Winston Whatoname headed home to Peach Springs, he was thinking about the number of times he'd made this trip over the past 20 years. This summer was almost over and soon he'd be returning to his job as professor of anthropology at Northern Arizona University at Flagstaff. He could have retired already, but the courses on native North Americans kept him in touch with his history.

His wife Georgina had supported his summer journeys to the North Rim and had, on a few occasions, come to stay for a day or two at his camp. Recently she had brought up the possibility of him staying home in the summer, but Winston was not yet ready to let go. He'd reduced his work load at the university and taught a couple of short courses in the spring session. Mentoring of graduate students allowed him even more time at Cape Final, as his first appointment with them was not until late October when facilities at the North Rim closed down. Winston took that as his time to move out as he didn't want to risk getting trapped by a snowfall. He'd return in spring after the North Rim re-opened.

Georgina herself had not retired and was still working as a family doctor at the clinic at Peach Springs, the Hualapai capital. Winston's thoughts turned to the text message his wife had sent. *Colby coming home soon. All I know. Love Georgina.* His last meeting with Colby had been brief and angry, like many that had preceded it.

"You're being a pain in the ass, Dad. The Parks Department just tolerate you. Nobody plays cowboys and Indians any more. You're playing at being the store-front Indian, the shim–sham shaman, making a fool of yourself. Give it up, for God's sake. It's like an addiction, a stupid god-damn addiction."

An addiction. You should know about addiction, Winston almost snapped back, but he had bitten his tongue and said nothing. When Colby was in his teens, Georgina discovered Colby hanging around with drug users. He knew Colby had experimented for a while, until one of his friends died of an overdose, getting to the clinic too late for Georgina to save him. The shock of his friend's death and Georgina's visible grief in not being able to save him had shaken Colby. A few months later, Georgina confided to Winston that Colby was clean and that he hadn't used drugs since that day.

"You've got no support," Colby had gone on. "The Hualapai have moved on. Years ago. Everybody has. Nobody in the Hualapai believes the legend, except maybe one or two of your friends. But you don't see them up there sitting on a pony and making like it's Halloween at the North Rim. And even if it was true, so what? Keeping a few ponies at Cape Final is not worth a hill of beans to the tribe. Nobody gives a shit! Except you! Smoke a god-damn peace pipe with The Parks Department and spend your summers with Mom. You were never there for her, never been there for me. Get a life!"

Winston had to admit that a lot of what Colby had said was true. He hadn't always been there for Colby. Winston had been drafted for the Vietnam War at the age of 20. He had fled to Vancouver, Canada, and his girl, Georgina, had insisted on coming with him.

A year later Georgina was pregnant and while Winston and Georgina felt welcomed in Canada and were convinced they had done the right thing, Winston persuaded her to return to Peach Springs, believing their child should be born on Hualapai land. By then Winston had become a prominent spokesman and figurehead in the anti-war movement, helping others like him to find sanctuary. He was often quoted in the Vancouver *Province* and it was picked up in American newspapers.

Just before Colby was born, Winston had slipped back into the U.S. and made his way to Peach Springs where he and Georgina were married. Winston might have remained there, but before Colby was a month old, word had come that the FBI had learned he was back and were anxious to bring him in. His reputation as a lightning rod for those seeking an escape from the war, which was now going badly, made him a prize worth grabbing. The protests in the U.S. were growing daily and Georgina convinced him to go back to Canada to help others rather than face imprisonment. It was seven long years before President Jimmy Carter declared an amnesty and he could return. By then, despite Georgina's best efforts, Colby was already distant because of his father's absence. He was also missing his grandfather, Winston's own father, who had been killed in a rafting accident on the Colorado River. Colby had harboured resentment at Winston not being there for his papa's funeral and it had added fuel to their estrangement.

When Colby was 12, Winston, now a probationary anthropology professor at the university, had taken him to the North Rim, hoping to interest him in the legend of Colby's great-great-grandfather Manukaja, also known as Johnny Whatoname. Winston had hoped Colby would join him in his desire to maintain the right to keep his ponies on the Grand Canyon lands of his choosing. General Crook, appointed commander of Arizona in 1868 by President Grant, had made this promise to Manukaja and his family's descendants.

After a couple of trips to the North Rim and Cape Final, the place Winston believed his great-grandfather had chosen and where Winston had set up camp, Colby had refused to go again. Winston had put it down to teenage rebellion, but it was more than that.

"You know what they call me at school? Colby *Cottontail*!" Colby was sporting a black eye.

"You win the fight?" Winston had countered.

"Do you care? Don't you know the kids know what you do? Dressing up like you're on the war-path and scaring the shit out of white tourists?"

"I'm sorry if I embarrass you," Winston remembered saying. "Playing the Indian helps pay a few bills and helps me to fight the government. Fighting the government makes me feel good. It's something I have to do. I admit, though, that I've enjoyed the dressing up. The tourists love it and it gives me a bit of fun too."

Winston's thoughts drifted to a few days ago and he couldn't help chuckling. A guide had just begun a talk to a large group at Roosevelt Point when Winston and a couple of Japanese tourists on his ponies had appeared on a ridge behind them. The Japanese men looked the part of Indian braves, decked out in war-paint and stripped to the waist like Winston.

None of the tourists noticed them until one lady had looked over her shoulder and called out, "*Mein Gott!* Kurt! Quick! Lookit! Indians! Up *dere!*" She'd pointed at the three sitting quietly on the ridge on their ponies. The whole crowd had turned to look and there were a few gasps. "What do *zay vant*, Kurt? Are *ve zafe?*" the lady with a German accent continued. The Japanese men, who spoke enough English to understand, were delighted. Winston gave a signal, and they joined him in a spine-chilling whoop, threateningly waving what looked like spears above their heads before they turned their ponies and disappeared from the ridge.

Winston had paused to eavesdrop on the crowd below. He knew the tour guide well. Gavin Bryant was one of the students from his spring courses last year. The same German lady was asking, "*Vere zay* real? *Vhat vere zay doing?*"

"Oh yes, Ma'm," Gavin replied, playing along, knowing it was Winston on the ridge with a couple of tourists, "they were real all right. But not to worry. They were just a few Hualapai war-party scouts. Probably riding back now to their camp for reinforcements, but that's a long ride and we'll have moved on before they get back. And there hasn't been a scalping for, let me see, when was it now?" He paused. "Gosh I can't remember when it was." He paused again then laughed. "Just kidding folks. But let me take a minute to tell you a little about the Hualapai and Havasupai, the first people here." Winston was grateful for guides like Gavin who took a little time to mention his people, hopefully garnering a few more supporters for his cause.

Winston's forays and guided trail rides brought in a little extra money, just enough to cover his expenses for his gasoline between the North Rim and Peach Springs and the upkeep of his vehicle and ponies. Money for legal fees was another matter and a dart that Colby, as he grew older, threw at Winston.

"All that money given to big-time lawyers. Gone! And nothing to show for it. Even if you won, what are you or our people going to get out of it? The right to pitch a tent, graze a few ponies? The Hualapai have nearly a million acres, for God's sake! They don't care about what some long dead General said nearly a hundred and fifty years ago."

"I know it's not gonna be a windfall for the Hualapai," Winston had argued. "I just want to prove a principle. I want the government to acknowledge that General Crook made that promise to your great-great-grandfather." Winston would have

THE GRAND GETAWAY   279

been happy with some kind of small monument erected at Cape Final, verification of General Crook's promise to Manukaja.

Winston had taken the government to court claiming he had a legal right to be there, not only because of the history of his people but also because of a diary from a missionary to the area. Fragments of a few pages had been found by Winston during his research in The National Archives. The diary pages showed evidence of having been in a fire. The entry was vague and alluded to a promise that General Crook had made to Manukaja when he had served as his scout in the pursuit of Geronimo and the Apaches. The promise was made, the diary said, because he had been instrumental in saving the General's life, but there were no details or dates, nor what the promise actually was. Further pages which might have shed more light on the matter had been lost or burnt.

It was true what Colby had said about being 'a pain in the ass' as far as the National Parks Department was concerned. Winston knew he was seen as a thorn in their side and when he'd first begun to set up his camp at Cape Final, they had tried to drive him off. He had spent a fair amount of money hiring two researchers to find more evidence to back up his claim and lawyer's fees had mounted up too. By the time the court agreed to hear the case, Winston had given up on lawyers and represented himself. In his presentation to the court Winston cited the oral history of his tribe, the diary evidence and the words of the Lakota Chief, Red Cloud, 'That General Crook had never lied to us. His words gave the people hope.'

The Government had claimed that when the Hualapai had been granted their reserve lands, all previous claims became null and void. One of the three judges considering the case was sympathetic to Winston's claim. He agreed that it could possibly have some validity on the basis that General Crook was acting on behalf of President Grant, but without further historical documentation, there was no way of knowing what that promise was.

Winston had ignored the court's ruling and continued to camp sporadically at Cape Final. The Hualapai's oral history told of Johnny Whatoname, a shaman and scout with General Crook, who had been shipped to prison in Florida along with other Hualapai and Havasupai scouts and surrendered Apaches, when General Crook was replaced by his bitter rival General Miles.

For most of the scouts the imprisonment had lasted for 26 years. But the story also told of Johnny Whatoname's escape en route to Florida and his lengthy journey back to his tribe, where, just a few days after his return, he died. His dying wish was that his ashes be buried at Cape Final, the spot which he himself had chosen based on Crook's promise. Superintendents of the park had tolerated Winston, not wanting to stir up a media frenzy if the park had tried to evict him. Winston knew that they were just waiting him out and when he died, that would be the end of the matter.

Winston and Colby had argued again when Colby, who had moved away to Sacramento, California, announced he had joined the army. There was no draft but to Winston it seemed that Colby was joining to spite him and to atone for Winston's failure to obey his own draft summons years before. Colby had quite a successful career in the army, rising to the rank of master sergeant, keeping in touch with Georgina with postcards while surviving George H.W. Bush Senior's short war against Saddam Hussein in Kuwait.

Winston had really raged at Colby over George Bush Junior's war against Iraq when Colby, home on leave at the end of 2001, announced his unit was going there.

"This war is Bush's war. He's plunging America into an illegal war for his own glory. First he steals the election from Gore in Florida, and now he's dragging us into this war for his own glorification. And where are the weapons of mass destruction the United Nations have been searching for? They don't exist. But he won't wait and let the United Nations finish the job. No doubt we'll win the battle. The Iraqis won't stand a chance, but how many innocent people on both sides will die? They lied to us about Vietnam and they're lying to us now. We won't bring freedom to Iraq, only turmoil and hatred and bitterness against America for years to come. Christ, Colby, I thought you had more sense!"

"You made your choice about Vietnam. I'm making mine about Iraq. I'm a soldier now. It's my job. It's done. That's it. I just came back to see Mom before I ship out."

Colby had returned with a purple heart and minus an arm, and with even more bitterness because he knew Winston had been right. Iraq, without Saddam Hussein, was a bigger mess than ever. Colby was damaged not only in body but in spirit.

Winston hadn't talked about the Iraq war when Colby returned. He was just thankful that Colby had come home alive.

Colby had always been good at drawing, and had dabbled at painting, but had abandoned it when he joined the army. The hand he used was now gone, but slowly he'd drifted back to his art. With the encouragement of a Hualapai girl he'd taken up with, he began some sketches, learning to use his left hand. He and Derica had married and presented Winston and Georgina with a granddaughter, Julia. Because of the animosity between Winston and Colby, Georgina and Winston had seen less of Julia than they would have liked as she grew up. Julia was now attending university.

Now Colby was coming home. 'Soon', Georgina had said, and Winston was sure all the old arguments would start up again. What I need, Winston thought, is what I've always needed, definite proof of General Crook's promise or something to bring it all to a head. But how?

CHAPTER 62

"That was a great supper, thanks, Charlie," Betty said. "Maybe I'll spring for breakfast tomorrow. Right now, I feel like celebratin'. Let's get our new lawn chairs and sit outside. It's a lovely evenin'. I'd like to watch the sun go down on the canyon. Arnie and I did that. I'll make us some of that frozen lemonade we just bought."

Charlie and Danny got the chairs set up and Betty mixed up the lemonade and poured them a cup each. "Would you look at those colours on the canyon? It's absolutely breathtaking. Let's drink a toast to celebrate our success. By rights it should be champagne, but a cold cup of lemonade will do fine. To us."

They raised their cups.

"It's hard to believe we're really here," Charlie said. "Five weeks ago, did you really think we had a hope of getting here? I sure as hell didn't."

Betty chuckled. "It was always a gamble. But we just had to give it a go. And I'm sure glad we did. Just think. We'd still be starin' at the same god-awful fuzzy wallpaper in the dinin' room at Cavandish."

"I have to keep pinching myself to make sure it's really happening," Charlie said. "I keep thinking I'll wake up tomorrow in my room in Cavandish with someone sticking their head in my door asking if I had a bowel movement. Thanks, Betty, you really made it happen."

"What! I made you have a bowel movement?" Betty guffawed and Danny joined in.

Caroline smiled and said, "bowel movement, bowel movement."

"Ah jeez, Betty." Charlie laughed. "You know you made this whole trip happen." He raised his cup. "To Betty, our fearless leader."

Betty refilled their cups. "Fearless my ass, Charlie. But thanks to us all. To Caroline for gettin' us The Smucker. To The Smucker herself, she didn't let us down. And to Danny for gettin' us all here safely. And to you too, Charlie, you mad trapper, for getting us food when we needed it and savin' me from drownin' in that mud pot in Yellowstone."

Charlie laughed. "Hell, you were standing on the bottom. You could have climbed out."

"Yeah, but you didn't know that." Betty patted Charlie's knee.

They sat up until dark, laughing as they reminded each other of the little mishaps and adventures they'd had along the way, jubilant over their accomplishment, but still incredulous that they were actually there.

They reminisced and laughed about the journey until the lemonade was gone and it was fully dark and the night was filled with stars. They fell silent then, looking up at the vast sky, until Caroline's cup fell from her fingers.

"Time for bed, everyone," Betty said. "Caroline's asleep. God love her."

They checked first thing that morning for any future cancellations at the campground and got their name on a list. They were told to check back as often as they could, as sometimes someone on the list moved on without taking a spot.

Charlie proposed a trip to Bright Angel Point which was really close by. It was touted as one of the highlights and he suggested they take a picnic lunch.

While they waited for breakfast at the lodge, Danny wrote the address of Malone's Auctions on two postcards he'd purchased to send to Gail. "I've never written a postcard in my life. What will I say?"

"Maybe we should send one to Bill Darlington at Cavandish too with something like, *Having a great time, but _tired_ out after our trip.*"

Betty groaned. "Charlie, we're sure as hell not sendin' a card to Darlington. Danny, just say somethin' like, *Made it safe and sound in The Smucker. That's what Caroline called our bus. It was terrific. Thanks for your donation to the cause. It sure came in handy. Everyone doing fine.* She won't expect a play by play of the whole trip."

After breakfast they drove the short distance to the Bright Angel Point parking lot, which was just to the south of the Grand Canyon Lodge. The trail to the Point was only just over a half mile, and Betty was certain she'd have no trouble getting there and back. They prepared a lunch to take with them. There were a lot of people using the trail, and shortly after they started they found themselves walking along a narrow path, which was mostly a paved ridge with the canyon on either side.

"My God," Betty said. "This is very scary. Hold tight to my hand Caroline. You think we should go any further? We didn't come all this way to fall into the canyon."

"This is fantastic," Charlie said. "I didn't realize we'd be walking so close to the canyon. If we stay right in the middle of the trail, we'll be okay. It's not too far to the end point. Let me hold your hand and Danny can take Caroline."

"Okay, but if it gets any worse, we're turnin' back."

They moved very slowly along the ridge. Caroline didn't seem at all perturbed by the precipice on either side of them and walked along holding Danny's hand, murmuring softly. Danny was a bit nervous at some spots where there were no guardrails at the edge.

Betty said, "I might have walked along this trail with Arnie. I think I'd have remembered somethin' like this, but maybe I was a lot braver then. Sometimes it feels like yesterday, but it was a hell of a long time ago."

"I think we're almost at the end," Danny said, "We'll make it."

"Yeah," Betty said. "But what worries me is we have to go all the way back again."

Charlie laughed. "We can blindfold you on the way back so you can't see over the edge."

"Oh, that'd make me *really* feel safe."

THE GRAND GETAWAY   283

When they reached Bright Angel Point at the end of the peninsula, they were amazed at how much of the canyon they could see before them. The panoramic views were outstanding and with the air so clear, they could just make out Grand Canyon Village, which sat on the South Rim.

"This guide says the village is 10 miles away from here," Charlie said.

"Yeah," Danny said, "But it's quite a drive to get around from here to over there."

They asked about a campsite twice more in the late afternoon, and again before settling down for the night, and it wasn't looking good. They decided that next morning they'd drive back to DeMotte, check out the campground there, and pick up a few groceries.

"I don't want to take a campin' spot at DeMotte in case we get lucky here," Betty said. "We have until Thursday mornin'. If we move to DeMotte, we'll be away from the canyon and have to drive back and forth each day. It just won't be the same."

"It's not all that far," Charlie said, checking one of the brochures they'd picked up. "It's six miles north of the entrance station or 18 miles in total from here. The next campground is way back at Jacob Lake. That's 45 miles north of here.

"That's way too far," Betty said. "And even DeMotte is a 36-mile round trip. Let's give it 'til tomorrow night. There's still a chance."

After verifying their bank balances at a bank machine at the lodge, Betty declared that their pension money came to a grand total of nearly $3000.

"Plus, I still have the $200 I took out of my account," she said. "I think that's plenty for gas and the groceries."

After two hours in DeMotte picking up groceries, they checked out the camping ground which was in a meadow just off Highway 67. It too was full.

When they got back to the North Rim, they spent the rest of the day sitting on their lawn chairs outside The Smucker. Danny studied the map but didn't want to press Betty about where they might go on Thursday, knowing she had her heart set on staying. He would suggest they spend the rest of that day doing a little sightseeing and then maybe try calling the South Rim in case they could find a spot there. It wouldn't be the same for Betty, but it was still the Grand Canyon.

They had no luck getting a new campsite Wednesday and were sitting down for supper when Charlie called out, "Hey, here's Winston What's His Face. He just pulled up."

"Jeez Charlie," Betty said. "For God's sake get his name right. It's Winston Whatoname. Go ask him in."

"Hi, folks," Winston said. "How's it going? Uh, sorry, I guess I'm interrupting your supper."

"That's okay," Betty said. "You can have a bowl of chili if you'd like. There's enough left."

"Thanks, but I'll just have a coffee if there's one going."

"We didn't get an extension on our campsite. We're gonna have to move on tomorrow mornin'." Betty sighed. "We're not sure where we might go now. We had our hearts set on stayin' on the North Rim. That was our plan."

Winston put a spoonful of sugar in his coffee, stirred it and took a sip. He looked around The Smucker. "You okay for food for a couple of days?"

"Yeah we are," Betty said. "We stocked up yesterday at DeMotte."

"I might have a suggestion. It's not great but it would allow you to stay on at the North Rim for a while. Not right here, though."

Betty's eyes lit up. "It doesn't have to be exactly here. We'd just like to stay on this side of the canyon for a while. We looked at the campground at Demotte and there's no guarantee we can even get a spot there. What's your suggestion?"

"Well," Winston said, "I'm heading up to my spot at Cape Final tonight, here on the North Rim." He paused. "It's kinda primitive. I truck up water and I have this old camper parked there. The toilet facilities aren't the best."

"We've camped in the bush before," Betty said. "Quite a few times as a matter of fact. We've washed up right here in The Smucker."

"The Smucker?" Winston looked puzzled.

"Caroline gave our bus that name," Danny said. "But go on."

"Well, I only have a chemical toilet in my old camper. I do have an old outhouse I haven't used in years out back, and a half-assed shower I rigged up behind the camper. It's no resort."

"We've used a half-assed toilet before, haven't we?" Betty chuckled. "It sounds a lot better than some of the places we've camped."

"And you managed with…" He glanced at Caroline who was chasing the last few chili beans around her bowl.

"Caroline's been fine. She's no problem," Betty said.

Charlie asked. "I thought you had to have a special permit to camp at Cape Final?"

"You do. But my little camp spot is in the pines just before you get to Cape Final. You could park right behind my camper in the trees." Winston drained his coffee and Betty offered him another, but he shook his head. "I've got to head up there in a few minutes, get my stuff unloaded and my ponies out of the trailer before dark."

"Didn't you say the government believes you're camping there illegally?" Charlie asked.

"They do," Winston replied. "I took them to court."

"You win?"

"Not yet."

"How long have you been camping there?"

"Best part of 20 summers," Winston replied.

"And they let you stay there?" Charlie pursued.

"That's right. They've basically ignored me."

"Look, we're holdin' Winston up," Betty said. "Are you sayin', if we want to camp at your place we should leave now and follow you?"

"Yeah, if you think you'd like to try that. If it doesn't work out you can always move on in a day or two, but I'd like to get there before dark."

"We're comin'," Betty said. "Thanks Winston. Give us five minutes to put away a couple of things and we'll join you."

They checked out of their campsite and followed Winston closely. He was driving quite slowly, and Danny had no trouble keeping up. Although the road was paved, it was, as Winston had warned, very winding. As they passed a number of marked viewing points, Charlie said, "If things work out for us at Cape Final we can come and take in the sights. Those two, Vista Encantada and Roosevelt Point that we just passed, are a couple of the best."

It was nearly an hour before they reached the turn-off for Cape Final. They appeared to be driving on an old narrow logging road that wound slowly uphill through a forest of Ponderosa pines. Danny had no trouble driving The Smucker, but there was barely enough room for Winston's truck and horse-trailer and a couple of times he stopped and reversed a little in order to make a turn. The road levelled out and they came to a dirt parking lot off to one side with a couple of cars. To their surprise, Winston drove straight on past a sign that said, *No Vehicles Beyond This Point.* The road became a narrow trail and Winston slowed to a crawl. Danny thought there was no way they could go any further and expected Winston's truck to get wedged between the trees or rocks at any minute when Winston signalled left, turned completely off the track and began to wind his way between the pines. As they followed, Danny caught sight of a faded, painted sign that read, *Indian Land – Please Keep Out.*

Danny wasn't sure how far they had come since they'd left the track as Winston made so many zigs and zags, but then an old camper, up on blocks and with a small deck built outside the door, appeared through the trees. Winston pulled in close to a small corral among the trees and stopped. He walked to the rear of the trailer and led the ponies one by one into the corral. "I'll be with you in a few minutes," Winston called. "I just have to give the ponies some feed and fresh water." The truck was filled with hay bales and a couple of large metal barrels that made sloshing sounds when Winston climbed in. He heaved a couple of hay bales onto the ground, then pulled the lid off one of the barrels and filled a five-gallon pail which he set on the tailgate. He then hauled it to a couple of wide rubber containers in the corral, sloshing the water into them. He refilled the pail and emptied it once more. Then he fed the ponies some hay.

"There, that should hold them for now. Every time I leave here, I get water to bring back. I'll fill the barrel by the corral and get this hay unloaded and then I'll pull around the loop. You can park alongside my camper and help me fill up the barrel that's part of my shower."

Danny helped Winston fill the water-storage barrel for the ponies and then both Charlie and Danny helped him make a little stack of the hay bales. The track continued on behind the camper in a loop, the only way possible to get back to the original trail. Winston moved his truck ahead and guided Danny to a level spot close to the camper.

Betty and Caroline climbed out of The Smucker. "Oh, smell those pines Caroline," Betty said. "Isn't it lovely here? So quiet and peaceful." They watched as Danny and Charlie helped Winston fill the shower barrel as best they could. Danny stood in the truck and on Winston's advice only half-filled the five-gallon pail for Charlie to take to Winston, who climbed a rickety ladder beside the barrel to fill it.

They gathered around Winston and he showed them how operate the spigot at the bottom of the barrel. A concrete paving stone sat on the ground below the barrel to prevent the user from getting muddy feet. "Sorry, there's no shower curtains," Winston said, "but it's pretty private back here. Remember the water is cold in the morning but the sun hits the barrel in the afternoon so you can have a warm shower late afternoon."

"Hey, Betty, maybe you and I could shower together to save water." Charlie laughed.

"You wish." Betty grunted. "Don't worry Winston. I'll make sure we don't waste the water."

Winston showed them the outhouse, which listed a bit to one side. It had a carpet of pine needles that had found their way in through a gap in the roof.

"Sorry, it's a bit of a mess," Winston said. "I haven't used it in years. I'll show you the chemical toilet in my camper, Betty. You and Caroline might find it a bit more comfortable."

"Thanks, Winston. We'll soon sweep this outhouse out," Betty said. "We'll make do. We really appreciate what you're doin' for us."

"I'll show you through my camper anyway. It's no palace, but you're welcome to use anything you need. I don't lock it up. Nobody should bother you. I'll be up real early in the morning. I'll try not to wake you. I have a couple of tourist gigs I booked a long time ago and can't let the people down. It'll be the same the next day and then I'm off, back to Peach Springs for a couple of days. I'll be back again about Tuesday."

Winston gave them a quick look inside his camper, telling them again that if they needed anything to just help themselves. "It's just a short walk to Cape Final from here. Great views. Just make your way back to the trail and turn left. You shouldn't have any problem driving out if you want to go sightseeing somewhere else. I'll see you all tomorrow night."

When everyone had climbed into their bunks and Caroline was the only one who had fallen asleep, Betty whispered, "I knew we'd get lucky."

CHAPTER 63

Danny was the only one awake. He was sure it was the sound of Winston leaving that had awakened him. He lay there, thinking, *Winston sure is generous letting us stay here. It's not like we did him any big favour. He did say he had a soft spot for Canadians. Nowadays someone's always talking about wanting to give back, when they're asked why they're doing something good.*

His thoughts were interrupted by Caroline waking up and speaking softly out loud. "That's where she said she's going and I'm going with her."

Danny was surprised to hear her say a complete sentence. Then she was repeating a word, one of her favourites. "Tenter, tenter, tenter." He hadn't a clue if it meant anything.

Betty stirred and sat up. "You're awake Caroline," she said softly. "Want to find the bathroom with me?" Betty saw Danny was awake and waved as she led Caroline out of The Smucker.

Betty was sure happy last night, Danny thought. *This is what she really wanted. I wonder how much she really remembers Arnie. Maybe she'd built it into a big romance over all those years. Had she really fallen in love with him back then? Wonder what poor old Charlie thinks about that? He loves Betty. That's for sure.*

His thoughts drifted back to that day in Cavendish when Betty had first broached the subject of the Grand Canyon. He remembered she'd said that the song, *The Impossible Dream*, had been running through her head. Now they were here.

The door opened and Betty was helping Caroline up the steps. Danny scrambled out of bed and pulled on some pants as Betty appeared.

"It's cold out there, isn't it Caroline?" She gave a shiver.

"Cold, cold," Caroline repeated.

"I'll get some coffee on," Betty said as Danny slipped on some shoes, grabbed a jacket and hurried out.

As Danny was returning, Charlie came stumbling out of The Smucker wearing a sweater, no doubt on Betty's advice.

He greeted Danny. "Jeez. Cold enough for ya? I never thought I'd be saying that here, this early in the year. I won't be trying out Winston's shower this morning, that's for sure."

Betty was serving bacon and eggs for breakfast. "I think we should just take it easy today," she said. "We can amble down to the view-point and take a look. But if it's like that Angel Point, I'm not coming. If it looks anythin' like that, you can bring me and Caroline back here. You two okay with just hangin' around here for the day?"

THE GRAND GETAWAY   289

"It's fine by me," Danny said. "I don't have to drive us anywhere looking for a new place to stay. Yeah, that'd suit me fine, just taking it easy. I'll see what's left in our book collection."

"And it's okay with me," Charlie said.

They spent the day as they'd planned, sitting for a couple of hours at two viewpoints they found. Betty was happy that the main trail they followed, which turned south and west through pines and cactus, was quite safe. Then they came upon the clearing overlooking a dramatic drop with a huge valley below, the eastern section of the Grand Canyon. Despite the fact that Caroline was sitting contentedly on a rock well back from any edge, Betty held her hand the whole time they were there. Betty declared that while the view of the valley below was amazing, the drop was terrifying. On the way back, they followed an intersecting trail through scrubby vegetation that took them eastwards to the very tip of Cape Final. Far below, a sandy curve of the Colorado River could be seen, although the river itself was hidden. Betty found this viewpoint even scarier and clung to Caroline, keeping well behind the large rocks that Danny and Charlie scrambled onto to look over the very edge.

"Don't you dare fall over, Danny," Betty called. "None of us can drive and I don't want to have to spend all winter here."

When Danny came back with Charlie, he asked, "So where do you want to spend the winter, Betty? Where will we head once we move out of here?"

"You think we might be able to move into some trailer or RV park? My pension money and Charlie's should easily cover the rent and leave us plenty for food. Hell, we might even be able to save some money."

"The Smucker doesn't qualify as a trailer or RV" Charlie said. "They probably have lots of rules. We'd have to have a huge RV like the ones back at that Walmart in Utah. They mightn't like any scumbags moving in beside fancy RVs or trailers that cost as much as a house."

"Hey! Who are ya callin' scumbags?" Betty snorted. "Our Smucker's served us well."

"It has," Charlie agreed, "but sitting in the middle of those fancy outfits it would look kinda outta place. You probably have to have power and proper bathrooms and a furnace for heat."

"Next time we go for groceries we can look out for information on trailer parks. Maybe we could find a used trailer for sale somewhere and put a down-payment on it. Or we could look into buyin' a small house somewhere. I heard house prices have been really low in the south of the U.S. in the last few years."

"You really think a bank would give us a mortgage?" Charlie laughed.

"Let's see what's available," Betty said. "We could probably find a cabin, cheap."

After lunch they sat outside The Smucker, mostly dozing, and Danny began reading R.L. Delderfield's *Come Home Charlie And Face Them* that Charlie had read and recommended.

When Winston returned just before suppertime, he was decked out as he had been the first day they'd met, complete with war paint. Charlie and Danny were helping with feeding and watering the horses when Betty called out that she would have a salad and spaghetti ready shortly and Winston was welcome to join them.

"Sounds great, Betty. Thanks," Winston replied. "I'll get this war paint off and clean up and join you."

"So how did it go today?" Winston asked as they sat eating in The Smucker.

"We had a restful day," Betty said. "It's lovely here. We walked down and took in the views. Gettin' there was fine, but at the viewpoints it's quite scary. We sat for quite a while, but Caroline and I stayed well away from the edge. We might go down again just before sunset. It's an easy walk."

"Maybe I'll join you. I haven't been down to watch a sunset for quite a while. Did anyone try out the shower? The water's real warm now."

"Not yet," Betty said. "I was thinkin' that me and Caroline would have one this afternoon, but I dozed off. Maybe we could have a quick one before we go for our walk. It was really nippy this mornin'."

"How was your day, Winston?" Charlie asked.

"I think it went really well. I had some fun. My clients enjoyed it. Took them on a half day rim tour in the morning then did my Indian schtick with a couple from France in the afternoon. Told them some legends, folklore, and then rode around a bit scaring a few tourists. I don't use any authentic native costumes. It's all fake stuff. I explain to the tourists that I don't use real costumes or sacred objects so my conscience is clear."

"Why do you do this?" Charlie asked. "You're a doctor, your card says. When do you see your patients?"

Winston laughed. "I guess I should get some new cards printed. I'm not that kind of doctor. I'm a doctor of anthropology. I teach courses at the Southern University of Arizona in Flagstaff. That's how I can spend a good part of the summer here."

"Anthropology?" Betty looked puzzled. "What exactly is that?"

"It's the study of the origin of people, their cultural development and so on. It lets me indulge my interest in Cape Final. I told you a bit about us, the Hualapai. My great-grandfather was given a promise by General Crook years ago, during the Indian wars against Geronimo." Winston went on to tell them the story about his great-grandfather, his escape and return.

"Was your great-grandfather buried here?" Charlie asked.

"No. It was our people's custom to cremate dead bodies then. It's possible his ashes were placed here, but we bury our dead nowadays."

THE GRAND GETAWAY   291

"Sorry to interrupt, Winston," Betty said. "I'd love to hear the rest of the story, but if Caroline and I are gonna have that shower we should have it now. Have another coffee. Danny and Charlie can do the dishes and tidy up. Then I'd like to hear more."

With Danny washing the dishes, Winston drying, and Charlie putting them away, they had everything in order to Betty's satisfaction when she and Caroline returned.

As they set off together down the trail, Charlie said, "You were saying Winston, that General Crook gave your great-grandfather the right to graze his ponies here at Cape Final, but there sure as heck isn't much grazing here. It's all pine needles and cactus. You're hauling in feed for your ponies."

"I believe it was more of a spiritual thing with my great-grandfather. I suspect General Crook probably knew how much my great-grandfather missed the canyon and wanted to give him a place to camp if he wanted. I think *to graze his ponies* was just some phrase used in the spirit of the agreement. That's really how it is with me too. I'm not looking for more land or any kind of compensation. I'd just like to prove that the promise was made. If I got some acknowledgement of that, maybe some kind of cairn erected, honouring my great-grandfather and the Hualapai scouts who'd helped General Crook, I'd be happy."

They had come to the intersecting trail that would take them to the point of Cape Final. Winston asked if they'd like to go that way and they agreed.

"How are you gonna prove it, your claim?" Danny asked. "You said you took the government to court."

"Yeah, I did, but I couldn't come up with enough evidence."

"What does your wife think?" Betty asked. "I believe you said she's a doctor. A real doctor."

"She is. She's indulged me all these years. She's been very patient. I'm here mostly in the summer but she's been hinting I should give it up. But I dunno. I'd hate to do that."

"So are you doing the same stuff tomorrow?" Charlie asked. "I mean doing your Indian stuff? And how does that help you prove anything?"

"It doesn't." Winston went on to explain about keeping a Hualapai presence there and following up leads when he was back teaching at the university. "After tomorrow I have to head home again. My son's coming home. Haven't seen him in a long while. Don't know if he's coming for a few days to stay or what, but I want to be there when he arrives."

"How old is he? What does he do?"

"He's... jeez... What is he now? 44... No. God, Colby's 45 now. He's an artist. Or at least he was. He's had some success. Lives in Sacramento. Married to a nice Hualapai girl. Here we are. You been up on the rocks to look over, Betty?"

"No. I didn't dare," Betty said. "Danny and Charlie did though."

"Come on Betty. It's okay, I'll hold your hand. We can all sit on the rocks. It's quite safe."

On the way back, Charlie asked, "Are you going to take your ponies back home tomorrow night?"

"Yeah. I have to. Can't leave them here unattended."

"Me and Danny could watch them. You've brought lots of feed and there's enough water for a few days."

"There is," Winston said. "I'll be gone no more than three or four days. I'd make a lot better time if I don't have to haul my trailer and ponies back to Peach Springs. You sure you'd be able to do this? You'd just have to feed them some hay in the morning and again in the evening and make sure they have enough water. It wouldn't tie you down. You could still go someplace during the day. Oh, there is one thing. I usually clean up the corral after them and dump the manure into a wooden box I take away in my trailer."

"I think we could manage," Danny said. "Just show us how much hay to feed them and leave the manure box here with a shovel and we'll take care of them."

"I'll be off early again in the morning, but I'll bring the ponies back mid-afternoon and get you set up. That way I could be home before dark. If by any chance you run out of water, you can get it at Cape Royal just down the road. You're sure you can handle this?"

"We'll be fine. Don't worry," Danny said.

The following day, late in the afternoon, Rudy Van Erk, a park ranger driving by to check on permits at the Cape Final campground, stopped momentarily as he passed Winston's campsite. He'd caught a glimpse of something different in the trees. He reversed. *What was that? Was Winston adding more stuff to his campsite?* He switched off his vehicle and climbed out, stepping into the pines.

Rudy and a couple of new rangers had joined the Parks Service a year and a half ago. Joe Daly, the park superintendent, filled them in on Winston Whatoname, saying, "Nowadays, there's no knowing what the courts might do. Let sleeping dogs lie. There's been quite a few reports in newspapers and the rest of the media about sit-ins in various parts of the country, blocking highways, and railway lines. I'm retiring soon and I want to step down without any reporter having stuck a microphone into my face, asking me to comment on some blockade because of an Indian claim here at the Grand Canyon. I want no interruptions to service for our visitors at the North Rim on my watch, so make sure you're not the cause of any conflict with the Indians, including Winston Whatoname."

As Rudy used his binoculars to peer at what seemed to be some kind of ramshackle relic of a bus, he caught the sound of singing. He focused his binoculars on someone holding out a handful of hay to pony in a corral and stroking the pony's face.

THE GRAND GETAWAY   293

What's goin' on? That isn't Winston Whatoname. That's some old white guy. As Rudy watched he heard the man singing the song *I'm An Old Cowhand.*

Rudy wanted to march through the trees, confront the old white guy who was obviously camping illegally, and write up a ticket, but Winston's *Indian Land* sign made him hesitate. The superintendent's warning gave him further pause. He went back to his vehicle and drove on, wondering how he should handle this situation.

CHAPTER 64

Having fed Winston's ponies and finished supper, Charlie and Danny were sitting outside The Smucker. Betty was doing a little tidying inside and Caroline was with her. Danny was, to no avail, trying to read his book – Charlie was in a talkative mood and had interrupted him a number of times. He had started by talking about Winston's ponies, but had moved on to reminiscing on the size of the cabbages his grandmother had grown in her garden. He was recalling visiting his grandmother and being sent out in the street with a shovel to scoop up the steaming pile of horse manure that the bread deliveryman's horse had deposited in the middle of the street.

"I think I was about five," Charlie was saying, "and the scoop shovel was heavy. There was fierce competition for horse manure since everyone in the neighbourhood had a vegetable garden and horse manure was a fertilizer. There was a kind of honour system. The manure belonged to you if it was dropped in front of your house. But old man Crosby, who lived next door to my gran, was always watching through his front window and if you didn't get out real smart to claim the prize, he would be out to grab it. I think he maybe had a 10-second rule or something and kept his scoop shovel at his front door. I was struggling with Gran's shovel and I arrived at the manure pile about the same time as old man Crosby.

"I hesitated, but old man Crosby didn't. He had most of the manure on his shovel before I could blink, leaving me with a couple of handfuls. I remember he laughed and said something like, 'Beat ya kid.' I tried scooping up the leftovers but only managed to flip the manure onto Crosby's shoes. He thought I did it deliberately and was about to give me a cuff to the head when a yell from my gran stopped him. She'd come out onto her porch and then the language flew between the two of them, words I'd never heard before – huh?... Listen." Charlie stopped talking and was looking into the trees in front of them. "Something's coming."

They caught a glimpse of a red half-ton as it wove its way up the winding track towards them.

"Could be trouble," Charlie said. He stood up. "What if it's a park ranger? What are we gonna say?"

"Let's see who it is first," Danny said as he stood up too.

The truck rounded the last turn and slowed, then came to a stop almost parallel to where they were.

A woman was sitting in the passenger seat. The driver climbed out. He walked part-way towards them, then stopped, looking puzzled. He was, Danny guessed, in his forties and maybe a native Indian. The right sleeve of his short-sleeved shirt was empty.

"Winston around?" he asked.

THE GRAND GETAWAY   295

"No," Charlie replied. "He headed home this afternoon."

The driver grunted and didn't look pleased. "Those his ponies?" He nodded his head towards them.

"Yeah," Danny replied. "We're looking after them for a couple of days 'til he gets back."

"You a *Hoolapie* too?" Charlie asked.

The man looked startled when Betty and Caroline suddenly appeared in the doorway of the bus.

Betty smiled and called out, "Hello there."

The man gave a curt nod, said, "Hi," then turned back to Danny and Charlie and asked, "So Winston asked you to look after his ponies?"

"That's right,' Danny replied. "He said he'd be back in a couple of days. Can we give him a message?"

"Thanks, but I'll catch up to him." He turned on his heel, walked back to his truck and drove away.

"Sheesh," Charlie said, "he didn't seem too pleased."

"No," Danny said. "I don't think he expected to find us here. I think he might have been Winston's son. He looked about the right age."

"You notice he had an arm missing?" Charlie asked. "Winston didn't mention that."

"Well he must know how to find Winston, said he'd catch up to him."

Betty had joined them. "What was that all about?" she asked.

"Danny thinks he might have been Winston's son. We're not sure," Charlie said. "He had a woman with him, only has one arm."

"The woman? I didn't notice."

"No. The guy! The guy!" Charlie said.

"Oh," Betty said. "I thought he looked a bit like Winston. Wonder what he'd have thought if he'd come earlier when we were away at the view points and only the ponies were here? You think he believes we might be campin' here illegally?"

"Well, we are," Charlie said. "Sort of."

"No. I mean without Winston's permission. We'd better stick close by tomorrow in case he comes back. I think I might do a bit of cleanin' in Winston's camper. It could do with a good dustin' and airin' out. You can help me, Charlie."

CHAPTER 65

On the way home, Winston stopped at the offices of *The Arizona Daily Sun* in Flagstaff looking for Josh Patterson, a reporter who had given Winston and his cause favourable coverage in the past, only to find that Josh had just left for his annual vacation. Winston hadn't spoken to Josh in quite a while, and since losing his court case, the story had fallen from the public's interest and media coverage had dried up. Josh had told Winston to keep in touch and Winston had been hoping he might get him to revive the story, but he had nothing new to offer Josh anyway.

As he drove on, Winston wondered what might draw attention again to stir up publicity for his campaign. Maybe he could organize a *pow wow* or some kind of Indian days with lots of drumming to create a fuss. But it was late in the year now, too late to organize anything, even if he could get enough Hualapai to participate. With winter closing in, the season was almost over. Maybe he could try it next year.

When Winston arrived home around supper time, Georgina greeted him.

"You're early. I didn't see you haul in the horse trailer. Did you have any trouble on the way?"

"No, I've got someone looking after the ponies for a few days. I don't have to go back until Tuesday morning for a couple of last gigs. Then I'm closing things down for the season."

"Good. Colby and Derica are arriving sometime tomorrow. And Colby is hinting that they might be considering moving back here, depending."

"Depending on what?" Winston asked.

"He didn't say exactly," Georgina replied, "but one condition would no doubt be how the two of you get on."

"He's setting down conditions?"

"No. For God's sake, Winston! He didn't say anything about conditions, but you know damn well the main reason he left was because you and he provoked each other so much. So please don't start an argument as soon as he gets in the door. I'd like to give him and Derica the chance to stay. Maybe he's looking for a change from Sacramento. I think he's reached a point in his career where he's looking for new subjects to paint, coming back to his roots. I don't know, but let's give him a fair chance. Okay?"

"Okay, okay," Winston raised his hands.

"So if Colby happens to get you riled up, and you know how quickly that can happen – I know, I know..." Georgina waved off the rebuttal she could see Winston was about to make. "It cuts both ways. But try to be cool. Don't be rising like a trout to the first cast he makes. Let him talk, let him feel his way."

"Okay, honey. I'll try. I really will."

THE GRAND GETAWAY   297

"Maybe with you here for a few days, you and Colby will have a chance to patch things up. I certainly hope you can. I don't want to find myself refereeing any more fights. I want him back if that's what he wants. I want peace. And if he and Derica do move here, we'll get to see more of our granddaughter. That'd be wonderful. Colby told me she's doing great in her first year at university."

Georgina was in the bedroom getting ready for bed, and Winston had almost dozed off in front of the TV, when the lights of a vehicle flashed across the front window of the house and there was a rap on the door.

Winston opened it and Colby and Derica stood there, suitcases in hand.

"Colby! Derica! You're early. Mom said you were arriving tomorrow. Come in, come in."

"We got here a bit quicker than we expected," Colby said, putting his suitcase down on the floor as Winston took Derica's case from her hand. "We stopped by Cape Final on the way. Thought you might be there. There's some weirdos camping at your place. Said they were looking after your ponies. Who are they? Looked like a bunch of gypsies. I thought you always claimed it was Hualapai land. They're no more Hualapai than I'm Santa Claus... Now it's looking like a refugee camp or a hippy colony. What the hell are ya doing?"

"They're friends of mine. Canadians."

"Canadians! You're not still thanking Canadians for letting you hide out in their country? God, that was years ago."

"They needed somewhere to camp."

"Surely you're not raisin' money by renting out camping spots? You been spending all your money on lawyer's fees again?"

"Colby! Derica! You're home!" Georgina rushed in and hugged both of them.

"Colby up yet?" Winston asked Georgina as she was setting the table for breakfast.

"He's gone."

"Gone! God! What did I say? Did I make him mad already?"

"No." Georgina laughed. "He left a note. He wants to catch the sunrise on some of the canyon around here and he's dropping Derica off at her folks' place on the way. He said they might stay overnight at her folk's place. He'll phone."

"Hmm. I thought we might have some time together. I have to be back at Cape Final Tuesday."

"Colby said he'd be back tomorrow for sure. Derica will stay a few days at her folks' place then come back here. He's excited again about his painting and the two new galleries who want to represent him. You've got to give him a chance." Georgina came and hugged Winston. "Please try to make it work."

"I'll try. I really will. I want what you want, honey." Winston bent and kissed her.

CHAPTER 66

Rudy Van Erk was frustrated. He'd spent the last part of his afternoon fending off an obnoxious kid throughout the short informal talk he'd given about the Grand Canyon to a group behind the Lodge. The kid kept insisting that what he said was impossible whenever Rudy mentioned anything about the canyon's age in millions of years. At least four times the kid had called out, "But that's not true. My dad says that the earth is only 6000 years old."

To make matters worse, the kid's father had been part of the group and rather than telling his son to be quiet, he'd stood there grinning proudly every time his loud-mouth brat had interrupted.

Rudy had gritted his teeth and was thankful when his talk ended. He finished his shift for the day and retreated inside the lodge to grab a coffee. Still chafing from the pain-in-the-ass kid, his thoughts turned to his trip out to Cape Final the day before. He'd found that the few campers at the campsite all held back-country permits, making his trip, as far as he was concerned, futile.

But then there was Winston Whatoname's camp and the old white guy with the weird yellow bus. Winston was camping there illegally, as everyone knew, so the old guy he'd seen with Winston's ponies was really breaking the law. He sipped his coffee, mulling over what could be done to handle that situation, when his thoughts were interrupted by a high pitched, staccato laugh from across the room that he instantly recognized. Vince Esterhazy, who was married to Rudy's cousin, Alma. He was sitting across the room with another cop from Coconino County.

Vince had been, until recently, with the United States Border Patrol and had lived in Quartzsite, Arizona, on Interstate 10. Alma had persuaded him to take a job with the Coconino County Police Force and move back to her home town of Fredonia so she could look after her ailing mother, who was having heart problems. Alma had hated Quartzsite, declaring it a dump. Vince got tired of Alma's complaining and had caved in. He was now sure that Alma had used her mother's illness, which seemed to have dramatically improved on their arrival in Fredonia, as an excuse to get out of Quartzsite. His mother-in law, in fact, appeared to be the one person in Fredonia least likely to have a heart attack. She wasn't overweight, had a boundless amount of energy and rode a bicycle all over town.

Vince found Fredonia, with a population of only a third of Quartzsite, much quieter. He was bored with catching the occasional speeder and he missed the daily action with the USCBP, pulling over and searching vehicles along the roads leading north from Mexico, searching for drugs and illegals. He was making less money, but Alma pointed out that now they were living with her mother they weren't paying any rent. That was true, but Alma's mother, from the time they'd arrived, had felt compelled to comment on his laugh, which she claimed was "peeling the paint off

THE GRAND GETAWAY   299

my walls." The only compensation was that Fredonia's summer heat was less oppressive than Quartzsite's.

As Rudy approached the table where Vince and the other cop sat, he was hoping that Vince wouldn't embarrass him with that ungodly, hysterical laugh of his. It reminded him of a lawn-mower starting up. At first it was just *heh, heh, heh's*, repeated a couple of times and then, like the motor catching and throttle stuck, it spiralled into a high-pitched ear-piercing crescendo that seemed to bounce off walls. For a large man, Rudy thought, Vince sure had a shrill laugh. He had noticed that Vince's laugh had drawn stares. Vince had told him once over a few drinks that he'd been asked, when he wasn't in uniform, to leave a restaurant because he was disturbing the other guests.

Vince caught sight of Rudy and greeted him loudly, "Rudy! You son of a bitch! Haven't seen ya in a while. What's been turnin' your crank, lately?" He almost broke into a cackle but he changed topic and asked, "You met my partner, Deputy Joe Balasko?"

Rudy and Joe shook hands as Vince waved him into a seat. "You want a coffee?" He called to a passing waiter carrying a coffee pot.

"What are ya doin' down here, Vince?" Rudy asked.

"Aw just takin' a break. Actually, we're off shift. Headin' back in a few minutes. Thought we'd take in a few of the sights. Gettin' kinda bored drivin' up an' down the same strip of highway. Joe, here, likes it though. Can catch up on his sleep while I drive. All we saw today was a couple of tarantulas and one scorpion crossin' the road. Flattened one of the little bastards." He let out a couple of *heh, heh, heh's* but cut it short. "Alma's happy though. Me, I miss the action with the USCBP. So, what's up with you? Anythin' excitin'? No illegals hidin' in the bottomless pit ya have here? Heh heh, heh."

"Well." Rudy looked serious, lowered his voice and quickly pulled his chair closer to the table to forestall Vince's oncoming laugh. Vince took the hint that Rudy was looking for confidentiality and quietened, leaning forward.

Rudy quickly filled in Vince and his partner Joe on the possible illegal camper on Winston Whatoname's camp site.

"Isn't that your jurisdiction?" Joe asked. "We don't get involved in park's business. Wouldn't you park rangers usually handle that?"

"That's true," Rudy agreed. "But it's a little tricky." Rudy lowered his voice a bit more and told them about Winston Whatoname and the Park Superintendent's concern with stirring up the natives.

"You're sure this guy you saw was a white guy? Did you get a look at the license plate on his vehicle?" Vince asked.

"Yeah, Alberta. That's Canada. And I'm pretty sure he's white."

"Could be an illegal. Maybe me and Joe here could take a look. Not today though. Got to get the patrol car back. How about tomorrow, Joe? We can come down and take a quick look. Whatta ya say? How far is it to this Cape Final?"

"About a good half hour each way," Rudy said.

"Okay, Deputy. Whatta ya say?" Vince asked again.

"Tomorrow's Sunday and we're off. I'm taking my wife to Kanab to visit her sister, been promising her for weeks. Monday we're going over near Bitter Springs to do some paperwork on a residential break-in. Tuesday afternoon would be the earliest."

"I guess it's Tuesday then, Rudy." Vince rolled his eyes. "We'll drive out there Tuesday afternoon and take a look 'n' report back to ya. Doin' somethin' different for a change, 'stead of flattenin' tarantulas and scorpions, *heh, heh.*"

"Guess we could take a look. No harm in that," the deputy agreed. "Won't be anything official, though. But we better be heading back."

CHAPTER 67

Winston was sitting on the deck outside his house, reading a book he was thinking of using in one of his spring sessions, when Colby returned late the following afternoon. He was carrying a couple of partly completed canvases which he set on the deck in the shade.

"Painting go well?" Winston asked.

"It did. I think I have the basis of a couple of saleable paintings. I should be able to finish them okay."

Winston glanced at the painting he could see where Colby had set it against the house wall.

"That looks really good. You captured the reflections off the rocks and water real well. It's a beauty. Different too, from the stuff you did before. I like it."

"Thanks. I'm trying something different. I guess it's a bit more impressionistic."

"You want a beer?" Winston asked.

"Yeah. That'd be good."

"Pull up a chair. I'll get us a couple."

As they drank their beers from the cans, Colby tentatively asked Winston when he was going back to Cape Final.

"I should be back there Tuesday evening. I have a gig Wednesday morning and another Thursday. Then I think I'll be packing it in for this year."

"Mind if I come back with you? I'd like to catch a few scenes in your area. Take a few photos. Do some outlines, sketches. I'll take my own truck so I'm mobile, pick up a few groceries and a few beers. That be okay with you?"

"Sure, it'll be fine." Winston tried to keep the surprise out of his voice. "The camper is small, but we can try not to get into each other's hair."

"I'll be out scouting out a few spots most days. I'd like to spend more than a couple of days there. I can stay on, if you decide to come back here. Derica will probably spend the best part of the week at her folks' place. Can I have another beer?"

"Sure thing."

Winston was pleased with the way things went between him and Colby in the following days. Colby hung around and worked some more on the two canvases he'd started. Neither of them mentioned anything about Winston's fixation with Cape Final or any other topic that might cause friction. At supper times they mostly talked about painting, Julia's university courses and her notion that she might follow her grandmother's footsteps and possibly go into medicine. "She's not sure," Colby said. "She's only mentioned it in passing."

"She's got lots of time," Georgina said.

On Monday when Georgina came home from the clinic, she was surprised to find Winston dressed in his Hualapai Indian costume as Colby sketched him while he sat on a chair on the deck. She smiled at Winston and squeezed his shoulder as she passed them and went into the house.

Betty was busy. She had delayed cleaning up Winston's camper until the day he was due back. In the morning she dusted most of the shelves and swept the floor with some help from Charlie. Then she had Charlie take some chairs and a few other pieces outside and sent him to get some water so they could wash the floor.

"Okay, Charlie. That's it for now. We'll go get some lunch. The floor won't take long to dry. We can come back later to put back Winston's furniture and we'll have to be happy with that."

They had a light lunch and Betty said she was feeling tired and she'd have a nap. "Wake me up about three. I'll come and give Winston's camper a quick once-over."

After Betty had gone to lie down, Danny, Charlie and Caroline sat outside The Smucker.

"Betty okay?" Danny asked.

"I guess so. Why do you ask?"

"She seems kinda tired. I noticed that yesterday when we walked to the viewpoint. She didn't seem to have a lot of energy. She's been napping a lot lately. When we drove up to the general store yesterday to get the milk and other stuff, she fell asleep on the way there and on the way back. She been sleeping okay at night?"

"I guess so. I've been sleeping okay myself an' she didn't say. Caroline fell asleep in The Smucker going to the store and back too."

"But riding in The Smucker always makes Caroline sleep. Betty usually stays awake."

"Yeah. But today she went hammer and tongs cleaning Winston's camper. Had me hopping too, for a while."

"Well, let her rest," Danny said. "I think she's done enough for today."

"You're right. Maybe you and I could get supper later. Give her a break."

"It's 3:30. Where's Charlie? I told him to wake me at 3.00." Betty was standing in the door of The Smucker.

"He went over to Winston's camper a little while ago. You were still asleep and we decided not to wake you. Thought you needed your rest. He and I are gonna make supper tonight so you can put your feet up."

"Hmmf. Okay. Surprise me. Has Caroline been sleepin' long, Danny?"

"'Bout an hour, I guess. I dozed off for a few minutes myself."

Betty sat in an empty lawn chair beside Danny. "I asked Winston to see if he could bring back any information on trailer parks, any mobile homes for sale we

THE GRAND GETAWAY   303

could possibly buy, maybe a place to tide us over for the winter. It'd be great if we could find a cabin or little house on a piece of land somewhere, have a room of our own, even a little garden. What do ya think, Danny?"

"Sounds like a dream, but I've no idea what anything would cost. You think your pension and Charlie's are enough to actually buy something? I've no idea if we could find anything. I've got no money and then there's Caroline to consider."

"We'll see what Winston comes up with. Hi, Caroline. I see you're awake. Let's go check on Charlie to see what the bugger is up to. Probably sleepin' in Winston's bunk. Come on."

Vince Esterhazy and Deputy Joe Balasko finished their official shift a half hour early and headed down the Cape Royal Drive towards Cape Final. Joe was asleep inside of 10 minutes.

Probably dreaming of his retirement a year from now, Vince thought. *How in hell am I gonna stick it out here for another 20 years?*

Vince was looking forward to a little action. He'd spent his Sunday trying to stay out of the way of Alma's mother, but she found a job for him washing the windows of the house for the best part of the morning. He was planning to watch the Diamondbacks play the Mets on TV as soon as his mother-in-law and Alma went for a bike ride, but he found himself repairing the front tire of Alma's bicycle, which had developed a puncture. By the time he got that fixed, and Alma and his mother-in-law left, the game was already an 8-0 blow-out in the fourth inning for the Mets and it wasn't worth watching.

The trip to Bitter Springs yesterday to do the paperwork on the break-in was even more tedious. He'd mostly stood around while Joe filled in the forms. They listened to a harangue from the elderly, very overweight, couple, Venetia and Jack Brennan, on the ineffectiveness of the police force and why they were paying taxes when anyone could just walk into your home and garage and steal your valuables. They had argued with each other over the list of missing items, when and where they'd bought each item and the value. Vince had interrupted in disbelief at one point as Joe was writing down 'Thighmaster' on the list, which Venetia claimed was worth nearly $2000.

In the car, Vince laughed. "I nearly choked when that woman said her Thighmaster was missin'. You see the set of thighs on her? There'd be no way she could find enough space between her thighs to use a Thighmaster. You think they just went through some catalogue to make up the list of 'stolen' goods?"

"That's a good possibility. But all part of the job," Joe replied. "We'll just file the report."

God! Another 20 years fillin' in forms on fictitious stolen goods. I'll go nuts, Vince thought.

"Hey, wake up buddy." He tapped Joe's thigh. "Nearly there. The sign for Cape Final just came up."

Betty opened the door to the camper and stepped inside with Caroline in tow. In spite of the afternoon sun, inside was quite gloomy because of the nearby pines and the camper's tiny windows.

"You in here, Charlie?" Betty called. "Where the hell ya hidin'?"

A sudden movement behind a piece of curtain that separated the living area from the bunks startled her.

"Ha paleface woman! Women," Charlie corrected, on catching sight of Caroline. "You come pay respects to great Indian chief?" Charlie flipped the length of curtain aside and stepped forward.

Betty gave a shriek and staggered back into Caroline. "Holy jeez! Is that you, Charlie, ya dumb bugger? What in hell have ya done to yerself now? What have you got on your face?"

"Relax, Betty. I'm just having a little fun. I found a collection of Winston's fake costume stuff. When we played cowboys an' Indians when I was a kid, the older kids always wanted to be the cowboy heroes from the movies an' made us young kids be the Indians. But we never looked the part. All we had were a few seagull feathers we taped to our foreheads. I found this Spider-Man mask in the bottom of Winston's trunk and couldn't resist. I don't know what it was doing in there."

"Well you sure scared the crap outta me," Betty said. "And no doubt Caroline too. Real creepy."

"Creepy, creepy, creepy," Caroline repeated.

Charlie laughed. "It scared me too when I opened the trunk. I was just about to creep out and scare the hell outta Danny. I could see him still dozing in his chair. Come on. Let's have a bit of fun. There's a couple of small head-dresses in the trunk. You and Caroline could dress up too. Be a sport, Betty."

"What do you think Winston will think if he finds you messin' with his stuff?"

"It'll only take a few minutes. He won't be back here for a few more hours. Besides, he does this all the time with tourists. We'll put it all back and he'll be happy we cleaned up his camper. Look, try this on." Charlie picked up a small head-dress, more of a set of feathers arranged in a band, and placed it on Betty's head. "Take a look in the mirror, here."

Betty stepped forward and looked at herself and laughed. "I look like a blonde, fat peach with feathers growing out of the top."

While Betty was looking at herself in the mirror and laughing, Charlie fitted Caroline with a similar garb. Caroline poked and prodded at whatever Charlie had put on her head and started patting it. "Soft, soft."

"We shouldn't be doin' this," Betty said. "This is foolishness. I'm sure Winston would be mad if he saw us dressed like this and foolin' around with his stuff." Betty was studying herself in the mirror again. She chuckled. "I'd never pass for a Hualapai maiden."

"No one will know if you're still a maiden. I won't tell anyone." Charlie laughed.

"You're a mad bugger, Charlie Bannister. Hey! You left a pile of dust when you moved Winston's trunk. I thought we'd finished cleanin'. Where's that broom?"

Joe Balasko yawned and rubbed his eyes as Vince slowed the police cruiser and made the turn down the trail to Cape Final. "So what's the plan? We're just gonna take a look, right?"

"Right. We're just takin' a look. We won't be fillin' in any report forms, 'cept if we happen upon somethin' really big."

"Like what?" Joe asked. "We're not even supposed to be here. Not our jurisdiction."

"Hell. We're cops," Vince argued. "We see something goin' down that's illegal, we can't ignore it."

"I thought we were just gonna report whatever we saw to your cousin. We're only dealing with a possible illegal camper."

"Yeah. That's what we'll do. But if we find any bodies, a big stash of drugs, a number of scalps hanging from trees..." Vince started laughing and went into full throttle, startling Joe, although he had suffered with Vince's laugh a number of times and had learned to put up with it.

"Jeez, Vince. Let's not draw too much attention to ourselves. Quiet down. We're coming by the official campsite."

"Okay, okay," Vince managed to choke off his laugh. Joe was sounding nervous.

"Let's keep this low-key," Joe continued. "We should have used your car or mine to check this out. We don't want to have to explain to the sheriff why a Fredonia cop car was joyriding way down here. Let's just quietly take a look and then take off. How far is this Winston Whatoname's campsite anyway? This trail sure twists and turns."

"Rudy said it wasn't far. We gotta look out for an *Indian Land* sign. Look, I think that's it up ahead. Yeah, we're here."

"Good. I gotta take a piss real bad," Joe said. "Drank too much coffee this morning."

CHAPTER 68

"Here, Charlie, pass me that dust-pan. There's a pile of pine needles back here too." Betty swept a small pile of dust and needles onto the dust-pan Charlie handed her. "Open that window a bit more, I want to shake out this broom, then we'll be finished."

"Darn! I can't see Danny," Charlie said. "He musta gone into The Smucker for a coffee or something. I'll give him a minute, see if he comes out again. We'll all creep out and scare the hell outta him."

"Never mind that," Betty said. "Let me poke this broom out the window to shake it off. Damn! The head of the broom fell off. Go get it, Charlie, would you?"

"See anything?" Deputy Joe Balasko whispered as he walked toward a pine tree, intent on relieving himself. Vince, who had jumped out of the vehicle as soon as he turned off the motor, was already peering into the bush with a pair of binoculars.

"Not much," Vince muttered. "An old camper and some kind of crazy looking bus with, yeah, Rudy was right, a license plate that says Alberta. Gotta be an illegal camper. But there's no one in sight, just three horses in a corral. Must be someone around somewhere, maybe inside the camper. Holy crap! Must be an Indian! " Vince gasped.

He trained the binoculars on the startling figure who had appeared on the deck outside the camper. *What in hell has he got on his face? And what's he got in his hand?*

Charlie had been forced by Betty to go out to dump the dust-pan and to retrieve the broom head but he was determined to play the part of his character. He looked over his shoulder, hoping that Betty and Caroline were following behind him, but no. Betty was still holding the broom handle, wiggling it around through the open window, obviously waiting for Charlie to retrieve the broom head and screw it back on.

Vince caught the movement at the window. "Shit! A rifle!"

No use usin' my revolver from here. He jumped to the cruiser, flicked open the trunk and pulled out a rifle, snapping a clip into it. He took cover behind a tree.

He aimed the rifle just above the head of the Indian, cautiously watching the wavering rifle poking through the window. He'd let them make the first move.

"Ahhhhhh," Joe Balasko sighed with relief as he got his pants unzipped and started peeing against the tree.

Vince glanced at Joe to tell him to take cover but he was well protected by the tree he was peeing against.

The Indian on the deck let out a yowl and suddenly raised his hands above his head as some kind of powdery stuff flew into the air. Vince was convinced that the

THE GRAND GETAWAY   307

puff of powder might have been from a rifle shot. He noted that the rifle poking through the window had stopped wavering and seemed to be pointing directly at him. *I'll fire off a warning shot just to be on the safe side.* Vince tightened his finger on the trigger, aiming high just above the camper.

Just as Vince pulled the trigger, Charlie yelled, "I am Charlie Spider... Shit!"

There was a crack of a rifle and the metallic whine of a bullet ricocheting off the camper's roof-top above Charlie's head and a second, almost instantaneous, clang as it hit some other metallic object.

Joe Balasko was so startled by the sound of the rifle shot that he automatically ducked, peeing all over the leg of his uniform. Then he saw the rifle in Vince's hand.

"Jeez! What the fuck are you doing?" Joe zipped up his pants, cursing over his wet pant-leg and ran to Vince, grabbing the rifle just as a couple more yelling figures emerged from the camper.

"Shit! You've stirred up a whole hornets nest of Indians, you dumb bastard. Let's get the hell out of here. Quick!" He grabbed Vince and hustled him towards their vehicle. Neither of them saw the naked old white guy who scampered out of the shower behind the camper.

CHAPTER 69

Joe dropped the rifle into the open trunk, slamming it shut. He thought about getting behind the wheel himself, but Vince quickly jumped into the driver's seat and was already reversing the cruiser to get it turned around. With the car moving, Vince yelled, "Get in!" Joe just managed to scramble inside before Vince tramped on the accelerator and the car shot down the trail, throwing up a shower of gravel and dust, as Joe struggled to get the door shut.

"Jeez! What were you thinking back there? Slow down! Why the hell did you fire?"

"I was sure I saw a rifle pointin' at us through the camper window. I was aimin' for just over the top of the camper when that Indian hollered and startled the hell outta me. I accidentally squeezed the trigger. I think someone in the camper might've fired a shot. I thought I saw smoke," he went on. "Heh, heh, heh. Once I fired off the rifle and I saw a bunch of Indians, I realized we should probably high-tail it outta there. Heh, heh, heh. Hot damn! It was the most excitement we've had since I moved up here."

"Never mind that, just slow down, Vince. Your cousin isn't gonna be too pleased when you phone him and tell him we poked a hornet's nest of Indians."

"We'll say nothin' about the rifle shot. I'll just tell him that there's more Indians campin' there. He won't do nothin' seein' as how the Park Superintendent doesn't want any trouble. Jeez! What the hell happened to your pants? You pee on yourself? Heh, heh, heh."

Vince's laugh burst forth to its full high-pitched squeal and Joe, who was already irked enough, rolled down his window to try to ease the assault of Vince's laugh on his ear drums.

"Holy shit! Look out!" Joe yelled, as they careened around a bend, narrowly missing a truck coming towards them and just managing to squeeze by another that was following close behind. Vince was still laughing as he got the car under control, only slowing down as they neared the Cape Final parking lot.

"I can't wait for my retirement," Joe muttered.

Winston was thinking about what Georgina had said just before he and Colby had left for Cape Final in their own trucks. "This is your chance, Winston. Colby is really making an effort. Please don't mess it up." She'd kissed him on the cheek as he'd started the engine.

"Holy mother!" Winston braked hard just a few yards from his campsite and stopped as a fast-moving police cruiser careened around the bend just ahead of him, narrowly missing his truck.

THE GRAND GETAWAY   309

Although the siren wasn't on, Winston heard a strange high-pitched squealing sound coming from the cruiser as it swerved past him. Now he looked anxiously in his rearview mirror and held his breath as the cop car fish-tailed a couple of times before it straightened out and sped past Colby's vehicle.

Damn lunatic. Had something happened at the camp? Winston instantly stepped on the gas, anxious now to get there and see that everything was okay. *If there was some emergency at the camp, why is the cop car speeding away in the opposite direction?*

On hearing the loud bang, Betty and Caroline had rushed out to find Charlie lying face down on the deck.

"Oh my God! Charlie!" Betty yelled. "What happened?"

Charlie raised his head and hissed, "Jeez, Betty, get down! Get down! Get Caroline down!"

"Why? What's goin' on?"

"Someone's shooting at us. Get down!"

"What! Come on Charlie, stop playin' the fool. Quit playin' this cowboys and Indians thing. You banged on the side of the camper, didn't ya? You scared the life outta me. You've had your fun. Now get up."

"I'm not joking. Somebody fired a shot."

"You wounded, then? I don't see any blood. Get up for God's sake! Oh my God! Danny! Have ya gone mad or what?" Betty started laughing as a naked Danny ran up onto the deck. "You comin' to play cowboys 'n' Indians too?" Betty hooted. "I see you brought your six-shooter. Now there's a lethal weapon if ever I saw one."

"Oh shit! Sorry, Betty," Danny hastily covered himself with his hands. "I was taking a shower when I heard a shot. I was sure a bullet hit the water barrel over my head and I just rushed out. I shoulda grabbed a towel. What happened? What are you all doing? What's Charlie wearing?"

Charlie sat up, laughing along with Betty and then Caroline joined in.

"Jeez. Everyone's okay then? I'll go grab my clothes." Danny said sheepishly.

CHAPTER 70

"Oh shiii...t." Betty stopped laughing as Winston's truck, followed almost immediately by a second, pulled up in a cloud of dust.

Danny made a dash for the shower but realized it was too late. Winston had obviously seen them and was already only steps away.

"What are we gonna tell Winston?" Charlie hissed to Betty. A second man had climbed out of the other truck and was standing staring at the tableau the three presented on the camper's deck.

"We'll tell the truth," Betty whispered to Charlie. "We must look a sight, especially you Charlie. But there's no harm done." She removed her feathered head-band as Charlie pulled the Spider-Man mask off his head and stood looking like a schoolboy who'd just wet his pants in class.

"What happened here?" Winston asked. "We just about got creamed by a cop car belting out of here. You all okay?"

"We are," Betty said. "Sorry we look a sight." She giggled.

"Cop car? What's he talking about?" Charlie muttered.

"What the hell's happening?" Colby had come over. "What are you running here, Dad? You importing fake Indians now? It looks like some kind of geriatric hippy colony. And who was that naked old guy who just took off?"

"Ah-hem... That was me. Sorry. I'm Danny." Danny appeared from behind Winston's camper, this time fully dressed. "I came dashing out of the shower when I thought I heard a shot."

"My God!" Colby said, angrily. "You haven't been dumb enough to bring any guns here, have you Dad? What are you trying to orchestrate? Some kind of stand-off with the cops? Another Wounded Knee? Christ! With fake Indians!"

"Cool it, Colby," Winston snapped. "These are friends of mine. They're just camping here for a few days. And no, there are no guns here."

"It was my fault," Charlie said. "We had tidied up your camper. Betty thought we could do something nice for you for letting us camp here. I found a box with some of your Indian costumes. I thought I'd dress up and sneak up on Danny, to scare him. He was sitting outside but when I came out, he'd disappeared. I guess he was in the shower then. We were just having a bit of fun. We thought you wouldn't be back for a while and we'd be all cleaned up before you got here. I'm sorry. It was my idea."

"That's okay. But what about the police?" Winston asked.

"Police?" Charlie looked puzzled.

"There weren't any police here," Betty said. "It was just like Charlie said. We dressed up, Danny thought he heard a bang and came runnin' out of the shower.

THE GRAND GETAWAY   311

God that was funny." Betty started to laugh. "Look, let's get cleaned up and we'll have a coffee."

"So there were no police here?" Colby asked. "What about the shot you thought you heard?"

Danny cursed the fact he'd blurted out hearing a shot. "Could've been a back-fire out on the road," Danny replied, knowing full well that it sounded lame. He'd heard the ricochet hit something above him and Charlie had obviously thought it was a shot too because he was lying flat on the deck when Danny rushed out of the shower. And with Betty crouching anxiously over him, Danny had thought Charlie had been hit.

"There's a hell of a difference between a back-fire and a shot," Colby said.

"It was me," Charlie said. "I just banged on the side of the camper to get Betty and Caroline to come out and join me, that's all."

"Look there's no harm done," Betty said. "Danny, please put on the coffee while the three of us clean up."

"I'm gonna take a walk down to the point," Colby said. "I'll see ya later."

"Wait, Colby," Winston said. "Let me introduce you to my crazy Canadian friends." He chuckled. "Charlie, I see you found my old Spider-Man mask. I'd forgotten I still had that. This is Betty, Caroline, Charlie and Danny... my son, Colby."

"Hello," Colby said. He still sounded suspicious and guarded. "I'll take a walk and give you time to get yourselves sorted out."

When Colby returned, he took a short cut through the trees towards the camper. Winston, Danny and Charlie were standing around the ponies, coffee cups in hand. The two women were sitting outside their crazy looking bus. Betty spotted him and waved him over with her coffee cup.

"You want a coffee? It's fresh and still warm and there's a clean mug right here."

"Thanks," Colby said. "I take it black." He waved off Betty's offer of sugar as he poured himself a coffee and stood awkwardly beside them.

"Have a seat. We won't bite," Betty said. "Look, I'm sorry if we got off on the wrong foot. We're really harmless. We hope we didn't offend you by dressin' up. I've heard that can sometimes be kinda insultin'."

Caroline smiled at him as Colby took an empty lawn chair between her and Betty. "I'm used to my dad going around dressing up tourists all the time. I think it's crazy, but he thinks he's protecting our heritage."

"Yes, I know. He told us about it," Betty said. "I think we understand. It's somethin' he needs to do. Sometimes, somethin' drives us to follow a dream. Getting' here was somethin' I needed to do."

"You had a dream to come and camp at Cape Final? Did you know my father in Canada?"

312   THE GRAND GETAWAY

"No, and I'd never heard of Cape Final. I'd been to the Grand Canyon years ago. I needed to get here one more time." Betty went on to give Colby a quick run-down of what had brought them there and who they were. Caroline, sitting on Colby's right, was talking quietly and she reached out and tugged at the empty sleeve of Colby's T-shirt.

Colby looked at her, startled, until Betty said, "Caroline has dementia. She means no harm. She's probably tryin' to get the wrinkle out of your sleeve. She does things like that. She loves to fold cloth, dish-towels and so on, smoothin' out the wrinkles."

Colby reached with his left arm and took Caroline's hand and smiled at her as Betty went on about how she had persuaded Danny and Charlie to go along with her dream.

"Sorry I got steamed up earlier, calling you geriatric hippies and stuff," Colby said.

"That's okay." Betty laughed. "You weren't far off. We are lookin' for an alternative life style. Certainly an alternative to a nursing-home. And we are old, although I've never really understood the word geriatric. Sounds like an exercise programme for oldies. Has a kind of circus act sound to it. I can picture the ringmaster... 'And now ladies and gentlemen I present Madame Zola's death-defying geriatric performance on the high-wire in her one wheeled wheel-chair.'" Betty laughed again and Colby joined in.

Over at the corral, Winston said, "I still don't know what those crazy cops were doing. I don't think they expected to meet me and Colby on the trail when they flew around that bend. Fools... Could've killed us. You say you didn't see any cops, so I believe that. But if they fired off a shot... Well who knows? Some cops do really dumb things." He paused.

"You did a good job with the ponies. They look well fed and happy. I have a couple of barrels of water to empty. You could give me a hand." As he looked back at his truck, he caught sight of Colby sitting with Betty and Caroline outside The Smucker. "Huh, Colby's back. Looks like he's getting on with Betty and Caroline okay. Let's stay here a little longer and give them a few more minutes."

Colby was telling Betty a bit about himself after Betty had prodded him. "My Dad and I have butted heads on a number of things over the years. His crazy quest he pursues here, me joining the army and ending up in Iraq. I lost the arm there. I was right handed. Couldn't paint anymore. My girlfriend Derica – my wife now – got me to try with my left arm when I couldn't make one of those artificial arms work for me. It never felt right, I needed to really feel the brush in my fingers. It took a long while but I'm painting again. My style changed too. A couple of galleries took me on recently. They like my stuff. I've come back here to paint and maybe reconcile things with Dad. I'm working on it anyway. Like me learning to paint again, it will take time."

"But you've got the time," Betty said. "You're young yet, and I know from the short time we've known your dad, he wants it to work too. I know he'd love to have you back. Give him the time. You can make it work, I'm sure."

"Sure, sure, that's what she said," Caroline repeated and Colby gently squeezed her hand and returned her smile.

Betty said, "Colby, you couldn't stop paintin' even after you lost your arm. It was somethin' you had to keep doin'. Somethin' that drives you. Would that be right?"

Colby nodded. "Yeah, I guess that's true. Something I must do."

"So... Like me being drawn back to the canyon. I remember in school, and that was a long time ago, my teacher readin' a poem about a sailor needin' to return to the sea, the sea callin' him back. It went somethin' like..." Betty paused.

"I must down to the seas again, for the call of the running tide
Is a wild call and a clear call that may not – or is it cannot – be denied.

Your paintin' calls you and maybe, in the same way, this little piece of land keeps callin' to your dad."

"I suppose..." Colby looked up as Winston approached his truck, got in and drove it back to where Danny and Charlie waited by the ponies. He watched them begin unloading some of the water.

He turned back to Betty. "John Masefield. It was John Masefield."

"Who?"

"It was John Masefield who wrote the poem. An Englishman. It's called *Sea Fever*. You had it right the first time, *That may not be denied.* I believe the poem starts with –

I must down to the seas again, to the lonely sea and the sky,
And all I ask is a tall ship and a star to steer her by.

It's a nice poem. One of my buddies in Iraq read poetry. He particularly liked that one." Colby lapsed into silence, lost in thought for a moment. Then he turned to Betty. "You hungry? I brought some charcoal and some steaks and baking potatoes. You all eat steak?"

"We do," Betty said. "We just haven't been able to afford it lately."

"Great. I'll go see if I can fire up the barbecue."

Before they reached Fredonia, Deputy Joe Balasko had gone over and over what it was that Vince should tell Rudy when he called him.

"Remember we just went there to take a look as a favour to him and all we saw was some more Indians. Don't say another damn thing."

"I got it, I got it Joe. Jeez. You've said it about a hundred times. Relax. I won't say anything about us firin' a shot."

"Us? Us? You! Not us! You dumb bugger. Just tell him you saw some Indians and leave it at that. And tell him to leave them alone. We don't want them talking about someone shooting or your cousin will be asking questions. Thank God you didn't hit anyone. It would be the biggest damn story to hit Coconino County in years and you can bet that it wouldn't be confined to our county. Look at the protests and riots that flared up all over the country because of cops shooting unarmed citizens. You've had your excitement, now leave it be."

CHAPTER 71

Betty was looking through a couple of real estate flyers Winston had given her. "Here's a beat-up lookin' trailer, 2 bedroom and bathroom somewhere in Flagstaff… Sheesh… $94,500. Here's another, Flagstaff. Looks a lot better, on nearly 2 acres. God! $178,000! And 10 acres, no house, near some place called Happy Jack. Looks like it could be on the Moon. Sandblasted. Not a tree or bush in sight, $149,000."

They were just finishing breakfast. Winston had left early with the ponies to do his second last trail ride with a few tourists. They hadn't seen any sign of Colby.

"There's not a lot I can see in these real estate flyers that are any use to us," Betty said. "We've got about a week before the North Rim officially closes down."

"There's Colby," Charlie said, pointing through the window of The Smucker. "Looks like he's been out early, painting."

"Yeah," Betty said. "See if he'd like some coffee, Danny, maybe some breakfast."

"Coffee would be great," Colby said when he came in. "I thought I'd remembered to pack everything, but I somehow forgot my Thermos. I left early and got some photos and a bit of painting started, but the need for some coffee forced me to pack it in."

"We can offer you a couple of bran muffins," Betty said. "Can't have any pancakes or cereal, we're outta milk. Winston said he'd pick us up some before he comes back later this afternoon."

"A muffin would be fine," Colby said.

While Colby was having his coffee, Betty said they'd have to find a campground outside the park and raised the topic of finding a place, at least for the winter. That led Colby to ask, "What were your long-term plans before you left that home back in Canada?"

"Long term!" Charlie laughed. "The home was called a long-term care home, but apart from checking on our bowel movements, and occasionally checking to see if we were still breathing, they didn't have any long-term plans for us and when we left, we didn't have any either. Just to get the hell outta there and get to the Grand Canyon. I guess you could say we've been making this up as we went along."

"I thought we might look for a trailer park where we might buy a trailer, you know, a mobile home, or maybe even a cabin somewhere on a plot of land," Betty said. "We'd have to save up our pension money to make a down payment and then we've no idea if we could get a mortgage. If we move on to some small town with a campground it'd give us more time to check things out."

"I'm not sure what's available nearby. I'd say that anything near the canyon will be full."

"Well we might head somewhere south. Like Charlie said, we're makin' it up as we go along."

Colby hung around the rest of the morning, making sketches and then, to their surprise, asked all four of them to sit and pose for him. Betty had a look at the sketch of her and said, "Is that me? I think you're either a terrible artist or a hell of a flatterer." She laughed. "I'm no Mona Lisa but you made me look a lot younger than I am. Jeez, almost good lookin'."

"That's how I see you, Betty," Colby replied. "You've got a strong face."

"Yeah. You are a flatterer. Thanks. You really caught Caroline's smile. I love that."

To Charlie and Danny's surprise Colby unearthed some of the costumes Charlie had been fooling around with a few days ago and did a couple more sketches of them dressed as Indians. "Just an idea I have that I might use in the future."

When Winston returned later that day, he said he'd got a call from the dean at the university. There was some kind of mix-up about the dates for some student interviews. "I'm meeting with them Friday after my last gig here and I'll be back here Saturday or Sunday. What are your plans, Colby?"

"I was thinking of heading up to Parissawampitts Point and maybe Timp Point. I haven't been up that way for years. It's off the beaten track. Maybe spend a couple of days up that way. But if you need me to stay here that's okay."

"Charlie, Danny, do you fellas mind looking after the ponies again for a couple of days?" Winston asked.

"No that's fine, Winston," Danny said. "And you go ahead Colby. We'll be okay."

"Okay great, thanks," Winston said. "After my gig tomorrow, I'll bring the ponies back, and when I get back from Flagstaff, I'll get ready to close down for the winter and escort you folks out of here. You might be able to get a day or two still at the North Rim Campground. Any idea where you'll head to after that?"

"Well we'll be movin' somewhere I guess," Betty said. "Maybe we'll have a plan by the time you get back."

"Danny! Danny!"

Danny sat up as Charlie shook him awake.

"What? What is it?"

"It's Betty!" Charlie whispered hoarsely.

Danny scrambled out of bed and stood beside her bunk. Betty was breathing heavily and seemed to be sleeping.

"What's the matter, Charlie? She's just sleeping, isn't she?"

"She is now. I heard her moaning. I think she was in pain. Maybe her heart."

"God! You sure?"

The first glow of dawn showed the worry on Charlie's face. "I think she's had a heart attack. When I heard her moaning, I asked her what was the matter, but she just said it was nothing and I should go back to bed. I've been listening to her breathing and hopping in and out of bed for the best part of an hour. I know she's been having some pain. I got her to take an Aspirin and some water, then she told me to bugger off."

Betty stirred again. Danny could see that her face looked pale and drawn.

"We'd better drive up to the lodge and call a doctor," Charlie whispered to Danny.

Betty's eyes flicked open. "No. No doctor. Let me be for now. I'll be fine. Just let me rest. You go callin' a doctor, we'll all be arrested an' shipped back to Canada with a hell of a bill. You want that? And I really don't want to be carted off to some hospital and put through all kinds of tests that'll cost more money than you could ever imagine. Charlie, just go and do something useful like makin' the coffee."

"But you need a doctor! Danny, let's get going now!"

"Charlie, stop it. I know what's happenin'. If you panic and go callin' doctors, ambulances, it'll end badly for all of us, particularly Caroline. Remember, before we started out, it was one for all and all for one."

"Danny," Charlie asked, "have you still got Winston's card? His wife is a doctor. We should drive to the nearest phone and call Winston. Maybe he could get his wife here to check Betty out."

"Charlie, Charlie..." Betty reached for his hand. "Leave it be. Just let things take their course. Let me rest now. If I need anythin', I'll call you. I want you both to promise me you won't go callin' any doctor. I know I got you into this, but I'd never forgive you if Caroline is taken away and locked up. Please... I beg you. Danny, promise me. Don't go plottin' behind my back."

"Okay, Betty, I promise," Danny said, "we won't do anything unless you agree, but Betty... like Charlie says..."

"No buts... You make phone calls to doctors, then the police will be involved. Charlie, you don't want to end up back in Cavandish. And remember, poor Caroline was goin' to be shipped to God knows where. And Danny, you'd be back to sleepin' in culverts. Look, if the worst comes to worst, my pension will still come in for a while. My bank card and the PIN number are in my purse. You'll be able to get money from my account. With Charlie's pension too, the three of you should be okay as long as you don't tell the bank I'm no longer around. You can keep Caroline safe."

"Jeez, Betty. We'd surely be arrested if we cash in your pension money," Charlie groaned.

"Look, for now, just look after Caroline when she wakes up. Take her to the bathroom and then get her some breakfast. God, all this gabbin' is makin' me tired. Let me go back to sleep."

"Okay, Betty. Call us if you need anything. Come on Charlie."

Caroline was still sleeping. Danny grabbed a jacket and indicated that Charlie should do the same, then he took Charlie outside.

"What if she's dying?" Charlie asked.

"She might be. But she's asked us to wait."

"God! But if she dies... What then?"

"I don't know. She's not going to listen to us. Today is Friday. Winston and Colby will probably be back tomorrow. Maybe she'll listen to them. But she's right. It wouldn't take long before immigration and the cops were in on it, once a doctor gets involved."

"But if she dies, isn't that gonna turn out the same?" Charlie asked.

"I guess so."

"Betty and I talked about dying back at Cavandish, but we usually just joked about it. You know how it is? I don't know what I'll do without her, if she dies." Charlie sighed.

"Betty might be okay later," Danny said. "Did she have any pains before?"

"Don't know. They gave her pills at Cavandish. If she had any pills with her, she used them up a long time ago."

"Well let's go back in and make some coffee. Caroline might be awake."

Danny volunteered to take Caroline to the bathroom when they found her awake. Betty had fallen asleep again. Danny left Charlie to make the coffee and took Caroline out to the outhouse. He found that he could cope okay and Caroline seemed to accept having Danny look after her.

He fed the ponies and they had a quiet breakfast before he took Caroline outside to sit while Charlie watched over Betty. About an hour later, Charlie came out to get Danny, telling him that Betty was awake and he needed help to take her to the bathroom. They managed to get her out of her bunk and helped her to the outhouse. She used her walker with Danny and Charlie alongside her to ensure she didn't fall.

"I can manage okay myself inside, but I may need a hand gettin' up off the seat," Betty said. "I'll bang on the door if I need help."

While they waited, Charlie walked a little way further past the outhouse and came back looking really worried. They helped Betty back to The Smucker where she sat briefly at the table and they brought her some warm water to let her wash.

"I feel better now," Betty said. "I think I'd like a cup of coffee and maybe sit outside in the sunshine with Caroline."

Betty managed to drink about half of her coffee and sat for a while holding Caroline's hand before she fell asleep in the lawn chair. Charlie got a blanket from her bunk and draped it over her.

THE GRAND GETAWAY   319

Danny was fretting but doing his best not to voice his concerns to Charlie. *It's only a matter of time before we are picked up by the authorities. And then what?* "If Betty dies, what in God's name do we do?"

"She says she wants us to bury her here," Charlie whispered, startling Danny, who hadn't realized he'd spoken aloud.

"What?"

"Here. She said if the worst happens she wants to be buried right here. She picked out the spot yesterday and told me this morning."

"So, she hasn't been feeling well since yesterday. But the ground is rock hard, how in hell...?"

"There's a small rocky ridge a little further back. She says that's where we can bury her. I checked it out when we took her to the washroom. The rocks seem loose. She said she couldn't rest peacefully if we involve any funeral home. That would mean disaster for us all. She made me promise and she said she would ask you to promise too."

"But, jeez, we'll be in all kinds of trouble if we try burying her here. You think Winston would go along with that?"

"Probably not. Oh Danny, she said she'd rest easy here. I can't handle this anymore."

Betty stirred. "Charlie, love. Don't fret so much. We've gone over this. You don't want to end up back at Cavandish and we don't want that for Caroline either. Look at her smile. She's happy here. Aren't you happy, Caroline?"

"Happy, happy, happy," Caroline chanted.

Betty patted her hand then turned to Charlie and Danny. "Whatever happens, I want you to go on as long as you can. Move on. I'd like to think of the three of you findin' some place to stay." She paused. "You think you could play Caroline's tape with her readin' her poems and crank it up so we can hear it out here? I'd like that."

Charlie found the tape. With the volume up and the doors to The Smucker open wide, they could hear every word clearly. Betty asked Charlie to rewind it as she reached over and hugged Caroline. Caroline's voice spoke the last lines again-

And our mothers always know
By the footprints in the snow
Where it is the children go.

Tears were spilling down Betty's cheeks when she nodded to Charlie to turn it off. There was a lump in Danny and Charlie's throats as they realized Betty was really saying goodbye to Caroline.

"I think I'll go in now and lie down again, rest some more," Betty said.

The afternoon seemed to drag on. Betty had woken several times while Charlie had sat by her bunk. As Danny helped Caroline prepare for bed and got ready to go to bed himself, Charlie was still sitting beside Betty's bunk. Danny noticed he'd fallen asleep, but he was reluctant to wake him. Charlie was where he wanted to be.

Betty stirred and Charlie was instantly awake.

"I'm here, Betty," Charlie whispered. "How are ya doing?"

"Not bad, Charlie, not bad," Betty whispered back. "What time is it?"

"Dunno. Late, I guess."

"Are Danny and Caroline sleepin'?"

"Yeah."

"You should get some sleep too, love."

"I've been sleeping. I'm okay."

"No. I mean proper sleep. Do you think you could squeeze in here beside me?" Betty asked. "Hold me, Charlie."

Charlie had taken off his shoes earlier and now he slipped off his jacket as Betty did her best to make room for him to lie beside her on the narrow bunk.

"Sorry, Charlie. I'm so fat. I take up so much room."

"That's okay, Betty. I'm skinny." Charlie squeezed himself in beside Betty as she did her best to turn on her side, then he pulled Betty's comforter over the two of them and held her.

"You're nice and warm, Charlie."

"I love you, Betty. I think I've loved you for an awful long time," Charlie whispered.

"I know Charlie. I've known for quite a while."

"You did?"

"Of course I did."

"But I never said..."

"You didn't have to Charlie. I just knew. A woman knows these things. I love you too, Charlie. Have for a long time. I think we were always on the same page. Just sometimes on opposite sides of it."

"Is that why we always argued?"

"Did we? I think it's just in our nature, but I was never cruel, was I? It was always in good fun, wasn't it?"

"Yeah, I guess so. But you did make me sell my watch."

"Oh, for God's sake, Charlie! Okay, I did. But it was for a good cause. It helped get us here."

"I'm glad we made it. It's been a great trip."

"Kiss me, Charlie."

Charlie raised himself and Betty turned her face to him in the darkness and they found each other.

"That was nice, Charlie. Kiss me again."

Betty felt Charlie sob against her and she squeezed him tight. "Charlie, don't. Hold my breast. Put your hand on me."

THE GRAND GETAWAY   321

Charlie slipped his hand inside Betty's nightgown and caressed her.

"Your hand is nice and warm, Charlie."

"Yeah. Warm hand, cold heart."

"That you don't have, Charlie. I wouldn't have fallen in love with you if you did." Betty kissed him again. "You're a good man, Charlie."

"You've got a lovely breast, Betty." Charlie pressed his head against her and his lips found her nipple.

"That's nice, Charlie. I've got two. You can hold the other one as well." Betty giggled. "Is this what they call gettin' to first base?" Charlie's hand found her other breast and he gently massaged it.

"I dunno, maybe second base. You have two breasts, nice ones too, but I never really understood that reference. I was no good at baseball. Betty, maybe we shoulda got hitched."

"What? And lived together in one room in Cavandish? I don't think they would have gone for that. Kiss me again, love… Mmn. We couldn't have done this at Cavandish."

"Yeah. We would've had to set up a schedule with Luis and Wanda, taking turns to use the laundry room."

Betty chuckled. "Oh Charlie, you kill me."

"Oh, Betty."

The sound of Charlie sobbing wakened Danny. It was dawn.

CHAPTER 72

It was early afternoon and they had spent the morning preparing for Betty's burial. It had taken a while. From the time Danny had woken on hearing Charlie sobbing and knew that Betty was gone, he had been busy. He had held Charlie for a while and let him cry, but realized that he'd have to give Charlie something to do or there was no way he would be any help to him. As soon as it was light, he'd given him the task of feeding and watering the ponies while he got Caroline to and from the outhouse. From there, he took Caroline with him to examine the rocky ridge where Betty said they could bury her. The rocks were loose but it wasn't going to be easy.

Caroline was her usual self and had some cereal and toast for breakfast, which they ate outside. Danny got Charlie to drink some coffee, but he wouldn't eat anything. He sat sipping his coffee and doing his best not to break down.

Danny said, "I think we should go for a walk down to the viewpoint and plan what we're gonna do, Charlie. Come on."

They walked slowly down to the viewpoint, Caroline chatting quietly between them, Charlie saying nothing until they were about half-way there.

"I'd like to dress Betty in her favourite dress before we move her."

"That'd be nice, Charlie. You can handle that?"

"I think so," Charlie said. He stopped walking and started weeping quietly again.

Caroline noticed and patted Charlie on the back which brought on more crying from Charlie and distressed Caroline who said, "Oh no. Oh no," and patted Charlie's chest.

Charlie gulped and gathered himself and said, "I'm okay, Caroline, love. Let's get to the viewpoint."

They walked the rest of the way in silence. They found a large rock to sit on and watched the sunlight brighten and change the rocks of the canyon and the distant ridges.

"You know, I saw this nature programme on TV about a year ago," Charlie said. "It was about people agreeing to donate their bodies to science after they died, for some kind of nature research on vultures. They took the bodies out to a remote part of the desert and left them there for the vultures. I think they were studying how vultures ate and moved their food around. I'm not sure. Probably had cameras recording it."

"God! That sounds horrible."

"Maybe that's how it sounds, but it is kinda natural. Lots of early man must have gone that way before they started thinking up rituals and religious stuff."

"You're not suggesting..." Danny said.

"No. No, not Betty. God no. But I guess for myself... Well I wouldn't care, really, would I? And I'd be doing something useful."

THE GRAND GETAWAY   323

"Jeez, Charlie. Don't go thinking like that. Let's look after Betty. Get it done before Winston or Colby show up."

"Yeah. It's what Betty wanted. I loved her, Danny, you know. She said she loved me too. Said so last night. Said she knew I loved her for a long time, too. God, I can't believe she's gone." Charlie's body shook as he tried not to cry.

"She got us here," Danny said. "She was really happy we made it here together. I know it's hard but let's get through this day. We need to look after Betty, and then decide how we are gonna handle Winston's questions."

"Betty was hoping we'd somehow find a place to live together. Sort of a happily ever after. She would've loved this morning, just sitting here looking at this view." Charlie wept again and when Caroline touched his hand, Charlie clung to her. Danny reached for the two of them and the tears flowed.

They sat for a few more minutes until Charlie shook himself and stood.

"Okay. Let's go."

When they got back, Charlie said he'd go and get Betty ready. Danny had been thinking about how they were going to move Betty in some kind of half-decent, dignified manner. The rocky ridge was over a hundred yards from The Smucker. Betty wasn't light and he couldn't imagine Charlie and him struggling with Betty's body through the trees and over rough ground without dropping her. A smile came to his lips as he imagined Betty suddenly sitting up, giving them hell. 'You stupid buggers! Quick! Pick me up! My rear end is being punctured by a prickly cactus.'

He picked up the small shovel they used for cleaning up the pony manure and then took Caroline back to Winston's camper. Another tool would be useful. As he opened the door of the camper, his thoughts still on moving Betty, he noted that the door hinges were held in place by three pins which could easily be knocked out to remove the door. He found a metal spatula and a small wooden mallet in the kitchen drawers and while Caroline looked on, he managed to pop the three pins upward and freed the door. Even if they had to set it down a few times, it would make it easier to move Betty if they carried her using the door like a stretcher.

Danny looked for any other tools that might be useful and picked out a wooden spoon and a couple of large slotted metal ones that they could maybe use to scoop out some soil. All he could find outside the camper was a scoop in a bag of lime that stood in a corner of the outhouse. He and Caroline wandered back to The Smucker just as Charlie stepped out.

"I gave Betty a bit of a wash. I think you're supposed to do that," Charlie said. "And, and..." Charlie choked back a sob. "I got her dress on. She looks good. Looks like she's sleeping. But she's heavy. It's not gonna be easy carrying her."

"You did good, Charlie. I took the door off Winston's camper – we'll move Betty with that. I think we'd better go up to those rocks and see what we can do before we try moving her. It might take a while."

They moved a section of the rocks at the edge of the outcrop and set them in a pile. A couple were heavy, and they had to pry them out with the help of the shovel and lift them together. Caroline began picking up some smaller stones and threw them on the pile but then started taking some from the pile and moving them around.

"That's okay, Caroline," Charlie said. "You can leave those."

"It's okay, Charlie," Danny said. "She thinks she's helping and she's keeping busy. She's not doing any harm. You think we've cleared enough now? Let's see if we can dig a bit of a grave. We'll want to make this look as natural as possible after we put the rocks back."

Danny started with the shovel and Charlie used the scoop as best he could. The soil was sandy but sprinkled with smaller rocks and they had to pry a few out. There were long roots from the scrubby grass which had gone deep, seeking any moisture, but eventually they had a shallow hole that the two of them agreed was probably long and wide enough, and they were tired.

Charlie voiced a question that Danny had been thinking. "You think the wild animals – coyotes, mountain lions – will dig Betty up? The grave's not very deep."

"I know, but it's about the best we can do. The rocks will hold them off for a while and with winter coming on..."

"Yeah. But we were able to move the rocks and so will the wild animals," Charlie said. "I guess it's nature..."

"There's a bag of lime in the outhouse," Danny said. "I read somewhere that in the past they sprinkled a body with lime. I think it helps them decompose."

"That might put the animals off too," Charlie said.

They made their way back to The Smucker and gulped some water. Danny suggested they take a short rest before trying to move Betty. They left Caroline sitting in a lawn chair and got the camper door. There was no way they were going to get the door out of The Smucker with Betty's body lying on it. Inside, Danny waited while Charlie bent and kissed Betty on the cheek one last time. Danny was sure Charlie would break down again then, but he saw him shake it off. He helped Danny drape and tie a sheet with some twine over Betty, suppressing a sob when Danny covered her face.

"We'll have to try lifting Betty out of her bunk and set her on the floor first. That's not gonna be easy, Charlie. I'll take her feet and you try lifting her shoulders. You ready?"

"Yeah," Charlie said.

"Okay. On the count of three," Danny said. "One, two, three!"

They strained and grunted but barely got Betty raised off the lower bunk before their strength gave out and they had to stop.

"She's heavier than I thought," Charlie gasped.

"We'll have to try sliding her sideways and hang onto her as best we can," Danny said. "It's a good thing she slept on a lower bunk! Pull the seat cushion off the

THE GRAND GETAWAY   325

kitchen bench and put it here on the floor. If we drop her, she'll have a soft landing anyway."

They slowly dragged Betty's body as far over the edge of the bunk as they could. It was a bit of a struggle, but they managed to lower Betty's body part way before they had to let her drop the last few inches.

"We're not going to be able to carry her so let's drag her to the door on the cushion," Danny said.

They got Betty's body to the doorway and were able to lower her body onto the camper's door.

"We won't be able to carry the door and Betty," Charlie said. "We'll have to drag it. We'll need some rope. The ponies! You think we could hitch one of them to pull the door for us?"

"It's worth a try," Danny said.

They brought back the pony they thought was the most docile, along with a selection of rope. They tied the rope around the door at the end where Betty's head rested. Whether they got the pony to drag the door or dragged it themselves, the front end of the door would have to rise off the ground if they were going to move it.

Hitching the pony to the door was a problem. There was no collar to put around the pony's neck or horned saddle to attach the rope. Winston had his tourists ride his ponies bareback.

"We need to rig something across the pony's chest and somehow keep it up so it doesn't fall under his feet," Charlie said. "We need some straps. What about belts?"

They found two plastic belts belonging to Betty in The Smucker which were useless. The sturdiest belts they had were the leather belts from their own jeans. They buckled the two belts together and they were long enough to go around the pony's chest. They tied a loop of rope to the belts and draped it over the pony's shoulders to hold the belts up. To prevent the rope from chaffing the pony's shoulders, they stuffed a cushion under it. Next they ran ropes from the belts along the pony's sides to hitch it to the rope around the door.

"Oh wait," Danny said. "We forgot the lime. I'll go get it."

The bag was almost full and it was heavy and when Danny returned with it he placed it alongside Betty's body on the door.

"You have any experience leading a pony, Charlie?"

"A couple of times on my uncle's farm, I led a horse pulling a cart with a load of hay. Give me that green plastic belt of Betty's. I'll put it over the pony's head and lead him with that."

"Okay, Charlie, let's give it a try. If it doesn't work we'll end up dragging the door ourselves. Try leading the pony forward. I'll come alongside and get Caroline to come with us. Come on Caroline."

Charlie made a clicking sound and pulled on the plastic belt around the pony's head. The pony moved along. The rope attached to the door tightened, as did the straps on the pony's chest. When he felt the weight behind him, he lunged quickly forward. Charlie was startled and had to scramble to keep ahead of the pony. Danny held his breath as the front of the door rose off the ground. For a moment he was afraid Betty's body would slide off.

"Jeez. Slow down, Charlie! Slow down!" he called. He trotted alongside the door and reached down to make sure the bag of lime stayed where it was.

For the first few paces the pony seemed to be racing, but then settled down to a steady walk when it realized that whatever it was hitched to wasn't nearly as heavy as it seemed with the first pull. The pine needles that covered the ground allowed the door to slide along easily.

Charlie coaxed the pony through the trees. They had to stop and start when the door went a little off course and Danny had to get Charlie to come back to help drag the door sideways to avoid getting snagged by a tree. They were about fifty feet from the rocks when the buckle from one of the belts broke off and they had to stop.

"Okay," Danny said, "we can't fix it, so we'll have to try dragging the door the rest of the way ourselves."

They freed the pony from his harness and tied him to a tree. Then the two of them began pulling the door with the rope. The door didn't rise nearly as much off the ground as when the pony pulled it, and they had to stop several times to catch their breath and rest.

"We'd never have made it without the pony." Charlie panted.

They rested for a few minutes, then struggled to slide Betty's body into the grave. Danny took Caroline's hand and they stood, he and Caroline on one side and Charlie on the other.

"You want to say something, Charlie? Like a prayer or anything?"

"Don't know many prayers, Danny, except maybe The Lord's Prayer and I don't think it fits. Oh, I'm gonna miss you, Betty, so much. I love you. Can you say something Danny?" Charlie was choked up.

Danny thought of the prayers he'd heard at some of the missions he'd gone to with his friend Pete, but he could only remember a few words. He cleared his throat.

"Thanks, Betty for being such a good friend to all of us, to me, to Caroline and Charlie. For keeping us going when we were ready to quit. You got us here. Like Charlie said, we're gonna miss you. Charlie loved you, and in our own ways, so did Caroline and me. None of us could've had a better friend." Danny paused. "And God… if you are really there, God, please take care of Betty. She may give you a bit of lip at times, but she doesn't really mean it. You know how it is. Anyway, she's a good woman. Look after her, God. Amen."

"Amen," Charlie mumbled. "Thanks, Danny." Then Charlie was sobbing again as Caroline repeated, "Amen, amen, amen."

THE GRAND GETAWAY

327

"Charlie," Danny said gently. "Why don't you go for a short walk? Leave Caroline here with me. I'll look after covering Betty. Come back when you're ready. You can help me with the rocks."

Charlie stumbled away and Danny quickly knelt and began sprinkling lime from the bag over the sheet that covered Betty. He thought maybe he should sprinkle it directly on her body but he couldn't bring himself to open the sheet and do that. When he finished with the lime, he started scooping soil into the grave, starting where Betty's feet rested. He was glad he'd got Charlie to go away. This was the hardest bit. He gritted his teeth when he had most of Betty's body covered, using his hands to gently put soil over Betty's face. Caroline was kneeling down, pushing soil with one hand into the grave near Betty's feet and patting it down with her fingers.

He had most of the soil back into the grave and was replacing rocks when Charlie returned. Charlie said nothing but knelt and began gently setting rocks. Caroline was sifting a small handful of soil from one hand to the other.

Danny was doing his best to set the last rocks in place so they blended with the part of the ridge they'd left undisturbed. Caroline pulled a rock from the ridge and placed it on top of another rock on the grave.

"No, not that way, Caroline," Charlie said, taking the rock she had moved and replacing it back into the ridge. Caroline then busied herself rubbing at something in the palm of her hand.

As Danny and Charlie put the last rocks in place, they stood back to examine their handiwork, bending here and there to adjust a rock or brush soil between any crevices. They were exhausted.

"What the hell are you doing?" The sound of Winston's voice startled them. They hadn't heard him approaching. "I saw one of the ponies tied to a tree back there and someone stole the door off my camper!"

CHAPTER 73

"We were just… just…" Charlie wasn't sure what he was going to say. "Oh, please don't get mad, Winston. Betty wanted to… to…" He trailed off again, lowered his head and started sobbing.

"Betty wanted, what? Why are you crying? You mean…! Betty died? You buried Betty? Here? My God!"

Danny nodded. "Yes, Winston. Betty died this morning and asked us to bury her here. She knew she was dying, begged us not to take her to hospital or call an ambulance. She didn't want to get us into trouble and get sent back, especially Caroline."

"Not get into trouble? You know what kind of trouble you'll be in now? I can't think of what kind of charges would be brought against all of you, all of us. She did die of natural causes, right?"

"Yeah, she did." Danny said.

"Look, I'm sorry about Betty. I really am. I liked her very much. She was a real feisty lady. A real character. I know you'll miss her terribly." Winston paused. "What about her relatives?"

"She hasn't any as far as we know. None living anyway," Danny replied.

Charlie had recovered. "That's right. She didn't have any. I'm sorry, Winston. She said she'd be happy if we buried her here. There was no way she would let us call anyone. She knew we'd all be arrested for coming here illegally, and she was frightened that Caroline would be locked away somewhere. She wanted us to stick together and look after each other. So we promised. Uh, sorry about your door."

"Forget the door. That's nothing. But how did you think you'd get away with this?"

"I don't know," Danny said. "What's done is done. We've been in the U.S. for nearly a month and a half now and haven't been caught by anyone. Betty believed we might settle down together somewhere and not really be noticed. We're just a few more old people and there's lots of Canadians living down here for the winter. I guess if they don't get into trouble, nobody bothers them. How long did you live in Canada?"

"Years, but Canada welcomed us. It was here I was a law-breaker. Our country isn't as welcoming as Canada was then, never has been."

"Canada probably isn't as welcoming now either," Danny said.

"Probably not," Winston said. "We've made everyone, everywhere, more paranoid. God! I've got to think. For now, let's get back to our camp. Let's pick up what we can and take the door back. We'll come back for the pony." Winston looked at the rocky ridge where Betty was buried. "You did a good job of making things look natural."

THE GRAND GETAWAY   329

Caroline was still kneeling, quietly talking. Charlie gathered up the tools and the bag of lime. He tucked the shovel under his left arm and grabbed the lime bag with his left hand. He then got Caroline to her feet while Winston and Danny went slowly ahead, carrying the door.

Charlie tried to take Caroline by her left hand but she had her hand closed in a fist so he held her wrist. They stumbled after Winston and Danny. They hadn't gone far when Caroline suddenly stopped. She bent down and Charlie attempted to keep her moving along, but Caroline was insistent, twisting her body and reaching down with her free hand.

"Come on, Caroline. Let's go."

She was struggling to pick up something at her feet. Charlie realized she'd dropped it from her hand. He let her pick it up and he stood with her as they both looked at what she now held. It was some kind of medal, scratched and quite dull. Caroline allowed Charlie to take it in his hand. He could see the words *General Crook*.

"Hey, Winston! Danny! Wait up!"

"What?" he heard Danny call.

"Winston, take a look at this."

They came back quickly.

"What is it, Charlie?" Winston asked.

"It's some kind of medal. Look. Caroline must have found it when we were buryin' Betty."

Winston was peering at the medal. "God, this is the proof!"

"Proof?" Danny asked

"Yeah," Winston said excitedly. "The U.S. Army issued medals to several native chiefs as symbols of friendship and services rendered, but this one is special. It has my great-grandfather's name on it. Look, General Crook must have had it made. It says on this side *Issued by Order of General George Crook Commander of Arizona Territory* and has crossed hands, a symbol of friendship like I've seen on other medals. On the other side it says, *Issued to Manukaja – Johnny Whatoname. Grazing Rights In The Place Of His Choosing*. See this little loop at the top? It would have had a piece of rawhide looped through it to wear around your neck.

"What a stroke of luck! I scoured a lot of this area before with the help of archaeology students and we found nothing. I wonder how my great-grandfather managed to hold onto this when he was being shipped to Florida and then making his way back here? No matter, this puts a whole new spin on things. Thanks, Caroline." He bent and gave Caroline a peck on the cheek as Caroline smiled.

CHAPTER 74

They all had showers and Danny had taken Caroline to the shower too. He gave her a quick wash, although he had felt really awkward about it. Caroline was more concerned with the temperature of the water, gasping a bit and saying, "Cold, cold," when the water first splashed on her. He remembered at Cavandish that sometimes male health workers had looked after Caroline's toileting and any embarrassment now was merely on his part. He wrapped her in a towel and patted her dry and then got her dressed in some clean clothes. He realized that from now on he and Charlie would be responsible for Caroline's care. It certainly didn't seem to bother her.

They had a light supper and sat outside. Winston was thoughtful, and still examining the medal in his hands.

"It's amazing that this should be found today, after all these years. I was about ready to pack it in. I wasn't getting anywhere. This changes everything."

"Will anyone say it's a fake?" Charlie asked.

"No. It can be easily authenticated, by the metal used at the time, its age and so on. There won't be any trouble with that."

"I'm glad something good came of Betty's passing. I know she'd have been thrilled by that," Charlie sounded wistful. He paused. "Too bad she... well... and Caroline finding it. Betty would've loved that too. It's a bit vague though, you know, where it says, *Grazing Rights In The Place of His Choosing*. That could mean anywhere in North America."

"Well I suppose there was some kind of document to go with that, but our tribe's oral history always suggested it was here at Cape Final and, as I said before, I just wanted acknowledgement the promise was made. The medal proves that."

"But what if some of your people disagree and want more?"

"They've moved on. Colby tells me that all the time. He says it's only me who hasn't. I won't make any big fuss."

"What about the newspapers and so on?" Danny asked. "The publicity?"

"I don't think that will be too big a problem," Winston said. "It might make a small splash for a few days, but then the media will move on to the latest earthquake, plane crash or the next presidential election. I may be able to persuade the Hualapai to perform a ceremony to declare this little patch sacred land. We could put up a sign. That should keep nosey-parkers out and keep Betty's grave safe."

"What are we gonna tell Colby?" Danny asked. "I mean about Betty."

"That will be a bigger problem," Winston said. "There's a chance he might turn up tonight. But if he does, I'll say nothing. But I'm sure he won't show until late tomorrow."

"It would be easier if we left real early. You could tell Colby we headed further south," Danny added.

THE GRAND GETAWAY   331

"We'll talk first thing in the morning. I see Charlie's asleep."

"Poor bugger," Danny said. "He's gonna really miss Betty. He's exhausted. I'm tired too. I think we should all turn in. It's beginning to get dark. I'll leave Charlie to sleep a little longer while I get Caroline ready for bed. It might take me a while."

"In that case, I'll turn in myself. It's been quite a day."

Danny wasn't sure if he heard Charlie sobbing in the night or if he'd been imagining it. Caroline had fallen asleep as soon as he'd got her to bed and when he tried to get Charlie to go inside The Smucker, he'd had trouble waking him up. Charlie was exhausted, almost out on his feet, and had tumbled into bed after struggling with his pants and shoes. He was asleep when his head hit the pillow. Danny too, had fallen asleep almost immediately.

He awoke to find Caroline standing beside Betty's bunk, trying her best to remake the bed. She had pulled the one remaining sheet almost into place and was smoothing it down with her hand, saying, "There, there." Danny and Charlie had left the sheet and blanket in a tangled heap on the bunk after they had removed Betty and the blanket was now on the floor around Caroline's feet.

Danny stretched and yawned. His shoulders ached from yesterday's exertions. He thought he'd better get out of bed in case Caroline tripped over the blanket on the floor and then he should take her to the outhouse.

He slipped out of bed and picked up the blanket. He found a pull-up for Caroline and grabbed her jacket. He decided he'd dress her properly when they got back. He glanced over at Charlie, who was still fast asleep.

When he returned with Caroline, he looked at the little alarm clock sitting on a shelf in the kitchen area. The time was 7:35 a.m. It was the clock Betty had given him the night before they left Cavandish. It seemed like years ago now. Charlie was still asleep.

Danny got Caroline dressed, then sat her at the table and found some cereal for her. He decided to make coffee and let Charlie sleep some more. He'd make breakfast when Charlie woke up. When the coffee was ready, he poured himself a cup and sat with Caroline. She finished her cereal without spilling too much on the table, and he said, "I'll get you some toast and jam, Caroline. Okay?"

He spread some margarine and jam on two slices of toast and cut the slices into four pieces to make them easier for Caroline to pick up. It was 8:15 a.m. by the clock. Time to wake up Charlie. He was usually finishing breakfast by now. He went to Charlie's bunk and gently shook him. "Time to wake up, Charlie. Coffee's ready."

Charlie didn't move. "Come on, Charlie. Breakfast time." Danny shook him again, this time harder but Charlie didn't open his eyes. He seemed to flop about like he was limp. Danny shook him again. "Charlie, Charlie. Oh no! Damn it, Charlie! No. You can't be..." But Charlie was unresponsive. Charlie was dead.

CHAPTER 75

Danny stood resting his head against the edge of his bunk, overwhelmed by the thoughts racing through his mind. He was devastated by the enormity of what had happened. He felt his body tremble. *There is nothing for it but to turn back. Take Caroline back to Canada.* Yesterday he'd thought there was a possibility of the three of them moving on, finding a place to stay.

But that was over now. There was only himself and Caroline. He'd thought he'd be able to cope with looking after Caroline, but he'd been counting on Charlie's help. And now Charlie was gone. *Jeez, Charlie. I was counting on you. Ya bugger. Sorry, Charlie, I know you didn't go and die on purpose.*

He felt Caroline's hand running over the back of his shirt. It was as if she sensed something was wrong. He turned and found her looking thoughtful. She started smoothing the front of his shirt. Danny found himself hugging her as Caroline stroked his back again. "Okay Caroline. We've got to go and talk to Winston. We're gonna need help."

Danny and Winston had put the badly scratched-up door back on Winston's camper the night before, and now Danny tentatively knocked on it as he stood outside with Caroline, trying to think how he should open the conversation. *We've got some bad? terrible? god-awful? news* or *You're not gonna believe this, Winston, but Charlie died during the night.* Or maybe, *Sorry, Winston, but we're gonna have to bury Charlie now.*

Danny was in the act of knocking on the door again when Winston suddenly pulled it open.

Startled, Danny blurted, "Charlie died."

"What!"

Danny nodded.

"Christ! What happened? He didn't kill himself, did he?"

"God! No! He wouldn't have."

"Then what?"

Danny noticed the dubious look that crossed Winston's face.

"Winston! I didn't kill him. He just died. In his sleep!"

"Come in. Come in. I don't know what to think."

Danny led Caroline inside and he got her to sit at Winston's table. He slumped into a chair, himself, and held his head in his hands. Winston poured all three of them a coffee and remained standing. Caroline busied herself by pushing some crumbs into a small pile on the brown linoleum-covered table, then lost interest in them as she ran a finger over the table's faded, zigzag patterns. The silence was interrupted by the chatter of a woodpecker outside.

THE GRAND GETAWAY   333

Winston turned to Danny. "Was Charlie ill? I mean like... what was his general health? How was he last night when he went to bed?"

"He was really tired. But you saw that. We both were. He fell asleep right away and so did I. I don't know why he died. He just did. He didn't complain of any chest pains or anything. I think losing Betty was a terrible blow. I know he was heartbroken. Maybe he just gave up."

"Why was he in that home in Canada to begin with if he was healthy?"

"When I first met him at the home, he told me he'd had a minor heart attack about five years before, but hadn't had any problems since then. I think his daughter and her husband talked him into going into the home. They moved away to the east coast. I know he wasn't happy there. Betty was what kept him going. He seemed to buck up and really get into the spirit of the trip once we took off."

"So what are you going to do now?"

"I was thinking we could maybe bury him beside Betty," Danny answered. "I can't think of anything else to do. Then head back to Canada with Caroline. Last night I thought all three of us might head south a bit further, have a little time to consider what to do next. But now with Charlie gone..." Danny trailed off. "I didn't see Colby's truck, so I take it he didn't get back last night."

"No. God, he's not going to be happy about this. Okay. Let's go over and see to Charlie. Check him out."

"He's dead. Believe me. You won't find any blood stains and I didn't smother him with a pillow or anything."

"Sorry, Danny. I believe you. It's just a hell of a shock. We'd be in trouble because we buried Betty without telling anyone, but if the authorities ever find out we buried two people here... God! I can't bear to think about it. The tabloids would jump all over this. Jeez, Georgina would kill me. The consequences would be disastrous, for me, the university, Colby's career, my grand-daughter Julia. And the whole Hualapai tribe – this isn't the kind of publicity they'd want. God..."

"Okay, Winston. I'll turn myself in," Danny said. "Tell them the truth, that it was me and Charlie who buried Betty when she died. You weren't even here. Report Charlie's death. An autopsy on Charlie and Betty would prove they died naturally. I'd only be charged with mishandling a dead body. Something like that. Maybe be in jail a little while and get sent back to Canada along with Caroline."

"No. Let's not go down that road. What's done is done. You and Charlie did what you thought was best for Betty, no matter what the legal procedures are. Sometimes the laws, for all their well-intended purposes, are not always right. Let's get it done. We have no choice and we're doing what's right for Charlie."

"You sure, Winston?" Danny asked

Winston nodded. "I'm sure, Danny. Let's go."

Danny sat Caroline at The Smucker's table and gave her an *Arizona Official State Visitor's Guide* to look at while he and Winston prepared Charlie's body for burial. They used one of Charlie's Spider-Man sheets from his bunk in the same manner as Danny and Charlie had used to cover Betty's body.

Danny said, "Charlie would be pleased. He was a big Spider-Man fan."

Then all three of them walked to the rocky ridge to prepare the grave.

They worked quickly, moving the rocks alongside Betty's burial place and scooping out a small grave beside hers. Caroline played with the freshly dug soil.

They hurried back to The Smucker and Winston explained that while it was undignified, putting Charlie's body over the back of a pony would be the quickest way to get it there.

Danny and Winston managed to lift Charlie's body out of his bunk and get him outside. He was considerably lighter than Betty. They got Charlie's body over the back of the pony and tied some rope around his legs. Then Winston ran the rope under the pony's belly and wrapped the other end over the sheet around Charlie's chest and arms. The pony snorted and stamped a foot, disturbed by a sense that this wasn't the usual way riders sat on him, and that there was something very strange about whatever was over his back. Danny asked if they should take what was left of the lime and Winston said, "It can't do any harm and may hold off the wild animals."

When Danny returned, Winston said, "Okay, let's go. You'll have to walk beside the pony in case Charlie starts to slip off." Danny caught the sense of urgency in Winston's voice, no doubt wanting to get this over before Colby showed up.

Everything went well. Charlie's body stayed put and Winston was able to lead the pony faster than Charlie had done the previous day. Caroline couldn't keep up, but Danny kept glancing back and saw she was following them, although slowly.

Once they reached the gravesite, he helped Winston remove Charlie's body from the pony's back and place it gently in the grave. The pony was jerking his head in an agitated manner, so Winston took him a little further away and tied him to a tree.

When he came back, he asked Danny if he had anything to say before they covered Charlie's body.

Danny took Caroline's hand and drew her close to stand beside him. "I'm not much for praying Winston, but, well... Charlie old buddy, we're gonna miss you. We've been really glad of your company. I know you were a good friend to Caroline here, long before I met you. I'll do my best to look after her a bit longer. I know you'd be pleased to lie here with Betty. God bless you, Charlie." Danny wiped tears from his eyes and squeezed Caroline's hand.

"If you like, I'd be glad to say a Hualapai prayer," Winston said.

"Thanks, Winston. I'm sure Charlie would like that."

Winston raised his head and gave a short prayer in his own language. At the end he gave a short whoop, then turned to Danny and Caroline. "I asked Creator to look

THE GRAND GETAWAY   335

after both Betty and Charlie, and to let them be together again in the beautiful land of the spirits."

"Thanks, Winston," Danny said.

Danny sprinkled the lime over the sheet that covered Charlie, then they covered Charlie's body with soil and knelt to begin setting the rocks in place.

About an hour later they came out of the trees and saw Colby's truck parked beside Winston's camper. Danny sighed. He'd been hoping that maybe he and Caroline could leave in The Smucker before Colby showed up. It would make things easier for Winston. He could have told Colby that all four of them had decided to move on before the snow flew and that way Colby wouldn't be involved. Now he came out onto the camper's deck as they approached.

"What's happening? I saw one of the ponies was missing. Thought maybe he took off and you were all off looking for him. And the door of the camper looks like maybe a bear decided to sharpen his nails! What's with the shovel?"

CHAPTER 76

They were sitting in Winston's camper. Caroline was tracing the patterns on Winston's table top with her fingers.

"So, what is it you have to tell me?" Colby asked. "Where's Betty and Charlie?"

"Gone." Danny said. "They..."

"Gone where? Did you guys have a fight about something?"

"No," Danny said. "They... died."

"Died! Both of them? How? Jesus, I'm sorry Danny. What happened? Some kind of accident? I hadn't heard anything. But then I've been kinda out of touch. I didn't listen to the radio or anything."

"No, Colby," Winston said. "They died naturally. Just one day apart."

"My God! That's real sad. Sorry, Danny. So you've arranged for the funerals?"

"They're over," Winston said.

"Already? God, that was quick. Were they buried together? I mean you had one funeral for the two of them, right? How long ago was this? I've only been gone a few days. When did they die?"

Danny and Winston looked at each other.

Winston sighed. "It's okay, Danny. I'll tell him. Betty died yesterday and Charlie died this morning."

"Jeez. So they're at some funeral home then. But... didn't you say their funerals were over already?"

"It was Betty's wish," Danny said. "She asked to be buried here."

"Here? The shovel...! Don't tell me. You buried her here!"

Winston nodded.

"Are you out of your god-damned mind, Dad? What in Christ's name were you thinking? You're fucking crazy. And what's Mom gonna say? Besides checking you into some hospital to have your head examined. And Charlie... You buried him here too?"

"He died in his sleep, last night," Danny said. "We'd already buried Betty before your dad got back. He had nothing to do with burying her. That was me and Charlie. When Charlie died so soon after, we decided to bury him next to Betty. They loved each other."

"Was this her plan all along? To drive down here from Canada, hang around 'til she died and then have you guys bury her? And then Charlie joins in the act. What about autopsies? An inquest? What will happen once this gets out?"

"We're not planning on letting it get out," Winston said.

"So how...?"

Caroline put a finger to her lips and made a shushing sound, then turned back to the patterns on the table.

THE GRAND GETAWAY   337

"Calm down, Colby. Just shut up for a minute, and listen," Winston snapped. "Betty died suddenly when I was away. Danny and Charlie had just finished burying her when I got back yesterday. I admit I was shocked. I didn't know what to think. My first reaction was the same as yours — we can't do this. But then I changed my mind."

"Why?"

"I thought of the consequences that would follow. First, for us as a family, and then, for Danny, Charlie, and Caroline, and I knew I couldn't do anything else."

"But that was before Charlie died, wasn't it?" Colby snapped. "You went ahead and buried him too!"

"We did. The consequences would have been the same whether we buried one body or two. But I understood Betty's wish. It was no different than my great-grandfather, Johnny Whatoname, who wanted to be put to rest here."

"But Christ! That was what? Over 150 years ago." Colby broke in. "That damned legend. It's lucky you didn't follow the Hualapai customs of back then. You would have had a huge cremation fire burning to dispose of the bodies and then you would have had to burn their crazy camper too, since that was their home. Hell! I'd have got here to find the whole National Forest Fire Service dealing with it."

"It was Betty's dream to return here to the Grand Canyon," Winston said. "She hadn't planned on dying here. She was hoping all four of them could find some place to settle down together for a while. But once she knew she was dying, she persuaded Charlie and Danny to bury her here — not to satisfy a wish of hers but to protect her friends. If they'd called anyone, they would have been arrested. Betty couldn't let that happen. And I couldn't either."

Colby sighed.

Winston went on. "Danny, Charlie and Caroline were planning to move on early this morning, before you got back. But then Charlie died overnight and complicated things. If you hadn't arrived when you did, I'd have told you they all headed south before the snow came. I would've been the only one who knew about Betty and Charlie."

"So now I know. What now? What if Danny and Caroline get picked up anyway? And what about relatives? Aren't they gonna wonder what happened to them? Report them missing?"

"Betty didn't have any," Danny said, "and Charlie was more or less abandoned by his family. Look, I'm sorry we dropped you and your dad into this mess. Believe me, we didn't plan it. We would've moved on any day now, and if I could change things, I would. When Betty died, Charlie and I did what we thought was best. It was probably a bad idea, but Betty made us promise. When Charlie died... well, some of the decisions I've made in the past haven't been great, and I guess this was another bad one. But burying Charlie with Betty just felt right. If you think we should call the authorities, then we should do it. I'll take the responsibility for burying Betty and

Charlie. Maybe... I don't know. If I could somehow get Caroline back to Canada... She has no family. We were her family."

"You want to call the police, the coroner, whoever you want, Colby, go ahead," Winston said. "Tell them Charlie and Betty died."

"Oh no. They died?" Caroline had a concerned look on her face.

"It's okay, Caroline," Danny said, "everyone is fine." He reached for her hand.

Colby looked at Caroline and sighed. "I need a coffee."

"I'll make some," Winston said, getting up and going to the stove.

Colby sipped his coffee. Caroline began turning the pages of a magazine.

"No matter what we do now," Colby said, "we've got a problem. Suppose we just let things lie. What then? If Danny and Caroline are picked up for any reason, it wouldn't take long before they were sent back to Canada. At least if Caroline is sent back to a home, she'll be looked after. Do you think you can look after her yourself, Danny?"

"I haven't thought that far ahead. Losing Betty and then Charlie... well. It was Betty's wish that we all look after each other, including Caroline. Especially Caroline. When we set out, none of us thought about dying. As Charlie said the other day, we were just making it up as we went along. I can't see myself turning us in to the authorities knowing I'd be responsible for whatever happened to Caroline after that. In my heart, I want to try to look after her, but none of this seems real anymore. Me, a former alcoholic and homeless bum, now responsible for what happens to someone else? I've never really had any obligation like that before. I'd hate to let her down. It's damn hard. What's the right thing?" Danny trailed off in a whisper.

"Right thing, right thing." Caroline repeated softly.

"I know... it is hard... doing the right thing..." Colby murmured. He was staring into space.

"In Iraq," he said quietly, "my buddy Doug Casselman and I got separated from our platoon, pinned down on the edge of a village by some Iraqis. We took cover behind a wall and returned fire, but the Iraqis cornered us when a couple more started firing from a nearby roof. Doug got hit. I put down my rifle to try to help him... turned him on his side to try to get at the wound in his back. He was bleeding badly... conscious and moaning. I tried to staunch the blood but then the firing got heavier and I had to lie flat. We were being fired on from all directions.

"I was about to reach for my rifle when a couple of Iraqis jumped over the wall. Doug was groaning loudly. I was covered in his blood. I lay still, got a kick in the ribs but managed to stay quiet. Someone grabbed up my rifle and then I heard them drag Doug away. I lay there expecting a bullet at any minute, but they'd gone. For maybe half an hour, I dunno how long, I listened to Doug's screams and their laughter as they did whatever it was they were doing to him. A couple of times he called... he called my name." Colby was weeping and his body shuddered with sobs but he caught his breath and went on.

THE GRAND GETAWAY   339

"I still had a grenade in my belt. It would have been easy to locate which abandoned house they were in by Doug's screams. But I didn't move. His screams... I waited 'til he stopped screaming. I heard the Iraqis laughing and I knew Doug was dead. Only then did I crawl forward. I pulled the pin on the grenade and tossed it through a window opening. Once the smoke cleared, I moved in. Two of them were still alive but badly wounded. My rifle was propped against a wall. I grabbed it and finished them off, but I'd let Doug down. I didn't help him when I should've. He would probably have died anyway, but I could have used my grenade to stop his pain. I didn't." Colby started weeping again.

Winston quickly stepped forward, knelt and took Colby in his arms. "Oh son, my son," Winston whispered.

Danny took Caroline's hand and led her outside to give Colby and Winston time alone.

CHAPTER 77

Danny busied himself giving the ponies some hay and topping up their water tubs. Caroline watched, more interested in the water than the ponies themselves. She dipped her hand into the water until a pony stuck his head into the tub and began noisily slurping up some water. She laughed, and tried imitating the sucking noise he made.

Danny was almost sure that Caroline really had no idea that Betty and Charlie had died. She was living only in that moment. That, he thought, was probably a blessing. He'd often wondered what thoughts were going through Caroline's mind when she spoke. She'd start with a few words, a short phrase, making sense for a moment. Then it became a jumble of regular words mixed with others that her brain conjured up as she pursued her point. Often she'd get stuck on some made-up word like *tenter*. Sometimes she would whimper, and then he wondered if she was having thoughts of something sad from the past, or was frustrated. And time. How did she experience time? Was an hour like a day, a day like a week? Still, she usually seemed happy. He looked at her now, laughing as the pony lifted his head from the tub and she cupped a hand to catch the water that dribbled from his mouth.

Time, he thought. He didn't have much of that to decide what to do next. He knew Colby's traumatic revelations were something that must have weighed on him for a long time, and were obviously a surprise to Winston. Right now, Colby and Winston needed some time.

It was getting on to evening. He'd have to think about supper for Caroline and himself. They went back to The Smucker and washed up.

Caroline was still finishing her supper, and Danny was sitting with her at the table, nursing a coffee, when Winston came over.

"How's Colby?" Danny asked.

"He's okay now," Winston replied. "He's been living with that Iraq memory for years. He'll still live with it, but Georgina and I will help him. I think that's what finally drove him home. He needs time to heal. He hadn't told anybody about it except his wife, Derica, and she persuaded him to come back home. She's kept him going, got him back to painting again, and he really needs that. It's his therapy."

"Did you tell him about finding the medal?" Danny asked.

"Not yet. I might tell him tonight. We've got a lot to talk about. He said he'd maybe like to come back up here with me in the spring, to paint and help me with the ponies. Finding the medal will change things, but I know I'll still be back next spring, and this time I'll have my son with me. Some of the arguments we've had over the years were Colby's way of coping, wanting to talk about what had happened in Iraq but looking for a way to avoid it. Today it came to a head. You all made it happen. The four of you were the catalyst. Thank you. The good news is that Colby has thought about what we did for Betty and Charlie, and he's okay with it now. He knows it was the right thing to do. So, what will you do now?"

"I'm still mulling it over. I think tomorrow morning Caroline and I will move back to the North Rim Campground. I hope we can find a spot."

"You shouldn't have any problem. There's quite a few vacancies now. It's coming up to closing time and there's some snow on the way soon. I heard it on the radio on the way back here. Long range forecast, maybe a few days away."

"Well, hopefully I'll have another day or two at the North Rim to think," Danny said. "Then either head south somewhere or back north, towards Canada. I need to figure it out. Right now I don't know what to do. I'll leave early and let you and Colby clean up here."

"I'd like to spend one more day here with Colby, talk some more. We'll probably see you in the morning, but if not, we'll look in on you at the North Rim Campsite before we head south. Goodnight, Danny, Caroline."

CHAPTER 78

Danny found it difficult to get to sleep. He couldn't seem to get comfortable. He tried to reshape the two sweaters that were stuffed inside each other. They never did buy any proper pillows after Betty had declared the ones she'd seen back in Calgary too expensive. They'd got used to whatever they were using. Charlie's Spider-Man pillowcase was stuffed with a heavy windbreaker. *What would happen to Caroline if, like Charlie, I didn't wake up?* He tried pushing that thought away. He couldn't. *I'll be a nervous wreck going to bed every night, afraid to sleep, and a virtual zombie trying to look after Caroline. God, it's a hell of a responsibility and a hell of a decision.*

Tomorrow they'd move back to the North Rim Campground. From there, he'd have to decide – head north back towards Canada, or further south. That's where they would have been heading if Betty and Charlie hadn't died.

Betty had said, 'One for all and all for one,' the motto of *The Three Musketeers*. It was easy to say, and probably easier to make work when there'd been four of them. Now he had nobody to really talk to – which, if he looked back on his life before meeting Charlie, Betty and Caroline, put him back at square one. At least Caroline was a lot more pleasurable company than anyone he'd come in contact with on the streets.

Gotta get to sleep. Once more he adjusted the sweaters under his head. He dozed, then, but woke with a start.

Colby had said, 'She'd be looked after somewhere in a home, no matter what. You think you can look after her now?'

Could he? He didn't know. There must be better care homes than Cavandish. But according to what Betty had said, Caroline had no real income. He remembered how many of the residents at Cavandish had spent their days sitting outside their rooms, most of them in wheel-chairs staring at the walls, waiting for their next meal. Even if Caroline didn't understand what was happening, could he bring himself to drop her off like an unwanted puppy?

Danny had the cash from Betty's purse and Charlie's wallet, for a grand total of $655 and change. It was more money than he'd had in an awful long time, but it wouldn't last, and then what? He could use the bank cards since he now had the PIN numbers, but he was nervous about using them. He was sure they would be cut off before long, and he and Caroline might even be tracked down. If he didn't use the cards, he and Caroline would be reduced to being homeless and destitute. They hadn't been far off it when they'd set out, he mused. Now there was only him and Caroline, and he couldn't ask for her opinion. What would she want to do now if she could tell him? He slept again, but it was a restless sleep.

THE GRAND GETAWAY   343

Just before he and Caroline drove off next morning, Winston came over. "You're off
then? Colby's still sleeping. I didn't want to wake him. We'll track you down
tomorrow morning. I know Colby will want to say goodbye. Have you come to a
decision on what you're going to do?"

"Not yet," Danny said. "Too much has happened, and so fast. I want to do the
right thing by Caroline, but I'm still unsure of what that is. What would she want? I
know for most people the answer would seem easy. Put Caroline back into a home
somewhere. But Betty and Charlie hated it. And look at Caroline now. Right now,
she's happy."

Winston poked his head into the cab of The Smucker. Caroline looked up from
pressing the buttons on the silent radio on the dash and smiled at him.

"There, there, there you are. It's you, you. That's what she said. There, there."

Winston reached for her hand. "I'll see you tomorrow morning, Caroline." He
let go of her hand and waved goodbye. Caroline smiled again and returned his wave
before turning back to the radio buttons, studying each one intently for a moment
before pressing it.

"Take care, Caroline. You too, Danny." Winston clapped him on the shoulder.
"See you in the morning.

"Yeah, 'til tomorrow."

Danny started The Smucker. *And now the news brought to you by Walmart!* He
and Caroline both leaped in their seats as the radio came on full blast and Danny
quickly fumbled for the off switch. "I guess you found the one station that didn't
crackle, Caroline."

"Oh yes," Caroline replied.

As he drove slowly out of their Cape Final campsite, he saw that Winston was
laughing and waving.

They managed to find a camping spot just a few places from where they had camped
before, and spent a pleasant day going for walks and resting in their lawn chairs. It
was still quite warm, and Danny was sure the forecast for snow was wrong.

After putting Caroline to bed that night he familiarized himself again with their
roadmap. Whether he decided to head back to Canada or to head somewhere
south, he would have to begin the journey by heading north to Jacob Lake.

If his decision was north to Canada, it wouldn't take long, provided The Smucker
held up. He'd have enough money and they could camp in real campsites with
proper toilets. Still, he knew the return trip would leave a bitter taste in his mouth
and there would be no joy in it. Going further south sounded attractive, and he could
always decide to turn around if he didn't go too far. But it wouldn't solve the problem
of Caroline's fate if anything happened to him or they got caught. He went to bed
knowing he would have to make the decision once he reached Jacob Lake tomorrow.

When Danny awoke the next morning around 7:00 a.m., he was surprised how dark it seemed inside The Smucker. Then he noticed that snow was covering the windshield and windows. When he opened the door, he was startled by the amount of snow that had fallen overnight. Huge snowflakes were still drifting down from the heavy grey clouds overhead. He bundled himself and Caroline in jackets and found a couple of caps before they headed for the washroom. Caroline grinned and tried to catch the falling snowflakes.

"The more it snows," Danny said.

"Tiddely-Pom," Caroline replied.

Danny laughed delightedly. "You remembered. Good for you." He gently squeezed her hand. He hoped the snow would stop soon. Getting as far as Jacob Lake might prove difficult in this weather. As they were finishing breakfast, a park ranger knocked on The Smucker's door.

"This snowfall is much heavier and a lot earlier than we expected," the ranger said. "If you get snowed in here, it could be days before we can get any snow plows in and you might have to be towed out. With this wet heavy snow, chances are you'll get stuck on the road out if you don't leave soon."

"Thanks," Danny said. "We'll pack up in a few minutes."

Damn. Winston had said they'd stop by that morning, but now they might miss them. "Finish your toast, Caroline. We've gotta get going."

"Going, going, yes," Caroline repeated as she chased some toast crumbs around her plate.

Danny mused out loud to Caroline, "I'd hate to miss Winston and Colby. But right now, we have to get out of here. Maybe we can stop over at the campground at Jacob Lake until the roads improve. We can't risk being pulled over by cops or getting involved with tow trucks. I do have Winston's cell phone number. I guess I could go look for a pay phone and try calling him. Lucky we filled The Smucker with gas last night, eh Caroline?"

"Yes, lucky, lucky."

There was another knock on the door and someone called out.

"Okay, we're just about to leave," Danny shouted. He glanced outside and saw Winston and Colby at the door. Colby had a broom and was already clearing the thick snow from the windshield.

"Thank God, it's you," Danny said. "I thought it was that park ranger again. We've been told to get out of here now."

"Yeah, that's right," Winston said. "We only just made it out of Cape Final. If too many vehicles start getting stuck they may close the road. You have gas?"

Danny nodded. "Filled up last night."

"Good. Colby's leaving his truck here. He'll come pick it up next week when the weather improves. We want to get the ponies out of here and we thought we'd make sure you got out too. Colby can ride with you. He'll add a bit of weight. You follow me, close as you can. If we make it as far as Jacob Lake, we might be okay. I just

THE GRAND GETAWAY   345

called ahead to the campground there. They won't take reservations, it's first come first served. We'd better leave now. This is a big snowstorm. If you get stuck or slide off the road, honk like hell and flash your lights. Colby will help you back out."

Danny strapped Caroline into the passenger seat and started The Smucker. He turned the defroster to high as Colby got the last of the snow cleared from the windshield, before directing Danny to reverse out of their camping spot.

As soon as Danny had The Smucker onto the main road out of the campground, Colby jumped in, tossing the broom into The Smucker's aisle, shaking snow off his jacket and stomping his feet. Clumps of wet snow slid off his hair and Caroline tried to catch them as they fell.

Colby laughed and blew on his hands. "Dad's just ahead there. Flash your lights and he'll pull out. Then follow him and take it slow. I guess you've driven in snow before up in Canada."

"Not really."

"You're kidding."

"No."

"Well let's see how it goes."

Winston's truck, pulling the horse trailer, was ambling ahead, and Danny eased The Smucker after it. Another large RV pulled in behind them and followed. He turned the fan on the heater to high as Colby took a seat at the kitchen table. Danny felt the wheels slip a little on the snow and eased off the gas, then he got some traction and lurched forward. He was going to have to learn to drive in snow real fast. Colby sitting behind him made him nervous, but he was also glad he and Caroline were not alone and, with Winston just ahead, he felt comforted. His responsibility for Caroline was already beginning to weigh heavily on him, but right now, he had to get them as far as Jacob Lake.

The snow had been beaten down on the roadway ahead by the number of vehicles that had already left, but it was covering the road again quickly and getting really deep along the edge. He concentrated on keeping in the tracks of Winston's truck and trailer. The snowflakes flew and swirled towards them and the wipers swooped back and forth, barely keeping the windshield clear. It was 45 miles to Jacob Lake, and it was going to be a long trip.

CHAPTER 79

Ahead of him, Danny saw Winston's brake lights come on and he eased The Smucker to a halt, hoping that the RV that had been following close behind him would stop in time.

"What's happening?" Colby asked.

"I dunno yet. Your Dad stopped. There's some flashing lights. I think there are cops up ahead."

Winston's left turn signals were on and he was moving to the side of the road. Danny did the same. Soon they were easing past a large RV that had skidded partly off the road and was blocking a good part of the right lane. A cop with a glowing red flashlight was directing them past in the left lane. The scene had an eerie look, with the red and blue emergency lights of his cruiser bouncing off the RV and the swirling snow. The cop waving them past was fast becoming a snowman.

Caroline, who had been sleeping, woke and said, "Christmas."

Danny chuckled as he pulled back in behind Winston.

It was another hour or so before the snow suddenly stopped, as if a switch on some giant snow-machine had been turned off. Bare black tarmac patches appeared on the road and the snow on the ground was only a skiff. When they reached the sign telling them they were arriving at Jacob Lake, there was no snow on the road at all.

"That's amazing," Colby said. "It was just a localized snowstorm, but we were lucky we made it out. Look, Dad's pulling up at the campground. You know, Danny, he told me about Caroline finding the medal. He was right all along. I've decided to help him get the promise made to my great-great-grandfather acknowledged."

"That's terrific," Danny replied. "I know your dad must be pleased."

"He is. I'm gonna stick around. But what about you and Caroline? What are you going to do from here?"

"First, I'm gonna get out and have a stretch. I was so tensed up driving in that snowstorm."

A sign at the campground entrance read, *Closing Date – Oct 20th.* Winston had pulled off the road into the campground entrance. Danny followed and stopped just behind Winston's trailer near a picnic area. Winston jumped out and greeted Danny at the door of The Smucker. "That was incredible. I've never driven through a snowstorm like that, and here there's no snow at all. You did great, Danny. So what now?"

"A bathroom break is the first order of the day," Danny said as he helped Caroline out of The Smucker. He flexed his shoulder muscles. "My shoulders ache."

"You need to rest," Winston said. "That's tension from having to drive in that blinding storm. Look, the sun's coming out. Colby, why don't you brew us some coffee. We'll have some lunch. Danny, you'd better not drive any further today. Camp here overnight and rest. I'll go check on a spot for you. This place will fill up fast."

"I gotta go," Danny said.

"Canada, then?" Colby asked.

"The washroom, before I wet myself. Come on Caroline."

It was 10 minutes before Danny and Caroline returned. He'd found a stall for the handicapped in the women's washroom. After cautiously peering in and finding it empty, he'd scrambled inside with her. He was going to have to get used to ducking into women's washrooms, he thought.

More RV's and campers were arriving and heading further into the campground, clumps of snow falling off their roofs.

Winston and Colby had arranged some food on the table in The Smucker. "I went and checked, and they only had a few spots left," Winston said. "I gave them my credit card number to hold a spot for you. I'll pick up the tab. We'll get you and Caroline set up before we leave. Come and eat. Colby found us some canned beans and the coffee's ready. There's some toast too."

"Thanks a lot Winston. I do have some money."

"That's okay, Winston said. "Our treat." As they ate, he said, "I guess this is where we part company."

Danny said, "That snowstorm made me think about how I hated pushing a grocery cart filled with pop cans and bottles down the back alleys of Calgary in the snow. The evening before Betty died, she said she'd like to think of the three of us finding some place to live and just keep moving on south 'til we did. Made us promise to look after Caroline as long as we could. But now with just me and Caroline, it'll only be a matter of time before someone catches up to us. A cop could stop me for breaking some traffic law or I could get turned in for hanging around women's toilets like some peeping Tom."

"But people would understand that once you explained," Colby said.

"Yeah, you think so? It's not like Caroline is my wife I'm looking after. She doesn't even know my name."

"And if you go back to Canada?" Winston asked.

"That's the dilemma. I'm all Caroline has now. I'll be breaking faith with Betty if I take Caroline back, but at the same time, I'm putting Caroline in God knows what kind of fix if anything happens to me and she's left alone down here. The easiest thing to do would be to drive to the nearest cop station and turn myself in. Get it over with."

"And you'd be okay with that?" Colby asked.

"Hell, no."

"You know," Winston said, "the baseball player, Yogi Berra, supposedly said, 'If you come to a fork in the road, take it.' I understand your dilemma, Danny. I guess you're at that fork now."

"You're right. I guess you could say I consider Caroline family now. Betty and Charlie were too. They took me in, when I was really feeling down. They made me part of their group. I might head a little ways south in a few days. I'm gonna stick with Caroline a little longer. I hope for her sake it's the right decision."

"Good for you, Danny," Winston said. "Colby and I will be back here Sunday to pick up his truck. You want to stay here until then, that's okay. It will give you time to decide where you're going. If you do head somewhere south, we could at least escort you part of the way."

"What do you say, Caroline?" Danny asked.

"Oh yes, say, say, say."

"Okay, Caroline, but after that I don't know where we're going."

"Well, we should finish lunch and take off soon. You okay with the plan to stay here until Sunday, then? I'll go to the office and confirm it. You have my phone number. If you do decide to leave earlier, give me a call. I'll understand."

"Okay," Danny said. "Thanks a lot."

Winston picked up The Smucker's keys from the table where Danny had left them. "I'll just turn on your radio and get the weather channel. Make sure we're not going to be heading back into a snowstorm."

"The radio's pretty crackly. You probably won't get much on it. We hardly ever use it," Danny said.

Winston put the keys in the ignition and turned on the radio. The song *South Of The Border (Down Mexico Way)* came crackling on.

"Boy! That's a golden oldie." He left it on the station for a minute.

"Mexico, Mexico, Mexico," Caroline repeated.

Winston laughed and let the song play a little longer before trying to find the weather station, but all he got was more crackling. He gave up and turned it back to the first station as the song came to an end.

"You know, my old buddy Pete and I often dreamed of going to the ocean some time, preferably somewhere warm," Danny said. "He'd ask me to tell him stories about us lying on a tropical beach, sunbathing and living on coconuts – particularly when he'd gotten into a bottle of rum."

"Well, you're a long way from the sea here Danny, unless you head all the way east through New Mexico down..."

He was interrupted by Caroline repeating, "Mexico, Mex, Mexico."

"Down to the Texas coast, I was going to say," Winston continued.

"You'd like to go to Mexico, Caroline, and see the ocean?" Danny laughed. "You think we might find a place to lie low somewhere in Mexico?"

"You know any Spanish?" Colby asked.

"Not a lot. Let's see... *Cerveza* and tequila."

"Boy! That should really help." Winston laughed. "Could be a problem."

"Yeah, I guess so," Danny said. "And getting into Mexico... Well that'd be like starting over again. We were fantastically lucky getting across the U.S. border."

"You're not really serious, Danny? Are you?" Winston asked.

"Nah. Just thinking out loud. Wondering what the odds would be of not getting caught, maybe finding a little place near the ocean."

"This is just crazy talk," Winston said. "You were trying to choose between trying your luck here in the States or heading back home to Canada. Now we're adding Mexico to the mix. I'll get the campsite confirmed here so you'll have some more time to make up your mind."

"There's always your cousin Edgar Havatone, Dad. Is he still in business?" Colby asked.

"I haven't talked to Edgar in ages," Winston replied.

"What kind of business is he in?" Danny asked.

Winston laughed. "Helping Mexicans, particularly if they are Mexican Indians, cross the U.S. border."

"Shouldn't be any harder going the other way," Colby said. "Probably easier going south."

"You think so?" Winston said. "Edgar lives in Ajo, where it's crawling with border agents. I'm off to the office to book your spot 'til Sunday."

After Winston had left, Danny asked, "You ever been to Mexico, Colby?"

"Yeah a few times. But not recently. You?"

"No, never. Where's the nearest town by the ocean south of here?"

"I'm not sure. Maybe Guaymas. Only place of any size, anyway. I went there a couple of times with Mom and Dad on holiday. Some years later I went again with a couple of my friends. It's a real small city, mostly a shrimp and fishing place, surrounded by low mountains. Quiet, sleepy kind of place, very laid back."

"How far is it?"

"Well, you'd go south past Phoenix and then through Ajo where Dad's cousin, Edgar lives, before you get to the border crossing at Sonoita. It's about another four hours at most from there to Guaymas."

"So about 12 hours driving?"

"Yeah about that. There's the fishing harbour there and a couple of nice beaches just north west of Guaymas. It gets hot there, but the sea breeze helps."

"Sea, sea, sea," Caroline said.

Colby laughed. "There you go, Danny. Another Spanish word for you, Si. Now you know three words. Means yes."

"I think I knew that one." Danny laughed. "What's the word for the real sea, the ocean?"

"*Mare*. You really thinking of trying Mexico?"

"Ah, I dunno. I guess I'm grasping at straws. I'm just dreaming."

"Too bad you can't hole up on our land at Peach Springs, but there's only temporary tourist accommodation there. There are rules about Indian land."

"Yeah. Well... If Caroline and I could stay anywhere to get our bearings, so to speak, a place by the ocean sounds attractive. Fish would be cheap anyway. Charlie would have liked that. Probably would've gone fishing every day." Danny lapsed into silence.

CHAPTER 80

"Winston, do you think you'd be able to contact your cousin Edgar in case we make a run for Mexico?" Danny asked.

"I could try. But are you sure about this?"

"No. I'm not sure about anything. Tilting at windmills."

"What's that?" Colby asked.

"It's from *Don Quixote*, the book by Cervantes," Winston said. "Don Quixote was a little crazy. Went around attacking windmills. Danny's referring to the impracticality, the romance of the idea, about going to Mexico. That right, Danny?"

"Yeah. *The Impossible Dream*. Betty lived by that," Danny said. "Maybe some of it has rubbed off on me."

Winston looked at Caroline who was busy folding a paper napkin. He lowered his voice. "You know, Danny, Caroline will only get worse."

"Yeah. I know that. But maybe in the time we've got left, I can help her have a half-assed decent quality of life."

"Okay. It's your call. I'll try calling Edgar. If anyone knows how to cross the border, he will. I'll tell you what he says, then you can decide. I checked the road report on my phone. The roads are good for now, but we'd better get going. It's still a fair drive home."

"Before we go, I want to give Danny something," Colby said. "It's in the truck. I'll get it."

"I don't know what information Edgar will want or if he can help," Winston said. "I'm sure he'll need your driver's license information and the registration of the vehicle. Betty said that none of you had passports. Getting across the border might be a long-shot, unless Edgar has some secret back road."

Danny pulled The Smucker's registration out of the small glove compartment and the licenses out of his wallet and handed them to Winston.

"You're kidding!" Winston said. "Caroline is the registered owner and she has a driver's license, but yours is only a learners? Holy crap! She doesn't drive, does she? Would that be legal?"

"I'm the only driver, and we didn't stop and ask anyone about it being legal. We're winging it."

"Jeez, you can say that again."

Winston was finishing copying down the information as Colby returned carrying a painting. "I used the sketches I did of the four of you dressed up like Indians. If you like it, I'd like you and Caroline to have it."

The oil painting depicted Winston and the four of them riding ponies along a ridge above the canyon with the side of the canyon in the foreground, glowing a bright orange in the afternoon sun. Danny could clearly identify everyone in the painting.

"It's beautiful," Danny said. "It's full of humour. I love it. Betty and Charlie would have loved it too. You captured us well, and you can tell we're not real Indians. We're all wearing something that gives us away. Betty with her sun hat and sunglasses, Charlie and me bare-chested with farmer's tans." Danny laughed. "Brown arms and neck and white chests. Charlie's needing a haircut. And he's wearing... on his belt. Is that a pocket watch? That's really good. He must have told you about Betty making him pawn his railway watch."

"He did." Colby grinned.

"And there's me," Danny continued, "looking a bit scruffy with a pony tail and wearing jeans with a hole at the knee. Is that a peace sign painted on my face?"

Colby nodded.

Danny laughed. "There's still a bit of the homeless look about me. Look at Caroline, shading her eyes and looking into the distance, smiling, wearing a pink headband and lipstick. Your Dad looks great too. But he looks the real thing. Genuine. You sure you want to part with it?" Danny asked.

"Yeah. I painted a small proof before I did this. I can pretty well put the four of you in any setting." Colby laughed. "I called it *Canyon Chicanery*."

"It's really great," Winston said. "I guess you were getting a dig in at me at the same time. But that's okay."

"Sorry, Dad. I couldn't resist. And I had to paint Betty and her gang as I saw them."

"Well we'd better get going" Winston said. "I may not have any answers for you Danny, but I'll see what I can do. See you on Sunday."

In the remaining days of the week, the weather was a bit cooler than it had been. Danny took Caroline for short walks, stocked up on a few groceries, and they generally took it easy. The campground was set among a forest of Ponderosa pines, and their own campsite was small but secluded. When it was warm enough, they sat in the lawn chairs outside.

Danny paid close attention to Caroline's chatter, particularly when she engaged him in one of her earnest conversations, although he didn't really understand anything of what she was saying. He tried to let her know he was really listening, nodding occasionally and laughing with her when she laughed as she apparently told him something funny.

Winston had given Danny a roadmap, and he looked over the route he might follow if he headed south to meet with Edgar. At Flagstaff, the highway became Interstate 10, a four–lane highway to Phoenix, then west to a place called Buckeye and from there south through Gila Bend to Ajo, the small town where Edgar lived. It wasn't far from Ajo to the Mexican border.

I'm getting ahead of myself, he thought. *We can play at being tourists a little longer, but may have to make the decision to head back to Canada eventually.* He wondered too, what would happen if he was stopped by police or the Border Patrol and they found he was in possession of Charlie and Betty's bank cards. That would no doubt open up a whole new line of questioning, and who knows where that could end. *Not well,* he thought.

He was up bright and early on Sunday morning, anxious to learn if Winston had been able to contact Edgar and if he'd agreed to help, or if the whole idea was just another impossible dream. He was itching to be on the move again no matter what. He lingered over a second cup of coffee as Caroline slowly ate her breakfast, and he found himself constantly glancing at the little clock. It was barely 8:00 a.m. when Winston's truck pulled up.

Danny had to know right away. "Winston, did you get hold of your cousin?"

"I got hold of him late Friday night," Winston replied. "Have you made a decision about heading for Mexico, Canada or elsewhere?"

"I'd like to give Mexico a try, if we have a chance of getting there. I've been getting antsy and we can't hang around here much longer. What did your cousin say?"

"He said there are risks, but he thinks they are reasonable. He told me he'd need to get some papers fixed up, so I gave him the info you gave me. I think he has some contact at the Mexican border. He needs a few days to get things set up. You want me to call him, then?"

"Okay," Danny said. "We'll give it a try."

"If it doesn't work out or you change your mind, phone me from wherever you are. I'll do my best to meet up with you if you need any help. Okay?"

"Yeah. Thanks, Winston. What about money? Won't Edgar want some money? I mean, if he has to pay off anyone or get us some fake papers."

"He was a bit closed-mouthed about that. I think he wants to size you up first. There will be money involved, but don't worry about that. I said I'd forward the money to Edgar in due course if all goes well. You don't have to bribe anyone. He did say that if you make it to Guaymas, you'll be on your own. And if Mexico doesn't work out, he said it would be very difficult to get back into the U.S."

"No matter what I decide, me and Caroline will be in limbo. But I have a little money. You don't have to pay for everything."

"That's okay. You and Caroline have saved me a bundle in legal fees. I had a meeting at the University of Flagstaff yesterday and talked to the leading expert on native historical artifacts. The medal Caroline found is definitely genuine. The consensus is that the National Parks will be more than happy to set up some kind of plaque or commemorative stone acknowledging my great-grandfather's historical rights at Cape Final, seeing as I won't be staking a claim for ownership of the Cape and us Indians aren't trying to take back our lands. So I owe you one, especially you, Caroline."

"'Specially you," Caroline smiled

As Winston pulled out his cell phone to call Edgar, Danny felt his heart thumping. He hoped like hell that things would work out. He wished he had some of Betty's boldness, her audacity. He glanced at her image in the painting that was now attached to the wall above her bunk, and even behind the sunglasses that Colby had painted on her, he was sure her eyes were mocking him. *Chicken-hearted*. That's what her eyes always said when he or Charlie were timid.

"Hello, Edgar, it's Winston. It's a go."

When Winston ended the call, he turned to Danny. "Edgar said the U. S. Border Patrol mostly focus on vehicles coming north. If you are a U.S. citizen going south, they just ask where you're heading and they wave you through. He thinks it should be the same for Canadians, but if they ask for I.D. it might be a problem. The main thing is to be polite. You might be okay with your driving licenses.

"Here's the important bit. He says that you should arrive in Ajo on Thursday afternoon between 3:00 and 3:15 p.m. and pull into the parking lot of the Roadrunner Motel. It's just north of Ajo on the highway. I described your bus. He'll meet you in the parkin' lot, but he won't show up until that time, so wait there. I got the impression that the fewer people who know his movements the better. I think the Border Patrol has had their suspicions about him and he's keeping a low profile. He also said you should arrive at the Mexican border next morning at a certain time, but he'll give you further instructions when he meets you.

"We'll go and get Colby's truck, and stop by here on the way back. We can guide you as far as Flagstaff this afternoon. We should be back in a couple of hours. It's up to you."

"I'd appreciate the escort. I'd like to move on today."

"We head west from here, Danny," Winston said. He and Colby had pulled their vehicles up at the junction of Highway 89 at Flagstaff and joined Caroline and Danny in The Smucker. "Take your time so you don't get to Ajo before Thursday afternoon. Edgar stressed that your time of arrival at the motel parking lot in Ajo is important. You know the time and the motel, right?"

"Yeah, I wrote it down."

"Good. You were saying you'd like to avoid Phoenix, and I think that's a good plan. If you make it to Wickenburg by Wednesday night you should have an easy drive to Ajo on Thursday. Finding campgrounds with vacancies might be difficult. Let me check on my phone and see what's available before you take off."

Winston studied his phone for several minutes. "Holy, these places are busy. Why don't I try this Cool Springs campground? If I can get a booking, I think you

THE GRAND GETAWAY   355

should take two nights there. You can easily make it from there to Wickenburg in one day."

In Wickenburg all Winston could find was a motel room at the Margarita Motel with single beds, and he booked that too for Danny and Caroline.

"Okay, everything's taken care of," Winston said. "You won't have to spend time searching for somewhere to stay."

"I've got cash. Let me pay," Danny said, but Winston wouldn't hear of it.

"It's been great knowing you, Danny, Caroline." Winston hugged both of them. "I wish you the best of luck. You're good folks. If you do get to Guaymas, send us a postcard. I promise you, Colby and I will look after Betty and Charlie's resting place. Goodbye Caroline, love." Winston hugged her and then Colby said his goodbyes too.

"Look after each other," Danny said.

"You too," Colby said.

Danny waited until Colby and Winston's vehicles had pulled away and wiped the tears from his eyes.

"Well, Caroline. Here we go. Should I put on some music?" He found the Barbra Streisand tapes. As Streisand began singing *People,* he found himself biting his lip. He glanced at Caroline. She was smiling.

CHAPTER 81

Danny guessed they were a little more than halfway between Gila Bend and Ajo. It was hot in The Smucker, and when he'd turned on the fan to try to get some cool air from outside, it felt like he'd turned on the heater full blast. He turned it off and settled for having the side windows rolled down, but the breeze that blew on them was just as hot. Caroline looked warm, but she had fallen asleep. The forecast on the TV in the motel in Wickenburg had been for a day with high temperatures. He was glad he'd dressed her in a light blouse and shorts. He was wearing his jeans and he'd found a T-shirt of Charlie's with Newfoundland & Labrador's provincial crest above the pocket and *Come By Chance* emblazoned across the front. Danny had asked him what *Come By Chance* was and Charlie had made a joke about it being a wet dream of a place or something like that. He'd never been to Newfoundland. His daughter had sent him the shirt. Anyway, Danny thought, it's the best Caroline and I can do to look like genuine tourists taking in the sights.

They had spent the last three days doing just that. From the Cool Springs Campground near Cottonwood, where they'd spent two days, they had explored some of the red rock attractions near Sedona.

As they'd headed further south, they had strolled the streets of Jerome, a small town set on the side of a mountain. Danny knew that Charlie would have made a far better tour guide, pointing out many more points of interest and historical facts to all of them. But it didn't matter to Caroline, and she had seemed content and happy with everything he chose to do.

At the Margarita Motel in Wickenburg, they'd slept in real beds for the first time since they had left Calgary. Danny had slept well, but as soon as he awoke, he felt anxious about the day ahead.

They'd left the motel after Danny had brewed some coffee that was provided in the room, and they had a picnic breakfast about an hour later out of town. Before they'd headed south to Gila Bend, Danny decided to try Betty and Charlie's bank cards once more. It could well be the last time he could use them. Meanwhile, having more money in his pocket, whether they made it to Mexico or not, couldn't hurt. He took $500 from both accounts.

The land they travelled through was now mostly flat sandy desert with low scrub and those tall cactus with what looked like a flexed arm jutting out. They reminded him of the ones he'd seen on the *Wile E. Coyote* cartoons. The air across the desert seemed to tremble in the heat, and he caught glimpses in the distance of hazy low-lying mountains.

The highway was now fenced off on both sides by a wide-mesh wire fence on which hung signs, spaced at long intervals that read, *Danger, Military Reservation. No Trespassing. Dangerous Explosives. Violators Will Be Subject To Prosecution.*

THE GRAND GETAWAY   357

Another announced it was the *Barry M. Goldwater Air Force Range,* while another warned *Danger – Keep Out – Unexploded Armaments.*

Danny glanced at the clock again. It was only 2:10 p.m. He checked the piece of paper in his shirt pocket with the time Edgar had said he should arrive at the Roadrunner Motel. It must have been the fifth time he'd checked it that day. Edgar had insisted on them arriving between 3:00 and 3:15 p.m. He decided he would drive past the motel if they were too early and find some way to kill time. Caroline had woken up and was studying the landscape.

A sign set in the scrub along the right side of the road announced, *Just Ahead – Lindy Lou's L'il Ice Cream Stand – The Best Tastin' Ice Cream In Arizona.*

"Let's stop and buy an ice cream, Caroline. How's that rhyme go? I scream, you scream, we all scream for ice cream."

"Ice cream, ice cream," Caroline repeated.

As they rounded a bend, he caught sight of the ice cream stand, a small trailer parked on the left. A school bus had pulled off the road just past the ice cream stand and a cluster of little kids were milling about the serving hatch. Two young women were distributing cones as they were handed through the hatch.

Danny pulled The Smucker off the road on the right, just short of the ice cream stand. Behind him a Border Patrol vehicle rounded the bend and coasted to a stop just behind The Smucker. Danny didn't notice it, as he reached over and unbuckled Caroline's seatbelt and stepped past her. "Here, the sun's hot out there, put this cap on your head. Okay, good." He put his own cap on. "Let's go and get that ice cream, Caroline." He opened the door and stepped out to help her down the steps.

"That ice cream is sure gonna taste good today, Rick. It's been a hot one."

"Yeah, ya got that right. And a heck of a borin' one. Hey, Tom! What kind of a contraption are we parked behind? Alberta license plate. God-damn weird paint job. Looks like some kind of hippy get-up. Let's check it out. Flash your lights."

Danny had his back to the Border Patrol vehicle as he helped Caroline step onto the ground, but he suddenly caught the flash of the vehicle's lights reflected off the side of The Smucker. He turned quickly to see a Border Patrol agent step out of the passenger side of the vehicle and begin to walk towards them.

"Damn," Danny muttered. He closed the door of The Smucker and took Caroline by the hand. *Best to act innocent,* he thought. *We're just tourists stopping for an ice cream.*

Another Border Patrol agent had stepped around the front of The Smucker. The name Bigalow was in large lettering across the right breast of his shirt. They couldn't go anywhere.

"Good afternoon, sir, ma'am. Where are you headed?"

"Just across the road to buy us some ice cream," Danny replied.

'It's real good ice cream," the other agent said. His shirt declared his name was Agnew. "We're thinkin' the same thing. But where are ya headed after that?"

"Just as far as *Ah-joe* today. We're thinking of taking a look at The Organ Pipe Cactus Monument tomorrow and then maybe head towards Tucson."

"You're from Canada?" the one whose name was Bigalow asked.

"We are," Danny said.

"Can we please see some I.D. sir?" Bigalow said.

Danny swallowed. This is it, then. He reached for his wallet in the back pocket of his jeans and pulled out their licenses and handed them to Bigalow.

Is there any hope they might accept this I.D. as enough? What if they questioned Caroline?

"You have the vehicle registration, passports?"

Behind Danny, agent Tom Agnew was dying for an ice cream. He could almost taste it. He was giving Bigalow a look that said, *Come on, Rick. Let's get that ice cream. They're just a couple of tourists. Leave them be.*

Danny opened the door of The Smucker and stepped in to get the registration out of the glove compartment, praying that it would be enough, otherwise...

Whaaam! Whaaam!

Danny jumped and staggered back as two sudden claps of loud thunder exploded overhead. The air above them reverberated and seemed to compress downwards as two low-flying airplanes flashed over them, almost nose to tail.

Danny hadn't a clue what kind of planes they were, only that they were loud and had scared the hell out of him.

But Billy-Joe Bigalow, standing with the other kids in his kindergarten class and licking his strawberry ice cream cone, knew exactly what the planes were. Fairfield Republic A-10 Thunderbolts. They were his favourite aircraft. "*Hogs,*" he yelled, tossing his half-eaten cone in the dirt and racing across the road after the planes.

Danny heard Caroline yell something, but whatever she'd yelled had been drowned out by the clamourous roar above them.

Danny and the two agents stared after the aircraft which had now gained altitude in a long curving turn to the north before banking south again, the second plane dropping a little further behind the first. They swooped low to level off, lining themselves up to attack a line of disused tanks set out on the practice range some distance from the highway.

Once 5-year-old Billy-Joe had crossed the road, he'd found a gap at the bottom of the fence large enough for him to squeeze under. Then he was on his feet again, racing after the planes and hoping he'd be able to see the actual attack. A couple of times his dad had taken him to see action at the firing range, which was occasionally open to the public. He'd watched all kinds of aircraft strafe and bomb trucks, tanks and even a mock village – and he'd loved it. But most of all, he loved the *Hogs,* or *Warthogs* as the Thunderbolts were nicknamed.

THE GRAND GETAWAY   359

Danny retrieved the registration and was about to hand it over to agent Bigalow when a young woman dashed up, looking panicked.

"We've lost a little boy," she cried out. "One of my class."

The agents turned to her, startled.

Agent Bigalow recognized the young woman as his son's kindergarten teacher, Monica.

Another woman had come running to join them, leaving the kindergarten class in the care of Lindy-Lou of the ice cream stand.

"Monica," she yelled. "One of the kids saw Billy-Joe run across the road and duck under the fence. He's run in there." She pointed.

"Billy-Joe?" Bigalow asked. "Billy-Joe Bigalow?"

Monica nodded. "Yes. I'm sorry. We were all watching the planes and..."

Brrrrrmmmmrrrrrt – Brrrrrmmmmrrrrrt – Brrrrrmmmmrrrrrt. At the firing range the first plane had started its attack on the tanks, its cannon spitting rapid bursts of fire, bright flashes exploding from its nose.

Monica glanced anxiously through the fence in the direction of the noise. A long way off on the ground, puffs of smoke and flame were visible.

She turned back to agent Bigalow. "I'm sorry. I was trying to get them all back on the bus when one of the girls said Billy-Joe had run off."

"Show me." Bigalow quickly handed the drivers' licenses back to Danny. "Thanks sir. You can go ahead."

But Danny wasn't going anywhere. Danny was in a panic himself. He took the licenses and ran around The Smucker looking for Caroline. He couldn't see her. *She'd been scared by the planes. Was it possible I hadn't seen her hop back inside?* "Caroline, Caroline!" He ran up the steps and quickly looked under the table, in the bunks, even checking that she hadn't crawled under one of the lower ones. There was no sign of her. He stumbled outside again and looked across the road to the ice cream stand. The other young woman was now there, getting the kids back on the bus. Caroline would have seen the kids. She must be with them, he thought. She could never resist little kids.

He raced across the road. "Did you see a woman? She's wearing shorts. She was with me." Danny gasped. His heart was pounding. He couldn't see Caroline.

The woman looked up surprised. "Oh..."

"Is she on the bus with the kids?"

"No. No... over there. Across the road." She pointed to where Monica and the two agents were at the fence.

"Oh God!" Danny ran back across the road. When he got there, Bigalow had clambered over the fence. Agent Agnew was there with Monica, who was looking worried and chewing on her fingers.

Inside the fence, a long way off, Danny glimpsed a tiny figure running up a low ridge and then caught sight of another movement. It was Caroline. She was about a hundred yards behind the little boy, walking as fast as she could. Danny grabbed the fence, intending to follow, when he was stopped by Agnew.

"I've got to go get her," Danny said. "She'll get lost if..."

"Rick should be able to catch him, sir. Your wife too. She musta gone after Billy-Joe when she saw him duck under the fence. Yessir! You got a great little lady there."

Danny stared through the fence. Bigalow was beginning to catch up, but now Billy-Joe disappeared, and Caroline was half-way up the ridge.

Brrrrrmmmrrrrrt – Brrrrrmmmrrrrrt – Brrrrrmmmrrrrrt. The second plane was making its attack, and the first had circled back and was lining up for a second run. To Danny, the sound was like the gruff chatter of the engine brakes of a big rig truck, repeated again and again. The flames had grown and clouds of black smoke were rising over the range.

He felt desperate just standing there as Caroline gained the top of the ridge. *What if the noise scared her off and she didn't follow the kid? What if she got lost in there? Oh God, please bring her back safe.* Under his shirt he could feel sweat trickling down his sides. The sun on his back burned through his shirt, but it wasn't just the sun that caused Danny to sweat. He was worried sick. The second plane fired off a couple of rockets and the explosions could easily be heard and seen from where he stood.

"Oh God." Danny grasped the mesh of the fence with both hands and pressed his face against the wire.

Agent Agnew patted Danny on the shoulder. "Don't worry, sir, Rick will bring 'em back. He'll be pretty mad at Billy-Joe. The kid's crazy about planes. Especially them *Warthogs.*"

Caroline had now disappeared over the ridge and Agent Bigalow was almost at the top. Danny found himself staring at one of the signs a few yards away attached to the fence that read, *Danger – Keep Out – Unexploded Armaments.*

"What about the unexploded armaments?"

"Ah. I believe those would be closer to the actual firin' range. I don't think there'd be any of those close to here. They'll be fine."

The planes made two or three more runs over the range, firing more rockets and dropping some bombs before finally breaking off and disappearing altogether. At the fence they could see flickering flames and hear the faint crackle of the fire. The columns of black smoke rose higher into the sky. It seemed to Danny that Bigalow was taking an eternity to find Billy-Joe and Caroline.

Bigalow crested the ridge and found the woman and Billy-Joe hand in hand, standing and looking at the distant smoke and flames. Both of them in turn were making blurting, raspberry noises, mimicking the sounds of the Warthog's cannon.

"Billy-Joe! What in tarnation do you think you were doin'? I've a good mind to give you a whuppin' right here and now."

The woman holding Billy-Joe's hand blew another raspberry and Billy-Joe immediately followed suit, then both of them burst out laughing.

"This lady is funny," Billy-Joe said.

"There they are." Monica gave a huge sigh, like she'd been holding her breath while they waited.

As they drew closer Danny could see the little boy was walking hand in hand between Bigalow and Caroline. Every now and then Danny could see Caroline bend towards Billy-Joe and say something to him. She was laughing.

As they approached the fence, Billy-Joe made a farting raspberry sound and laughed and Caroline joined in.

"These two have been doing that since I caught up with them," Bigalow said. "They're playin' *Warthogs*. Gave up tryin' to get them to stop."

"They okay?" Agnew asked as Billy-Joe dropped to his knees to scramble under the gap in the fence. Caroline bent down when Billy-Joe did, but when he scrambled under the fence, she looked a bit puzzled.

"Come on lady," Billy-Joe squirmed past Danny and stuck his head through the hole under the fence. Caroline immediately lowered her head to Billy-Joe's and crawled under. Danny hugged her close and made a bit of a show of dusting her off. He wanted to get her back to The Smucker and take off as quickly as possible. He knew it must be getting close to the time they were supposed to meet Edgar, but Bigalow had other ideas.

As he scrambled over the fence and jumped to the ground, he said, "What's your wife's name?"

"Caroline," Danny replied.

"Well, if Caroline hadn't been here and gone after Billy-Joe, who knows how long we might have been searchin' for him, or how far he'd have gone. When I caught up to them, she was holdin' Billy-Joe's hand. She'd have brought him back."

Danny wasn't so sure about that. More likely she'd have gone further into the firing range if Billy-Joe had been intent on getting closer to the planes.

"Let's go get those ice cream cones now. My treat."

"Aw, that's okay," Danny said but Bigalow wasn't listening. He'd turned to Monica. "Here, Monica, take this little bugger back to the bus. He'll get a good talkin' to from me and his mom tonight," Bigalow said.

"'Bye lady," Billy-Joe made the raspberry sound again and laughed as Caroline repeated it.

"Don't encourage him, Caroline," Bigalow said, but he and Agnew were laughing too as Monica led Billy-Joe away. "Come on, let's get those ice creams."

They stood under the small awning that hung from the roof of the ice cream stand, licking their cones. Danny was helping Caroline with her chocolate cone, doing his best to keep it from running down her wrist with a couple of paper napkins. Bigalow had insisted on ordering double scoop sizes, although Danny had said a single cone would be fine for Caroline and himself. Bigalow had looked at Caroline and said, "Nah. On a hot day like this you'd like a double, wouldn't you Caroline?" Caroline had given Bigalow a big grin and said, "Oh you," which Bigalow took as a yes.

"Billy-Joe really took to Caroline, here. He's often quite shy with strangers. What do you do, Caroline? Or are you retired now?"

Caroline had taken an extra large slurp of the ice cream and her mouth was full. "Mmn," she said.

"She was a grade one teacher," Danny answered. "She loves little kids."

"You can say that again. She hardly paid any attention to me. She was totally focussed on Billy-Joe. They were sure havin' fun."

"Yeah, when she's with children she gets carried away."

"You said you're just goin' as far as Ajo today? Where you gonna stay?"

"Er. The Roadrunner Motel," Danny blurted. He didn't know the names of any other motels in Ajo. He thought it best to stay honest.

"Ya got a booking?"

"Um, no," Danny said.

"Not a bad motel. We'll help you get fixed up," Bigalow went on.

What did he mean *help you get fixed up?* Danny hoped that as soon as they finished their ice cream they would be able to get going. Edgar had probably come and gone by now.

"It's been a long day," Danny said. "About time for us folks to get to the motel and have an afternoon nap. We've had enough excitement for one day." He practically wolfed down the remainder of Caroline's cone. "Thanks for the ice cream, Mr. Bigalow."

"It's nothin'. Thanks for your help with Billy-Joe, Caroline. We'll see you down the road to the motel. Just follow us. Come on, Tom."

Danny got Caroline back to The Smucker and groaned after he buckled her in and looked at the clock. It was 3:44 p.m. They were half an hour late. Now what? Edgar would have given up on them.

Bigalow started the car and pulled back onto the highway, waving with his arm out the window for Danny to follow.

A few yards down the highway, the emergency flashing lights on the Border Patrol vehicle came on. Danny followed as they picked up speed.

Five minutes later, with the Border Patrol car's lights still flashing, they coasted up to the office of the Roadrunner Motel. If Edgar had been still hanging around, there was no way he'd show his face here now. Danny was at least grateful that their escort hadn't included the sirens. He got out of The Smucker, hoping the two border agents would just back out and drive away. Then he could get back into The Smucker and wait, hoping against hope that Edgar might still show up. He was surprised to

THE GRAND GETAWAY   363

see a smiling Bigalow step out of the patrol vehicle, walk to the motel office door
and stand expectantly holding the door open for him.

"Here ya go, sir."

Danny stepped into the office. There was no one there, but Bigalow slapped his
hand down on the bell on the counter and a smiling, middle-aged woman appeared
through some curtains.

"Welcome to the Roadrunner," she said. "How may I help you?"

"I see your sign says you got a vacancy, Mabel. This man and his lovely wife need
a room for the night. You got a good one? They're friends of mine. I'm picking up
the tab." He pulled a credit card out of his wallet and put it on the counter.

"Jeez. Thanks! But you don't have to do that," Danny said.

"I'm payin'. Say no more. I owe you and Caroline. It's on me."

"We have a lovely couple of rooms on the south end," Mabel said. "Would you
like a double bed or two singles, sir?"

"Er. Singles. I'm a restless sleeper and Caroline likes a good night's sleep."

"Okay fine. Here's the keys. Room number 9. It's got a great view of the desert.
There's coffee fixins in the room. I'll just have you sign the guest book. And if you
need anythin' just pick up the phone."

"Thanks," Danny said. He signed the guest book as Bigalow signed the credit
card slip.

"Well, thanks again. Enjoy your stay. We've gotta go sign off on our shift. All the
best, sir, ma'am."

Danny took the keys to the motel room off the counter as Bigalow held the door
open for him again.

"Have a good trip," he called as he headed for the patrol car.

"Thanks a lot," Danny said as he walked to The Smucker to drive it down to room
number 9. Their encounter with the Border Patrol had turned out much better than
he'd feared, thanks to Caroline, but it had probably cost them their chance of getting
to Mexico. He didn't have any way of contacting Edgar. Still, they'd have a good
night's rest and it was free. Betty would have loved that.

CHAPTER 82

Danny opened the door of the motel room and scanned the parking lot. It was about the fifth or sixth time he'd done that, hoping to see someone who might turn out to be Edgar. The trouble was, he had no idea what Edgar looked like. It was probably a forlorn hope, considering they'd done the opposite of everything that Edgar had instructed them to do. They'd missed the meeting time by forty minutes, checked into the motel when they should have waited in the parking lot, and arrived with a Border Patrol escort. He was sure they'd scared Edgar off completely. He couldn't blame him. If Edgar had witnessed their arrival, he had probably high-tailed it out of town. The Smucker was plainly visible, parked at the very end of the motel. But it was getting on to evening and it didn't look like Edgar was going to contact them.

The room had seemed like an ice-box when he and Caroline had come in after the heat of outside. Danny turned the air-conditioner down. Caroline had fallen asleep on one of the beds and he'd covered her with a blanket. He made a sandwich and brewed some coffee. Caroline was still asleep, so he put her sandwich in the small fridge in the room. He took one last look outside at the parking lot. It was now dark. He lay on his bed after turning the TV on low volume, and fell asleep in the middle of a news report about the Border Patrol. They had picked up about 20 Mexicans crossing into the U.S. just south of Ajo.

When the phone rang beside his bed, he awoke startled, not sure of where he was. It rang three times before he managed to find the switch for the bedside lamp and pick up the phone. Panic and then relief flooded through him as he said, "Hello?" It had to be Edgar.

"Hello. Is this Danny Carroll?" The voice on the other end sounded familiar.

"Yes. It is. Is this..."

"It's Winston."

"Winston! How..."

"I just talked to Edgar. What happened? He said you were escorted to the motel by the Border Patrol."

"We were. But everything's fine. A Border Patrol agent paid for our motel bill for the night."

"What! You're kidding. You're not under arrest, are you?"

"No. Nothing like that. We're free to go but we were late. We missed our appointment."

Danny gave Winston a brief account of what had happened. By the end of Danny's story, Winston could hardly stop laughing. "That's unbelievable, but I'll have to get Edgar to believe it. That won't be easy. He's spooked. I'll phone you back in a few minutes and confirm that he'll meet you. Don't leave the room. Talk to you in a bit."

THE GRAND GETAWAY   365

"Thanks, Winston."

Danny took Caroline to the bathroom and 20 minutes later the phone rang again.

"Danny. Winston here. I had a hell of a time convincing Edgar you are on the up and up. He knows Agent Bigalow and says he's one of the most hard-assed agents around. He can't imagine him treating anyone to an ice cream cone, let alone paying for a motel bill. Here's the plan. You have to meet him at the Chevron gas station about 150 yards south of your motel. Pull in there on the side where the washrooms are. Go into the station store and buy an Oh Henry chocolate bar. I know this all sounds cloak and dagger, but Edgar still thinks maybe Bigalow is pulling a fast one. If Edgar is sure you're not being followed, he'll follow you out of the store and hop into The Smucker."

"How will he know me? The Oh Henry bar?"

"Yeah. I guess so." Winston laughed. "But I described you and he can't miss The Smucker. Don't mess this up, or you won't get another chance. Good luck to both of you."

"Thanks a million, Winston."

Danny got Caroline's shoes on, but then he couldn't find his own. He got panicky when he could only find one under the bed, but when he stood up, he found Caroline holding the other shoe in her hands. "Thanks, Caroline." He slipped on his shoes and tried to calm down. If Edgar was already spooked, it wouldn't help if he arrived all nervous. It would only make him more suspicious.

He pulled into the service station lot. Two cars were at the pumps getting gas. As he stepped past Caroline, he said, "I'll be back in a couple of minutes, love. Just wait here, okay?" He locked the door and went into the service station store.

One of the customers who'd been getting gas was standing at the counter paying. Danny glanced around but didn't see anyone else.

"Can I help you?" It was the man behind the counter.

"Yeah, I'd like to get an Oh Henry bar, please," Danny said in a fairly loud voice, glancing down at the display of candy bars on the side of the counter. He couldn't see any Oh Henrys. *Christ,* he thought. *Where are the Oh Henrys?*

"Sorry. All out of Oh Henrys. You like something else?"

"Gee. That's too bad. You're all out of Oh Henrys." Danny spoke loudly again. "I kinda had my heart set on an Oh Henry." *God, Edgar, it's not my fault they're out of Oh Henrys. It was you that suggested Oh Henrys.* "Darn! No Oh Henrys."

"No. No Oh Henrys." The storekeeper waved his hand over the selection like Danny was blind or deaf. Maybe both.

I have to buy something. I'll look like a fool now if I don't buy anything, but maybe Edgar is waiting outside for me to come out of the store with the Oh Henry bar. God, this is getting ridiculous. "Okay, I'll take a couple of those Reese's Pieces."

"Good choice," the storekeeper said. "That'll be two-fifty."

"Yeah. Reese's Pieces are good," someone behind him said as Danny paid. "I'll just take this newspaper, Al."

"Sure thing, Edgar."

Danny tried not to stare at the slimmer version of Winston who was now paying for his newspaper. Danny picked up the Reese's Pieces and hurried outside to The Smucker, trying not to look over his shoulder.

He opened the door and climbed in. Caroline was talking quietly to herself. A second later there was a tap on the door. Danny opened it and Edgar got in. "You did good. Just drive a little further down the highway to Jacko's Tacos. Drive around to the take-out and we'll talk. I'll order us some tacos."

"I have money," Danny said.

"That's okay," Edgar said. Then he laughed, "I'll add them to Winston's bill."

They were parked at the edge of the parking lot and the overhead lights of Jacko's Tacos were bright enough to light up the inside of the bus as they ate at the table.

Danny had just finished recounting, for Edgar's satisfaction, how Agent Bigalow had come to pay their motel bill.

"That's fantastic. I didn't really believe it when Winston told me. Rick Bigalow has a reputation. He blows his own horn about how many people he's arrested around here trying to cross illegally. Keeps a tally like the old gunfighters used to notch on their six-shooters. He stops anyone that strikes his fancy, no matter which way they're goin', north or south."

"He seemed like a regular guy to me," Danny said. "Just worried about his kid."

"Well, you got a hell of a break there," Edgar said. "If his kid hadn't run away, you wouldn't be here now. I know for a fact he's been keepin' tabs on me. I've had to lie low. Stayed away from the import business, if you know what I mean."

"Just Mexicans. Right? You're not into drugs, are you?"

"Hell no. Just helpin' people find a better life."

"Well you seem to be well known around here. That storekeeper..."

"Yeah it's a small town. Everyone knows everybody. Sorry about the Oh Henry bars. My mistake. Just tryin' to make sure you were the right guy." Edgar laughed. "Great tacos, huh?"

"Yeah they are. Don't know how you can eat those hot peppers on yours, though. Just seeing you swallowing them makes me sweat."

"You might get a taste for them in Mexico. Winston told me a bit about you and Caroline runnin' away from a home or somethin'. What are you runnin' away from?"

"We're not really on the run from anything," Danny said. "Caroline has dementia and I'm trying to keep her out of one of those long-term care homes. Trying to help her get a bit more out of life as long as I can. I made a promise to someone." Danny didn't mention Betty and Charlie. He wasn't sure how much Winston had told Edgar. "I thought maybe Mexico was an option."

THE GRAND GETAWAY   367

"Okay." Edgar spread his hands. "I won't ask anymore. If you're finished, Danny, I need to see your registration and drivin' licenses. I have to make sure I've got the spellin' and everything right on these tourist cards."

Danny got The Smucker's registration and handed over their licenses. Edgar studied them against the papers in his hand. "Okay, everything checks out."

"What about a permit for our bus? Winston said something about that."

"You're in luck there. You're only goin' as far as Guaymas, right?"

Danny nodded.

"Well, you can get as far as Guaymas without a permit. You'd only need a permit to go beyond there."

"How many people have you helped get into Mexico?" Danny asked.

"Mexico, Mexico," Caroline repeated.

"Yeah, we're going there, Caroline," Danny said, patting her hand.

"To answer your question," Edgar said. "None. You're my first. Everyone else I've helped was comin' north. I've missed the thrill, the excitement, so when Winston called, it whet my appetite, for one more play, even if you are headin' south.

"It's been gettin' harder and harder to fool the Border Patrol, what with fences, helicopters, more and more agents, and now locals joinin' in – vigilantes actin' like bounty hunters. Then there's the drug smugglers. Once you get through the border, I wouldn't advise you to stop in Sonoita. I haven't been there in a while. There's been a lot of killings lately, gang members, cops, innocent people. Make sure you have a full tank of gas and some food. I wouldn't stop until you reach Guaymas."

Danny swallowed hard. "Holy crap! I hadn't counted on getting caught in any shoot-outs. So what's the plan?" Danny asked.

"Here's what you do. Get to the border after 10:00 a.m. tomorrow, maybe get there around 10:20 – 10:30. My contact comes on shift at ten. He owes me a favour. I helped get his sister, her husband and their kids into the U.S. some time ago. Look for the agent wearin' a Toronto Blue Jays baseball cap. He's a fan so I got him a couple of caps. He'll stamp these fake tourist visa cards with an official stamp."

"Does he have a name?" Danny asked.

"Yeah. It's Enrique Rodrigues. But don't ask for him. Just look for the guy with the Blue Jays cap. He knows your name and he's expectin' you. Once Enrique stamps your tourist visas, you're on your way. Now, if you'll drop me off up the road at the Cactus Grill, I have my car there. I'll let Winston know if you make it across the border."

Edgar shook Danny's and Caroline's hands when they reached the Cactus Grill. "Good luck to you, Danny, Caroline. Hope everything works out okay for you."

CHAPTER 83

Danny and Caroline were up and dressed at 8:00 a.m. He made breakfast for Caroline. He wasn't really hungry, his stomach in knots about what lay ahead. He didn't want to think about things going wrong at the border and hoped he wouldn't run into any U.S. Border Patrol agents who had nothing much to do and were likely to stop them just because they were bored.

It was about 9.00 a.m. when they left the motel and got on the road. They were only out 20 minutes when a helicopter buzzed over them. Danny braked, momentarily startled. He checked the speedometer, but he was well below the limit. The helicopter with clear markings of the U.S. Border Patrol skimmed low over the highway ahead of them, its clatter vibrating in the warm air. It dipped lower and for a moment Danny thought it was going to land on the highway, but it suddenly seemed to have a change of heart and veered off, heading westward.

He now knew the differences between organ pipe and the cactus called saguaros. Danny pointed them out, repeating the names to Caroline. It took his mind off things and became a game. Caroline mostly responded with, "Oh, yes," but he was finally rewarded when she repeated "saguaro, saguaro, saguaro," then it became "carro, carro, carro". Danny laughed and she laughed along with him.

Just past the small town of Why, a sign told him they had entered Organ Pipe Cactus Monument, which Danny thought was a strange name for a natural park. A sign for the Kris Eggle Visitor Centre appeared on the side of the highway, informing them that it was just a mile ahead. In the motel, Danny had read about Kris Eggle, a young patrol officer who'd been shot while in pursuit of a drug smuggling gang back in 2002. Danny glanced at the clock. It was still early.

"You think we should stop for a few minutes, Caroline, just in case Enrique Rodrigues is late for work? What do ya think?"

"Yes. Late for work, work." Caroline smiled at him. Danny turned off and pulled up outside the visitor centre and park headquarters. He thought they would maybe just sit in the vehicle for a few minutes before going on. Two other vehicles were parked outside. It was getting hot and he rolled down the window completely. He stepped back into the kitchen and got some water and found a couple of cookies to go with them.

A vehicle pulled in beside them, but Danny was busy wiping some water from Caroline's blouse and didn't notice it until he caught a glimpse of it in his mirror. It was a Border Patrol vehicle.

"Danny!" It was Bigalow grinning at him through the open window. "Good to see ya, Danny, ma'am." He tugged at his cap. "Hope the motel was okay."

"It was fine, really fine. Thanks again," Danny said.

THE GRAND GETAWAY   369

"You been inside yet?" Rick Bigalow indicated the building. "It's worth a look. No charge."

"Uh. No. Just havin' a snack. We'll go inside in a few minutes. How's Billy-Joe?"

"He's fine. Gave him a real good talkin' to last night. Told him I'd never take him back to the firin' range if he pulled a stunt like that again. Real grateful to you, ma'am." Bigalow stuck his head in the window, smiling.

"Oh you. It's you. Yes." Caroline grinned back at him.

"Well thanks again." He indicated his partner behind him. "We'd better get on. Have a great day." He and Tom Agnew headed inside the visitor centre.

When the agents came out and waved at them before climbing into their vehicle, Danny waved back and breathed a big sigh of relief as they drove north up the highway.

He took Caroline inside and headed for the washroom. Afterwards they had a quick look round at the displays of the different types of cactus and other vegetation, along with a number of creatures native to the area, like the Gila Monster lizard. All were stuffed, but nevertheless looked alert and, he thought, ready to pounce at any moment, especially a selection of vicious looking snakes, spiders and scorpions. He was glad that Caroline hadn't encountered the likes of those when she'd ventured after Billy-Joe. She paid little attention to the displays, being more interested in a little girl who was visiting with her parents.

Now anxious to get going, Danny headed for the border crossing.

It was 10:40 a.m. when they reached the border. He slowed and brought The Smucker to a halt, pulling up at a small parking area beside a half-ton truck with Mexican plates just outside a fence marking the border. He looked ahead and saw two booths through a small gate in the fence. There was one man ahead of them, presumably the owner of the half-ton, standing at a booth where the agent was indeed wearing a Blue Jays baseball cap.

Danny got Caroline out of The Smucker. He had the registration, licenses and the tourist cards Edgar had given them in his hand. He bent down, pretending to tie Caroline's shoelace, keeping his eye on the booth where the agent with the baseball cap was still dealing with the man. He hoped that the other agent would not wave at him to come forward. If he did, they would be in trouble. He could always go back into The Smucker, pretending he'd forgotten something.

Out of the corner of his eye he caught a movement. Another agent, also wearing a Blue Jays cap came out to a booth. *God Almighty, Edgar. How in hell do I know which one is Enrique? You said you sent him two Blue Jay ball caps. Did Enrique give one to the other guy?* The first agent was now finished with the driver of the pick-up, who was climbing into his truck. He drove around The Smucker as someone raised a barrier to let him continue into Mexico. The first agent now motioned to Danny and Caroline to come forward. Danny held his breath. *God help us, Caroline.* Danny took her hand and walked slowly towards the agent who was studying them.

When they reached the booth, the agent said, "*Nombre?*"

What the hell was nombre? It sounds like number. Do I have to have some number?

"*Nombre? Nombre, por favor, señor?*" the agent repeated, then said, "Your name, *señor?*"

"Uh. My name. Uh, Danny, Danny Carroll," Danny spluttered, placing the tourist forms, licenses and registration into his outstretched hand.

The border agent looked briefly at the papers. "*Y Caroline.*" He smiled at Caroline, pronouncing her name with a heavy accent. He was still smiling as he said, "*Sweet Caroline.* You know that song, *señora?* Neil Diamond. *Sweet Caroline.*"

Caroline smiled and said, "Oh yes."

"Beautiful song, beautiful lady." He stamped the tourist visas with a flourish and handed them back to Danny who only then noticed the name E. Rodrigues printed on his shirt pocket. "Have a wonderful trip, *señor, señora.*"

About a half mile down the road they passed a sign, *Bienvenidos A Mexico.*

Danny gave a whoop. "Let's have some music, Caroline. I think this calls for your favourite. As Enrique said, 'Beautiful song. Beautiful lady.'"

He looked at Caroline tapping her hands on her knees in time to the song. She looked happy. In fact, most of the time he'd known her she'd seemed happy. How long was it now? Was it only June when he'd wandered into Cavandish and met her, along with Betty and Charlie? It seemed such a long time ago. And now, looking after her on his own, his regard and admiration for her had grown immensely. She asked for nothing and accepted everything she encountered. Admittedly, she was probably unable to complain or protest about anything. In his promise to Betty, he had vowed to look after her, but now he knew there was more to it than that. As he looked at her beside him, he didn't entirely understand his feelings for her, but he knew being with her, he didn't feel alone. Whatever awaited them in Mexico, they would meet it together.

CHAPTER 84

It was their fourth day in Guaymas. Danny was beginning to like the place. It was a pretty town, with its harbour surrounded by low dry hills dotted with saguaro cacti. They had spent the last three days in a small RV park just a few blocks from the harbour. It was fairly quiet, and nobody bothered them. Yesterday they'd discovered a small market just two blocks away, and fruit and vegetables were cheap.

Danny didn't know how long they could stay where they were. That would depend on how long the money lasted. He thought they should be okay for a while without using Betty and Charlie's bank cards, which he was reluctant to do again. He was fearful they might somehow be traced to Guaymas and the banks would get suspicious and cut the cards off.

He and Caroline were sitting on a bench facing the harbour, watching a small number of pelicans standing on a breakwater a short distance beyond the harbour entrance. Danny had tried pointing them out to Caroline, but after glancing in their general direction she had become much more interested in a small boy and girl who had arrived a few minutes ago with their mother. Danny guessed the boy was maybe five years old, his sister about three. Their mother sat off to their left. The boy had a crudely carved wooden boat with a length of string attached that he tossed into the water as far as he could and then dragged back to shore. He did this a number of times until his sister began throwing stones into the water near where his boat was floating. He moved away from his sister, pulling his boat out of range of her stones, which brought him directly opposite Danny and Caroline. Caroline tried to speak to him, but he was intent on launching his boat and pulling it back to shore and didn't hear her.

His mother called out, "Miguelito," then added something else in Spanish that Danny didn't understand, but he thought was probably, "Be careful." She smiled at Danny when he looked in her direction.

Miguelito launched his boat again and was towing it slowly back to shore when the string got snagged on something. The boy tugged harder and only succeeded in pulling himself towards the edge of the wooden pier. He pulled harder, then tripped and toppled off the harbour edge into the water. Danny heard his mother scream and call, "Miguelito! Miguelito! *Dios mio!*" The boy was floundering and splashing in the water and calling, "Mama, Mama." Danny jumped off the dock into the water which barely came up to his waist, grabbed the boy and hoisted him back onto the dock. The boy's mother reached them as Danny was pulling himself out of the water, but the boy was still hanging onto the string and pointing. *"Mi barco! Mi barco!"* he yelled.

Danny glanced over his shoulder. The string was still snagged on something. Danny lowered himself into the water again, waded out a few more feet and untangled the string from a rock. Miguelito pulled his boat to shore.

Miguelito's mother, a pretty woman in about her late thirties was full of apologies and thanks as Danny hoisted himself out of the water again. In Spanish and some broken English, Danny understood that she wanted him and Caroline to come with her. "You come. *Mi casa.* I fix *ropa,* clothes. *Me llamo,* Dolores Castellano. *Venganse.* Come. *Ven,* Lupita." She called her little girl and took her hand. Taking Miguelito by her other hand, she indicated that Danny and Caroline should follow. Danny and Miguelito left a trail of water behind them, but it was only a block from the harbour to Dolores' house, a single storey Spanish colonial style with a coating of pink plaster. Adjoining the house was a small repair shop with a sign that read, *Alberto Castellano — Servicio Automotriz.*

Inside the house, Danny sat Caroline on a couch in a large kitchen. Dolores took Danny into a bedroom off a small, open air courtyard and quickly pulled a colourful red floral shirt and a pair of tan pants from a wardrobe. She placed them on the double bed, then rummaged in a dresser drawer and pulled out a pair of boxer shorts. She held them up as if measuring them against Danny, gave a small snort, smiled and said, *"Mas grande,"* and added them to the clothes on the bed.

"Deme su ropa." She indicated Danny's wet clothes. "I wash. Give me. Pronto."

Dolores came back a few minutes later and chuckled at the sight of Danny in the borrowed clothes, particularly the pants, which were very wide and short. She picked up his wet clothes and dropped them into a plastic basket and indicated he should follow her. He found Caroline sitting with the two kids on the couch chatting quietly to them as they looked at her with puzzled glances, trying to follow what she was saying. Miguelito was now wearing dry clothes.

"Cafécito?" Dolores asked, holding a coffee pot in her hand.

"Yes. Uh, *gracias."* Danny answered. She poured a small cup for Danny and added two spoons of sugar before Danny could protest.

"Y Señora?" Dolores pointed to Caroline.

"Uh no. She's okay. No coffee, thanks, *gracias."*

Dolores picked up the clothes basket and went into a small alcove off the kitchen. She came back a short time later with his clothes, and went out to the back yard of the house. He could see her hanging them on a clothes line in the sun. When she came back, Danny had finished his coffee. *"Vengan.* Come." She took Caroline by the hand and led her through the front of the house to the street as Danny and the kids followed. Outside they turned into the wide-open door of the garage. An early sixties half ton truck had been driven up onto a short, low ramp that raised it off the concrete floor. A pair of feet protruded from underneath the vehicle, their owner grunting and panting loudly, struggling with something under the truck.

"Alberto," Dolores called.

There were more grunts and then what sounded to Danny like a curse.

THE GRAND GETAWAY   373

"Alberto," Dolores called again more loudly, tapping one of Alberto's feet with her shoe.

"Que? Que?" Another curse followed.

"Alberto!"

"Hijo de la... Que quieres, Dolores? Estoy occupado. Tanto importa?" There were more grunts and the protruding feet appeared to raise then slam back to the floor, followed by another curse.

Danny squatted and looked into the sweating face of Alberto, who was struggling with a heavy transmission. It was resting on a short piece of plank and the whole thing was strapped onto a floor jack. Alberto was trying to get the bolt holes on the transmission aligned with the bell housing. As Danny watched, Alberto was struggling to ease the jack a tiny bit backwards, but it rolled too far and he cursed again.

Danny slid under the body of the truck as Alberto stared into his eyes. Then Alberto eased the jack forward slightly checking the alignment, then looked at Danny. "Hay que levantar el gato un poco." Alberto pointed upwards and then indicated a tiny space between his fingers, and repeated, "Poco, poco."

Danny understood and nodded. He gently pulled down on the jack handle and Alberto grunted. "Bueno. Un poco, un poco asi... dele... dele... eso, that's it!" Danny saw him slide one of the top bolts into its slot then grab another and slid it into place. "Fantastico. Gracias, hermano. Gracias." Alberto was fumbling for the other two bolts which Danny quickly found on the floor and handed to him. Alberto slid each one into place. Satisfied the transmission was connected properly, he quickly tightened the bolts. Danny slid from under the truck and Alberto removed the strap from the transmission and followed, pulling the jack after him.

As Alberto wiped the sweat from his forehead with the back of his arm, Danny saw that he was almost a foot shorter than himself and quite a bit heavier. He realized Alberto was staring at him, looking puzzled. "Dolores por que tiene este gringo mi ropa? Mi mejor camisa?" Alberto pointed to the shirt and Danny immediately put his hand on the shirt front, leaving a perfect oily hand print, in addition to the other oily stains from the floor.

"Y mi mejor pantalon tambien?"

"Si, Alberto," Dolores replied. "No te has puesto el pantalon desde el carnival hace seis anos." She turned to Danny. "He no wear por... for six years."

"Por que? Por que? Why? Why?" Alberto repeated.

"Porque el señor salvo a tu hijo, lo saco del mar. El señor save your son from sea," she repeated for Danny's benefit.

"Miguelito? Mi hijo! He save?" He pointed to Danny.

"Si. Si." Dolores nodded. "Ese hombre."

"I didn't really," Danny began. "The water was..." but Alberto was patting Danny on the shoulder, adding more oil to the shirt.

"Y mi barco, Papa. Y mi barco," Miguelito shouted.

CHAPTER 85

"Mama, I'm going to build a big sandcastle," Lupita said in Spanish. "Will you help me?" It was Sunday afternoon and they were on a sandy beach. To Danny, it felt like a very pleasant day, though it was near the end of January. He and Caroline had dabbled their feet in the water, much to Caroline's delight, but Alberto, Dolores and the two children considered the water much too cold.

In the nearly three months that had passed since they'd arrived in Guaymas, Danny had picked up enough Spanish to understand the gist of the conversation between Lupita and her mother. "Okay, I'll help," Dolores replied. "But Grandma Caroline would like to help too."

"But sometimes she just plays with the sand," Lupita complained quietly.

"I'll help too, and I'll help Grandma Caroline," Danny said. "She likes to build sandcastles."

Danny understood Lupita's frustration, remembering the last time they had built a sandcastle together. Caroline, trying to be helpful in gathering sand, had swept the entire outside supporting wall away, causing a large portion of the castle to collapse.

"Okay, *un castillo grande*," Danny said. *"Y un castillo pequeno para Caroline.* Caroline, we'll build a little castle for you and I'll help Lupita build a big one over there."

In the week following Miguelito's rescue, Danny and Caroline had dropped by the garage on Alberto's invitation for morning coffee breaks. While Caroline had played with the children in the little courtyard of the house, Danny had hung around the garage with Alberto. Alberto soon discovered that Danny knew a lot about the older vehicles that came to the market with their fruit and vegetables.

Danny and Caroline had been to supper at the Castellano's house a couple of times, and Dolores witnessed how Caroline related to her two children. She learned about Caroline's dementia and discovered that they were not tourists as she'd first thought, but had come to Mexico with the intention of staying there. She found out where Danny and Caroline were living and visited them in the RV park. She had grown fond of them and knew that when summer came with its temperatures into the forties, it would be unbearable in their little bus. She had come home with a proposal for Alberto. He had often talked about how Danny appeared to have some knowledge and was skilled at repairing the vehicles in his garage, and Dolores suggested that Alberto offer him a part-time job.

At first Alberto showed some reluctance, arguing that a gringo from the north would not work for the low wages he could offer. Dolores suggested giving him a trial and part of the deal would be free accommodation. She further argued that with an extra hand in the garage, Alberto could catch up on the work. He always had too much, never taking a day off.

Alberto agreed to give Danny a try-out, and Danny and Caroline were offered the use of a spare bedroom off the courtyard, which Dolores fixed up with single beds.

Most of the work entailed replacing exhaust pipes, batteries, gasoline tanks with holes in them, clutches, transmissions and run of the mill repairs. That suited Danny just fine, and he was quickly relearning skills he thought he'd forgotten and adding some new ones. Alberto was particularly impressed with Danny's knack for adjusting carburetors, getting the vehicles running smoothly far faster than Alberto ever could. Although Danny did not earn much working for Alberto, it was more than enough. With the free accommodation on top of his wage, he and Caroline easily met their needs. Danny destroyed Charlie and Betty's bank cards.

Dolores often took care of Caroline's needs when Danny was helping Alberto in the garage. She loved the way Caroline had taken to her two children. The children, who had no living grandparents, called Caroline and Danny *Abulita* Caroline and *Abulito* Danny. Danny had taught them to say Grandpa Danny and Grandma Caroline in English. He was enjoying the role. The children enjoyed listening to the tape of Grandma Caroline reciting the poems about snow and frequently asked to hear it. They had heard it so often they could recite some of the lines by heart, and particularly liked chiming in with *Tiddely-Pom* from *The House at Pooh Corner*.

The Smucker had been retired from the road. It now served as a chicken coop in a corner of the back yard. Danny thought that Betty would have found that delightful when he recalled her thoughts of finding a cabin somewhere and raising chickens. He and Caroline took frequent walks to the harbour, and on Sundays, often went with the rest of the family to the beach at San Carlos. On extremely hot days, they took it easy in the coolness of the little courtyard in the house, watching the tiny lizards scramble up and down the walls and between the plants.

Danny had sent a post-card to Winston and he had replied. He was going to retire after this spring session at the university and he and his wife planned to come and visit them. He also included the news that a small monument would be erected at Cape Final in honour of his great-grandfather shortly after the park opened for the season.

Colby's painting had pride of place in Danny and Caroline's bedroom. Danny often talked about the people in the picture with Caroline, although he was sure she really didn't recognise anyone in it. He knew Caroline would eventually get worse, but Dolores had promised that they would look after her and himself, assuring him that they could end their days as part of the family in the Mexican fashion.

The day Danny had stopped off at Cavandish to warm up seemed a distant memory. His life had changed so much he could hardly believe it. The camaraderie he had shared with Betty, Charlie and Caroline was something he would always treasure. And what an adventure they'd had together! Truly it had been the road trip of a lifetime. Danny couldn't have asked for more.

SOURCES AND ACKNOWLEDGEMENTS

Disobedience by A.A. Milne

Sing Ho! by Jeanne De Lamarter

White Fields by James Stevens

Sea Fever by John Masefield

The More It Snows from The House at Pooh Corner by A.A. Milne, 1928

Frank O'Keeffe moved to Canada from Dublin, Ireland shortly after finishing high school. He is the author of several children's/young adult novels including Guppy Love, Weekend at the Ritz, Harry Flammable, and Nancy Nylen, which was short-listed for the R. Ross Arnett Award for Children's Literature. Frank now lives in Calgary, Alberta.

This is his second novel written for adults. His recent historical fiction novel *Woodbine* is set in Africa, Ireland, France and England, with a dynamic young protagonist, Lise de Tassigny. It covers the period from the late 1800s to 1935 – a sweeping saga weaving history with unforgettable characters across decades and continents. *Woodbine* is also available on Amazon.

Made in the USA
Columbia, SC
23 May 2023

16309709R00231